THE Al

NEW WORLD

DAVE

CHRIS CERVINI

DIVERTIR
PUBLISHING
Salem, NH

The Adventures of New World Dave

Chris Cervini

Cover design by Kenneth Tupper

Published by Divertir Publishing LLC
PO Box 232
North Salem, NH 03073
http://www.divertirpublishing.com/

ISBN-13: 978-1-938888-26-7
ISBN-10: 1-938888-26-X

Library of Congress Control Number: 2020941506

Printed in the United States of America

Dedication

This book is dedicated to the wonderful, warm, and resilient people of Mexico.

Table of Contents

CHAPTER 1

History as we know it

IN THE SPRING of 1519, Hernán Cortés arrived at the shores of Mexico to conquer the Aztec Empire and claim its gold for the glory of Spain. Aiding his effort was one of the greatest coincidences in history—the Aztec belief that, at the exact moment of Cortés' arrival, their civilization was to be visited by Quetzalcoatl, the light-skinned and plumed Aztec god of wisdom.

Mistaking Cortés for Quetzalcoatl was a fatal, civilization-crushing error.

In slightly more than two years—and with support from local tribes weary of Aztec rule—Cortés and his small band of Conquistadors swept through the valley of Mexico, destroyed the Aztec Empire, and established a firm European foothold on the continent of North America.

That's what the history books tell us.

But sometimes, right in the middle of the history we know, somebody goes and does something to change one important detail, and the world is never the same.

CHAPTER 2

The account of Efraim Ramirez, written in May of 1536

MY MASTER AND friend asked me to tell my story so that my children may know the truth about the incredible events that brought me to these hills and this simple life of peace under the sun of a new god.

It was Holy Thursday in the Year of our Lord, 1519. We were a proud group—the sons of Spain—brought together on a grand quest for new souls for the Lord Jesus Christ, for gold to fill the coffers of his majesty the King, and for eternal glory for ourselves and our commander, Hernán Cortés.

In my memories, I can still feel my body shake with excitement as many of the men by my side worked quickly, eager to board our small tender boats and make landfall. From our ship, less than a league from shore, the jungle looked to be impossibly thick and forbidding. Thankfully, it appeared less impenetrable than the tangled mangroves we had observed just weeks before on the shores of what the local Indios called the Yucatan.

Commander Cortés was standing proudly on the forecastle deck of our flagship, the Santa Maria de la Concepcion, surveying the coast with his hand to his brow. He turned and whispered something to Malintzin, our Indio interpreter, who was supplied to us by the Tabascans down the coast just a few weeks before.

Malintzin pointed to a spot on the coast just north of us, and Cortés spent a few moments straining to survey the land in the midday glare. He smiled. This would be the place—the true beginning of our expedition into the heart of Mexica and the storied riches of the Aztec Empire.

"This is where we land," Cortés bellowed. "Send a signal to the other ships and prepare to disembark."

With his order, we hastened our work loosening the ropes on the tenders and preparing the ladders for our descent to glory. In less than an hour, we were aboard the landing boats with the sun blazing at the top of the sky. I carried with me a small satchel of clothes, a powder bag and shot, and my musket. I remember the sun baking me in my heavy metal breastplate and helmet.

I was in the third landing boat behind Cortés, who stood tall on the prow of the lead tender in his moment of glory. The banners of our beloved Spain and the Church of Rome fluttered behind him. This was our grand entrance into the New World—an undiscovered place, a place that would someday bear our names.

I remember I was laughing with Jose Acevedo from my home city of Granada when we noticed a peculiar line of white smoke streaking toward the Commander's lead tender at an impossible speed. The streak connected with the bow of Cortés' tender, and a vicious explosion opened a yawning hole in the front of his boat, sending splinters in all directions.

I strained to see Cortés, wide-eyed and confused, clumsily trying to keep his balance on his shattered boat. He quickly turned to Malintzin, gesticulating wildly as if trying to demand an explanation. Malintzin appeared stunned by the blast, a red gash now above her brow. She shook her head violently and covered her ears as if indicating she had no knowledge of what had just happened.

We heard a loud crack come from the shore and beheld the exploding shoulder of Cortés, chunks of flesh ripped from his body. Cortés slumped as the crew members on his sinking tender recoiled at the blood and horror.

A quiet shock came over us; it would only last a few moments, as the air became filled with loud, repetitive cracks punctuated by dozens of speeding smoke lines hurtling toward our fleet.

Jose screamed, and I looked over at him. He had two smoking holes in his armor—center chest and left belly. He crumpled to the deck of the boat writhing in agony. I jumped on top of him, trying to pry his chest plate from his body. Two more men on our boat slumped over, Rodriguez with a hole blown in his face, and Garza with three holes across his chest. Feverishly, my hands worked to free Jose of his armor, but his screaming began to ebb, and his life slipped away under my hands.

I looked back on our fleet. I counted seven of our eleven galleons on fire, and the other four being consistently raked by the rapid-firing devil's contraption on shore. One by one the men in my boat were killed by this terrible calamity— and one by one they either toppled into the surf or fell on top of me and Jose, blood emptying from their bodies.

Sheltered from the violence by the weight of my dead comrades, the sounds of the massacre became muffled, save the hollow clunks of shot hitting bodies and the groans and screams of my dying friends. I squeezed my eyes shut, my body evacuating itself as I prayed to the Lord Jesus for my deliverance.

CHAPTER 3

1999—in a new timeline created after the Aztecs miraculously defeated the Spanish on the shores of Mexica in 1519...

The case of Santiago Villa De Esparza

I N HIS DREAM, *David Aragon saw a city he knew well but had never visited before in waking life. Gray and cold, he approached it like he always did—in a large ferry motoring through a choppy harbor. Spires stretched up into the clouds. It was all in a dream, but he knew it so well that it felt undeniably real to him. His ship was called the TATEN—at least that's what he saw imprinted on the gangway platform—and while that big, gray city across the harbor had no name, it was darkly magnificent.*

A swift elbow to his ribs snapped him back to reality.

"Heads up, David," Johnny said, "we're on final approach."

Dave sat upright, shook off the sleep, and suddenly remembered where he was—on a jet airship flying into the forbidden Empire of the Aztecs.

Coming into the Grand City of Tenochtitlan from the air was always an adventure. The bumpy updrafts caused by the high mountains and volcanoes that ringed the city made even the least pious flyers consider praying to their chosen gods or saints, depending on their persuasion. The triple engine Singh V airship pitched forward slightly as it came out of the mountains and began to coast on its final descent into Emperor Moctezuma XXI International Airport.

Ding. "Good afternoon, and welcome to the Pan Aztec Empire," came the soft, soothing female voice over the intercom, speaking perfect Spanish. "Please remember to have your immigration documents ready, and roll up your sleeves for your entrance immunizations."

Johnny Fiver, Dave's partner on this assignment, shook his head as he began to roll up his sleeve. "Freakin' Aztecs, right? What makes them so clean that they gotta make us into pincushions just for the honor of being in their presence," he whispered under his breath, but loud enough for Dave to hear.

Dave smiled and showily unbuttoned his sleeve. Johnny was a crack, no-nonsense field agent for the Colonial Spanish Foreign Service, but Dave was learning in just their first few hours of being on assignment together that he had a habit of not being terribly diplomatic or culturally appropriate.

"You'd be xenophobic too if your civilization had almost been wiped out by foreign diseases," Dave said.

Johnny rolled his eyes. "You can't even get with an Aztec girl without her spraying you down with disinfectant and making you wear a condom—which, I might add, our Holy Father has said will put us on a fast track to hell."

Johnny was rough around the edges, having spent the first eleven years of his life in foster care in New Amsterdam. When he was twelve, he was 'adopted' by a Colonial Catholic relief agency out of Havana. Such agencies sprouted up throughout the Spanish Empire starting in the mid-1500s when it became apparent Spain's moves into the New World would be stymied by much better organized and equipped *Indios*. The Pope and the crown demanded souls, and if they couldn't conquer the native peoples to get them, they had to get them from somewhere.

These relief agencies housed, fed, and taught orphans from around the world in exchange for a bended knee to the Lord Jesus Christ. Over time they went from frightening houses of abuse to relatively benign religious prep schools, and orphans brought from abroad through the program received automatic Spanish Colonial citizenship and generally did well getting into colleges, finding careers, and assimilating into Spanish culture.

"Have a lot of experience with Aztec girls, do you?" Dave asked, throwing Johnny a sideways glance.

"Yeah, I dated one in New Madrid for a bit when I was in the Foreign Service Academy," Johnny said. "She was on Hispaniola through an exchange program a few years after they decided to open up their society."

"Obviously it was an enlightening experience," Dave said as he brought his chair to its full, upright position.

Inside, Dave was bubbling with excitement and anticipation. In addition to this being his very first field assignment in nine years as a Spanish Colonial Foreign Service lawyer, it was also his first time back to the Grand City of Tenochtitlan since he studied Aztec culture for three semesters at the University of Tlateloco, just north of the city. He always remembered his time as a student in the city with great fondness because—much like how he felt at age nineteen—the city then was fresh and alive, flooded with new ideas and new freedoms.

Back then, some twelve years before, the Aztec Green Revolution had just ended nearly 750 years of absolute monarchy and an endless era of human sacrifice. In an unexpected move that shocked the world, Aztec Emperor Nachuila Moctezuma the 26th abruptly issued a decree opening Aztec society to trade, allowing women into the lower levels of the priesthood and bureaucracy, and—in an unprecedented and historic moment—he appeared at the top steps of the Templo Mayor to personally issue a proclamation abolishing human sacrifice and slavery in the empire.

At first, the people who lived under the fist of the Aztec monarchs did not know what to make of the bloodless massive shift in Imperial policy. For two weeks, the city trembled in fear as people were afraid to leave their homes, go to work, or even attend the market. What did this change mean? Was it some kind of a ruse to smoke out the progressives in society who, for decades, had secretly plotted to abolish human sacrifice?

Realizing his people were paralyzed with fear, the emperor emerged again, this time at the Xochi markets just south of the Great Causeway. He walked among his awed subjects, even buying mangoes and rice from a stall. International and local media reports quoted him telling the stall owners that day, "The terror is over. Do not be afraid, live peacefully, and live as you please."

Those calm and simple words were disseminated widely by the High Directorate of Information from the Dry River Territories of the north to the Incan Protectorate in the south. The words soothed the entire empire and lifted an unbearable weight off the society. Within a year, the first woman was admitted to the judicial priesthood, and many more had entered the bureaucracy as analysts and clerks. It was in this new and open society—this electric atmosphere of change—that nineteen-year-old David Aragon of New Madrid, Cuba, found himself as a young exchange student.

But as with all things kept behind the veil of the Imperial Court, no one ever knew the motivation for the Emperor's change of heart. Scholars surmised he was pressured by a priesthood that had grown more liberal as the world changed and became more interconnected. However, there was also ample evidence that elements of the high priesthood were deeply concerned about the societal shifts and that the Emperor had acted in an effort to reduce their powers—especially the moratorium on human sacrifice, which the high priests of the Jaguar Sect had mercilessly used to frighten dissenters and keep control of the society for centuries.

The Green Revolution, as it became known, launched the Aztec Empire into an era of creativity and secular scholarship. Writing and art flourished and, for the first time in its history, the empire began exporting its vast oil and precious-metal reserves—ushering in a period of stunning economic success that was enjoyed by both the nobles, piplitzin, and by commoners alike.

Young David Aragon was granted a student visa, in part because he came from connected and wealthy Cuban land-owning stock. He was one of the first outsiders permitted to study at an Aztec university. This was an amazing feat because he was considered by the Aztec medical examiners to be "biologically imperfect." Dave had a small metal plate in his skull that was implanted after a horse-riding accident on his grandfather's ranch when he was fourteen.

But Dave's academic record, his ability to quickly pick up Nahuatl, and a hefty 'donation' by his family to the charity running the exchange program made him a top choice for one of those prized first student visas. He made wonderful friends during his time in the Empire and even had an Aztec girlfriend—T'shla.

When he left, he promised to return.

But time and distance, as they often do, have a way of pulling people apart and making promises go unfulfilled. Dave lost contact with his dear friends and lost touch with the youthful exuberance that first brought him to Tenoch. Now he was just over 30, single, and a middling bureaucrat lawyer, tortured by strange dreams and living a simple and solitary life for the Colonial Foreign Service of New Spain, Hispaniola District.

Dave smiled as he looked out the plane's window. They were now over the grand lake at the heart of the bowl created by impossibly high snow-capped mountains. At the center of Lake Texcoco was the Templo Mayor, the ancient heart of the Aztec religion and government. Templo Mayor, unaltered since the mid-1500s, was a stepped pyramid gleaming mostly white. It had dual shrines at the top in honor of the leading Aztec deities of the 1400s, Huitzilopotchli and Tlaloc. Those deities had been out of fashion for centuries in favor of the Quetzalcoatl and Jaguar sects, which now dominated society. Three huge causeways stretched from the shore to the island. The broad causeways were lined with buildings and were home to markets, restaurants, nightclubs, and theaters. Along the shore and stretching to the foothills of the mountains were endless neighborhoods and broad thoroughfares.

The plane banked over the University of Tlateloco on the northern shore of the lake and leveled off for final approach into Moctezuma International Airport.

"So have you had a chance to look over the Esparza file?" Johnny asked.

"Yep. Committed it to memory," Dave said, lightly tapping his forehead. Dave didn't do field extradition work at all, and he wanted to impress his street-savvy partner, who got his start as a Havana police agent before transferring to marshal duty for the foreign service.

The air servant came by with the inoculation gun. "Smallpox, chicken pox, or MMR?" she asked. She was an attractive Aztec girl wearing a silken flying shawl in the traditional colors of the Empire—red, green, and gold.

"MMR, I believe," Dave said. "I think I'm caught up on the others."

The air servant calibrated a dial on the gun, pointed it at Dave's upper arm, and pulled the trigger. "And for you, sir?" she asked Johnny.

"Hell, I'm looking forward to having a good time. You better hit me up with everything you have," Johnny said with a playful wink.

Dave rolled his eyes as the air servant smiled politely and administered the shots. "Great. Very smooth. I'm sure she's never heard that one before."

Johnny smiled. "You think she liked me? Because for a moment I thought I felt some kind of thing happening there between us."

Dave reached under his seat and pulled out his leather satchel. "Here, put your mind on this," he said, handing Johnny the Esparza file.

Santiago Villa de Esparza was a Spanish colonial citizen from the Florida Peninsula. He was a petty thief who had done several short stretches of incarceration in various spots throughout the Spanish and French colonial islands. Four days before, he was arrested in Tenochtitlan on charges of conducting a human sacrifice.

Spanish Colonial officials on the island of Hispaniola were informed of the arrest by the Aztec diplomatic attaché who, in the interest of openness, encouraged the colonial Spanish government to send legal representation.

Though Dave was a bookish, office-bound attorney, his past experience as a student in the Aztec Empire made him a perfect candidate for this job, as very few outsiders could boast the kind of in-country and linguistic background he had. However, despite being an adventurous student, Dave rarely traveled and had not taken a vacation off the island of Hispaniola in his past nine years as a government worker.

Helping him get this high-profile assignment was the lead consular officer of Tenochtitlan, Marta C'de Baca, who happened to be a close childhood friend of Dave's and was, herself, a shooting star in the Spanish Colonial Foreign Service. Rumor had it she was on track to be chief of the entire ministry before age forty. Marta had been quite persistent in trying to get Dave to take this assignment, calling him four times to nudge him. Maybe she saw something in him that he didn't see in himself.

Johnny leafed through the dossier on Esparza as the airship landed and skidded to a stop on the runway. "What a scumbag this guy is," he muttered.

"He's a Spanish citizen and should be afforded a fair opportunity to explain himself," Dave said as the mechanical stairs attached to the belly of the jet, signaling that all passengers were free to gather their luggage and prepare to disembark. "Why would a Spaniard—a Catholic—conduct a ritual sacrifice of another human being? It doesn't make sense."

Johnny shrugged as he undid his seat belt and stood up to stretch. "I don't know. Drugs? It's usually drugs. Anyway, let's get a move on, compadre."

The two departed the plane, crossed the sun-soaked tarmac on foot, and entered the great hall of the airport's rather small and outdated foreign arrivals terminal. Immediately upon entering, they were greeted by official agents of the Empire.

"Greetings and welcome to the Aztec Empire. My name is Tlacatan, and we will be your official escorts and drivers during your stay with us. I am your, how do you say, official diplomatic liaison. Would you gentlemen care to check in with your consulate first or see the prisoner?"

Tlacatan's Spanish was terrible, but Dave understood him. He was a slight, bespectacled man in an electric blue European-style business suit. He was joined by two hulking men wearing shiny gold lamè business suits and the telltale forest green capes of the Jaguar order. Jaguars—especially their security agents—had a reputation for being no nonsense brutes. They were typically used as muscle, body guards, and soldiers, and they were generally not to be messed with.

Dave looked sidelong at Johnny letting him know he'd handle this and cleared his throat. "Thank you for your hospitality, and my deepest gratitude and respect to His Highness Moctezuma the 26th," Dave said in his best, but rusty Nahuatl. "If it is no trouble, we would first like to see the prisoner in question."

"What'd you say?" Johnny asked.

"Prisoner," Dave said.

"Goddammit," Johnny said, "we can see that moron tomorrow. It's not often you get a visa to come to Tenoch—and free drivers, too. We should have an evening on the Spanish Crown's peseta before we get down to business."

Dave put up his finger signaling to their guides that they needed a moment to confer. He gently put his hand on Johnny's elbow and led him a few feet away.

"Listen, I know this is just another case for you, but we're dealing with the Aztecs here, and there's a lot at stake," Dave said. "These guys have done a lot of work to get away from the image of sacrifice and blood-stained pyramids. They take this shit seriously. We should talk to our guy to try and figure out his story—then we can have dinner with our consulate people."

"I get it—some idiot Spaniard ritualistically kills an Aztec. I can see why they're so worked up," Johnny said. "But it's no different than what we see on a daily basis in some of the bad neighborhoods back home."

"No, you don't get it," Dave insisted. "These guys are extremely embarrassed about their history with sacrifices, and they are trying to turn over a new leaf. They're a world power now, and they can't have their people—or worse, some crazed foreigners—running around sacrificing people. Understand? This could blow up in the media and become an international embarrassment."

Johnny put his right hand reassuringly on Dave's shoulder. "My friend, relax—did you get a look at those Aztec cops? Our guy ain't going anywhere. He can sit on ice for a few hours."

Dave pressed. "In three weeks, Colonial Governor Archuleta will make an official visit to talk about lifting trade limits so we can get more access to Aztec gold and oil. The last time I checked, our government likes gold and oil."

Johnny softened a bit. "You're a sad man, David Aragon. All that time riding a desk, and the first time you get into the field you think the global economy rides on the success of our little mission to defend some creep."

Tlacatan loudly cleared his throat. "I hate to disturb you two, but the prison is a thirty-minute drive from here through difficult traffic, and the day is aging quickly."

"Ma xinechtlapohpolhui," Dave said, an offering of apology rolling off his rusty tongue. "We're coming." He felt a little giddy getting to use the official Aztecan language again.

"Wonderful," Tlacatan said. "This is terribly important business, and the sooner we can get to it, the better."

§ § §

If the Aztecs took great pride in their capital city, with its glass spires and manicured boulevards, it certainly didn't trickle down to their jails. Detention Center 3 was located just off the Grand Western Causeway. It was an ancient, dark, rotted tooth of a building set in the middle of the light and cheery Tenochtitlan Garden District with its bright flower shops, nurseries, and arboretum.

Once inside the main gates of DC3, the car was guided by a walking guard down a ramp and into the basement parking lot. The walls of the basement were wet with lake seepage, and the smell was heavy and dank, assaulting their nostrils as soon as they exited the car.

"We like to keep our detainees comfortable," Tlacatan said. "That's why the temperature in the facility never gets above 24 degrees centigrade."

"Like a dark and cozy cave," Johnny remarked.

"This way, gentlemen."

Dave and Johnny followed the guards and their guide to a stairwell, but instead of going up, they went down—three flights to Cell Block 1. After having their papers and visas checked at three guard stations, Dave and Johnny were escorted to a small visiting room which had a simple table, a chair, and two lights which shone down from a pitch black ceiling.

They waited there for several minutes. "Claustrophobic?" Johnny asked Dave, who was pacing the walls, nervously looking up into the ceiling.

Dave looked at Johnny, pulled out a pen, and quickly scribbled something on a legal scroll, which was lying on the table in the center of the room. *Don't think this is a confidential room*, Dave wrote.

Johnny nodded.

"Let's not accidentally incriminate our guy," Dave wrote.

Johnny read the second note and shrugged. "Whatever gets us out of here quicker," Johnny said. "If our guy did it, he did it," he added, under his breath.

Just then, the door at the far end of the room slid open, and a short, pudgy Spaniard wearing brown prison pajamas was escorted in, flanked by two Aztec guards each standing at least a head above two meters. Holding Esparza by his elbows, they led him to the solitary chair at the table. Esparza had a bulging right eye and a badly swollen nose.

11

"Do you need anything?" Dave asked. "Some water, bandages?" Esparza stared blankly down at the table and gave no response as the Aztec guards exited the room.

Johnny stepped forward. "Santiago, we have three questions that must be asked," he said. "One, as a citizen of the Spanish Empire, do you want Spanish representation in the Aztec legal system?"

Esparza looked wearily in Johnny's direction. After a moment, he nodded.

"Two, do you understand the charges that are being leveled against you?" No response.

"Three, did you..."

"I didn't do it." Esparza's voice was weak and scratchy.

"What?" Johnny asked as Dave nervously looked up at the pitch black ceiling.

"I said I didn't kill that guy," Esparza said, his voice stronger, more composed.

"Do you know who did?" Dave asked, his voice soft and soothing—almost a whisper.

Esparza sat back in his chair. "I was paid on the spot to lure him out of the bar. I don't even know what his name was."

Johnny pulled out a picture of a stately looking Aztec man standing with a woman and two children. "His name was Ventli, and he had a wife and two children. He ran a non-profit social-service agency that provided health-care clinics in the rural areas of the Aztec Empire."

"I didn't kill him," Esparza insisted, looking at the picture.

"Well, they say you did," Johnny said.

Dave coughed, glowered at Johnny, and stepped forward again, bowing down so that his mouth was scarcely three inches from Esparza's ear. "Help us help you," Dave whispered. "Who paid you? Who killed Mr. Ventli?"

Esparza sighed deeply. "I was here on vacation. I was at a bar. This guy came up to me and struck up a conversation—seemed like a nice guy, but he was big, intimidating." Esparza then became very quiet and conspiratorial.

"He had a Jaguar bracelet on his wrist," he whispered. "He told me he'd give me 250 pesetas, Spanish, if I lured this other guy out of the bar and into the alley. That the guy owed him money or something." Esparza looked nervously from side to side.

"What?" Johnny asked.

"I lured him out the best way I know—by picking his pocket," Esparza said. "I know, I am not a smart man." He started to whimper.

"And the victim, Mr. Ventli, he followed you?" Dave asked.

"Yes, out into the street and around the corner," Esparza's voice trailed off.

"Then what?" Johnny asked.

"Then, this guy, the one with the Jaguar bracelet, he was waiting there with a shiny sword. He yelled something in the local language, and before I could do anything he swung the sword. In one swing the man's head came straight off and fell to the ground with blood, lots of blood." Esparza shuddered.

"That's it, I guess," he said. "The man took the head, put it in a sack, and just like that he was gone. The police arrested me a few hours later as I tried to leave my hotel and get out of town. They told me several patrons in the bar described me from when I picked the man's pocket and ran out of the bar. The bartender knew I was a Spaniard, so I guess it wasn't hard for them to track me down."

Dave and Johnny both stood erect and looked at each other. Johnny took the legal scroll, jotted down, *We need to talk,* and showed it to Dave. Dave nodded.

"So, can you help me?" Esparza said, his voice cracking.

Dave looked down and offered a hopeful smile. "We'll see what we can do. Sit tight."

Johnny went over and knocked on the visitors' side door. "We're done here," he called out.

"Please help me," Esparza pleaded. "I didn't mean for this man to get killed." Johnny avoided his gaze as the doors on both ends of the room opened simultaneously and the jail guards emerged to return Esparza to his cell.

Back in the car, Dave was silent, not wanting to say too much in front of their Aztecan minders. Johnny sat next to him in the back seat, looking through the Esparza file.

"This doesn't say anything about another suspect; it's just Esparza's rap sheet and the details of the crime scene," he said softly and quickly in Spanish so that it would be hard for Tlacatan and the Jaguar Agents to make out.

Tlacatan looked over from the middle seat of their three-row Incan-made SUV. "We can now take you to your hotel," he said in broken Spanish.

"Okay," Johnny said, now eager to relate his observations from the questioning session to Dave in private.

"No," Dave said. "I'd like to speak with the judicial priest overseeing this case. Can you please take us to him?" Johnny and Tlacatan both looked surprised.

"Judge Priest Decoyan is a very busy man. It will be difficult to arrange a meeting on such short notice," Tlacatan protested.

"Tell him which case it is," Dave said. "I'm sure he'll find time to see us."

Tlacatan nodded reluctantly and reached into his suit pocket for his phone.

§ § §

Judge Priest Decoyan's office was in the Central Judicial Complex just outside the Sacred Precinct and the Templo Mayor Complex, which was home to the highest levels of the priesthoods. It was on the island just over the causeway from the detention center.

"Wow," Johnny said as he exited the car and gazed upon the pyramids of central Tenochtitlan, gleaming white and gold in the late-afternoon sun.

"It's different than I remember," Dave said. "The blood stains are largely gone."

Tlacatan cleared his throat. "This way gentlemen."

"Blood?" Johnny asked.

"Yeah," Dave said. "They used to conduct human sacrifices at the top—700 years of blood stained the tops of the pyramids. It was still there when I lived here. They must have re-plastered them since then."

When Dave had come so many years before, the pyramids were covered with an uneven sheen of dried black blood from centuries of death. Such displays were not befitting the new, modern capital of the Aztec Empire in a post-Green Revolution era, so the Emperor ordered a citywide modernization program to cleanse the capital of all references to sacrifice and slavery. If one looked hard enough, one could still find traces of the city's history—tourist shops here and there selling replica sacrifice blades—but such displays were frowned upon and quickly covered up or taken out of circulation.

The office of Judge Priest Decoyan was well appointed and immediately comforting to Dave, as it was decorated with Spanish Colonial Art from the 16th and 17th centuries. It reminded him of his grandfather's library back in Havana.

"Your excellency," Dave said with a bow as they entered the room.

"Come in, boys," Decoyan said. He was an elderly man, his once long black hair now stringy and salt-and-pepper. He wore traditional priestly robes, with wide green metallic stripes going from the shoulders down the sleeves, indicating a fondness for the Quetzalcoatl order. "As the judge priest in this case, I'd like to remind you that meeting before our initial hearing tomorrow is highly irregular."

Dave stepped in tentatively. "I understand, sir, but I also understand from our briefing that you have a record for fair and thoughtful jurisprudence. A maverick, some might say."

Decoyan scoffed. "Nonsense. If I were a true maverick, do you think I would be here, in these robes." Decoyan turned and noticed Johnny, who was admiring a wood carved retablo depicting San Sebastian pierced with arrows. "Do you like it?" Decoyan asked.

"Yes, it's beautiful," Johnny said.

"Yes, yes," Decoyan said. "It's one of my favorite pieces—it's an old family heirloom. The carver of this piece was Spanish and lived here way back in the 1500s—he's legendarily one of the first Spanish our people ever encountered."

"Interesting," Dave said, heartened to know this priest seemed to have a wider world view and cosmopolitan tastes. Often, priests lived secluded, fanatical lives, drowning in ancient texts and meting out justice according to the cruel, ancient ways. At first blush, Judge Priest Decoyan offered a ray of hope.

"You'll find it's often not the piece, but the story behind it that truly provides meaning and value," Decoyan said. "Looking at the poor soul in this retablo makes me think of the suffering of the poor soul who carved it."

"I'm surprised, your Excellency," Dave ventured. "You are a high priest. I cannot imagine this collection of Christian artifacts is smiled upon."

Decoyan laughed. "Not a high priest, just a lowly old judicial priest. There is a difference, and it's about 50,000 of your Spanish pesetas a year."

"My apologies," Dave said.

"To answer your question, yes, I do sometimes get questioning looks from my peers and superiors over at Templo Mayor. However, my record of fairness and loyalty to the emperor has given me a certain amount of leeway to explore the other faiths of the world," Decoyan said as he headed to his chair. "Now, you gentlemen asked to see me so close to the end of the day. How can I help you quickly so as not to be separated from my family for much longer."

He motioned for Johnny and Dave to sit. Tlacatan and the two Jaguar agents were still in the office, standing by the door.

"If you don't mind, sir," Dave said.

"Oh, of course. Please, give us a moment," the old judge said to Tlacatan and the two guards. "Trust me, no state secrets will be passed here." Tlacatan left the room, taking the guards with him.

"Jaguar agents, eh?" Decoyan said, as if confiding in Johnny and Dave. "Somebody thinks a lot of this visit and this Esparza character. So, how can I help you?"

"Santiago Esparza says he didn't kill Ventli and that he was paid to lure him out of the pub," Dave said. Decoyan sat back in his leather chair, looking off into the space just above the heads of Dave and Johnny. "He said the man who paid him was a Jaguar. Or, at least, a big guy wearing a Jaguar bracelet."

Decoyan betrayed no emotion. He leaned forward and leveled his gaze at Johnny. "You haven't spoken much. What have you to say?"

"Well, sir, this Esparza's kind of a puny little shit, if you ask me—a weak and petty criminal," Johnny said. "I have a hard time believing he could lop the victim's head off as cleanly as it appeared to have been separated from the body, according to the crime-scene pictures I saw."

A smile crept across Decoyan's face and he leaned back in his chair. "That's what I thought," Decoyan said with a deep sigh. "Though, your Esparza has been silent in my questioning of him. I guess it's only fair he would trust a Spaniard to profess his innocence. But still, there is nothing from the police canvass of the people in the bar about a Jaguar being involved."

Decoyan seemed to get lost in thought for a moment before Dave pulled him back. "So, is there significance that someone tied to the Jaguar Sect might be involved?"

"Don't look at me, I'm a devotee of Quetzalcoatl. I cannot speak ill of those who adhere to the simpler faiths," Decoyan said. "But, let me just say that if you can prove a Jaguar is somehow involved, I would not die of shock at this fact."

"So…" Dave started, but Decoyan quickly put up his hands.

"You're smart boys. You get off the airship less than two hours ago, and you've already raised some doubt about the government's case in just one questioning of the suspect."

"Don't sound so depressed," Johnny said.

Decoyan slowly stood up from his chair and went over to a veranda behind his desk, opening the door to behold the tops of the pyramids in the Sacred Precinct. "Mr. Aragon, you were here before," Decoyan said.

"Yes, sir, I was, when I was in college," Dave said, suddenly feeling at a disadvantage that Decoyan seemed to know more about him than he let on.

"Don't worry," Decoyan said. "I know all about you—I've known all about you from probably before you were chosen by your government for this mission."

Dave stood up. "Listen, we're just here to represent a Spanish citizen in your system. How or why we were chosen or our past experience in your empire is irrelevant. We just want a fair trial for our countryman, and you just indicated there's some doubt. That's enough for me to ask you to lessen the charges to aiding and abetting—which, under Aztec code, does not carry the death penalty."

Decoyan nodded gravely. "Come here a minute, boys," he said, motioning for them to join him on the balcony behind his desk.

Dave and Johnny went behind Decoyan's desk and stepped out into the late afternoon sun. The city was filled with the sound of traffic and street vendors selling their wares to the lower level bureaucrats leaving their jobs in the Templo Mayor complex.

"We've come a long way, haven't we?" Decoyan asked, taking in the majesty of the Sacred Precinct. "I'm not going to reduce the charges against your man," he added after a long pause.

Dave and Johnny were silent. "Mr. Aragon, do you remember when the tops of those pyramids were red with blood?"

"I do," Dave said, searching for a read on this most peculiar judge.

"Did you ever, in all your time here after the Green Revolution, hear of someone sacrificing an offering by beheading them in an alley with a sword?"

Dave cocked his head in consideration. "No," he finally offered, "most sacrifices, historically, were offerings of the heart, cut out with a stone blade—the blade of the high priests, kept in the temple."

"Precisely," Decoyan said. "My superiors," he pointed to the temple complex, "are concerned about how this grisly crime looks to the outside world. They're afraid it makes us look backwards and unstable. But you know and I know—and in their hearts even the high priests know—that this killing is not the Aztec way. It's very tidy for me, and for my superiors, to have a foreigner commit this crime."

"So," Dave said, "how do we make this more complicated for you and your superiors?"

Decoyan smiled wide and reached out to pat Dave on the shoulder. His bony fingers clenched Dave's tunic and he pulled him close. Decoyan looked back into the room and then over at the Templo Mayor. "Find me this mythical Jaguar-bracelet-wearing executioner," he whispered softly into Dave's ear. He let go of the tunic and smoothed it out. "Or, find me some other strong evidence that corroborates your Spaniard's claim—then I'll reconsider his fate."

CHAPTER 4

2013—London in our timeline

A determined kazillionaire with too much time on his hands

SIR IAN DAVID Boddington ruled the world from his roost in London's Financial District. Like many of the billionaires of his generation, he got his start in computers, essentially inventing one of the first dummy-proof operating-systems—"The Q"—when he was just out of Oxford at age twenty-three.

The Q was more practical than Windows and more intuitive than the Mac-OS. For five years, Sir Ian presided over his growing empire as his operating system began to be a real threat to both Microsoft and Apple.

Then he got bored.

At twenty-eight, he sold his controlling stake in The Q for $14 billion. Without his vision, The Q quickly became a middle-of-the-pack computer operating system and was soon relegated to a few government platforms around the world.

Sir Ian quickly turned to the entertainment world, buying a webcast network, starting a pop-culture and gossip Web empire—*IDB! News*, and producing young talent. His work gave the world The Harmonious Krew, or THK, a Brit-pop boy band whose infectious hits paved the way for the boy band craze of the late 1990s.

At thirty-six and now worth $22 billion, he grew bored with being a media mogul and took a year off to train, literally. He culminated the year, on his thirty-seventh birthday, by besting the individual record for rowing across the Atlantic Ocean by twelve hours and thirty-six minutes.

That success inspired him to create *12:36 Adventures*, a company catering to the extreme-sports whims of the upper classes. From kayaking in Ushuaia, to the Active Volcano Hiking Experience in the Philippines, to a deluxe week spent living with a real tribe of headhunters in Micronesia, Boddington's company lived up to its tagline—"Adrenaline…On Demand."

He was living a dream beyond the wildest expectations of the middle-class asthmatic boy who grew up just outside Leeds, the child of an accountant father and school-administrator mother. It was those memories—the ones of being stuck in his room on bad-air days—that drove him toward his latest adventure.

Boddington sat in his 3,000-square-foot office looking out over London. In his hand were the latest reports from Dr. Kopplewicz on her development of the machine and its revolutionary abilities. He clenched the papers tightly. They were close, very close to success. It could be days, Kopplewicz said. Days and about $6 million more in Rhodium for successful completion.

Rhodium sold at about $6,000 an ounce—four times more than gold. This project had probably made Boddington and 12:36 Adventures the single largest holder of Rhodium in the world. He probably held more Rhodium than was left in the earth. Boddington pressed the call button on the arm of his chair, a nod to his childhood love of Star Trek.

"Yes, Sir Ian?" His assistant's voice was calm and soothing.

"Betsy, would you please have Deneven come in here?"

"Right away sir."

§ § §

Brian Deneven was a financial whiz kid, plucked from Wall Street by Sir Ian three years earlier when Sir Ian wanted to take 12:36 Adventures public. Always the Long Island social climber, Deneven jumped at the opportunity to work for the eccentric genius who turned everything he touched to gold.

Little did he know what being swept into Boddington's circle would mean.

"Yes," Brian was saying, finger to the faulty Bluetooth device that he could never get properly affixed to his ear. "It goes without saying that mercenaries do raise eyebrows, of course. But you have to understand, Sir Ian is a genius, and if he says the project needs mercenaries, then, well, it probably needs mercenaries." Brian heard a beep indicating he was getting buzzed on the other line.

"Hold on a sec," he said, "I have another call coming." He clicked over to the other line. It was Betsy.

"The boss wants you in his office," she said.

Brian sighed deeply. "Okay, be right there." He clicked back. "Listen, I have to go." There was another pause. "Yeah, I mean, no, sure." He listened for a moment. "Okay," he said, "just tell the shareholders to have a little faith."

With that he hung up and started down the long hall to Sir Ian's suite.

Sir Ian's office was decorated in shiny black obsidian and ancient statuary. He seemed inordinately fond of pre-Colombian Mexican statues—Mayan, Tlaxcalan, and Aztec in particular. In fact, his prized possession was a reclining Quetzalcoatl statue under glass that he had made into an elaborate coffee table.

Sir Ian was sitting at his desk with his back to the door, staring out at the city. "Deneven, we're going to need more Rhodium," Sir Ian said, wheeling around in his chair as Brian entered.

Brian had anticipated the request. He dutifully pulled out his iPhone and scrolled to the commodities quotes. "If you don't mind, Sir Ian, it appears Rhodium is trading at a 26-week high. It might make sense to wait and buy at a lower price," Brian said.

Sir Ian stroked his salt-and-pepper beard. "Eh," he said, "we're going to need about $6 million worth at the current price in order to finish the project. I'm not too concerned about the market. We make this work, and the market won't matter."

Crazy talk, Brian thought. "Okay, boss, I'll arrange the order."

"Great," Sir Ian said, leaning back and smiling. Spending money always seemed to give him a strange sense of euphoria. "Make sure the goods get shipped directly to Kopplewicz's team in the lab complex."

"Of course," Brian said, his head down and his thumbs now tapping wildly on his iPhone. "I just placed the buy order with our broker." He held up his phone and waved it showily as if to prove to Sir Ian that he had accomplished the task.

"You know, without me..." Sir Ian said.

"Yes, I know," Brian said, "we'd still be using teletype machines and couriers."

"Exactly," Sir Ian said, a smile of self-satisfaction creasing his lips. Brian turned to leave. "Hold on a second," Sir Ian said.

"Yes?"

"Am I losing the shareholders?" he asked.

"Well, sir," Brian began, carefully putting his phone back in his suit pocket. He took a breath and opened his mouth to speak. "Ahhh..."

"I'll take that as a 'yes,'" Sir Ian cut in.

Brian chose his words carefully. "I'd be lying if I said there weren't questions."

Sir Ian rose from his desk and meandered over to Brian, arms folded across his chest, brow furrowed. "What types of questions?" he asked.

Brian knew this was his opportunity to be frank with his boss. "Well, sir, there is a real concern about your perceived acumen. There are questions about shareholder funds being used to buy precious metals at the top end of the market. And, well, there are questions about the mercenaries."

"Which are?" Sir Ian asked.

"Why do we keep a squad of mercenaries on the payroll?" Brian asked.

Sir Ian chuckled. "Because they are the best at what they do, of course."

"Yes, but they're ruthless killers, and they are on our payroll," Brian said. "That will raise eyebrows. It has raised eyebrows."

Sir Ian waved his hand dismissively. "We have clients engaging in some very dangerous adventures around the world—tell them we need the mercenaries as an insurance policy in case one of our very wealthy adventure-seeking clients needs a quick extraction. What's that Warren Zevon song? 'Lawyers, Guns, and Money'? Well, we have the lawyers and the money—now we also have the guns on the payroll."

"I'll try to make that point, sir," Brian said, moving toward the door.

"Deneven," Sir Ian called. Brian turned halfway around. "I'd be lost without you, boy. Seriously lost."

Brian nodded with a half-smile and continued on his way out the door.

CHAPTER 5

1999—Aztec time

T'shla gets a phone call

T'SHLA IXTAPOYAN WAS working late at the Ministry of Health's Internal Services Division going over the details of a recent major mainframe security breach in which the health records of 6,200 Aztecs had been stolen.

T'shla arched her neck to stretch it out and give her eyes something to look at other than the endless lines of computer code she had been poring over for much of the past four hours. How was it that others were becoming incredibly wealthy working with computers, yet she was a mid-level cubicle drone charged with monitoring co-workers and investigating digital improprieties?

"Did you get something?" her coworker, Shetla, asked from across their small office.

"Just a stabbing pain in my neck," T'shla said. She looked back down at the stacks of computer readouts from the last fourteen days. Every login to the Aztec government system by every employee, official, and priest for that period.

The crime was committed at some point in the prior fourteen days. They had such a wide window because the Aztec government's mainframe backed up only once every two Julian weeks. They were upgrading to a backup of data once every ten days in accordance with the Aztec calendar, but T'shla had often sent memos to the High Priest Directorate for Technology that data needed to be backed up daily to improve the ability to track down attacks on the system. She never received a response.

"I can't believe we still can't sort these logins digitally," T'shla complained. "Or at least be able to digitally narrow down the window on when these records were stolen."

Shetla shook her head. "Well, Miss Computer Wizard, you could write a search program and make all of our lives easier."

A sudden chill went down T'shla's back as she considered the thought. "You do know only high priests can authorize new programs on the official government mainframe," she said.

Shetla rolled her eyes. "Well, what are they going to do? Fire you for making our jobs easier?"

T'shla laughed self-consciously. "So, do you have plans tonight?" she asked.

Shetla was a few years younger and lived the life of a single Aztec girl without a care in the world, hopping from boy to boy. It was exhilarating for T'shla to hear the stories.

Shetla smiled. "Serpin finally asked me out. He's taking me to Xochimilco for dinner." Xochimilco was an area of ancient canals just south of the city. It was a place for lovers to take long boat rides and discreetly show affection in public.

"*Eish* girl, very romantic," T'shla said.

"And you?" Shetla asked.

"Not much. I'll probably stay here another hour, grab some food at the Pantitlan Market, and head home."

"Ay, T'shla, you need to get a life," Shetla said as she began to pack up her things and switch from her office shoes to her commuting sneakers. "And I don't mean staying home writing computer code you will never get to use. A computer code can't keep you warm at night."

"You live enough for the both of us," T'shla said, not mentioning how lucky she felt every day that she could get up, breathe the clean air of her homeland, and live her simple life.

Before leaving, Shetla went over to T'shla and loosened her hair until it fell to her shoulders. "That's better," she said. "Wish me luck tonight."

Once Shetla left, T'shla got back to work, promising herself to look over at least 100 more login records before she would go home for the night. It was at that moment her cell phone chirped, signaling an unknown caller.

She flipped open the phone. "Hello?"

"Is this T'shla Ixtapoyan?" the masculine voice asked. It was unsteady but in a strangely familiar Spanish accent.

"Yes," T'shla replied. She felt the hair on the back of her neck go up. She did not receive too many phone calls.

"Hi," the voice started. "I'm sorry to bother you. I know it's been a very long time, but it's...it's David, David Aragon, from Tlateloco—you know, from way back when." The voice trailed off.

"Coatlicue!" T'shla exclaimed in excitement, her heart pounding. "How are you? How did you find me?" She heard what she took to be a sigh of relief on the other end of the line.

"I'm here in Tenoch," he said. "I'm a guest of the government here representing a Spaniard who got himself into a little trouble. I called the Main Phone Exchange Ministry and asked them to do a search of listed cell phones. They got me your number in five minutes. It was strangely efficient. I truly didn't expect to be able to get you so quickly. I'm sorry if I crossed some line by calling you. It's just...I'm in town and I wanted to reach out."

T'shla was at a loss for words. "Wow. Just wow." Her mind raced back ten years to a young, cute, brown-haired Spanish boy who showed way too much interest in an Aztec virgin. They had three classes together and often found themselves in the same study groups or at the library. Their mutual attraction was instant. And being of college age, they soon found themselves doing more than just studying.

Within a month, she was no longer an Aztec virgin. Their relationship was secret and forbidden. Not because the Aztec Government expressly forbade it, but more because this sort of thing just wasn't done, even in post-Green Revolution Tenochtitlan. Their relationship was, by turns, breezy and non-committal and then intense and serious—lost in talk of her leaving the Valley of Mexico for the exotic Caribbean Islands of Colonial New Spain.

But it wasn't to be. His student visa expired and was not renewed. Her ties to her culture were reinforced by her 'uncle,' Coaxoach, a corrupt high priest of the Jaguar Order. Somehow Coaxoach had gotten wind of her tryst and summoned her to his Jaguar Temple office, reminding her, rather sternly, of her responsibilities as an Aztec "Saved One"—an orphan girl once slated for ritual sacrifice, but given a reprieve by the emperor's order to suspend the awful practice. At the time of the edict ending ritual executions, T'shla was third in line to be sacrificed. If the order were ever lifted, she would have to report to the Temple and take up her place in line as a sacrifice to Coatlicue, the goddess of the earth who gave birth to the moon and stars.

After Dave left, T'shla recommitted herself to her traditional role as an orphan 'niece' of a high priest and chaste Saved One—save a few short relationships here and there; she was only human, after all. She finished her education and embarked on a life of honest, hard work, and waited piously for the order to end sacrifice to be rescinded, as was her obligation.

"I'm sorry to call you like this," Dave said. "Since I learned I'd be coming here, I've been thinking a lot about you."

T'shla smiled, biting her lower lip. "Don't apologize," she said in halting Spanish—a language she hadn't used in years, "but please bear with me as I, well, as I feel at a bit of a disadvantage."

"I understand," Dave said in Nahuatl. "I was just calling to see if you wanted to get together for dinner or a drink. I should be here for about three or four days."

T'shla laughed. "I feel terrible because your Nahuatl is so much better than my Spanish."

"So what do you say? Can we make plans to meet up?"

Hearing his voice and the prospect of seeing him again made the endless lines of computer code vanish from her running list of immediate concerns. "How about tonight?" she asked, as she gathered up the piles of printed-out login records and shoved them into her ample messenger bag. "I'm getting off work in just a few minutes. Where are you staying?"

"Plaza Central Templo Mayor, right on the island," Dave said. "Teotihuacan Internationale Hotel."

"That's five minutes from my office," she said. "I can meet you anytime."

"Why don't I meet you somewhere else? I'm pretty heavily escorted and, well, you know, I'm sure there are still prying eyes everywhere in this town, especially at the fancy hotels that cater to off-landers."

"Sure," T'shla said. "You must have come back to my city as a very important Spanish person to be so nervous about being seen with a little computer drone like me. Meet me at Le Clerq—it's a French place just down the street from your hotel toward the Northern Causeway at the corner of Temoc and Coatepec."

"Perfect," he said. "See you at the hour of the cricket, about 45 minutes."

§ § §

Dave had dinner plans with Johnny and his old friend Marta C'de Baca from the consulate office, but since he obtained T'shla's number so quickly, he was sure they wouldn't mind a change of plans.

He spotted Johnny on a hotel lobby couch looking like he was trying to read an Aztec newspaper. The Teotihuacan Internationale, or TI for short, seemed almost too fine for government workers. Aside from gold and oil wealth, the luxury of the TI brand was one of the Aztec Empire's first exports to the rest of the world post Green Revolution. There were five-star boutique TI's in every major city—Paris, London, New Amsterdam, and Edo. Dave's many years of not traveling made his experience of the TI seem that much more over-the-top. *Why not live a little*, he figured. *Why not come back to Tenochtitlan in style?*

"Did you read the story on our guy?" Dave asked as he approached Johnny.

"Read," Johnny said. "You can read this?"

The Aztec written language was a complex and ornate pictograph system which took years for outsiders to learn. Dave had only a very cursory knowledge of the written language. "Not really," Dave said. "A little bit—it's been a while."

Johnny folded the newspaper and put it down on the seat beside him. "I've been looking at the pictures to see how Esparza and his case are playing in the local media," Johnny said. "Rule Number One of any field assignment, compadre. Take a nice hot steaming bath in the local media to get a better feel for the local chatter and how stories were playing out in the press."

Dave was taken aback by Johnny's professionalism. He had seemed to be little more than muscle with street smarts when they were paired together, but ever since they landed he had proved to be quite savvy in both the interview with Esparza and their later meeting with Decoyan.

"So, where are we going to eat?" Johnny asked.

Dave put his hands up as if to stop Johnny from going any further. "Listen, I got in touch with an old friend I haven't seen in years, and she wants to meet up with me in about 30 minutes. Is it all right if we go over this stuff later or in the morning?"

Johnny smiled. "And I'm the one with no work ethic? The one who just wants to screw around on this assignment?"

"Well," Dave said, "if you're looking to work, why don't you try looking for the head of our victim and whoever might have possession of it—after you check in with Marta at the Consulate, of course."

Johnny stood up and adjusted his pants. "Yeah, I'll be sure to do that. I'll just go out speaking Spanish or English and try to get these people to understand me."

Dave laughed and put his hand on Johnny's shoulder, pulling him close as he looked around the lobby. Two Jaguar soldiers—different from the ones who drove them around this afternoon—were at the front of the lobby.

"Listen," Dave said. It was almost a whisper. "If you go out, ask the hotel to call you a Red Cab—those are typically airport cabs, and the drivers are usually bilingual."

Johnny nodded. "Red cab," he repeated. "What about our friends?"

"I'm going to tell them I want to grab a bite and do some shopping and that I don't necessarily need an escort," Dave said. "You should do the same if they question you."

"I don't trust those guys," Johnny said.

"You're smart not to," Dave said. "If Esparza's telling us the truth that this killing was done by a Jaguar, that means the killer is a blood brother of the goons who are assigned to watch over us."

Johnny shook his head. "What is the deal with this place? It's so, I don't know—loose. Loose in some places and then restrictive in others."

Dave leaned in even closer. "This is what happens when you open things up but then want to keep all your secrets secret. This government is all over the place. Corrupt bureaucracies, priests on the take, rules that apply to some but not others—depending on the day or prevailing wind. Everything here is built on shifting sands, and you will never know who to trust."

"Right, right," Johnny said, eyes widening. He then stiffened, straightened his jacket, and created some distance between he and Dave. "Have fun on your date tonight, partner."

CHAPTER 6

Efraim Ramirez's continued account of the events of 1519…

A bloody, heaving mess at the bottom of a boat

I HEARD THE waves pounding stronger and stronger, louder and louder. I knew I was getting close to shore, and felt I was also getting closer to the end of my life. Thankfully, the loud cracks of those strange and awful weapons and black powder explosions subsided. I feared my entire fleet and all my comrades were now dead. My bloody clothes and armor must have made me look as if I had suffered a thousand wounds, but I was physically unharmed save a few lacerations from the splintering wood of our craft.

Above the sound of the surf I heard voices, dim and strange, yelling. Then I felt the boat jerk as it came under the power of men, wrestling it to shore. The voices grew louder—it was a tongue not dissimilar to what we heard a few weeks before on the Yucatan. Not dissimilar, but not the same. Little by little, the dead weight of my comrades lessened as their bodies were pulled off me—their black sticky blood still dripping down and soaking my hair.

Finally, the light of day reached me and I stirred; surely this was the moment I would die.

An Indio warrior with a feathered eagle headdress who had climbed into my boat to unload our bodies and weapons noticed I was still alive and jumped back in shock, falling out of the boat and onto the beach. His comrades laughed heartily at his reaction.

For what seemed like an eternity, the Indios talked among themselves. I can only imagine they were trying to figure out what to do with their lowly prisoner who now cowered in the blood and splinters of what was left of our landing craft.

The group grew silent. I hunkered lower, and my breath grew short. Suddenly, a large Indio came upon me, grabbed me by the hair, and dragged me out of the boat in one swift move. He was a man of my height, with the skin of an animal draped over his shoulders and the head of what appeared to be a large spotted cat crowning his head. His bronze face was painted with spots. In his hand was what I could only imagine was some sort of pistola, except it was small and made of a black unpolished metal or wood.

The Aztec warrior, Tuxla I would learn, seemed to be in charge of the other

Aztecs on the beach. I counted some thirty in total. All except Tuxla had some kind of long rifle, only they were much shorter than any musket I had ever seen. Were these the savages who reduced Cortés' fleet to ruin?

I fell to my knees in the waves and used the saltwater to wash the blood from my skin. As I was washing, the Aztecs dragged another survivor from a second nearby landing boat. He was wounded in the arm. They roughly threw him in my direction. He fell to his knees just feet from me—broken and bleeding.

"What ship were you on?" I whispered.

"The Mendocino," he said. "My name is Juan Pierre Miera."

"Efraim Ramirez," I responded. "Let me help you clean your wound."

Juan sat back in the water, immersing his wounded arm under the waves. I untied a kerchief that was around my neck, rinsed it off in the water, and began to dab his wound as he winced in pain. "I think the ball is still inside," I said, not feeling an exit wound. "But it appears to have missed the bone in your arm." Admittedly, I knew little of healing, but I also knew I was all Juan Pierre had at that moment. My uncle was a hair cutter and healer in Grenada, and I sometimes helped him as a boy. But I had no avocation for the healing arts and instead turned my life's quest to the hunt for adventure and gold.

The Aztecs watched us curiously. How could they have developed such weapons? With this kind of achievement in weaponry, why were they not broaching our shores?

Just then, the Aztecs were distracted by several men dressed very differently from them. The men, who also carried similar weapons, were dressed in the colors of the nearby jungle. There were six men; four were European, while two were clearly African. They did not speak, but rather deferred to a seventh man, a small character with black-rimmed spectacles. His skin was darker than the Europeans, and he had facial features in common with the natives.

The little man spoke to Tuxla. Tuxla replied to the little spectacled man and motioned back to me and Juan. The little man looked over as if noticing us for the first time, lifting his spectacles to his forehead and squinting in our direction.

He then motioned in a number of directions, and the Aztecs began to disperse, getting back to the work of going through our landing craft, sorting out bodies, and taking what was useful to them—belts, satchels, muskets, and other items.

"Are we the only ones left?" Juan asked, surveying the scene.

"I don't know," I responded. "I don't know anything anymore."

The Aztecs stopped their work all at once and looked to the sky, transfixed. Juan and I looked up and beheld a green, gold, and red-winged beast. We then heard its buzz grow over the sound of the waves. It flew along the beach, into the sun, and then out to sea as if surveying the scene. Was it a bird? I was not sure. It appeared to hold a man inside of it somehow, but I was not sure of that, either.

"Dios mio," Juan said, "what kind of witchcraft is this?"

The little man with spectacles was trudging our way. He paid scarcely any attention to the wondrous flying machine and instead knelt in front of us. "Are the two of you unharmed?" he asked us in Spanish, which surprised me.

"I am fine," I said, "but my friend has a wound in his arm."

The man reached into a small satchel he carried on his shoulder, pulled out what appeared to be a clean bandage, and began working on Juan's wound. Our attention—much like that of the Aztecs—quickly returned to the sky, as we watched the colorful flying machine bank back and forth as it circled overhead.

I knew I was in no place to ask questions, but I couldn't help it. "What is that thing?" I asked, pointing to the sky.

The little man looked up, almost as if noticing it for the first time. "Oh that," he said. "That's Quetzalcoatl."

CHAPTER 7

1999, Aztecan time

Reunion

DAVE WAITED OUTSIDE the cafe. It was bustling for a weeknight. He couldn't put his finger on why, but for some reason the Aztecs were mad about French cuisine, and the historic district was practically littered with bistros, patisseries, and French cafes.

Dave felt a soft tap on his shoulder and turned to see T'shla standing before him. She was as strikingly beautiful as he remembered, but now had the look of a confident and professional woman.

"Hey there," she said, coming in close for a hug. They embraced. Her hair smelled of mango.

"You look fantastic," he said, pushing back to take her in. "I really never thought I would get to see you again."

"You're not so bad yourself," she said. "I'm glad you called me," she said after a long moment of them taking each other in. They got a table near the door but out of view of the street so they could be assured of a modicum of privacy.

"So, are you still, well, a ward of the state?" Dave asked after they were seated. T'shla put her fingers to her forehead and closed her eyes tightly. Dave could tell immediately this was not a fun topic for her.

"I'm sorry. It's just it was something that was always looming over us—I mean, looming over you. I couldn't imagine what it would be like to live day-to-day with this thing hanging over your head."

"It's alright," she said. Dave was probably the only non-Aztec to know of her predicament. "They haven't freed us of our holy obligation, so to speak. We're all still supposed to be, well, chaste, and waiting for the day when the Emperor reverses his decree against sacrifice."

Dave smiled. "Well, if that's the case, I have some good news."

"Oh really?" she asked.

"Believe it or not, human sacrifice is one of the reasons I'm here in Tenoch," he said. "Your government is so petrified of the bad public relations regarding human sacrifice, they have me and a partner here investigating why some Spaniard allegedly beheaded an Aztec man three nights ago."

T'shla's eyes widened. "That's insane. But, you know beheading is not the way of our old religions. Are you sure this isn't something connected to one of the Island religions—the newer ones, Santeria, you know the ones that mix tribal and Christian beliefs—what do the French-Africans call it, voodoo?"

Dave hadn't thought of Santeria or voodoo and thought it was probably wise to probe Esparza about his personal beliefs and practices in these areas.

"Either way, the fact that your government is so worried about this should put you on safer footing. I mean, they're launching this major dual-government inquiry into one silly little murder in a city of twenty-one million people," Dave said.

A sickly look came over T'shla's face. "I don't know if I'd call a beheading a silly little murder."

"You're right," Dave said, "that was a poor choice of words. I'm sorry."

T'shla gave Dave a warm smile and a wink. "I've lived my whole life with a blade inches from my breast waiting for sick Uncle Coaxoach to do me in. Trust me, I'm not offended."

Dave took a sip of fruit wine and felt a warm wave of peace wash over him. It could have been the mescaline infused in the wine, or it could have been finally seeing T'shla after all this time. Either way, he felt the years melt away.

"Not to bring up more painful subjects, but how is your uncle these days?" Dave asked.

Coaxoach Ixtapoyan had been in the highest circles of the Jaguar priesthood. As an orphan slave girl set for sacrifice, it would have been Coaxoach who wielded the blade and carried out T'shla's execution. Once the Green Revolution occurred, T'shla was given Coaxoach's family name, Ixtapoyan, and was made his official ward, or niece. It was his job to support her and ensure she maintained a life connected to the Aztec ways so she may remain a worthy sacrifice should the Green Revolution end and ritualized executions resume.

"Still lurking," T'shla said. "He left his position in the Order of the Jaguar to become a devotee of Quetzalcoatl, if you can believe that."

"Wow, that's a big life change," Dave said. He never met the looming Coaxoach, but always imagined him to be a stern zealot, willing to kill children as blood sacrifices. Quetzalcoatl was the green feathered serpent, the god of civilization and learning. Dave found it hard to believe that a man such as Coaxoach would turn to such a reasonable deity.

"Yep," T'shla said, "Quetzalcoatl is very much in vogue these days – top god of devotion twelve years in a row."

"I noticed," Dave said. "On the way in from the airport, I saw they built a new shining temple complex in Quetzalcoatl's name. It was very impressive—almost as big as the Templo Mayor."

"It's huge, isn't it? That's where my uncle now works and worships. They started building it way back when you were here—financing the construction with all the new oil and gas money," T'shla said.

"Why the newfound fascination with Quetzalcoatl?" Dave asked.

"I honestly don't know," she said. "Rumor has it the Emperor became enamored of Quetzalcoatl years back and that led him to open the society and end human sacrifice, 'ushering in an age of peace and prosperity for the Aztec people.' At least that's what they say in the media."

"It'd be nice if that were completely true," Dave said. "And since when did you start speaking like you were an official government press release?"

T'shla laughed. "Well, in a sense, what the media says is true. Quetzalcoatl is a symbol. For whatever reason, the Emperor and his advisers realized the society needed to change to be able to compete in the modern world, and there were these things holding us back. They used the imagery of Quetzalcoatl to re-educate and re-orient the people. To inspire us to succeed and to free us from fear."

"And it worked, I guess," Dave said.

"Damn right it did," T'shla said. "You know me. I'm no big fan of any system that oppresses its people and holds women back. I grew up in the old regime. The Green Revolution changed everything. You were here at the start. You experienced it. I now have a good government job with real skills—that was unheard of for women before."

"I get you," Dave said. "The Aztec Miracle."

"Well Quetzalcoatl was the symbol the government used to make it happen—who cares how or why, I'm just glad they did it," T'shla said. "Without that movement, I'd be dead."

"Then why does your uncle still keep tabs on you?" Dave asked.

A worried look crossed T'shla's face as she stared into her drink. "Because, for all we have achieved, when this emperor dies, his institutional changes and decrees die with him. And with that, a return to the old ways. I hear his son, Moctezuma 27, is a fan of the Jaguars—and that might not be good for me."

Dave shook his head. "I don't buy it. Your country has enjoyed so much success in the world. Your trade, your fashions, your oil and gas—it would be insane to turn back."

T'shla took a sip of her wine. "Not here. You see, for all we have done, we still have not instituted a democratically elected parliament to set policy. A lot of the day-to-day is run by directorates of high priests which are susceptible to superstition and inefficiency. So, say a new emperor comes to the throne and his close circle believes we need to close off our society and re-institute sacrifices—just like that, we are back in the past."

"Insane," Dave said.

"Welcome to my world," T'shla said with a shrug.

"Still, though I never personally met him, I can't picture your uncle an enlightened devotee of Quetzalcoatl," Dave said, remembering the occasions T'shla would show up at his dorm room petrified she was being tailed by one of good old Uncle Coaxoach's Jaguar goons.

"I know what you mean," T'shla said. "I guess he just understands power and is smart enough to see which way the wind blows. He's just a pragmatic zealot, if there is such a thing."

"There's one in every crowd," Dave said.

§ § §

Across town, Johnny had a cab driver take him to Caribe, the bar named in the dossier—the one where Santiago Esparza met his alleged Aztec victim. It was a dive bar specializing in liquor derived from the blue agave plant. The bar was in Tenochtitlan's Park District, a neighborhood of nightclubs and general debauchery in the shadow of Chapultepec Hill, which is a hill and park off one of the great causeways southwest of the city's main island.

Chapultepec is the gateway to a vast and overgrown urban park, but it's not the type of park where Aztec parents take their children for weekend strolls. The Park of Chapultepec, in the shadow of the great hill that houses the Emperor's residence, is the place to go in the city for drugs, illicit sex, illegal gambling, and any manner of black-market goods deemed off-limits by the High Priest Directorate for Moral Virtue.

The HPDMV didn't have much pull in modern, post-Green Revolution Aztecan society. It had recently successfully banned pornography depicting unprotected sex. But generally, its official actions were derided and mocked by most secular Aztecs and the mainstream media. Short of outright banning immoral practices, it did have the ability to "Orange Stamp" materials it found below acceptable virtue but not bad enough to ban. The "Orange HPDMV Stamp of Shame" was enough to drive such material underground or "into the park" as the Aztecs liked to say.

Though a shadow of its former self, the HPDMV retained patrons in many of the high priest brotherhoods, particularly among the powerful Order of the Jaguar. These priests persuaded the Emperor to weaken, but not abolish, the Directorate in the days leading up to the Emperor's proclamation of freedom. A man of deep moral convictions, Emperor Moctezuma the 26th agreed that it was wise to have at least a portion of the bureaucracy focused on virtue, and he let the HPDMV endure, though with less power and a smaller budget.

Johnny paid his cab driver, Tototl, 200 Spanish pesetas to take a few hours off his normal route and help him translate and navigate the city's underbelly.

Tototl was a scrawny and good-natured man in his mid-forties, black hair graying and his shoulders a bit hunched over from twenty years spent behind the wheel of his cab.

They entered the bar, which was a rowdy and loud place with a jungle theme. Caribbean-Afro beats pounded through the speakers. It was crowded for a mid-week night. There were several whites there—mostly European tourists and *Norte Americanos*, Johnny surmised by the looks of them.

"Hey Choco," Tototl said to the bartender. Choco was an outdated generic term that entered the Aztec lexicon when the Aztecs finally established trade relations with the Spaniards one hundred thirty years before. Spaniards referred to the skin color of people who were particularly dark as *chocolate*. The term seeped into the Aztec language and had now became an innocuous "hey man" or "hey you" construct.

The bartender lifted his chin in acknowledgment of Tototl. "This whitey wants to know who was working the night that guy got killed," Tototl said, motioning to Johnny. "What was it, three nights ago?"

"Who is he, and why does he want to know?" the bartender asked, his eyes narrowing on Johnny.

"What'd he say?" Johnny asked.

"Shh." Tototl put his hand up. "Some Spaniard. How do I know? Maybe his brother."

The bartender nodded and came around to the end of the bar. "I was working that night—but I didn't talk to the guy who got killed," the bartender said, nodding in the direction of a small, waif-like waitress who was taking an order toward the back of the bar, near the restrooms. "Keela, she served the man who got killed that night," the bartender said. "The police agents spent a long time talking to her afterward."

Tototl strained on his tiptoes to see the waitress. He spotted her at the far end of the bar and elbowed Johnny in the ribs, nodding in her direction. Johnny reached into his wallet and handed the bartender a 10 peseta note before rushing to catch up with Tototl, who was already weaving his way through the crowded bar in the direction of the waitress.

"Come on," Tototl said, turning back to make sure Johnny was following.

Johnny caught up just as Tototl was introducing himself to Keela. Johnny couldn't hear much in the loud bar, but could see Keela was visibly nervous to be speaking to them out in the open. She escorted Tototl and Johnny back to a quiet corner near the restrooms.

"The guy who was killed was a nice man—named Ventli. He had a wife and kids and liked to help the poor," she said.

"Did you know him?" Johnny asked and Tototl translated.

"A little," Keela said. "He had come in a couple of times before—he was always kind and quiet, never looking for trouble—just a drink after work here and there, I guess. I read in the papers that his office was not too far from here. Who are you by the way? Why do you care?"

"I'm a Spanish Colonial official, and I've been asked to look into it by my government because the Aztec authorities arrested a Spanish citizen in the incident," Johnny explained.

Keela became quiet.

"Yesterday, the police asked me to look at a lineup to see if I recognized anyone from that night, and there was a Spaniard in the lineup. I pointed him out, but I also told the police that I never saw the Spaniard and Ventli talk to each other," Keela said as she started to fidget, touching her hair, wringing her hands, and smoothing her palms out on her skirt.

"Don't worry—it doesn't mean the Spaniard did it," Johnny said. "It just means it's enough to detain someone indefinitely until the truth gets sorted out by the judicial priests."

"Listen," Keela said, "I have two young daughters. I don't want any more trouble—I feel like I've told you enough—plus, there's been a rash of beheadings all over the city. The paper today said seven in the last two months."

Tototl translated and Johnny visibly recoiled in surprise. "Seven?" Johnny asked, exasperated. "How come I haven't seen this or heard about it anywhere?"

"Yeah, it's been all over the papers," Tototl said. "That's some preparation your government gives you, eh?"

"I need to get back to work," Keela said, nodding toward the bartender. Johnny turned to see he had begun to pay close attention to their conversation.

"Okay," Johnny said. "Thank you for taking the time to talk to us. If there is anything else you can think of that might be helpful, please feel free to call me." He handed Keela a business card as Tototl was translating. "I think if you dial '453' that's the country code, then the cell number, and you can reach me directly."

Keela put the card in her apron. "Just one more thing," she said softly, almost a whisper. "There seemed to be a few Jaguar agents in the bar that night, keeping a low profile. It was just, well, we don't normally see too many of them in this part of town, much less in a bar pretending to be having a good time."

Johnny nodded at the translation and tried to thank Keela for her help, but she was off and back to work before Tototl could finish.

Tototl turned to face Johnny, poking his index finger into Johnny's shoulder. "Jaguar agents? Really, Spanish? This night just got a lot more expensive. You're going to have to pay me another 200 pesetas if Jaguar soldiers are involved."

"Settle down, buddy, we're bona fide—the colonial governor will pay you well," Johnny said, suddenly feeling the confirmation that their Spanish prisoner

Santiago Esparza was somehow just a patsy who happened to be in the wrong place at the wrong time.

Tototl rolled his eyes and put his hand down. Just then, they both turned to see two large men moving through the crowded bar in their direction.

Tototl looked toward the rear exit of the bar and reflexively tugged on Johnny's arm. "We have to go, my friend," he said. "Not the front door—let's go back here by the bathrooms."

Both Tototl and Johnny headed in the direction of the restroom hall. Johnny made the hallway first. His heart starting to race. He didn't look back but felt a wave of commotion behind him as the two men pushed through the crowded bar to cut them off. He felt Tototl's hand clench the back of his jacket and propel him forward past the restrooms and through the back door of the bar which led to a poorly lit concrete and cinder block corridor. Empty kegs of beer and casks of rum and agave nectar littered the space.

"Which way?" Johnny asked, frantically.

"You think I know?" Tototl said.

"Shit," Johnny said as he turned right and began to trot down the corridor. "I don't even know why we're running. We didn't do anything wrong."

"Just run, whitey, don't ask questions," Tototl said. "Those looked like plain-clothes Jaguar agents." He skidded to a stop at a door in the corridor and tried the knob. It was locked. Quickly, he shuffled to another door—it was open. "Here, down here," Tototl said, swinging the door open. Johnny turned around, ran back, and scooted through the door.

Tototl followed, closing the door behind him and enclosing them in a pitch-black and stuffy room. "Shh," Tototl said, ear to the door. Johnny came up next to him in the darkness. He, too, put his ear to the door.

On the other side, the Jaguar soldiers were already in the hall. Johnny heard the sound of what he thought was a pistol being cocked. Heart pounding, he crouched lower. There had to be at least eight doors in the corridor—how long would it take before they began to try them to see if they were locked.

Quietly, frantically, he began to feel the back of the door for the locking mechanism. Just above the handle was a deadbolt. He thought to himself very quickly about why it was called a deadbolt. He felt the metal of the latch between his fingers and slowly began to turn. It started smooth and finished with a nearly inaudible click, but a click nonetheless.

Johnny heard Tototl's heavy breathing next to him and felt his own heart pounding in his throat. They heard the footsteps in the hall come up to the door. The man these footsteps belonged to stopped. One jiggle at the door with just a hand. One jiggle with a shoulder against it for extra force. Then footsteps shuffling away.

Johnny felt the blood drain from his face. He sat on the floor by the door and breathed a sigh of relief. He opened his cell phone, and the small room was illuminated by the dim greenish light. It was a supply closet for the bar, filled with cardboard boxes of coasters and glassware.

Johnny waved the cell slowly around the room. "No booze," he said. "Just my luck."

"Yeah, well, for this nonsense you're putting me through, tonight's going to cost you another 200 pesetas," Tototl said.

"What?" Johnny asked.

"Damn right, Spanish," Tototl said. "I'm a decent, law-abiding, working man. I don't need to be running from government goons."

Johnny exhaled loudly. "Listen," he said, his voice a harsh whisper. "I am an official guest of your government. I have no idea why the fuck I'm running from those agents anyway—you're the one who pushed me through the door."

Tototl put a finger to his lips and his ear to the door. "I think it's clear," he said.

Johnny put his hands to his eyes, rubbing them in disbelief. "We should probably sit here for a while. If they think we're still here, they'll be expecting us to leave once we thought it was clear."

"Good point," Tototl said, sitting down and getting comfortable.

"So, what do you think of all this?" Johnny asked. He didn't really care what Tototl thought; he just wanted to buy a few moments from Tototl's rambling so he could put it together in his head.

"Two things, really," Tototl said. "One, I don't think your guy committed this crime. Unless your person has been here for several weeks, he couldn't have beheaded all the other people that have been in the papers."

"Good point," Johnny said, now paying more attention to the cabbie.

"And second, the fact that this case has attracted so much attention from the Order of the Jaguar tells me right away that things aren't as they seem."

Johnny pulled his legs in campfire style. "So, the Jaguars don't have the highest reputation?"

"No, no, no, they have an impeccable reputation. In fact, I don't ever recall anyone, ever, speaking out against them in public or otherwise," Tototl said. "I might add, of course, that I grew up in a Jaguar neighborhood and am a Jaguar by birth, of course. Non-practicing, as are most regular Jaguars these days."

"Well, you're certainly not as scary," Johnny said.

"Listen, I signed up to translate for you—this, this is ridiculous. What am I even doing here—trapped in a closet, hiding from the authorities?"

"Apparently you're earning 600 pesetas," Johnny said.

CHAPTER 8

Efraim Ramirez's continued account of the events of 1519...

Moving out

AFTER ABOUT THREE hours of sitting under the shade of mangrove trees and watching the *Indios* and their compatriots comb through our boats and pile up the bodies of our comrades, they ordered us to stand and gave each of us satchels of equipment and supplies to carry. There were now seven of us—seven survivors from a fleet of eleven ships.

The little man with the spectacles—we learned his name was Vargas—was well practiced in the healing arts and was able to treat the minor wounds of three of my comrades with techniques and materials I had never seen before. Tuxla, the Aztecan warrior and clearly the leader of the *Indios* who were assembled, barked orders to his men. Obediently, they formed up in two rows, their short, rapid-firing muskets slung over their shoulders. They lined us up in a single file between the two rows of warriors. Vargas made one last pass with water and to check on our wounded. I was tired and hot and resigned to death—so I spoke up.

"What will become of us?" I asked Vargas as he passed me with a clear container of water.

Vargas shrugged. "Honestly, I'm not sure," he said. "We did not expect to see any survivors."

"So we may still be killed?" I asked.

"If you survive the jungle, then I assume, yes, you still may be killed," Vargas said. "But, either way, you belong to the Aztecs now." With that, Vargas worked down the line, and I thought how cruel he was to heal us knowing that we would all likely soon die.

Tuxla barked another order, and the Aztecs began marching us forward, off the beach and up into the jungle.

§ § §

The Adventures of New World Dave

2013—London in our timeline

Brian Deneven lay cocooned in a soft, down comforter in his West End flat. It was a Saturday, 9:30 a.m.—a cold, dreary February day. Brian's girlfriend, Becca, had to leave at seven to visit her parents, who lived north of London, and now his flat was blissfully quiet.

Brian rolled over and pulled the warm covers in closer. He was not going anywhere today. He might not even leave his bed. He had a million pound city view out his bedroom window, but the day was gray and bleak so he closed his eyes.

Just as he seemed to drift back to sleep his phone chirped the familiar ring. It was Sir Ian's personal ring. One of Brian's hands ventured out of the cocoon of covers, snatched up the phone on the bedside table, and pulled it back inside.

"Where are you?" Sir Ian's voice crackled through the phone.

"I'm home, in bed," Brian said. "It's Saturday."

"No, no, that won't do at all," Boddington said. Brian couldn't tell if Sir Ian was speaking to him or to someone else.

"Excuse me," he ventured.

"My boy, you've been working for eight months on this project, hiring killers, buying up three-quarters of the world's Rhodium, and keeping me clear of the stockholders—don't you want to see what it was all for?"

Brian stretched out in his bed. He actually didn't really care what Boddington was up to. He was just doing his job—making deals, fixing problems, and pulling down $1.5 million American to do it.

"Uh..." Brian started.

"Uh nothing," Boddington said. "Be at the heliport in an hour." And with that, Boddington was gone.

Brian lay in bed for another few minutes considering his options and knowing he really only had one. He pulled himself up and out of bed and hauled himself off to the shower.

§ § §

1999, Aztec time

T'shla and Dave talked for hours at the café, catching up, reminiscing, and discussing how the reality of daily life can sometimes take your dreams off their tracks. She never figured she'd be a computer programmer. Well, up until the age of seventeen she never thought she'd live to see her twenty-eighth birthday.

They closed down the café, and Dave offered to walk her to her apartment. "I'm going to be tired in the morning," T'shla said as they approached her building.

"You're a bureaucrat like me. I can't imagine you need to be bright-eyed to get through the day," Dave said. "I certainly don't."

T'shla smiled. "I wish that were the case, but I'm on a deadline researching a large and potentially embarrassing identify-theft scandal."

"Not your fault, I hope," Dave said.

"Me? Never, I'm too good for that," she said. "Looks like it might have been an inside job, though." They were now at her door—it was a four-story walk-up, painted in bright greens and yellows. She wanted to leap out of her skin and kiss him, but knew in Tenochtitlan there were eyes around every corner.

"Would you like to come in for some maté?" she asked.

Dave looked around nervously. "I would love to," he said. "But I just don't think it's a good idea. Prying eyes."

T'shla cocked her head. "In the grand scheme of things, we're really not all that important," she said. "Besides, it's just maté."

Dave stepped closer and embraced her, gently stroking her hair and kissing her forehead. "I can't risk it," he said. "Maybe when this case is sorted out I can, uh, come up for maté."

T'shla smiled. "Who says I'll even have maté for you then?"

Dave rolled his eyes. "It's a chance I'll have to take."

When T'shla got up to her apartment, she went over to her window to look out on the street below. It was midnight, the hour of the Panther, and all was quiet except for the distant sound of traffic on busy Avenue 1519, which ringed Lake Texcoco and connected the three main Causeways. Under a light across the street from her building she noticed a tall man smoking a cigarette. He stood there for several minutes, surveying her building, not looking in her direction, just standing there like a pillar.

Dave was beginning to make her paranoid.

She turned on her home computer, and while it booted up, she went to the kitchen for a glass of water. No maté tonight—it would have kept her up till dawn.

Back at her computer, she opened a secure connection to her work desktop. Maybe she could crank through a few hundred lines of data before bed. Each line was a human life, someone whose health records had been compromised. One by one, she went through the data, trying to determine a pattern. It was a wide population—men and women, from all regions of the empire, all ages except for the very young, all ethnic groups and income levels. There were priests, soldiers, farmers, and bankers. Six thousand in all, and she had so far gone through about half of them. Many of the names stuck with her and would creep into her daily life.

Charity Neezup, an English name on an Aztecan woman—*it was very pretty*, T'shla thought. She would go through her day and the names would pop into her head. T'Dore Vashmug—a woman's name on a man. *How strange.*

T'shla was blessed or cursed with near photographic memory. In school she never needed to take notes; she just memorized the readings and lectures. It was why the vocational priests suggested computer programming and computer forensics as an avocation. She could remember lines of code and rarely made errors when inputting data.

Still, she longed for something more. She wanted to travel, to see the world outside the Aztec Empire. As someone waiting to be sacrificed, she was never allowed to go more than fifty miles outside the Imperial District which included Tenochtitlan and the mountains that ringed the city. It's one of the many things that would doom any potential relationship with Dave. When her uncle got wind of their college tryst, he personally saw to it that Dave's student visa was not renewed, even though all of Dave's fellow foreign exchange students had their visas renewed.

T'shla longed to see the ocean and the islands of New Spain, New Portugal, and New France. She longed to see the capitals of Europe and China. Her degree was in Asian History, a subject frowned upon by the more conservative priests who would rather their students look inward. But, they allowed her to follow her academic dreams, knowing she would forever be chained to the capital.

All these thoughts of what might have been and the reality of a life lived chained to a computer—existing at the whim of the emperor—gave her a sudden flush of anger.

She hazarded another look out the window and the smoking man was gone.

§ § §

When Dave made it back to his hotel, there was a large manila envelope waiting for him on his bed. It seemed hastily stuffed with papers. He opened it and emptied the contents onto the white satin bedspread. It was copies of three newspapers and a handwritten note from Johnny. *More beheadings, compadre. Talk more in the morning. JF*

Dave opened the newspapers and began looking through them. At first glance they were normal—some recent copies of the *Aztec Daily Rag* and *The Tenochtitlan Evening Scroll.* Dave noticed some of the pages had been dog-eared. He immediately turned to the pages to find articles circled in red.

"Beheaded teacher remembered as caring mentor." It was a *Daily Rag* article about a woman from north of the sacred precinct in Tlateloco who was found beheaded in an alley near her apartment. No head was recovered. The story was from six days prior.

Dave then picked up the other newspaper—the much more trashy tabloid, *Tenochtitlan Evening Scroll,* which local intellectuals derided as the Tenochtitlan Evening Stool.

"Body count to five as head-hunting madman terrorizes city." It was a sensational story about a series of beheadings—including a reference to the most recent killing of Mr. Ventli. It said the killings had started several weeks ago and listed the victims as Ventli, Tomas Tsebuem, D'arg Kenyon, James Fetoosh, and Nazca Ledi, a teacher. It said inept police work was slowing the investigation as Chapultepec Police Command was not communicating with Central Command or Tlateloco Command about the details of the cases.

"And I thought the Spanish legal system was flawed," Dave said under his breath as he walked over to his luggage and pulled out his copy of the Esparza file. In it, clear as day, it listed Esparza's "stamp-in" date as exactly seven days after the first beheading had occurred, according to the timeline from the *Scroll*.

Dave felt a huge weight come off his shoulders. Case closed. No matter what Esparza's petty role was in this whole affair, he was no head-hunting mad man. A stupid criminal, for sure, but clearly not a killer.

How the hell did we not know this before? Dave thought. Newspapers and local media reports rarely left the continent, so all the news about the Empire generally came through word of mouth or the official Aztec news agency—which basically stuck to fluff and commodities reports. *Still, our Consular office here should have seen this and communicated it in the briefing documents. Someone dropped the ball.*

Dave heard a knock at his door. *Johnny probably can't wait till morning*, he thought as he went over to see who it was. He opened the door to reveal T'shla, smiling nervously in the hallway.

"Hello," Dave said, truly not knowing what else to say. "I didn't expect…"

T'shla stepped through the door and quieted him with a full kiss on the mouth that knocked his glasses askew. "Shh," she said after a long, passionate kiss that pushed Dave back into the room. "Don't say anything."

She closed the door behind her and led him over to the bed where she sat down and began to undo his pants. Dave felt his heart pounding like he was a teen again. He stroked her smooth, jet-black hair, noticing for the first time a few stray strands of gray. It made him want her even more.

Wordlessly, they groped at each other, kissing, feeling, and rubbing. Her body was exactly what he remembered, but slightly different. Her hips were more full, her breasts softer. Gone were the boney angles, replaced by slightly more rounded, toned flesh.

They spent hours getting to know each other again. Long, steamy showers, late-night room service, and sex that would definitely be deemed 'deviant' by the HPDMV.

It was the most perfect five hours anyone has ever had.

CHAPTER 9

DAVE WAS HAVING that dream again, and somehow this time he knew it. *He felt the brisk harbor air as he walked down the boat ramp toward the cement pier. He heard the hustle and bustle of the city—car horns, screeching tires, the ruffling sounds of the masses getting ready to start their day. It was still drizzling. He looked up at the tall buildings in wonder and amazement. They were buildings he had never seen before in waking life. But deep down, something told him he knew this place well. He knew the building where he worked and how to get there, and knew there was a great place for coffee and pastries on the way.*

§ § §

The very real smell of coffee pulled him from the dream. He opened his left eye and caught a side view of T'shla's perfect naked back as she poured him a cup.

"I hope you don't mind, but I ordered room service again," T'shla said. "I figured we could use the coffee."

Dave rolled over and kissed the small of T'shla's back. "That sounds great— I've been a good boy, so the Spanish Crown owes me a lavish hotel stay. What time is it?"

"It's getting close to eight," she said. "I am going to be late to work." She sounded as if she didn't care. It was something Dave had never heard in her voice before, like the burdens of her life were no longer on her shoulders. "What are you up to?"

Dave sat up and rubbed his eyes. "I guess I am going to try and figure out more about your legal system," he said. "I think circumstances are now strongly pointing in the direction of innocence for my guy, well, at least lesser charges. We have a preliminary hearing this afternoon in front of the judge on the merits of the case."

T'shla got up and walked across the room for her purse. It was larger than the purse she carried when they met for dinner. She pulled out fresh underwear and a fresh change of clothes. Dave immediately knew T'shla had made up her mind to sleep with him way back when she asked him to come up for maté. Silently, he thanked her for her boldness.

"I'm impressed, Mr. Aragon. You exonerated your person in the short time between when you left me and when I arrived?" T'shla asked.

"Sure did," Dave said, getting up and walking over to the hotel desk. He handed her the newspapers. "Somebody's been beheading people since a few days before Esparza ever got here."

T'shla stopped getting dressed and sat back down on the bed to begin flipping through the newspapers. Dave went over to his suitcase and began pulling out his clothes for the day. A court hearing meant he'd have to wear his lucky socks, the ones from when he won his first case.

He was halfway dressed when T'shla immediately put down the papers and began dressing hurriedly.

"This is bizarre," T'shla said, still focused on the papers strewn about the bed as she dressed. "Can I borrow these papers?"

"Uh, they're the only evidence I have in favor of my guy right now, but I can make a copy for you down in the hotel business center."

"Sure, that's fine," T'shla said, visibly distracted.

"Are you okay?" Dave asked. T'shla walked over to Dave and caressed his chin with the palm of her right hand. Their eyes met, and he saw immediately something was troubling her. "What is it?" Dave asked.

"I, I don't quite know how to tell you, or, well, if I should tell you."

"Is this some Aztec thing? Secret society stuff you can't tell me?" he asked as he took her hand in his and gently kissed it.

T'shla's shoulders slumped and she pulled away. "It just might be."

"Try me," Dave said.

"I recognize two of the names from *my* identity-theft project right here in the news stories," she said. "The teacher, Nazca Ledi, and this Ventli gentleman."

Dave was shocked.

"Coincidence?" she asked. "I need to check the other names in these news stories with my database of stolen identities to see if there are any more matches."

"Are you sure about this?" Dave asked, going back to collect the papers strewn across the bed.

T'shla pointed to her head. "Do you know me at all? My memory got you through two semesters of organic chemistry."

"Of course," Dave said.

After they dressed and pulled the newspapers together, they left the room and rode down to the lobby. Dave had a message from Johnny on his phone, but ignored it for the time being. Once they made copies of the news stories, they spent a brief moment on the sidewalk outside the hotel. Back under the gaze of prying eyes, they suddenly both felt self-conscious about what had happened the night before.

"Thanks for these," T'shla said, stuffing the copies into her over-sized bag.

"No problem. Let me know what you find out."

T'shla nodded. "I'll give you a call." With that, they parted. No kiss, no hug, and no acknowledgment of the wonderful night they had just shared.

As soon as T'shla was off in her cab, Dave reached for his cell phone to retrieve his message from Johnny.

"Dave...hey...Dave, I went ahead to the jail this morning to check on our guy. He's still here, and there's a lot of crap I have to tell you about from last night. It's about 7:30 now; just head to the consulate when you get this and we'll compare notes with Marta...hey, what the fuck are you doing... get your hands off me...Dave...meet me at the consulate! Da..." The message cut out.

Dave ended the call and warily took in his surroundings. There were two Jaguar agents at the door of the hotel, eyeing him. He assumed they were his escorts. Dave turned away and redialed Johnny. Straight to voicemail. He closed the phone again, frustrated, and turned back to the Jaguars. They were now joined by Tlacatan, the diminutive guide who this morning was wearing a rumpled seersucker suit.

Tlacatan offered his hand, a nod to the European custom of the handshake. "Mr. Aragon, good day to you. I am glad to see you out and about so bright and early this wonderful morning."

Dave was puzzled and agitated. "Where's my partner?" he asked, his tone bordering on demanding.

Tlacatan looked legitimately confused. "Mr. Fiver. I assumed he was running late," Tlacatan said. "Are you all right, Mr. Aragon? Do you not know the where-abouts of your compatriot?"

Dave put his phone in his coat pocket and sized up Tlacatan and the Jaguar agents. "Can you take me to the Spanish Consulate and then to see Judicial Priest Decoyan?" he asked. "I have some important information for him."

Tlacatan straightened. "Your hearing with Priest Decoyan is not until 16:00 this afternoon, the hour of the cresting eagle."

"I know," Dave said. "There are just a few things I need to clear up with Priest Decoyan before the hearing." Dave had no idea why he felt he could trust Decoyan, but the judge was the closest thing to a friendly official Aztecan face.

Tlacatan still seemed confused. "So, Judge Priest Decoyan or the consulate first?" he asked.

"Consulate, please," Dave said, pointedly. "Thank you." He couldn't say why, but he had a hunch these official minders didn't have anything to do with Johnny's cryptic message, but he couldn't be sure.

Tlacatan motioned to one of the Jaguar agents who nodded gravely and opened the car door for Dave. Once inside the vehicle, Tlacatan turned to Dave. "So, your partner is not in the hotel?"

"No," Dave responded. He was becoming more convinced Tlacatan and these particular Jaguars didn't know what happened to Johnny, because they would be in deep trouble with the Justice Directorate if they didn't have a good bead on their charges at all times. Dave quickly redialed Johnny's number. Straight to voicemail again, indicating the phone was off.

"Oh dear," Tlacatan said, reaching for his phone.

"What are you doing?" Dave asked.

"This must be reported to my superiors. We do allow certain freedoms of movement, as you say, during off hours—like your romantic dinner last night with one of the Saved Ones, but we do get in a certain amount of trouble if we don't have tabs on you during official business hours," Tlacatan said, fidgeting in his seat, fiddling with his phone and giving away what appeared to be the beginnings of a panic attack. "You do not understand, Mr. Aragon, we simply cannot lose track of our official visitors. This could result in a most stern reprimand, or even worse, a one-way ticket to a posting in the northern desert and the Dry River Territories."

Just then, in the middle of traffic along the busy Cuauhtemoc Parkway, the Jaguar driver skidded to a sudden stop, knocking Dave and Tlacatan forward and interrupting Tlacatan's fit. The cars around them erupted in honks.

Nefarayit, their driver and meat-hook handed guard, turned in his seat and leveled a sneer at Tlacatan. "No need to call the superiors, protocol officer, we'll take care of this oversight," Nefarayit grumbled in a low voice that very much matched his imposing figure. There was a rumor that steroids were rampant among the highest levels of the Jaguar security ranks, and Nefarayit very much looked like he partook.

Tlacatan shrunk back in his seat, appearing to be chastened by the stern countenance of their driver.

"How do you suggest you find him?" Dave jumped in, remembering Esparza's chilling words about the frightening Jaguar with the golden sword. He was sure there was likely a tight network of these guys that probably went back to the Angola War or recent police action in the French Northlands. If they didn't know who Ventli's killer was, they probably had a strong inkling. And if Johnny was getting close to the truth, these goons probably knew what stones to turn over.

Nefarayit turned forward and accelerated back in the direction of the Spanish Consulate. "Never you mind, Mr. Aragon. You do your lawyer work; we'll find your partner."

The Spanish Colonial consulate was located on the long Southern Causeway that connected the Sacred Precinct with the neighborhoods on the southern shore of Lake Texcoco. The Southern Causeway was the longest of the three main causeways and went two miles over the lake, marshes, islands, and famed Floating Gardens of Xochimilco. It was easily a quarter mile wide and was home to some 100,000 people—many of whom lived and worked in the floating gardens and sold their wares in the markets that lined the giant bridge. The floating gardens were an iconic image of Tenochtitlan, and the food grown there made up about ten percent of the city's produce. These days they were more of a tourist trap, and eating mangoes from them was merely something every tourist visiting the city simply had to do. Like taking gondola rides in Venice.

The Spanish Colonial Consulate was just off South Causeway Boulevard on Ramirez Road. The road was named in honor of one of the first Spaniards to set foot in Tenochtitlan back in the early 1500s. When the Spanish Colonial government first established a consulate here eight years before, the Aztecs named the street in his honor and in honor of their newfound diplomatic relationship with a long regional rival.

The building was Spanish in design, but was painted the color of ripened squash. The vibrant yellow-orange of the building mixed well with the smell of fruits from the nearby stalls and the cool breezes coming off the lake. It was built on the edge of the causeway bridge, probably so the Spanish consular bigwigs could have nice views of the lake and Chapultepec Hill along the tourist district of the Southwestern Shore. At the top of Chapultepec Hill, Dave could faintly make out the spires of the Emperor's residence peeking above the lush trees. At the bottom of the hill and to the north was Chapultepec Park and the famous Park District near where poor Santiago Esparza got into so much trouble with all this beheading business.

Tlacatan and the Jaguar guards waited by the car while Dave went inside. Because the consulate was considered Spanish Colonial territory, and because so few exit visas were ever granted to Aztecs who wanted to travel, Aztecs were generally very afraid to set foot in consulates even though there were no formal rules against it. The only time an Aztec would enter a foreign consulate was if he or she had a visa and the requisite immunizations for the country they'd be "visiting."

Once inside the building, Dave was hastily taken back to the consulate's legal office by a young male receptionist. Marta Cabeza de Baca, or C'de Baca for short, was Head Consulate Officer and was very interested to see Dave.

Her office was cramped and clinical—few personal effects—but she did have one of the million-peseta views. Her window looked directly across the lake and had a direct view of the imperial palace on Chapultepec Hill.

"Mr. Aragon," Marta began brusquely, looking up from her paperwork as Dave entered. "I'm so glad you could find the time to join me. Why didn't you or your partner check in last night?"

Dave was taken aback at being in her presence again and by her air of formality. They had grown up together, after all. Her family was sugar sharecroppers on a portion of his grandfather's ranch. As kids they were the best of friends. They would play and ride horses together. She was with him when he had the horse accident that ultimately led to the implantation of the metal plate in his skull.

When the accident happened, she feverishly rode back to the ranch house to get help and later stayed by his side at the hospital throughout the whole ordeal.

When he was fourteen, his grandfather reminded him of his place in the Colonial upper classes and that it was not appropriate for him to be so friendly with people who were of a lower caste. Dave rebelled and was sent to San Juan, Puerto Rico, for boarding school. He and Marta lost touch. Though they would never admit it, they both kept tabs on each other and followed each other's careers. Marta was, by far, more successful. It was Marta who personally appealed to the Colonial Foreign Service that Dave should be tasked with this specific opportunity in Tenochtitlan, even though Dave had never before been on a foreign assignment.

"It's a simple question. When your hotel informed me you had already checked in, I had half a mind to go over there myself and read you and Fiver the riot act. Not to mention our working dinner appointment that you completely blew off."

"Wait," Dave cut in. "Johnny was supposed to..."

"Supposed to what?" Marta said. "I got nothing from him and nothing from you. My time is more valuable than your time. There are incredibly important things happening here—and I can't go into all of them with you. But regardless, I need you on top of your game. And that means checking in with me as soon as you land, dammit. There's an internal power struggle between the Jaguars and Quetzalcoatls, and this case is playing into it. We do not, I repeat, DO NOT, want shit-heel petty Spanish criminals anywhere near this internal Aztec bullshit— especially ahead of important trade talks."

She stood up behind her desk and exhaled loudly. She was part African by ancestry, her tight curly hair less puffy in the more temperate and dry Aztec climate. She had soft rounded features and alluring almond eyes. Dave forgot how lovely she was. He always had a bit of a crush on her when they were kids.

"Where is Johnny, anyway?" she asked curtly.

"That's why I'm here," Dave said. "He told me to meet him here, but it was a voicemail that got cut off by some commotion—I was hoping he made it here so we could compare notes. There may be a break in the Esparza case."

Marta sat back down. "Can I hear the message?"

Dave handed over his phone. "My pass code is 9823," he said.

Marta listened to the message for herself, saved it, and then handed the phone back to Dave. "What the fuck have you guys gotten yourself into?" she asked, her tone less angry than the words she spoke.

"I'm sorry," Dave said. "I told Johnny to keep the evening appointment with you. I'm guessing he never made it. We were able to see the accused as well as the judge and prepare..."

"Prepare to what? Jeopardize our legal standing in this matter?" Marta cut in.

"Huh?" Dave was confused.

"I had someone tailing you to make sure you both were safe," Marta explained. "Trying to influence the judge who is hearing the case is frowned upon in this system. And having sexual relations with the adopted niece of a powerful priest is, oh, I don't know, probably the dumbest thing I have ever heard of. Imagine my joy this morning to spit my coffee all over the surveillance report as I read it."

Dave slouched down in his chair, his heart both sinking and racing at the same time. Marta rolled her eyes.

"If seeing the judge is frowned upon, why would our guide and bodyguards let us do it so easily?" Dave asked, trying to keep the subject away from T'shla.

Marta shrugged. "Don't know. Could be they are under strict instructions to take you wherever you want to go. Could be that they want to use their legal system to their advantage and make the argument that you are subverting the process."

"I met Judge Decoyan—I can't say why, but I trust him," Dave said.

Marta softened. "Well, it could also be that they don't like their judge and wanted to prejudice him and get a better, more favorable judge selected. You know, a real hardliner – maybe a Jaguar. Decoyan is seen as a radical liberal, an outsider-lover—he's only in his position because he comes from a powerful family."

Dave reached for his bag. He needed to prove to Marta he wasn't the wrong choice for this assignment, and he needed to get aggressive, fast.

"I don't know why you're all over me this morning—when you clearly have not been keeping up on the local news." He pulled out the newspaper articles Johnny had left for him. "We just got our guy out of his murder charge, because people have been getting killed the same way all over town—well before Esparza was even in country."

Marta flipped through the pages in silence. She fidgeted in her chair.

Dave got up and walked over to Marta's coffee maker and poured himself a cup. "My question is," he said, feeling cocky and composed for the first time since he left T'shla, "how the hell did your top-notch operation not just, oh, I don't know, read the fucking newspapers and put this together?"

Marta put the pages down with a sigh. "These are tabloid trash sold in the poor neighborhoods in the outlying areas," Marta said. "This never made the news or the media briefs of the more legitimate national daily papers. It would have been easy for our intel ops to miss this."

Dave confidently sipped his coffee, gloating like a lawyer who had a witness cornered. "That doesn't fucking matter. You have agents who can trail me and Johnny to make sure we're not screwing up, but they can't gather basic intel like finding out the Spaniard being held for these crimes couldn't possibly have committed them. Instead you have to fly out two hot-shots from Havana to come and take care of business and solve the case in, what has it been, fifteen hours?" Dave said, looking at his watch for effect. Deep down, he felt a twinge of heartburn, because he also knew that, while he was romancing his ex-girlfriend, Johnny was the one actually figuring it out.

Marta softened as she put the papers back in the envelope. "This is good evidence and may get us off the hook diplomatically," she conceded, "but we still have to present this at the hearing today. Let's hope the high priest directorates—especially the Jaguars and Quetzalcoatls—don't consider your little pre-meeting with the judge as grounds to postpone the hearing or throw a monkey wrench into the proceedings. Remember, it's generally good for all of them, and for the new Aztec national image, if they can pin this killing—or these killings—on an outsider."

Dave nodded. He knew when it was time to play it by the book and follow the orders of his superiors. "Now onto other things. What do we do about Johnny?" he asked. "I have to prep for the hearing this afternoon, but I want to make sure he's all right."

"I'll try to find Fiver while you meet with Esparza and prepare for this afternoon. But if you see him first and he's okay, let me know so I can call off my agents."

There was a long silence in the room as Marta looked Dave over.

"What?" Dave asked.

"We're done here," Marta said, motioning for the door.

Dave slowly stood. "I am sorry for…you know, everything. Not staying in touch. Not coming by. Last night. Lots of stuff."

Marta leaned back in her chair. "I just want you to get through this hearing and get your partner back. But I would like to meet up with you to discuss another important matter. Let's plan to meet up after the hearing this afternoon. I'll meet you at your hotel."

"Understood," Dave said. He turned for the door and let himself out. He wanted to ask her how she was and spend some time but knew that would probably not be possible—at least not right now.

§ § §

Marta waited to be sure Dave was out of the building when she reached into her purse and pulled out her personal burner cell phone. She dialed the one number in the address book.

"He finally checked in with me just now," she said. "Do you have custody of his partner?" She paused to listen to the voice on the other end. "Yes, he seemed to vanish after an early morning visit to the jail. I assumed it was you who grabbed him."

Another pause.

"Okay, yes, I got it. We can bring him in to see you after the hearing this afternoon. He still has his official duty to take care of."

CHAPTER 10

2013—London in our timeline

THE 12:36 Adventures corporate Black Hawk hovered low under the clouds and was flying south of the London suburbs and into the countryside of gentle hills, hedgerows, and ancient stone walls. Brian had only been out to Sir Ian's country estate by land and was surprised at how soon it took for the house to come into view by air.

Scarcely thirty minutes out of the city and Brian saw the main house of the stately Boddington Manor, Whitestone, on the horizon. To its right, just down a tree-lined lane, was the four-story modern industrial building where Sir Ian conducted his experiments and kept his toys.

The 12:36 Black Hawk shot out beyond the estate and out over the coast at Dover, banking wide over the sea to take in the white cliffs. Brian felt his stomach churn as the wind, rain, sea, and updrafts from the cliffs seemed to buffet the helicopter all at once.

"Wheee, hooo," the pilot exclaimed over the radio as the chopper leveled off and began to turn back toward the coast.

In minutes, they were back at Boddington Manor. The mansion, and Sir Ian's ghastly eyesore of a toy box, dwarfed all that was around them. Locals initially balked at the nouveau riche billionaire's purchase of the property so close to England's iconic Dover Cliffs. They later came around when Sir Ian endowed the UK Trust to Preserve the White Cliffs with a fourteen-million-pound donation.

Brian had not been out to Whitestone since the spring and was always surprised to see the four-story metal warehouse structure erected about 300 meters from the main house. "It's so damn ugly," Brian commented into his microphone.

The pilot smiled. "He has the money to do anything he wants, even build a tool shed that's larger than his mansion," the pilot said as the Black Hawk began its descent to a helipad between the house and the over-sized metal structure. The Black Hawk touched down gently onto the rain-soaked helipad, and the pilot cut the power.

Waiting at the helipad was Dr. Hans Gaummer, Dr. Theodora Kopplewicz's chief assistant and second in command of Sir Ian's personal research and development team. Gaummer approached Brian with an umbrella.

"Welcome to Whitestone," he said with a friendly smile. "It's not often that we get visitors out here in the country." Gaummer was a German particle physicist recruited away from the Hadron Supercollider at a cost of 350,000 pounds a year. Brian knew this because he had to try and explain to the 12:36 corporate board the necessity of having a particle physicist and a nuclear physicist on the payroll. Gaummer also had expertise in imbuing alloys with nanotechnology, something he contended—in several academic papers—would someday allow for the human incorporation of alloys into their bodies to regulate systems or even send emails just by thinking about them.

Dr. Theodora Kopplewicz, the chief scientist, was plucked from Los Alamos National Laboratory in New Mexico for 500,000 pounds a year. Every time Brian saw Gaummer or Kopplewicz, he couldn't avoid thinking of their salaries and the fact they were exhibits A and B in the board's forthcoming attempt to oust Sir Ian from the company he started.

"Sir Ian is excited to see you," Gaummer said as they walked in the direction of the workshop, which now towered over them. "Without your business acumen and knowledge of the commodities markets, none of this would have been possible. I can't say enough how much this means to all of us who are involved."

Gaummer and Brian stepped through a metal door and into what appeared to be a simple machine-shop office space with a few cubicles, some drafting tables, and a conference room off to the right. In the conference room, Brian noticed that the table was stacked high with black duffel bags, assault weapons, and what looked like munitions boxes.

"Planning an invasion, I see," Brian said. He began to feel sick as if realizing for the first time that his boss wasn't just eccentric, he was outright insane.

"Just a small police action, my boy, nothing more," Sir Ian said, coming up from behind and putting his arm around Brian's shoulder.

"Wha, what is all this?" Brian managed.

Sir Ian looked him over with a smile that burst through the day's rainy gloom. "It's the beginning of the greatest adventure in the history of mankind."

§ § §

1999, Aztecan time

T'shla made it to her workstation and immediately set about cross-referencing the names in the newspaper stories with her massive identity-theft list. Nazca Ledi, check. Ventli, check. Tsebuem, check. Kenyon, check. Fetoosh—an off-lander name, did not appear in her data file.

T'shla looked up from the screen. The newspaper clippings did not name all of the victims. These tabloid scrolls often didn't bother with basic facts or telling the complete stories. They reveled in the blood and fear. "Head hungry killer on the loose in the park." She let out a big sigh and put the papers down on her desk.

"You look busy," Shetla said. T'shla hadn't even noticed that Shetla had arrived and was already working at her computer.

T'shla smiled. "Just trying to power through this data—it's killing me."

"Want some coffee?" Shetla asked, standing up and grabbing her cup. She reached for T'shla's cup.

"Thanks."

"Huh?" Shetla said, pausing and looking in the direction of the main entrance to their floor. "Morality police." She motioned with the cup to the reception area.

"What?" T'shla asked, startled and turning toward the entrance. She saw a man and a woman, both with orange arm-bands signifying they were officers from the HPDMV, the High Priest Directorate of Moral Virtue. She put her head down and bit her lower lip. *Fuck.*

Quickly and quietly, she gathered the newspaper clippings and put them in her bag. She also grabbed the printouts of information about the people who had their identity stolen and stuffed them inside as well, happy for a brief instant that she had slept with Dave the night before, if only because it meant she had the larger purse this morning.

"They're headed this way," Shetla said, abruptly putting down the coffee cups, turning back to her computer, and sitting, eyes down, trying to make herself as small as possible.

"*Shit,*" T'shla said under her breath.

"It's not that bad, little girl. We're here to help," crooned a male voice from behind her. T'shla turned and looked up. The HPDMV agent smiled, but his face betrayed no friendliness whatsoever. He smiled likely because he was a creep who loved his job and relished making people uncomfortable. That's the type of characters the HPDMV attracted. "Can you come with us for a quick chat?"

Slowly, T'shla rose from her chair, knowing all eyes in her office were now on her. She was careful to sling her bag over her shoulder and keep it close. Obediently, she followed the morality police to the glass-walled conference room where the female agent was waiting. Once inside, the female agent drew the curtains.

"Ms. Ixtapoyan, I have to say, first, how honored I am to be in the presence of one of the Saved Ones—your enduring sacrifice touches us all, deeply," the man said, hand on his heart to show her how earnest he was being. T'shla could not make out the name on his name tag. Behind her, she heard the woman putting on latex gloves.

"How can I help you, officer…" T'shla asked.

"Sintapa, and this is X'tara, my partner," he answered.

"Sintapa," T'shla finished.

"I don't take any pride in this," Sintapa said. He was lying and T'shla could tell. They probably wouldn't even have to pay him and he'd still keep showing up to harass women or anyone who was targeted for acting outside the fine moral standards of the Aztec people. "But I have to ask you a few questions."

"Okay," T'shla said, her heart pounding and a shakiness to her voice that made her feel disappointed in herself.

"Did you engage in sexual relations this morning?" Sintapa asked. "Be careful how you answer; you are a Saved One, after all."

"I fail to see how this is the business of the HPDMV?" T'shla asked.

"We report to the upper priesthoods, and you are a ward of the priesthood and of a high priest. It, and he, have a right to know that the status of its honored property is unblemished," Sintapa said. "Officer X'tara can administer a physical examination if need be."

X'tara stepped forward. She had already lubed two finders on her gloved hand. T'shla stepped away, one foot toward the door.

"Don't make this difficult," Sintapa said.

"My sick uncle put you up to this—I'm sure of it," T'shla said. Maybe it was seeing Dave, but suddenly T'shla felt a strength she had not felt even the day before. She was empowered and done with all the false piety and trying to live according to the standards of others. Her earlier nervousness was now gone.

"Your uncle is very powerful, and he gets things done. And it's all, always, for the betterment of our society and its people," Sintapa said. "Now bend over and lower your undergarments so we may inspect you."

"Fuck you," T'shla said. "Put that in your morality report. My uncle is a pervert, and so is anyone who works for the Directorate of Moral Virtue."

"That's enough," Sintapa said, eyes wild as he motioned for X'tara to move in behind T'shla.

T'shla felt a cold hand at her back working to pull down her skirt. She wiggled away, realizing her attacker's other hand was held up and away from her, two lubed fingers aloft. With a swift stomp she landed her short heel squarely onto X'tara's foot, sending the woman reeling backwards in pain. T'shla now had her back to the door with a clear path of escape. She held up her hands.

"You want the truth? I fucked that Spaniard," she said, head held proudly. "And we didn't use your royal prophylactics, either." Sintapa stood erect, tight faced and barely able to maintain composure while X'tara recovered her footing. "And he's not the only one, either—I've had five or six lovers since I've been a woman," she said, defiantly. "I'm done with your nonsense. Tell my uncle he can take his virtue and shove it." T'shla left the conference room and hurriedly went to her desk.

"What happened," Shetla whispered.

T'shla was flustered and shaking. "I think I just had a revolution of my own," she said, feeling heat in her cheeks as she gathered her belongings. "Tell our director I need to take a few days." Behind her, Sintapa and X'tara emerged from the conference room, straightening their tunics and watching T'shla as she hastily walked toward the elevators.

§ § §

Dave emerged from the Spanish consular offices to find his Aztec keepers enjoying maté at a nearby hot-drink stall.

"Do you want one?" Tlacatan asked when he saw Dave approach.

"Sure," Dave said, joining Tlacatan and the Jaguars at the small table that was set up near the stall.

"Well, on to Judge Decoyan's chambers like you instructed?" Tlacatan asked, finishing up and throwing his cup in the trash.

Dave thought about Marta's advice against prejudicing the judge. "You know, I've changed my mind—I'd like to check on the prisoner, first."

"Fine by us," Tlacatan said. "By the way, we've asked around about your partner—no sign of him being taken in by metro police or by the Jaguar Order. We have a full effort on to find him—if something bad happens to him, it would not reflect well on us. I hope you realize that."

"Understood," Dave said. He felt he might have a chance to learn more about Johnny's disappearance by going to the jail. Maybe Esparza said something to him that should not have been said. "My government is on it as well," Dave said, motioning back toward the consulate building.

He sipped his maté through the traditional straw. Maté came to the Aztec Empire in the 1730s when the Aztecs marched through the Amazon and conquered parts of the Argentine Pampas. "You fellows don't say much," Dave said to one of the Jaguars, the driver Nefarayit, who snorted and turned away.

Tlacatan tried to interject, but the other Jaguar cut him off. "We are not paid to speak," he said, his voice higher and more lilting than Dave would have expected.

Dave felt an opportunity, so he grabbed it. "So, this Spaniard I'm representing, you know, the little guy who they said chopped that Aztec man's head off? Well, he says a Jaguar man did it—a big warrior with a Jaguar bracelet. You fellows have any ideas about that? I know your network is really tight."

Both Jaguars stiffened. Tlacatan nervously put his hand on Dave's forearm. "I think we should be on our way," he began.

"Listen, Spanish lawyer. You think because we Jaguars are the tip of the Aztec spear that it must be a Jaguar who can commit this terrible crime?" Nefarayit said as both Jaguars stood to clear their trash and head to the vehicle. "Minister Tlacatan is correct. It's time to go to the detention center."

"I, I'm not accusing you or your people," Dave stammered. "I guess I felt it was just worth asking."

Tlacatan offered Dave a helpful pat on the shoulder. "You're trying to defend your countryman, I understand. And I'm sure our friends here understand as well," he said, motioning to the Jaguars.

"I truly meant no offense," Dave said. The last thing he needed was to have his official minders irritated with him.

Nefarayit nodded grudgingly and opened the car door for Dave. As Dave stood to head to the car, he felt a buzz in his pocket and reached for his phone. It was a text message from T'shla.

Meet me at Reno's Bookstore. I left work and need to talk.

Dave looked at the time—10:00—he could probably get to the detention center and out to Reno's before the hearing at 16:00. Reno's was near the university—it was a place T'shla knew Dave would remember.

Everything okay? he texted. *Can be there after detention-center drop-by.*

"Mr. Aragon, are you coming?" Tlacatan asked from the waiting car.

Okay, T'shla buzzed back, *but get here as soon as you can.*

Dave got in the car already thinking about how he could lose his escorts for a little while.

§ § §

Santiago Esparza entered the visitors' chamber visibly surprised to see Dave. "I spoke to you partner this morning—what are you doing here?" he asked.

Dave handed Esparza a note. *Partner disappeared after seeing you—tell me about meeting with him,* the note read.

Esparza read and became visibly distressed—he motioned for Dave's pen and began writing. *Asked if I had connections to religious or violent criminal groups here,* he wrote.

Dave took the paper. *And?*

"And nothing," Esparza said aloud.

Dave opened his briefcase and pulled out the file. Esparza, being an ex-convict, would have trouble securing a visa. In his file it said his sponsor was an Aztec by the name of Jidge Axtulla. Dave pointed to the name in the file.

Esparza began writing. *Jidge is an old friend, served together in Angola War. Invited me here for a new start. Good guy.*

Dave leafed back through the file. He knew Esparza had military service, but didn't know he was in Angola—a short-lived conflict about ten years before during which Colonial New Spain allied with the Aztecs to protect the diamond and gold trade from the racist South African Dutch regime. It was the first time Aztecs and Spaniards fought side by side, allowing for many people from the commoner classes of both cultures to truly get to know each other.

Jidge law-abiding? Does he associate with violent or radical types? Dave wrote.

Esparza considered the question and asked for Dave's pen. *Has security job at Quetzalcoatl Temple,* he wrote. *Devoted to Quetzalcoatl and giving people second chances. Has become very religious, but in a good, peaceful way.*

"Did you tell my partner the same information?" Dave asked aloud.

Esparza nodded, and then said, "Your partner was the one who brought him up, asking me all sorts of questions about him. How long he'd been employed by the Quetzals, whether he was a former Jaguar, what his family was like—he was really interested in Jidge."

Dave was puzzled. *What was Johnny on to?* "And?"

Santiago looked annoyed that he had to relay this information again. He held out his hand impatiently, and Dave gave him his pen. Santiago wrote, *He was a former Jaguar who converted to Quetzalcoatl worship. He has become a lot more mystical than when I knew him, saying he has actually been in the presence of Quetzalcoatl – the living, breathing god. Which is crazy. He's quite peculiar now—but not violent, not a killer. No family. Very lonely.*

"Anything else discussed with my partner?" Dave asked.

Esparza shrugged. "Nothing. He just said he had something that raised doubts about my case."

Dave gathered his files and began putting them back in his briefcase. He took the pen and pad and began writing. *Some media reports say other similar killings happened before you got here. This will be enough to get you out of murder charge, but not the luring of the man to the alley. Need to be able to show you are a common patsy, tricked into helping these criminals to lessen any other charges. Spanish Gov't might sign off on that.*

Esparza read the note and seemed to understand that, though the news may be good on the murder charge, he still might be in for a prison stretch.

"Just sit tight and let me do the talking this afternoon," Dave said, standing. "Agent Fiver's absence might force a delay if it is in any way related to his conversation with you this morning," Dave said, loud enough to be picked up by any bugs that might be in the room. "Remember, the eyes of New Spain are on the Aztec empire. There is a lot riding on whether this case is handled appropriately."

Dave grabbed the scratch paper that contained their conversation and tore the page in two pieces. He hazarded another glance around the room—no visible cameras. Dave took half the paper, wadded it up, put it in his mouth, and began to chew. He handed the other half to Esparza, who did the same.

Dave emerged from the detention center to see his official minders waiting by the car. "I'm going to need to work on my presentation for the judge this afternoon, so why don't you gentlemen go grab lunch," Dave said as he approached the car. "I'm just going to find a place to camp out and work."

Tlacatan gave Dave a cock-eyed look. "We can take you someplace where you can work," he offered.

"It's okay, I'll be fine," Dave said.

"I will have to report this up to my chain of command," Tlacatan said, pulling out his cell phone. "You understand our job is to staff you during working hours—this is, well, irregular. Especially given the absence of your partner."

"That's fine," Dave said. "I just need to get some work done, and it doesn't make sense for you to sit around. So, tell who you need to tell, but I'm going."

Dave walked toward the street to a cab stand near the entrance of the detention center grounds. "I need a ride to Reno's Bookstore in Tlateloco," Dave told the attendant, a young Aztec boy barely older than sixteen.

"Oye," the boy called, whistling for the next cab in the line to come forward.

A small, green three-cylinder Chinese Rickshaw taxi sputtered into action. The Rickshaw's were the smallest, clunkiest cars on the road, getting only a maximum speed of 45 miles per hour. Dave rolled his eyes. It would take him at least a half hour to get across two causeways and to Reno's in a Rickshaw.

Just then a Red Cab—a beefy *Norte Americano*-built eight-cylinder roared up from out of nowhere and cut off the Rickshaw. The cab stand attendant forcefully slammed his palm on the fender of the Red Cab, yelling Nahuatl obscenities—pointed questions about the red cabbie's business ethics and upbringing, from what Dave could surmise from the stream of words and tones. The green cabbie began laying on his horn, joining in, telling the red cabbie to get back to the airport and let the green cabs get some work in the city.

Dave stepped in, holding up his hands, knowing this commotion was likely drawing the attention of his official minders. "Boys, boys, please," Dave said, moving toward the door of the Red Cab. He reached into his pocket, pulled out a twenty-credit Aztec gold note, and handed it to the attendant. "Life is short," he said, using a standard Nahuatl opening meant to cool down tense situations. "There will be other passengers, my friend."

Dave slid into the Red Cab and breathed a sigh of relief he was in a better car. He looked over and saw Tlacatan and the Jaguar agents looking in his direction. Dave sat back. "Listen friend, can you please run me by the Hotel TI at Northwest Shore?" He needed Tlacatan and friends to think he was heading back toward the hotel to work. It didn't answer why they couldn't have brought him back to the hotel and he didn't just catch a cab from there, but Dave was not accustomed to working in the field. He was a desk jockey, not a man of adventure.

The Red Cab shot out into traffic and merged onto the north causeway access road.

"Once we get going a few blocks, please change direction and take me to Reno's Bookstore and Cafe in the Tlateloco University District," Dave said.

Without warning, the driver slammed on the brakes, and Dave's face came forward, smashing into the front-passenger neck brace. Before he could react, the cabbie turned around and swatted the top of Dave's head with a newspaper. "You Spanish idiot," he said in broken Spanish.

"Excuse me, sir," Dave sat up straight, indignant.

The cars around them began beeping their horns. Tototl accelerated and merged back into traffic. "You, Spanish, and your work ethic, pfft." Tototl made a derisive fist pump at the windshield. "It's 10:45—10:45—and I saw your friend get jumped and put into a car more than two hours ago. What's wrong with you, Spanish?"

Chapter 11

Back to Holy Thursday, 1519, on the coast …

TUXLA LED THE way on what I assumed was a well-worn Aztec trail through the jungle and up into the hills just off the coast. I could feel in my weary bones that we had a steep climb ahead of us. There were seven of us: myself, Juan Pierre, Pedro Aguirre, Juan Sanchez, Cristobol Salas, Jesus Morales, and Diego Ventura.

Most of us were afflicted with some form of injury related to the fearsome attack on our fleet. This made me thankful, but filled with guilt, that I was one of the few to have not suffered a physical injury. The man called Vargas was apparently a physician, as he successfully stopped the bleeding of both Juan Pierre and Diego by packing the wounds with a powder and applying pressure and clean dressings. Still, Diego could not walk, and Aguirre and Salas were tasked by the European and African soldiers with putting Diego on a litter to be carried.

"I can take over when you get tired," I offered. Salas nodded. Of all the survivors, Salas was the only other man from my ship.

One of the burly soldiers who was clearly not Aztecan—I counted six of these men in total—shouldered his short musket and approached Vargas. He pointed at me but spoke to Vargas in a language that sounded like English or German.

Vargas approached me. "What did you say to that man?" he asked in Spanish.

"I told him I'd help carry our comrade if he grew tired," I said.

Vargas nodded in approval and walked back to tell the European who, from that point on, kept a wary eye on me.

After a few more minutes of climbing through the jungle, we crested a hill which looked out onto the water. I could tell much of the vegetation had recently been slashed away and redoubts dug into the side of the hill. This was apparently the lookout from where they fired the larger weapons that destroyed our fleet. I could see out into the sea. I strained to make out the remnants of our fleet, which now was gone beneath the waves. On the beach were the smoldering pyres where they had burned the bodies of Cortés and the others who washed ashore. Our entire proud fleet and all of our people and horses were gone forever.

The European and African soldiers gathered up several large bags and walked over to us. They dropped the bags at the feet of me, Sanchez, and Morales muttering something in a language that I could now make out was English.

Vargas came back over to me. "Healthy enough to carry your friend, healthy enough to help us carry our equipment," he said.

Three of us, who were all much smaller than the Europeans and Africans, struggled under the weight of the bags as we hoisted them to our shoulders. The contents seemed pointy and hard, with sharp edges just under the canvas of the bags. One of the African fighters barked an order to the rest of his comrades, who all at once shouldered their weapons and began marching deeper into the jungle beyond the redoubts they had recently dug.

Morales looked at me shaking his head. "Gracias," he said, pushing forward.

The Indio Tuxla barked out some commands and the Aztec soldiers, who were apparently under his command, began following the Europeans and Africans. Slowly, we all followed. What were we to do? They destroyed our entire fleet—eleven ships—in a matter of minutes. We all grasped at that moment that running meant certain, painful death. So we dutifully pushed forward, bounded on either side by our Aztecan captors and their comrades.

As I passed the redoubt I admired the quality of the position. My father, Efraim Gonzalez y Ramirez, was a solider and a master of the cannon.

"What are you looking at?" Juan Pierre asked.

I pointed to the redoubt and then out to the sea. "Excellent placement," I said. "With their weapons we didn't have a chance. No chance at all."

"The weapons are miraculous," Juan Pierre whispered. "Why are these people not invading our shores?"

I nodded. So many questions, and I would likely be dead before learning any of the answers.

Using blades designed to cut through thick jungle, three Aztecs led the way, widening the trail they must have used to reach the beach. It was only the spring, but the heat was oppressive, and the weight of our burdens drained our strength with each step.

After about an hour of trudging into the jungle, we began to see Indios from the nearby city of Cempoala lining our route. They were mostly women and children, standing silently and with stares of curiosity. The Cempoalan women were strikingly beautiful and covered in heavy seashell necklaces. They were not laden with the gold of the Aztec soldiers.

Up ahead, I could see the jungle melt away into a clearing. A black pyramid constructed of volcanic rock came into view. It was surrounded by thatched-roof huts and several other low-slung volcanic-rock built structures.

On top of one of the flat structures was what Vargas called Quetzalcoatl. But this apparently was not an animal; it was some kind of mechanical flying machine painted a brilliant and shiny red, gold, and green. Standing near it on the platform were two Europeans, an Aztec—I could tell by the gold—and what I took to be a Cempoalan because he was dressed ornately in robes and feathers, but not adorned in the gold of the Aztecs who attacked us.

"Everyone take a break," Vargas said to us in Spanish. He pulled clear containers of water from his pack and passed them to us, starting with Diego, our most severely wounded comrade.

I sat next to the heavy pack I had been carrying and was immediately approached by several Cempoalan children, staring intently at me. One, a little girl with impossibly long black hair, hazarded a tug on my beard. The Aztec Tuxla and one of the African soldiers walked over to the platform to confer with the Cempoalan and the men who were standing by the metal flying beast.

"What is this place? What is happening," Diego asked, weakly.

Vargas went over to him and checked his forehead. "This man needs a cold compress," Vargas said, handing his water and a kerchief to Salas. Vargas stood and arched his back, staring in the direction of the impromptu conference.

"We didn't expect there to be any survivors," Vargas said. "We were tasked with turning back the invasion, not taking prisoners."

"Invasion?" I asked. "What do you mean, invasion?"

Vargas swept his hand over our group. "All of you, your invasion of Mexico. We stopped you before you could land."

Slightly emboldened, I pressed. "We were not invading, as you say. We were coming here to bring the word of His Lord Jesus Christ. This is a holy mission."

Vargas snorted. "You think they need the Lord Jesus?" he asked, motioning to the city. "They seem to be doing just fine, and probably have been for hundreds of years."

"But who will save their mortal souls?" I asked in disbelief.

"Who says it's your job, Spaniard?" Vargas asked. "Your path of disease, steel, and fanaticism would have destroyed civilizations and murdered hundreds of thousands of people—and we put a stop to it."

I was dumbfounded. "How can you say such a thing—it's inconceivable."

Vargas snapped to as if realizing or remembering something. He went to his bag, rummaged, and then fell to his knees intently pawing through it. "Here," he said, pulling out a kit and what looked like a silver pistola. He affixed three small glass vials into the heel of the pistola and quickly came up to each of us, pointing it into our upper arms and pulling the trigger. He moved so fast we couldn't protest.

"Relax," he said to me softly, pressing the device into my upper right arm.

"What is this?" I asked, suddenly feeling a sharp pain shoot through my arm and shoulder.

"Medicine," he said, "meant to stem the spread of foreign disease these people have never been exposed to before."

I shook my head. It was clear to him I didn't understand.

"Europeans carry many diseases the people of the New World have never been exposed to. Why do you think the native populations of the Indies have been so decimated? It's because of the diseases you carry—small pox, etcetera. I'm trying to prevent the same thing from happening here. This vaccination will cure many of the diseases that have been so ruinous to these people."

I rubbed my arm in an attempt to deaden the pain. "So, I can tell you are clearly not Aztec. What are you—where are you from?" In that moment, I could tell Vargas was confused about how to answer the question. But more than confusion, I could also sense a kernel of conflict creep across his face.

"Hold on," he said, standing and walking over to where the leaders were having their conference.

"What did he say to you?" Diego asked me, weakly. "What did he do to us?"

"He said he was giving us medicine," I said, "meant to protect them from us." I pointed to the natives who were still gathered around staring at us with curiosity.

After several minutes of conferring with the men atop the volcanic pedestal, Vargas walked back, wiping his brow with a white kerchief. "It looks like you have all been approved for a flight on the Quetzalcoatl. You are all going to Tenochtitlan."

"What do you mean, flight?" I asked.

Vargas pointed to Quetzalcoatl. "You're all going to fly to Tenochtitlan. Trust me, it's a better alternative to walking. The Aztecs will be walking, if you want to join them, but they may sell you as slaves to some of the cities along the way in exchange for food or souvenirs."

I felt my chest begin to tighten and heard my comrades begin to grumble with unease.

Vargas held up his hands. "We didn't anticipate survivors," he said. "The warriors could just as easily have killed each and every one of you, but they didn't. The Aztecs wanted to sell you to the Cempoalans as slaves or sacrifices— but our leader said 'no'—he said we'd take you all back to the capital. So trust me—this is the best alternative for you at this time."

§ § §

1999—Aztecan time

Coaxoach Ixtapoyan leaned back in his chair, ear to his phone. For a high priest of the Quetzalcoatl Order, his office was small, cluttered, and had no windows. That's what happens when you're a lifelong devotee of the Jaguar and now find yourself a recent convert to the ways of Quetzalcoatl. Many of his powers and privileges translated, but not necessarily the office space. There was a four-year wait among priests seeking an office with a window in the shiny new Q-Temple.

Sitting across from him in the cramped office was another somewhat recent convert to the ways of Quetzalcoatl, Jidge Axtulla. Only Jidge wasn't a priest; he was a hardened war vet and now a low-level security worker at the temple. Coaxoach liked him because he did was he was told without asking too many questions.

"Very well," Coaxoach said, twirling the cord of the phone with his right index finger. Sintapa, on the other end of the line, had just left T'shla's office and sounded nervous as he gave Coaxoach his report.

"Is that all, then, sir?" Sintapa asked. He was calling from a public phone across the street from the Information Ministry offices. The HPDMV still did not equip its agents with cell phones, viewing them as tools that engender immoral behavior by making it easier for spouses to communicate with their lovers.

Coaxoach shrugged. "I guess you did all you could. If the girl won't submit to an inspection, what am I to do? She's a Saved One. It never looks good to arrest a Saved One. They're public symbols of the wisdom of His Highness and the Holy Quetzalcoatl."

Jidge shifted in his chair. Coaxoach noticed and held up his hand, indicating he should remain patient.

"Well," Sintapa stammered, "I must say that X'tara and I did our best—the girl certainly was shaken. If that was your aim then I think you achieved it."

A smile of satisfaction slowly crept across Coaxoach's wrinkled face. "Yes, it'll do." He couldn't say why, but he delighted in torturing the girl. He couldn't sacrifice her, not yet at least, and until that day came, petty harassment would have to do. Just the fact that she was entangled again with this Spaniard and the beheading case was enough of an excuse for his fingers to poke her yet again.

"So, are we done?" Sintapa asked.

"For now," Coaxoach said, "but you still owe me one more favor, and don't you forget it."

"Of course," Sintapa said, sounding deflated. "Our purpose is to serve."

"Take your partner to Sirnicho for lunch today, on me," Coaxoach said, moving into position to hang up the phone. "I have an account there, and the chef owes me a favor."

Coaxoach hung up the receiver and again leaned back. Awful office not withstanding, he was still at the heights of his powers. Coaxoach learned when he was a boy that the priesthood was more than a path to the gods; it was the fastest route to wealth and power the lower castes had. Most in the priesthoods took their duties with great seriousness and pride. For Coaxoach, it was a chance to seek out the little advantages in life.

And that fact made him a very effective and sought-after priest.

While most priests spent their days and nights reading ancient scrolls and divining from the stars, Coaxoach was not of their ilk. He was a procurer. When a priest needed a special ticket to an exclusive event—he went to Coaxoach. When someone in one order had a family member in trouble with another order, they called Coaxoach to fix it. He was a valuable acquisition for the Quetzal Order, as the Quetzals were always so dour and serious. They needed a priest like Coaxoach who could grease wheels and get things done.

For Coaxoach, the move made sense. After twenty-five years of wheeling and dealing with the Jaguars, his act had worn thin. Too many favors, too many toes stepped on. That, and the fact the Jaguars were becoming too secular for his taste, and the conversion made perfect sense. Coaxoach's act only worked when he was the loosest priest in the room. As the Jaguars made moves to appeal to more mainstream and progressive Aztecs to compete with the soaring popularity of the Quetzalcoatl devotees, the priesthood began to change. Sure, the Jaguars still espoused a need to teach the "old ways," but they were now just words. Too many free thinkers were working their way up the Jaguar Order for Coaxoach's taste. Now, it was the Quetzals that were seemingly opening their doors to more and more hard liners—and that suited him just fine.

Coaxoach acknowledged Jidge, who still sat uncomfortably in a chair too small for his frame. "Oye, Jidge, you have served your order well," Coaxoach said, reaching into his desk. He pulled out two small stacks of Aztec gold notes.

Jidge looked at the notes on the desk. It was probably more than he made in two months. "I have given my life to Quetzalcoatl. I do not do your bidding for money," Jidge said, though it likely pained him greatly to turn down the cash.

"Really?" Coaxoach asked, legitimately surprised. He left the bills on the desk. It was always easier to control people if they took money, and this was a quandary for him.

"All I ask is another chance to be in the presence of Quetzalcoatl," Jidge said. "That is payment enough."

Coaxoach sighed. About a month before, he had gotten Jidge into the back of an Imperial Court chamber session in which Quetzalcoatl himself made a brief appearance. It was a fluke, because Quetzalcoatl was usually only known to be in the presence of the Emperor, close family, or the highest levels of the Quetzalcoatl Order. Coaxoach had seen him twice at a distance but had no interactions, so getting Jidge another sighting might be dicey.

"Quetzalcoatl will be there, walking beside you on your passage to death," Coaxoach said, trying another tack. Maybe this fellow was a legitimate zealot.

"I know, m'lord," Jidge said.

"Well, I will see what I can do, but remember, a life in unquestioning service to Quetzalcoatl will yield you a personal audience with him on the other side," Coaxoach said. *Religion was certainly handy*, he thought.

Jidge slunk in his chair, shoulders deflated. "Thank you for trying," he mumbled, weakly but earnestly.

Coaxoach sat back, satisfied.

"Good, good," he said. "Now, I have an assignment for you coming from a contact all the way up in the Imperial Palace. He was very grateful for your earlier help offering up the fact that you had an outsider visiting you, and he apologizes for your friend getting mixed up in this nasty business. It's just that it's easier for everyone if these crimes appear to have been committed by an outsider. You can imagine how bad it would look if an Aztec were seen to be engaging in sacrifices, especially with our outward positioning these days—tourism and whatnot."

He could tell Jidge was barely following.

"That's why he wanted to pay you for your troubles," Coaxoach said. "My contact in the palace truly did feel bad about your friend getting mixed up in this whole thing."

"It was not good what happened to Santiago," Jidge said. "He is a friend, and I feel bad for telling you he was visiting."

Coaxoach could feel his teeth grating. He detested speaking with imbeciles. "Yes, yes, and that's why we wanted to pay you as thanks for your troubles, my boy," Coaxoach said.

"I serve Quetzalcoatl," Jidge said.

"And Quetzalcoatl appreciates your service," Coaxoach said. "That's why, in addition to the money, I asked you in here to do one more assignment."

"Yes, m'lord?" Jidge asked, leaning forward eagerly in the too-small chair.

"There are those—much higher up the chain than me—who know the case against your friend is flimsy. They feel Santiago might get out this afternoon after his court hearing. If that's the case, we'd like to see him in our custody, you know, to keep him safe here with the Quetzalcoatls."

"That's sounds mighty right," Jidge said, his demeanor brightening.

"Fabulous," Coaxoach said. "So, just be around the courthouse this afternoon and await instructions. You might have to drive your friend over here or somewhere else. I will make the arrangements with the court to release this unfortunate Santiago Esparza into your custody should he be released from the detention blocs after the hearing."

Jidge nodded and started to rise from his seat.

Coaxoach gathered up the stacks of bills and again offered them to Jidge. "Take these, my boy," he said.

Jidge reluctantly held out his hand and took the bills.

Coaxoach held up his finger and shook it to drive his point home. "Take this money and make sure you put it in a safe place before you go to the court-house—*before*. Put it in a bank or something. I don't want you driving around with a bunch of cash. It's unsafe."

Jidge nodded and rose to exit. Once he was gone Coaxoach again picked up his phone. "Exchange, can you put me through to the office of Judge Priest Decoyan..."

§ § §

On the cab ride to meet T'shla, Dave learned from Tototl that, by all accounts, it appeared Johnny was not grabbed by Jaguar agents but by someone else entirely. White people, and probably not Spanish colonials, so Tototl surmised, by their fair skin and light hair.

"So, why were you helping him?" Dave asked.

"He, well you, you owe me 600 pesetas, well now 800 pesetas considering the time I have spent," Tototl said.

"That's it?" Dave asked.

Tototl shrugged. "He's a nice guy," he said. "We spent a lot of time last night hitting newsstands in the bad neighborhoods and getting stories about the beheadings. I took him to the hotel so he could drop off the papers to you, then we went to an all-night diner, and then back to the jail to see the Spaniard they have locked up."

Dave sensed Tototl was more invested than he was letting on. "What else do you know?" Dave asked.

"What do I know, eh, fuck you, what do I know," Tototl said. "I know a nice guy I saw get jacked, man, that's not right."

"What kind of car were they in?" Dave asked.

"An Incan Spider—'97 or '98—nice car," Tototl said. "The whites were in suits—black—similar to European business guys I have taken around town. But these guys had a car with Tenochtitlan plates, so they obviously can drive here."

It was very rare for visitors to have driving privileges in the capital, partially for liability reasons, as driving in the Tenoch 'speedway' was a life or death proposition even for the most experienced of motorists. Also, restricting access to vehicles allowed the government to better control the movement of foreign visitors.

"Johnny left me a voicemail as he was being grabbed. I told my consulate about it, and we are making official inquiries. If he wasn't taken by your government, then I need to alert my diplomatic contact that we might be dealing with something completely different," Dave said.

"That's fine man, but all I know is you don't trust anyone—your guys, the whites, especially the Jaguars—this whole thing is about more than just some Spanish guy in jail," Tototl said, his free hand waving wildly about his head.

Suddenly, Dave felt a piercing pain at the top of his head where his metal plate was located. "Ahh," he cringed, falling back into the seat and losing all muscle control as he felt something akin to a switch in his brain turn on.

"Hey, Spanish, you all right?" Tototl asked, but Dave could barely hear. The back of his head felt like it was on fire. Dave squeezed his eyes shut and flashes of light and images from his dream—of riding the boat to the gray, rain-swept city of impossibly high towers that stretched into the clouds—all poured into his mind.

His boat, the "TATEN", was moored to a pier, and workers attached the gangway ramp. The boat's horn bellowed deeply in the rainy morning. Slowly, the crowd moved to the gangway to disembark. Dave was gripping a leather satchel of some kind. With his free left hand, he grasped the handrail on the gangway and stepped onto it, walking off the boat in a single-file line. Was he dead? Was this purgatory?

Toward the end of the gangway, his foot slipped on a metal part of the floor where the rubber traction strips had worn thin. He felt the weight of his body come out from under him, and for an instant he seemed to be flying. The weightless sensation ended when the back of his head hit the railing and his body crumpled down the rest of the gangway.

The next thing Dave felt was a warm hand cradling his face.

"David," came a soft feminine voice with an Aztec lilt, "Please, wake up."

It was T'shla. She had crawled into the back seat of the cab. Tototl was leaning over the front seat. He had a concerned look on his face. T'shla moved her arm around Dave's head and gently massaged the back of his neck.

"Lady, do we go to a hospital?" Tototl asked T'shla.

"No," Dave answered weakly, "I'm all right." He sat up slowly. "What happened?" he asked.

"You complained of head pain and went into a seizure of some kind," Tototl said. "I got you here, went in, and grabbed your friend, and that's when you came out of it."

Dave took a deep breath, still confused and weakened by the visions he had seen, but not wanting to alarm T'shla. "I guess I needed to get something to eat," he said. He looked out at the café, filled with students and their laptops working in the open air of a bright spring morning.

"This is perfect," he said. "Tototl, can you please park the car and come in and join us?" T'shla's brow furrowed.

"It's okay," Dave said, "I think this guy's here to help, somehow."

Once inside, T'shla took Dave to a quiet table in the back. "Are you sure you're okay?" she asked.

Dave nodded, still trying to get his bearings. "I don't know—I blacked out and almost…dreamed, I think…but it was so real—real as right now. It's been that same recurring dream for as long as I can remember, but this time I can remember so much more. This time I remember slipping and falling..." Dave reflexively felt the top of his head, running his fingers along the seam of the metal plate.

For Dave, this recurring dream began soon after his childhood surgery to reconstruct his skull. Throughout his academic and bureaucratic careers, he had to answer questions about the plate and about the dreams. Would this injury, and these dreams, impact his mental capacity? Could he properly carry out his job? Could he be trusted to serve and support the diplomatic corps in times of high stress?

Dave had no doubts about his abilities, but the nagging questions chipped away at his confidence, causing him to stop taking risks and to stop asking for exciting foreign placements. In fact, he would never have been on this assignment had it not been for Marta C'de Baca personally pulling strings and asking for him.

"We should get you some water, sweet man," T'shla said, motioning for the waiter and holding up three fingers.

Dave finally felt himself returning to normal, shaking off the effects of the seizure. "Okay," he said, "I am back. I am all right now." He paused, eyes refocusing on the restaurant. "You asked me to come; your text seemed urgent."

T'shla cast her eyes down to the table and then carefully looked from side to side. "Yes. They know about last night—they sent two agents from the morality police to 'inspect me' this morning."

Dave reached for her hand. "Are you okay?"

"I wouldn't let them lay a finger on me. This is my life," she said, her eyes meeting his.

Dave nodded. "Can they do anything to you?"

"I don't know. But for whatever reason, they were watching me last night— they haven't really watched me in years. That tells me what they are really doing is watching you."

Dave slowly drew his hand away and looked around the café. "When I tried to get your number it probably tipped them off," Dave said. "I'm so stupid. I'm sorry."

T'shla shook her head. "No, don't ever be sorry. I am very happy you took the risk and called me."

Tototl arrived from parking the car and drew up a chair just as the waiter was delivering water. "You feeling better, Spanish?" Tototl asked, a note of genuine concern in his voice.

Dave nodded. "Any sign of anyone following us?" Dave asked.

Tototl shrugged. "They're professionals—if they were following I would never know it."

Dave motioned to Tototl. "He was my partner's driver last night and saw him get grabbed outside the detention center early this morning. He's also into us for about 800 Spanish pesetas."

"Jaguars?" T'shla asked.

"No," Tototl said. "Whites, a business guy and girl, black suits—they drove their own car."

The waiter returned to take their order. Dave kept it to tortillas and lime broth, T'shla had a coffee, and Tototl ordered two eggs, beans, tortillas, Xalapan chile, and pork stew.

"Your crown's getting this, right Spanish?"

"Sure, but leave room for dessert," Dave said.

When the waiter left, T'shla reached into her bag. "My visit from the authorities is not all I wanted to talk to you about," she said, producing copies of her spreadsheet and the newspaper clippings. "Are you sure we can trust…" she motioned to Tototl.

Tototl grunted to convey that he was insulted.

"He stuck around after my partner was taken to alert me," Dave said. "He can be trusted about as much as anyone else, I guess."

"A ringing endorsement," T'shla said.

"I ordered my food," Tototl said, "so I'm not leaving. You want to go all chippy-chippy telling secrets you can get another table."

"Okay," T'shla said, refocusing on the documents, pushing them forward and eagerly moving cups and condiments out of the way, "we've hit on something." She laid out the spreadsheet. "Many of the names match. Of the folks who were killed—almost all appeared on the list of people whose medical records were illegally downloaded."

"Meaning what?" Dave asked.

"Meaning this is one hell of a coincidence—or it's no coincidence at all. 224 million Aztec citizens, 6,200 health records stolen, nearly all the victims of this recent spate of killings appear on this list. I did the math—there's a 99.924 percent chance that the stolen health records are connected to these killings. In other words, I bet if we go back and do some kind of a regression on the rest of the people on the list—the 6,200—we'll find some kind of a data point in common."

"Impressive," Dave said after a few moments of looking over the spreadsheet and the names marked in red that matched those killed in the tabloid news reports. He was still having some trouble fully concentrating. "But, I don't know if this is something I can bring up at the hearing today—it starts knocking on some dark, secret Aztec doors that I don't think I need to be knocking on in order to get my guy out of this murder rap."

T'shla recoiled and sat back in her chair, folding her arms. Dave knew immediately this was not what she wanted to hear, and deep down he didn't want to sound like he was going into full bureaucrat mode, but some habits are hard to break.

Tototl studied T'shla closely and Dave noticed the cabbie's eyes brighten. "Wait a minute, I know you—you're T'shla Ixtapoyan. You're famous," he said, voice becoming a conspiratorial whisper.

T'shla shot Tototl a glare. Tototl sank in his seat. The waiter arrived with Tototl's order and the three sat in silence until well after he left.

"This is important," T'shla finally said, her eyes burning into Dave. "People are getting killed, and the who's or why's behind this are directly related to my data breach. That breach happened on my department's watch—our asses are on the line. Are you just going to leave me hanging out there?"

Dave was somewhat annoyed. "How am I leaving your ass hanging out there? Your internal Aztec data breach has nothing to do with Esparza. Esparza gets off because the killings were happening in the days and weeks before he arrived. Open and shut as far as I'm concerned."

T'shla leaned in. "Zheeee!" It was the Aztec verbalization of extreme frustration. "How can you be so narrow? Where do you think you are? Nothing about this will ever come out from an Aztec source. If I try to release it, I would be neutralized before I get within a kilometer of a microphone. It has to be a foreigner. I know there's a risk to me, and I am willing to take it—especially if it will smoke out what's behind it all. The only way there is ever light on this is from some outsider stumbling into it. That will make the media pay attention. That may save the lives of some of the people on this list. You know, the ones who haven't been marked red yet." She was now pounding her right forefinger on the papers, rattling the cups and saucers.

Dave leaned back and stretched. This whole subject made him very nervous. He cast a glance at Tototl, who nodded, apparently in full agreement with T'shla.

"So I have to be the guy—the foreign schlub who stumbles onto this as part of the investigation into Santiago Esparza," Dave said, deflated and feeling like a pawn. "I don't like it."

"Whatever," T'shla said, pushing away from the table and folding her arms. "Good for you."

Dave knew he was sunk. Sudden sadness washed over him. He knew he blew his chance and knew he disappointed her and likely crushed any faith she had in him. But he was afraid—afraid of the spotlight this revelation would cast on him. Afraid of what his superiors would think. Afraid about how this would conflict with his comfortable life back home, a place he desperately wanted to be right now. This was an Aztec matter best left to the Aztecs. Who could say if his revelation would actually do anything for the other people on this list?

He sighed deeply. Dave leaned in again to look closer at the list and attempt to re-engage with T'shla. "You said almost all?"

T'shla unfolded her arms and began gathering her papers. "Yes, a few of the people were non-Aztecs, people visiting—work visas," she said. "Since I don't have access to the foreign visa databases and those health data points, there is no way for me to cross reference to see if there is something innately medical that ties them to the other victims. I'd ask you to see of you could connect me to the Spanish victims' families, but I do recognize that's not part of your official job description."

Dave did not move. He sat, impotent.

"I guess we're done here," she said, rising from the table. "I hope you find your partner and get someone to check out your head problem. It was really nice seeing you." With that, she glanced at Tototl, cocked her head, and walked out of the restaurant, leaving Tototl and Dave to finish in silence.

Later, back in the car, Dave closed his eyes tightly. Images of T'shla and his recurring dream flashed before him. He reached for his pocket and pulled out his phone. He dialed Johnny's number—it went straight to voicemail. Next he tried Marta C'de Baca on her cell. No answer.

"Where to, Spanish?" Tototl asked curtly.

"Judicial District—take me to the courthouse," he said.

"Ehhh," Tototl began, "best I take you to your hotel—that's where your government minders are probably waiting for you."

"Oh yeah, right," Dave said. He was absent, ashamed, and regretted ever being chosen for this project.

After a few minutes of navigating light traffic back in the direction of the hotel, Tototl cleared his throat loudly. "How'd your government let some amateur get this job?" he asked.

"Excuse me?" Dave responded, sitting upright in the back seat.

"Yeah, you heard me," Tototl said. "Your partner would have never rejected a girl like that. He would have blown the cover off this whole thing."

"Yes, cab driver, you know my partner so well. For all we know, he's probably knee deep in whores right now." Dave immediately regretted saying that.

"*Eh-fa!*" Tototl exclaimed. It was the Aztec idiomatic equivalent of go fuck yourself, and Dave knew it. "You think I want to risk all the money you owe me by making you angry? Of course I don't. I want more than anything to have you pay me so that I can get away from you and this whole mess. But guess what? I can't now. Agents have probably been tracking me since last night, and I'll probably end up on some rock pile in the Chihuahuan Desert."

Dave reached into his wallet and began peeling off notes.

"There are no breaks for average guys like me. All we get is the chance to dream that we can one day do something different—be somebody. And here you are, some fancy Spanish lawyer, flying on planes, going different places, and you have less *cojones* than me—a simple guy who only ever went on two planes in his life—and that was to be a cook in the army."

"You wouldn't understand," Dave said in a resigned tone as he passed 1000 in peseta notes up to the front of the cabin.

Tototl took the money without looking at it and stuffed it into his inside jacket pocket. "I understand plenty," he said. "I understand that my life was predetermined from the time I was born—lower caste, field workers, Oaxacan stock. That today I am a cab driver marks the highest achievement of anyone in my family, ever. They see me as the Big City Tototl with his glamorous life. And to them, that's true. But I know the real truth. I know my station. And that lets me know how special it is to come across people who can flit anywhere they want—island to island—making love to beautiful women, taking vacations, changing jobs, doing what makes them truly happy. And then I see someone like you who has it all, and you confine yourself to monotony. You, always following the rules, never crossing lines that aren't supposed to be crossed. You make me sad, Spanish. Why should somebody like me aspire to be anything more when I see people like you who have the world but choose to be a dull asshole?"

Dave let Tototl's words sink in. He was right. Dave was a man of the New World, unburdened by the nobilities of Europe or the rigid caste systems of Aztec society. He could do anything, but he chose a life of least resistance. All his life he was that way, always choosing the timid over the bold. The only time he didn't was the year of his life spent right here in Tenochtitlan.

"Mister, I don't know what you are going to do," Tototl said, his voice softening. "But think about what I said, and then think of the girl. All her young life marked for death. She has no other path but to do her duty and wait for the emperor to have a bad day. She looks at you like I look at you. Consider her sadness when she watches you sit there like a lump—free from any real repercussion—and deny her one chance to shake things up. You should be ashamed."

The cab pulled up to the hotel. Dave exited without a word, and Tototl drove off into the early afternoon.

CHAPTER 12

The account of 1519

To the Grand City

THE IMPOSSIBLY COLORFUL and shiny Quetzalcoatl was a bare gray and metal beast on the inside—no flesh or blood, and no way to tell how it achieved flight other than the large rotating black blades that circled above it. Several of my comrades vomited as the beast roared with heart-bracing thumps and left the ground. It was witchcraft on an unimaginable scale. With these powers at their disposal, the Aztecs would never bend to the Lord Jesus Christ.

"Ramirez," Juan Pierre managed. I could hardly hear him above the thumps. "What does this all mean?"

I soothed his head with a wet towel provided by one of the non-Aztec warriors. "I don't know, friend. Try to rest."

The metal tube was no god—it was an invention of man, and it roared loudly for the better part of two hours, screaming through the sky and taking us deeper and deeper into the continent. Courage or foolhardiness caused me to hazard a look out the small window. We were higher than any human could possibly be, higher even than the birds that flew below us. I saw the jungle recede into hills and hills become a snow-topped mountain. The mountain passed at eye level, and beyond it was a bowl with a massive lake in the middle of it. At the center of the lake I beheld the greatest city on earth—larger than Madrid or Seville, perhaps even grander than Paris. A city on islands with a tall-stepped pyramid temple at the center.

The roar slowed as the great machine crossed the lake and came near the central tallest temple, one with twin towers at the top. The machine heaved, and then it all stopped with a soft bounce as we settled to the ground. After a few moments, the side of the machine opened to let in afternoon sunshine and the sounds of distant music.

We stepped out and into a city of exploding color as far as the eye could see. We were on the island on top of what I would later learn was the main temple and palace complex. From my vantage, I could see three broad bridges stretching out to the shore—they were filled with the bustle of vendors. I saw little fishing and commerce boats traversing the lake in a confusing jumble of movement. Behind me and towering above was the main temple, its steps painted red-black with the blood of sacrifices. Upon seeing the dried and caked-on blood, I now felt my life would end—perhaps very soon—at the top of that structure.

Vargas emerged from the flying beast and approached three European men and a woman wearing clothes similar to the European and African warriors who had joined with the Aztecs to destroy our fleet. I could tell one of the Europeans was definitely the leader—he wore a colorful flowing scarf the colors of gold, green, and red. Atop his head was a shiny plumed helmet. He looked to be a man about Cortés' age, and there was a flair about him that reminded me of our fallen leader.

Vargas spoke in English to what I now assumed were his superiors. The woman, hair pulled back and dark glass lenses over her eyes, walked over to me and began inspecting me and my comrades as if we were animals. She looked into our mouths, shined a light into our eyes and ears, and made one of the European warriors open each of our trousers. I was shamed. Vargas hurried over and spoke to the woman in English. I did not understand their conversation, but apparently she was inspecting us for signs of malady.

Vargas, to our assembled group, and in a soothing Spanish voice, said, "Calm boys, she is looking for any evidence of disease to make sure you don't infect any of us or the Aztecs."

I reached to my shoulder where Vargas had pricked me a few hours before. "But what about your pistola?" I asked. Apparently, as one of the healthiest of my comrades, I was somehow singled out as the leader and speaker for my group.

Vargas pushed his hands down in an attempt to quiet me, but it was too late. I had drawn the attention of the woman, who went up to Vargas and started to talk to him in English. Though I could not make out the words, I could tell she was somehow upset that Vargas had established a rapport with us. The other men and their colorful leader took notice of our exchange and started walking over.

I was going to die. My countrymen were going to die. I knew it. There was nothing to lose, so I grabbed Vargas' shirt in desperation. "Translate, translate!"

Vargas stepped back and pried my hands off his shirt. One of the African warriors came up and put his weapon to my head.

The scarf-wearing, helmeted leader reached in and put his hand on the warrior's gun. "*Calmate*," he said in a perfect Spanish accent. His cold blue eyes looked right through mine. "What is your name, young man?"

"Efraim Ramirez, son of Efraim Gonzalez y Ramirez. I am a carpenter by trade from Granada," I answered. If this man was going to kill me, I was going to give him no satisfaction of showing him fear.

"Are you the leader of this group?" he asked.

I looked around at my wounded comrades sitting wearily in the shade of the metal beast's tail. Juan Pierre, who had listened to the exchange, nodded his approval at me.

"I am," I said. "We are merely servants of his majesty, King Charles, and of the Lord Jesus Christ. You have bested us at arms, and in the name of my fleet and my fallen commander Hernán Cortés of Medellin, I surrender and plead for mercy on behalf of my men."

The man cradled my face in his hands and smiled. "I am Quetzalcoatl, plumed serpent, god of wisdom of the Aztec Empire. Welcome to the Grand City of Tenochtitlan."

The man took his hands from my face and turned to Vargas, the woman, and the two other men. He spoke in English to them and then walked off in the direction of what I would later learn was the central palace.

Once Quetzalcoatl and his entourage had gone, Vargas gathered us all together. "On behalf of Quetzalcoatl…" He stopped, took a breath, and rolled his eyes in obvious disdain. I could not tell if it was disdain for Quetzalcoatl's ruling or for Quetzalcoatl himself. "You are now guests of Tenochtitlan, subject to the laws of the Aztec Empire. We will provide medical treatment for your wounded comrades and provide quarters and food for you."

A few Aztec litter bearers approached and helped carry off our wounded—Sanchez, Ventura, and Morales—to a waiting mechanical cart with fat black wheels. Once the men were in the cart, one of the burly soldiers boarded the front, and the cart loudly roared off without the assistance of horses.

"Where are you taking them?" I asked, again astonished by this level of technology. Juan Pierre, Aguirre, and Salas came up next to me.

"We have better medical facilities at our main base outside the city," Vargas said. This confused me. This city's scale was awesome to me. How could the best medical facilities not be in the center?

"You are not Aztecs," I said, expressing a fact I suspected since not long after I was pulled from the boat.

Vargas shrugged. "That's observant of you," he said.

One of the men who was part of Quetzalcoatl's earlier entourage—a younger, handsome man with short brown hair wearing dark-rimmed spectacles with clear lenses—emerged from the palace and came over to us.

In halting Spanish he addressed Vargas, but I could tell he wanted all of us to understand. "These men have secured quarters in the palace," he said. "I mean, we have secured quarters for these men. They must get scrubbed completely. The others will be reunited with them once they have been medicine treatment."

Vargas nodded and looked to us. "*Comprende?*"

We all nodded and were led inside.

CHAPTER 13

Boddington's Whitestone facility—2013

Rhodium

BRIAN DENEVEN HAD become an expert in the rare alloy these past several months. You don't help your company become the world's single largest holder of the metal without learning a thing or two about it.

Rhodium was first discovered in 1803 by English scientist William Hyde Wollaston. It is an inert, incredibly rare metal similar to platinum but with a different electron makeup. It has a silvery white, highly reflective appearance and is mostly used in industrial settings such as in the catalytic converters of engines and as a corrosion-resistant bonding skin on jewelry and other metals. It is more resistant to heat than most metals and has a higher melting point than platinum.

So, why all this international business intrigue about a shiny metal that only commodities traders and scientists cared about?

That's a question the business community around the world was starting to ask. In fact, Sir Ian had bought so much Rhodium that a unified group of car makers including GM, Renault, Ford, Toyota, and Hyundai were about to bring a lawsuit in U.S. and international trade courts claiming 12:36 Adventures was going to impede international commerce by constricting the availability of the metal for use by the auto industry, which needed it for engine parts. All this international business intrigue about a shiny metal that only commodities traders and scientists cared about. Just what was Sir Ian doing with all that Rhodium?

Brian was led by Sir Ian from the workshop's office through a steel door and into the facility's metallurgical laboratory where Drs. Gaummer and Kopplewicz were stationed.

"I believe you have already seen Hans this morning," Sir Ian said.

Brian nodded acknowledgment. Gaummer was a short, paunchy man with hunched-over shoulders, gray stubble, and thinning hair.

Theodora Kopplewicz, on the other hand, was his exact opposite—bright and seemingly full of life and curiosity. She was a triathlete, which is what first drew Sir Ian to her. She not only was his chief scientist, she also was Boddington's workout partner and sometime lover.

"Good to see you, Brian." Theodora bounded over to him. She was always so damn bubbly; Brian couldn't help but be happy to see her despite her profit-draining salary. "This is indeed an exciting day—a day you helped bring about." She clutched his hand and gave him a sisterly punch on the shoulder with her other hand.

Brian was a little surprised by the physical gesture, seeing as how he had only met her a few times before—and all in the cold confines of Sir Ian's offices. Clearly she wasn't so bubbly about seeing him—she was more high on the science they were about to commit.

Theodora put her glasses on her forehead and motioned to Hans. "Hans, get me the gift for our colleague."

Hans went over to a cabinet on the far side of the lab near what Brian assumed was some kind of an industrial metal press. He retrieved a small, dark blue box with a white velveteen ribbon around it. He returned and handed the box to Theodora. Sir Ian was smiling broadly throughout.

"Here, for your work and…support, without which, today would not have been possible." Theodora handed Brian the box.

Brian did not want to open it. He wanted to politely say 'thank you' and put the box in his pocket, hoping for the awkward moment to pass so they could get on with the show or demonstration or whatever it was he was here to see.

"Don't be daft, boy, open it," Sir Ian chided.

Brian smiled and took a deep breath. He unraveled the bow and opened the box. Inside was a shiny, engraved ring with the stamp "12:36 forever."

"Oh," he said, "this is very…very thoughtful." He pulled the ring out and went to put it on his right ring finger, but it didn't quite fit. Instead it only fit his pinky. A pinky ring. Wonderful.

"I hope you like it," Theodora said. "We made it ourselves."

"Of course he does, doctor," Sir Ian said. "Brian has become quite fancy since coming to London."

"Made it yourself?" Brian asked.

"Yes, it's pure rhodium—a pure rhodium ring—and engraved of all things," Theodora said. "Incredibly rare."

Brian felt his heart begin to pound and suddenly began to feel the heat rising in his body. He looked more closely around the lab and saw scraps and chunks of what he now knew to be very expensive rhodium lying all over the lab. In fact, a sharp, bent shard that was about half a pound was just lying near his feet like a crumpled fast food wrapper.

"Are you fucking kidding me?" he asked.

"Whoa, whoa, whoa, my boy, no need for sour language," Sir Ian said.

Brian did a quick calculation in his head as he looked around the room. "There must be something like $12 million in rhodium scraps just lying around this one lab—not to mention this," he said, pointing to his ring.

"I really thought he'd appreciate it," Gaummer said under his breath, sounding like his feelings were genuinely hurt.

Theodora shook her head. "That's not very nice. Hans worked late into the evening on the ring—and he did it AFTER all of his other work."

"Work?" Brian asked. "What kind of work, exactly? I mean, we just bought a globally significant amount of a very precious and rare metal, something that the world business community, regulators, and most important—our shareholders—have begun to take notice of…and you and your 'scientists' are grab-assing around your own private playscape. Sir, this does not look good. The shareholders will revolt."

Sir Ian put his arm around Brian's shoulder. "Shush, shush, my boy," he said, trying to soothe Brian's ire. "I have never been wrong my entire career. Do you think I would do all this to be wrong now?"

"I don't even know what that means," Brian said.

"It means: Do you trust me?" Sir Ian's intense stare and countenance overpowered Brian.

Brian considered, but after a moment visibly softened. "Of course I trust you, but others think you are absolutely crazy—and that will not help you hold onto your business. You have to give me something to take back and ease the shareholders—convince them there is a method to this madness."

Sir Ian laughed and gave Brian a hearty pat on the back. "We're way past that now, boy. Dr. Kopplewicz, let's continue the tour."

Theodora stepped out ahead of them and led Brian to the other side of the lab and another set of steel doors. "Well, you have seen the metallurgic lab and processing facility," Theodora said. "All apologies for the mess."

Theodora took out her ID badge. "The entire facility is badge protected, and behind this door is the highest level of security—only about ten percent of the team who worked on site was ever permitted past this point. When you see the scale of what's behind this door you will understand why the security has been so tight."

With that she swiped her badge through the card reader and the light went from red to green.

Through the door was the massive superstructure of the Whitestone facility—which in reality was a huge hangar. Fitting snugly inside some three stories tall was a fat-throated craft that seemed to be the bastard child of the Spruce Goose and space shuttle. Its belly, below the cockpit, had an opening wide enough to accommodate large vehicles and cargo. It was completely skinned in shiny rhodium plating.

"So that's where all the rhodium went," Brian said under his breath, trying to comprehend this craft, and more important, why it even existed.

"There and that little bit on your finger, of course," Theodora said.

"Space," Brian said. "You've made a space craft and figured out that rhodium will somehow...what, make it sturdier, more easily able to handle atmospheric re-entry?" Brian was puzzled, but for all of Sir Ian's eccentricities, he could possibly sell a space vehicle to the shareholders.

Sir Ian walked over to the massive craft's underbelly. His hand caressed the smooth and reflective metal. "Think bigger, my boy," he said.

Theodora walked over to Sir Ian with a small towel and wiped clean the area where he was caressing his toy. "No touchy," she said.

Sir Ian took his hand off the wing and patted Theodora on her head. "This genius, this wonderful genius—and your fantastic ability to procure rhodium has created this—the world's first vehicle that has the ability to bend the temporal continuum and travel through time."

Sir Ian let the words hang there for a moment as Brian looked at him incredulously.

"And we're going to take it out for a spin today," Sir Ian concluded, a broad smile crossing his lips.

§ § §

Back in the hangar's break room, Brian turned on his iPhone and immediately tried to find a nearby cab company. No signal—data or cellular. *Shit.*

Hans Gaummer came into the break room and poured himself a cup of coffee.

"This is fucking insane," Brian said. "I have to get out of here, polish my resume, and talk to a lawyer. You all have been spending too much time around molten metal fumes—you need a doctor or some kind of intervention—the whole lot of you."

Hans slowly stirred his coffee and took a seat next to Brian. "Don't discount us or Mr. Boddington so easily," he said. "Where else is a man of Boddington's drive to go? He always has to push the bounds of what's possible."

Brian was rubbing his temples. "He's got nowhere left to go, no more mountains to climb, so why not flame out in complete insanity?"

Hans considered. "You could say that, but you could also say that after Eli Bramstoke conquered commercial space travel, you would only expect a man like Boddington to try and push the envelope one step further."

Boddington was always looking up to Bramstoke, who was fifteen years Boddington's senior and always seemed to be achieving glory for one deed or another, usually knocking a Boddington adventure off the front page.

"So, you think this is legitimate?" Brian asked.

"You probably don't know this, but I am widely considered the finest particle physicist working today, and from a science perspective, I am not even the top dog here. Theodora is brilliant on an Einstein level, and she has been working with an unlimited budget—thanks to you and your shrewd financial management. I have seen the theoretical models Theodora worked up, and they are sound. She has developed the first controllable, portable, and sustainable cold-fusion reactor—a patent that, when filed, will make 12:36 larger than all of the oil, gas, and energy companies in the world—combined. Add that massive power output to the positively charged ionic rhodium skin I designed on that vehicle, and we have the power and stability to create a seam in the space-time continuum. A seam that we can pass through and come out on the other side in another time and place. It's remarkable."

"This is all moving so fast," Brian said. "You said sustainable, controllable cold fusion reaction?"

"Yes, I've seen two successful demonstrations so far—one done three days ago," Hans said.

"Then why the hell don't we come out and release that, win a ton of Nobel prizes, and make every other power source on earth obsolete—why this time-travel scheme?" Brian asked.

"You work for Sir Ian; that's not his way. You know that," Hans said. "If he's going to do something, he's going to blow the doors off of it."

Just then, Theodora entered the break room, went to the refrigerator, and pulled out a bag of leafy greens and a bowl of fruit. "Smoothie?" she asked, to no one in particular.

"No, thank you," Hans said, holding up his coffee cup. Theodora shrugged and began painstakingly chopping up the fruit and greens.

"Is he still shitting on our science?" Theodora asked, pointing the knife in Brian's direction.

"I think he's trying to understand," Hans replied.

Brian got up and walked toward Theodora, causing her to stop her chopping and look Brian over, quizzically.

He stuck out his hand. "I want to shake the hand of the woman who brought the world cold fusion—that is on par with the invention of fire," he said.

Theodora put down the knife and shook Brian's hand. "Thank you." She paused. "And, again, thank you for creating the wealth to allow us to get it done."

Brian went to pour himself a cup of coffee. The banker in him wanted to force a stop to all this crazy time-travel talk and get Theodora and Sir Ian immediately in front of money people to demonstrate the cold fusion reaction. But the little boy in him was inspired by the science fiction tales of gallivanting time travelers, and he was damn curious to see if Boddington could actually pull it off.

"So, what does he have in mind for the time travel?" Brian asked.

Theodora pointed to her forehead. "I don't betray the boss' secrets," she said.

"You have to ask him. I'm just going along to ensure the fusion reactor operates at full functionality and that Gaummer's Folly doesn't peel apart under the rigors of time travel."

Brian noticed Gaummer shrug at Theodora's assertion. "You worry about the fusion and leave the time travel to me and Sir Ian. Sure, your cold fusion will change this world, but my time travel, well, that will change the fabric of the universe."

Theodora completed dumping her ingredients into the blender and fired it up.

§ § §

Outside the break room, Sir Ian was consulting with his chief logistician and team doctor, Antonio Vargas. Antonio was a former Emergency Room physician and U.S. Navy corpsman who completed two tours of duty in Iraq. He knew the military, he knew medicine, but most of all, he was completely bilingual in Spanish and English and had a working knowledge of the Nahuatl dialect of the Indian communities of central Mexico. It was a weird requirement for the job, but 12:36 paid really well, and he was the best candidate.

Sir Ian needed to make sure they had enough of everything for their trip and was personally overseeing the final loading into the wide open maw of the *Cyrus-Alexander*, as Sir Ian had dubbed his glorious machine. He named it after the two greats: Cyrus the Great, a thoughtful Persian emperor who was widely considered one of the first rulers to be accepting of different peoples and different religions, and hot-headed, blood-thirsty conqueror Alexander the Great. Sir Ian lived his life believing he was the embodiment of these two world views—the thinker and the conqueror—expressed in modern form. In business Sir Ian was the conqueror, buying companies and vanquishing competitors, while at the same time, as the thinker, he was bringing a new ethic of social responsibility to the corporate world. Inside Sir Ian, these two were in constant turmoil. Some days Alexander would win, some days it was Cyrus.

"Two lightweight four-wheel drive Jeeps?"

"Check."

"Black Hawk helicopter?"

"Check."

"Cirrus SR20 personal airplane?"

"Check."

"70 AK-47 WASR rifles with 1,000 rounds each?"

"Check."

"Three M-60 machine guns with 3,000 rounds each?"

"Check."

"Four RPGs with 100 rounds?"

"Check."

"Two Tow Missile Launchers with 100 rounds?"

"Check."

"Six elite mercenary commandos formerly from the French Foreign Legion and SAS?"

"Check."

"C rations and potable water for a month for all crew?"

"Check."

"Medical supplies?"

"Check."

"One ton of candy and mini liquors?"

"Check. That's the whole package, boss," Vargas said as he and Boddington double and triple checked the manifest. "It's going to be a heavy load—I don't know if the *Cyrus-Alexander* can handle it all."

Boddington smiled. "Fuel?"

Vargas quickly flipped through the manifest. "I assumed that with the new fusion engine…"

"I meant fuel for the vehicles," Sir Ian corrected.

"Oh right," Vargas said. "It's being pumped now—two bladders, one for the aircraft fuel and one for the ground vehicles. I suggest we take it easy on both because we do not have the ability to drill for oil or refine it wherever and whenever we're going."

"Excellent," Boddington said. "You really do keep the trains running on time, my boy." He gave Vargas a hearty pat on the ass.

Vargas straightened uncomfortably. This was the strangest job he ever had, and he suspected the same would be true for anyone in Boddington's employ.

"I need you to add rations and water for one more," Boddington said.

"Certainly," Vargas said. "The ship's quarters are jam packed with supplies though. Who are we adding?"

"I'm adding Brian Deneven," Sir Ian said.

Vargas looked uneasy at the suggestion. "Sir, everyone on the manifest has a mission-critical role. Are you sure it's appropriate or necessary to add a finance person to the crew?"

Sir Ian shrugged and waved his hand dismissively. "I could use an assistant. Plus, Brian's a good egg—he could probably help you manage the supplies while we're out in the field."

Sir Ian always had the last word and Vargas knew it.

"T-Minus 45 minutes to launch," Sir Ian said with a chipper, boyish lilt, as he walked away to grab his bags.

§ § §

Theodora and Hans left the break room, loaded up their duffels, and headed to the small bridge at the nose of the *Cyrus-Alexander*. Brian followed along and was surprised at how small and ordinary the bridge of the ship was. He expected the Enterprise from Star Trek, and what he got was just about twice as big as an ordinary jumbo jet or large military transport cockpit. The rest of the crew would be strapped into the seating compartment that was immediately aft of the flight deck. Brian spent some time talking to the mercenaries. They were pretty funny guys—all veterans of gnarly operations throughout Africa and the Middle East—nothing Brian had ever heard of on the news, but he assumed there was a lot of clandestine carnage happening in parts of the world he'd be hard pressed to find on a map.

Sir Ian came through the cabin and the jocularity of the mercenaries subsided. Sir Ian approached Brian.

"My boy, I am so glad you came aboard," he said. "We have a jump seat for you inside the flight deck. I think you're going to love it."

Brian was perplexed, but he'd be lying if he didn't feel a shock of exhilaration at being asked to come along for this test flight. "Me?"

"Absolutely—you made this happen," Sir Ian said. "You should be on board for the maiden voyage—it is history, after all."

"I...I just, I haven't packed anything," Brian said.

Sir Ian held out his arms to show his sleeve length. "We're about the same size, you and I—and I never go anywhere without a full steamer trunk. You'll be fine, and besides, I insist."

Brian's heart was racing. From threatening to quit a mere thirty minutes before to this crazy whirlwind of activity—the sounds of forklifts beeping as they loaded pallets of gear, the smell of fuel being pumped into the stern of this great machine, the sight of weaponry—*Why weaponry?* Brian thought—but the sight of the green crates only added to the sense that some kind of a crazy adventure was about to take place.

"So, if you're coming, follow me to the flight deck," Sir Ian said, moving past Brian in the aisle and up toward the cockpit door. Brian dutifully followed.

T-Minus 20 minutes to launch.

Sir Ian, Brian, Theodora, Hans and Black Hawk/time-machine pilot Silvestre Arenas had taken up their positions in the *Cyrus-Alexander's* flight deck. Silvestre was going through pre-flight preparation, but all of this was so damn theoretical, it was unclear how the ship would behave in actual flight conditions. It was supposed to behave similar to a helicopter, but no one really knew for sure. It was powered by seventy-two small thrusters coming off the cold fusion power plant. The controls were similar to those of a helicopter.

Brian sat in the fold-down jump seat, or flight-attendant seat, as Vargas had called it, at the very rear of the cockpit.

Theodora turned from her display and tapped Sir Ian on the shoulder. "All right, I need to spool up the fusion drive because it will take about eighteen minutes for the reaction to get to stasis."

Sir Ian looked at his watch and appeared to do a few calculations in his head. He nodded to Theodora. Theodora spun back and began flipping the switches to bring the power plant online. They all felt a low and steady hum vibrate up from deep within the ship. The vibration came up through the chair, and Brian could feel it throughout his entire body.

Fidgeting nervously, Sir Ian undid his seat belt and stood. "Hans, how are we on the timing?"

Hans swiveled to Sir Ian, gave him a thumbs up, and then turned back to his workstation.

Brian leaned in. "So," he said, "where are we going?"

Sir Ian pointed to Hans. "According to the physicist, we are not going to *go* anywhere."

Hans finished inputting some data into his computer. When he was done he turned back to the group. "The ship is not really designed to move much at all," Hans explained. "We don't even have the capacity to roll ourselves out of the hangar.

"The fusion power energizes and charges the rhodium skin of the *Cyrus-Alexander*. The rhodium is a catalyst, which continues and intensifies the reaction until it reaches critical mass, creating a hole in the time continuum. Once that happens, the ship slips to another point in time corresponding to where the Earth was at this exact location in the past," Gaummer explained.

Brian squinted. "I'm not following."

Hans took a breath and slowed down. "Okay, we can now map and predict every location for the Earth as it has rotated and circled the sun from the deep past well into the future. Of course, the Earth has moved and wobbled quite a bit throughout history, but all of this is also, generally, predicable and knowable. So, when our ship slips through time, it is not moving in space at all; it is merely moving through time. The Earth is the thing that's moving, and we 'land,' so to speak, at a different time and place."

Brian started to understand. "So the Earth moves under the ship and the ship reappears at a different time."

"Exactly," Theodora said. The ship slowly began to glow a bright, whitish blue that seemed otherworldly and permeated everything—even and especially the rhodium skin.

"So this has everything to do with when the reaction starts—if that's not timed correctly then…" Brian started.

"Then the ship re-materializes in a mountain or out in space somewhere," Hans said.

Brian stiffened. "So, how solid are your calculations, and where exactly in the past will this ship appear?"

"Valley of Mexico," Sir Ian said. "Mid-February, 1519, about 400 feet over Tenochtitlan, the great capital of the Aztecs." Brian could tell that the only other person on the flight deck for whom this was not news was Hans.

"Should I have brought more sunscreen and a swimsuit?" Theodora asked.

"Don't worry, Dr. Kopplewicz," Sir Ian said. "If Hans is a second off on the engage command, we'll materialize above a glacier 15,000 years ago. Be glad you packed layers."

The jocular talk made Brian feel much less at ease. *Who were these jokers and why did it seem like they were all flying by the seat of their pants?* "So, why the Valley of Mexico in 1519?" Brian asked.

"Because it was glorious," Sir Ian said. "Imagine a culture untouched by the West—a great city at the head of a great and powerful Empire. Silver and gold and blood, the smells of fruits, and a valley of floating gardens in bloom. A huge temple complex on an island with three wide bridges connecting it to the shores. It is the place of my childhood dreams." Sir Ian sat back in his chair and buckled his safety harness, eyes misty. "We calculated to land right near the time that the Aztecs were said to be visited by the winged serpent god of wisdom, Quetzalcoatl. Our arrival will coincide with that prophecy."

Brian may have been a number cruncher, but he did know a thing or two about history. "Didn't that already happen?" he asked. "I mean, didn't Hernán Cortés do that very thing? Arrive and pretend to be Quetzalcoatl?"

"Cortés and his men were bloodthirsty murderers," Boddington said. "They enslaved and destroyed a great people, killing millions by spreading disease and slavery all in the name of religion, gold, and glory. He used the guise of Quetzalcoatl to decimate an entire culture. I will use it to save it."

Brian sat back in his chair. This was crazy. Cortés may be seen by history as a ruthless conqueror, but messing with that, well, he had seen enough sci-fi to know there were probably good reasons not to go back into the past and change things around.

"I know what you're thinking," Hans said as he continued to input commands into his workstation. "All that jazz about changing something in the past having an effect on the future, etcetera, etcetera."

"Well yeah," Brian said, "it does stand to reason."

The blue glow began to intensify and permeate everything. Hans and Dr.

Kopplewicz slipped super-dark sunglasses on while the rest of the group squinted to shield their eyes from the intensity.

"We are spooled up," Kopplewicz called out as she reached up to an overhead hand lever.

Gaummer held his finger up. "I suggest you do some reading of my research into multiverses," Hans said. "The leading thought in the field is pretty confident that changing something will not impact this universe but instead create a new and alternate timeline. So, in some senses, what we're doing can be considered a sand-box or playground."

"Hans!" Theodora exclaimed, hand still on the reactor lever.

Hans dropped his hand, signaling Theodora to pull the lever. She pulled down and pushed it home into the console. Within seconds the vibration ceased and the blue light that was enveloping them shot outward as normal color returned to the inside of the ship. From inside the cockpit, the view of the hangar became obscured by an impossibly bright, white light.

Hans looked into a scope on his console. "We have split the time continuum. We're ready to go."

"Time till we hit the 1519 window?" Boddington asked.

"Seven seconds. Hold tight, I don't exactly know what will happen."

The seconds ticked down, one crossed over to zero, the blue light pulsed outward, and the view of the inside of Boddington's hangar instantaneously became bright blue sky at midday.

CHAPTER 14

1999—Aztecan Time

DAVE SAT ACROSS from Santiago Esparza in a simple holding room just down the hall from the Imperial Court of Justice Salon Three, Judge Decoyan's courtroom. The guard could come at any minute to let them know they were on.

Santiago fidgeted. Dave could hear the tremors in his breath. This was a preliminary hearing, but Dave was confident he had the evidence to at least get the murder charge reduced and to reopen the investigation. What he was nervous about were the documents sitting in his bag, the ones that tied T'shla's data breach to the beheadings that were happening all over town.

Aztec court hearings were still a huge mystery to outsiders. There were no rights to face the accuser in the court system. Accused were often placed in a holding room while the prosecution presented its case. There was also no video or audio feed, so Dave and Santiago had no idea what was being said, what witnesses were being called, and how the judge was reacting to it all. It was maddening.

"What do you think?" Santiago asked, knee shaking under the metal table.

Dave shrugged. "I'm as in the dark as you are."

The one good thing was that Spanish colonial media were allowed in the courtroom. The Aztecs did not typically let press cover live proceedings of trials, instead letting reporters review transcripts after rulings had been handed down. When the offense involved a foreign national, the Ministry of Justice often loosened those rules to avoid more international scrutiny and negative media coverage. T'shla was right; this was probably one of the few opportunities to shine a light on something dark in Aztec society.

"What?" Santiago asked.

"Nothing, just, when we get in there, keep your mouth shut and let me do the talking," Dave said. He checked his phone again. No missed calls or voice mails. Nothing. He knew he was supposed to meet Marta from the consulate soon after the hearing, but she had gone radio silent, too.

Dave put his phone in the front pocket of his briefcase just as their bailiff arrived letting them know the judge was ready. Dave gathered up his documents. He nodded to Santiago, who stood, still visibly nervous. Dave offered a weak smile, but he knew it did nothing to allay Santiago's worries.

The doors of justice and wisdom are golden, said the Nahuatl inscription in stone above the gilded doors of Decoyan's Courtroom. Two guards in rich green suits with dark wooden staffs opened the chamber, with the guard on the right entering ahead of Dave and Santiago, announcing, "Judge Decoyan, vessel of the great wisdom of our ancestors, I present Santiago Villa de Esparza from the Colonial Republic of New Spain, accused of premeditated capital murder, larceny, and lesser offenses." He banged the base of his staff on the sandstone floor three times, sending echoes through the courtroom.

Dave and Santiago entered and stood just inside the doorway. Per custom, no one took a step forward toward the judge until he invited you in. It was a barren, cavernous room with mossy green walls. There was no electrical lighting, per court custom that overhead artificial lighting shielded law givers from the heavens and from the sun. Instead, the courtroom was ringed with open clerestory windows about twenty feet up the walls and just below the ceilings. In the silence of these opening moments, Dave could hear the faint sounds of city traffic and feel some of the late afternoon fresh air on his face.

Around the entire room was a stone bench carved into the wall. To each side were reporters and TV cameras representing the media pool. Dave could tell one of the reporters had a Diario Havana ID badge. Diario was the biggest and most influential newspaper in the Colonies. The TV camera was from CSNS, or Colonial Spanish News Service, which was a satellite TV network. Dave wondered if this was being beamed live back to the islands. Dave also noted what he assumed to be a handful of Aztec reporters and cameras, probably allowed to be there because the Spanish press had been granted access. To their right was the prosecution team, sitting sternly, arms folded and showing off red armbands indicating their role. Near them was a woman, who Dave recognized from file photos as Ventli's wife, and two small children. She was obviously distraught with red eyes, holding her children close.

In the center of the courtroom sat Judge Decoyan on an elevated throne, carved out of shiny obsidian. It was four steps up on what appeared to be a small pyramid. The four steps symbolized the Four Agreements, an Aztec philosophy about life and civility that schoolchildren learned from the earliest days of primary school. On each step an agreement was carved so that the accused could see them. *Tell the Truth, Don't Take Offenses Personally, Don't Assume, and Always Do Your Best.* These were not laws, just good ideas about how to live and get along. Behind Decoyan sat court clerks and official recorders with laptops.

"Who comes to be judged?" Decoyan asked, his soft voice barely carrying through the room.

Dave nodded to Santiago. Santiago took one step forward. "I am Santiago Villa de Esparza," Esparza said, voice cracking with nerves.

Decoyan was wearing what appeared to be a gold lamè robe festooned with green and red feathers from exotic jungle birds. His face was framed by a golden feathered headdress that came down around his jowls. He held his palms up to the ceiling and looked up. A shaft of afternoon sunlight bathed his brown, wrinkled face.

"Lords of wisdom and justice. Please grant me the capacities to sit in judgment of this man," he said, slowly bringing his palms down and making eye contact with Dave. "Who else enters my courtroom this afternoon?"

Dave knew all this theater was for the official record. He actually kind of enjoyed the pomp of it all. He stepped forward.

"My name is David Aragon de Rodriguez, and I am an official representative of the Colonial Republic of New Spain. I am here as attorney in fact, representing Mr. Esparza and the interests of my government."

Decoyan nodded and waved his hand to empty spaces on the bench on the opposite side of the room from the prosecution and Ventli's family. Dave and Santiago took their seats. The inquest was about to begin.

As was custom, Decoyan began by explaining the case against Santiago, outlining that the prosecution had made a credible case implicating Santiago directly in the murder of Ventli. Under modern Aztec law, circumstantial evidence was enough to win a conviction and life imprisonment, but not a death sentence. And there was a mountain of circumstantial evidence against Santiago. Witnesses placed him at the bar and saw him engage with Ventli. The bartender on duty that night reported Ventli yelling to him, "That little Spanish man just stole my wallet," before giving chase out the door.

The bartender then reported he called the bouncer over to explain what had happened. The bouncer reported he then left the bar to see if he could help Ventli, ultimately finding his headless body in the side alley. There was no security footage of the incident from the alley camera, which the bar owners admitted was merely there to deter staff from stealing alcohol and spiriting it away via the alleyway.

Within thirty minutes of the crime, a capital-wide all-points bulletin went out alerting all units to knock on the doors of all Spaniards staying in the city—there were 1,452 Spaniards with visas in Tenochtitlan that night. The police search narrowed from 1,452 to one about two hours later when a hotel clerk at the modest Hotel Nezacoatl reported a Spanish guest returning to the hotel with an obvious bloodstain on his jacket and acting suspiciously. The police captured Santiago hiding in Chapultepec Park before sunrise. Case closed.

"Señor Villa de Esparza," Decoyan said, his voice strained from his recital of the case rundown, "what say you or your representative about the facts of this case as they have been presented?"

Dave rose and walked to the center of the courtroom, standing in front of Decoyan and ten feet before the steps of the Four Agreements. He heard the clicks of cameras from where the media were seated.

"Honorable and wise Judge Decoyan," Dave began. He wanted to show maximum respect and homage to Aztec ways, so this next part was important. "You are the twentieth of your name, descended from the Tabascan Peoples, the Xalapan Hill Peoples, and the Peoples of Macuiltepec. Your reputation for learned scholarship on the laws of man and the heavens is legendary and spreads well beyond the borders of this great empire. Because of your mercy and dedication to truth and fairness, I must, with all respect, disagree with your words on this matter." Dave took a deep breath; any nerves he had felt were gone. This was his element, and for the first time in days, save a few moments with T'shla, he was comfortable.

Decoyan straightened. "Very well, Spanish lawyer," he said. "Please point out any objections you have to the facts of the case as they have been presented."

"Honorable and wise Judge Decoyan, I do not make any objection to the facts of the case as you have so meticulously described. Everything you said is completely truthful and accurate," Dave said. He noticed Santiago fidgeting a bit in his chair. "And by the standards of Aztec law, my adversaries on the prosecution side can very well win some kind of a conviction with what you have laid out."

Dave faced the prosecutors and gave a respectful and slow bow as was custom when addressing the opposing counsel.

"Per the Aztec ways, my adversaries are rightfully concerned with winning a conviction in this case, even if they can only win a conviction at the lowest threshold, which is the threshold of circumstantial evidence. It is altogether fitting and proper that they do this," Dave said. Dave was referencing the fact that Aztec prosecutors were not truth finders; they were bureaucrats, and their bureaucratic duty was finding people guilty and putting them in jail. That's how their pay levels and bonus structures were set. It was not Dave's place to question or criticize this system—it's how it had always been done. However, he did have room to point out that there was more to this case than the circumstantial evidence.

"Proceed," Decoyan said.

"I know your character," Dave said. "I have read your scholarly articles on jurisprudence and your philosophy about what happens and what should happen within these hallowed walls."

Decoyan began to shift in his seat a bit, appearing to be not altogether comfortable having his philosophies or writings referenced. Dave sensed he may have gone too far and decided to dial it back a bit.

"I'm talking about the truth, and that it is the role of the judge to seek truth, always," Dave said. "There is one truth today that has not been spoken by the prosecutors."

"Well then, what is this truth?" Decoyan asked, his clipped tone telling Dave that he best get to his point, and quickly.

Dave strode confidently to his briefcase which was on the floor near Santiago's feet. He knew the cameras were following his every move. He reached into his briefcase and pulled out a handful of documents.

"I present to you and to my esteemed adversaries of the prosecution, new exhibits of evidence that cast doubt on the guilt of my client. Number one: A certified copy of Santiago Villa de Esparza's entrance visa indicating he arrived on Aztec Day One in the Trecena of the Vulture." Dave handed copies of the document to the bailiff, who passed them to both the judge and the prosecution.

"We know this," Decoyan said. "We are very strict on our visa policies; we know exactly when Señor Villa de Esparza came to our land."

"Number two," Dave said, almost running over Decoyan's sentence. "I present neighborhood newspaper articles outlining a rash of beheadings, no fewer than six, but four of which occurred before Señor Villa de Esparza ever entered the country. And in the case of the two others, my client was sightseeing in the north—Zacatecas—as is reflected in his hotel receipts from Zacatecas and the travel stamps on his visa which indicate where he was and when he was there."

Dave handed copies of the newspaper articles to the bailiff.

"Therefore, a rash of shockingly similar crimes has been happening in your capital city for weeks now, and my client was only physically in proximity to one of these incidents. I submit that my client is stupid and unlucky, but not a murderer. He has said to me that he did not kill this man. He even told me of a man who paid him to lure Mr. Ventli out of the bar that night. He said this is the story he told his police questioners."

Dave knew better than to bring up the Jaguar angle. He knew there was a chance the prosecutors knew it, and he did not want to be seen as the outsider breaking the news that Santiago was essentially accusing a member of the venerable Jaguar Order of these crimes.

"Is there a chance that this man before me is copying the actions of others?" Decoyan asked, turning his head and looking behind him.

A court employee came up from the back. "Honorable Judge Decoyan, our mental assessment of the accused does not support that this man is necessarily of a violent nature, nor has he the inclination for behaviors consistent with someone who would copy a violent act such as this."

Decoyan seemed more than a little annoyed. "Then why did you recommend conviction in your mental evaluation?"

The clerk, a slight woman wearing a plain brown robe that nearly matched the floor, cleared her throat. "My lord, we concluded that this man was a base criminal, motivated by money, and that motivation could be strong enough to make violent actions possible in certain circumstances."

Decoyan rubbed his forehead. "So, your report said this man could commit violent crimes in a general sense, but your statement here indicates that this does not necessarily mean he committed this crime?"

The clerk searched for words. "What, I, we mean, was that this man was found with blood from a murder scene. Eyewitnesses placed him with the deceased before the death, and our mental examination found that under certain circumstances, he could commit a violent crime—murder—ergo, when we combine all these circumstances, he is likely the killer."

Decoyan shook his head. "If you examine anyone in this room you will likely find that there is something that can drive each and every one of us to murder," Decoyan said. He then motioned to the prosecutors. "It's simply not enough."

One of the prosecutors rose. "With all due respect, honorable Judge Decoyan, only one of the people in this room was connected to a gruesome crime scene."

Dave watched this exchange with utter fascination. The Aztec legal system was a bureaucratic mess, and he could clearly see Decoyan was out of his mind in frustration.

"I don't like this," Decoyan said. "And I don't like that the ugly cracks in our system must be viewed by people all over the world." He motioned to the cameras.

He slumped in his chair. "On second thought, maybe it's a good thing the outside world can peer in and set us straight, like when Quetzalcoatl visited our people and vanquished the enemies at our shores."

Dave didn't understand the reference, but it was clear this case was going his way. Decoyan stood up and came off his elevated throne. It was common for judges to walk around their courtrooms during trials, so his movement was not surprising.

The prosecutor cleared his throat. "But judge," he said, "these trashy newspaper articles have never been accepted in a court of law as evidence. We all know these papers are printed in neighborhoods to get locals to buy them and use the businesses that advertise in them. There is no foundation in law for using newspaper reports as a reason to acquit a suspect."

In a way, the prosecutor was right. The trashy neighborhood tabloids were nothing more than gossip rags, and there were twenty-three of them in the city— all fighting for ad revenue. Using them in a courtroom would be considered very untoward.

"I know the sources of these stories," Decoyan said. "But, if we were to check with the police districts throughout the city, would we not find these people missing—at the very least?"

The prosecutor considered. "I cannot say, m'lord."

Decoyan closed his eyes and then opened them slowly. "Well then, how about we do that simple check before we convict this man." He walked over to Ventli's family, touching his widow on top of the head and kneeling down to be eye level with Ventli's two small children, a boy and a girl.

"I am so sorry for your terrible loss," he said. "By all accounts, Ventli was a good father and a pillar of our society—helping the poor, loving his family. I know you hurt very much and you think the strange man behind me killed your father. But it is very likely not true." He straightened and went over to the prosecutors. "You have to do better. This is ridiculous," he said.

Having only read about what happens inside an Aztec courtroom, Dave was fascinated. He wondered if these interactions were typical or if Decoyan was pumping them up for the media.

Decoyan made his way back to his throne and sat down in a heap. "I cannot let the accused go," he said to Dave. "Though you have presented credible evidence, there are still too many questions about this case and the incident on the evening of Vulture Day Seven. I am sure you would agree that Señor Esparza's actions directly led the deceased out of the bar, which ultimately resulted in his murder. At best, Santiago is a larcenist; at worst, he is an accessory to murder and perhaps involved in a conspiracy that has resulted in the murders of several others."

Dave nodded. He understood there was no way Santiago would go free and that he likely did not deserve to go free. His job was to prevent a quick murder conviction and to get the Aztec court system to the next level of inquest, which was the search for truth. He wondered how many poorly defended innocent people had gone to prison or been executed because they could not get out of this initial phase of 'he looks guilty, he probably is guilty' Aztec justice.

"My orders are the following," Decoyan began, speaking loudly. "Santiago Villa de Esparza will be remanded to the Quetzalcoatl Order to be kept in the Grand Temple of Quetzalcoatl, under the direct custody of his official visa sponsor, Jidge Axtulla."

This was strange. It seemed like it would be a conflict for a judge who was a Quetzalcoatl devotee to order a defendant to serve house arrest in the main temple, much less be put into the custody of a known associate.

"He will not leave Tenochtitlan until this matter is settled to the complete satisfaction of the Emperor," Decoyan continued.

Dave could see the judge was becoming more and more agitated. Decoyan leveled his bony finger at the prosecution. "Send word to your investigators," he said, his voice becoming more strained as his volume increased. "There may be a killer on the streets of our city, and though Spanish defense counsel would not say it in open court, I will. The killer is likely a Jaguar soldier. That's what the accused has described under questioning."

Dave and the rest of the spectators were stunned. It was unheard of to have any official, much less an esteemed judge priest, identify a suspect by his order of religious sect. As a Quetzalcoatl, this was a direct attack by Decoyan on the Jaguar Order—naming them in court and in front of the media. Dave looked around the courtroom and could only imagine the Jaguars in the room stiffening in their seats.

Decoyan turned his attention back to Dave. "Anything else?" he asked.

Now would have been the ideal time for Dave to bow and humbly get out of the courtroom before a Jaguar-Quetzalcoatl civil war broke out. But something strong was tugging at him. Maybe it was Decoyan's theatrics or that he knew, somewhere, T'shla was probably watching. For the first time in his adult life, Dave felt like crossing a line.

"Actually, Judge Decoyan, I do have one more thing," he said, making his way back across the courtroom to his briefcase. Dave reached in and pulled out a stack of papers and returned to his prior spot at the foot of the judicial pedestal.

"In the course of our investigation, we came across a strong correlation between the names of the people who have allegedly been killed by beheading and a recent data breach in the Ministry of Records where the medical histories of more than 6,000 Aztecs were compromised. I will not draw any reckless conclusions, but I strongly believe this deserves notation in the official record of these proceedings because the people whose data were stolen deserve notification for their own well-being."

Rather than pass the documents through the bailiff, Dave took two steps up the pedestal and handed the stack of papers directly to Decoyan.

Decoyan took the stack and leafed through it, pausing to review the circled names. Decoyan looked pained as he flipped through the pages, and Dave wondered if this had just complicated not only Decoyan's life, but also the lives of high priests well above Decoyan's pay grade.

"How did you come about this information?" Decoyan asked, leaning forward on his judicial throne.

Dave felt heat in his temples, and he wondered if his face was reddening. He had to be careful here. Decoyan, as a judge, had many tools of investigation at his fingertips. He must've known about Dave's rendezvous with T'shla the night before. But, then again, maybe Decoyan didn't know. Was the judge asking Dave to name T'shla as the source of this information? What purpose would that serve? Maybe he was overthinking it. Dave heard a clerk's cough echo in the chamber and realized he had been silent for quite some time.

"In the interest of discretion I will respectfully not answer your question to protect the people who had the courage to discover this connection," Dave said, recognizing he was probably going to have to trade his luxury hotel for a dank holding cell in the Tenoch Detention Center.

Decoyan sat back and clasped his hands together. Dave knew Decoyan had the power to throw him into the TDC until he answered the question, diplomatic immunity or not. This would certainly make this more of an international incident than it already was. If the judge let him go, the Supreme Judicial Council would likely have a fit and perhaps appeal the decision to the Emperor on the grounds that no foreigner or trade deal, no matter how important, was greater than the preeminence of Aztec law and its ability to compel the truth from all who appear before a judge. This was the foundation of the entire system. No one on Earth, except the emperor, was above the judicial system. At least that's how the Supreme Judicial Council viewed the world.

"All right, Spanish lawyer, I will allow you this bit of discretion. For now," he said, waving for his clerk to come over and take the list of Aztecs whose data was stolen. "But I will also confiscate your visa. You cannot leave the country until this matter is satisfactorily settled." This was a formality, of course. The government likely knew who passed him the information and had probably already dispatched agents to knock on T'shla's door. Dave hoped T'shla was safe and for a moment regretted opening his mouth on the data breach angle because he knew the danger she faced was real, regardless of her status as a Saved One.

"This hearing is closed," Decoyan announced abruptly, quickly descending his throne and going back over to the prosecution bench.

§ § §

Across town, T'shla clicked off her television monitor. The hearing was carried live on at least two networks. She walked to the window of her apartment's living room and looked out. It was a typical golden afternoon. People were starting to come home, and children were out of school, playing on the ball court at the playground across the street.

She sat in a soft chair near the window and let the breeze cool her flushed face. It would probably only be a matter of minutes before they came for her. Still, she could not help but well up with happiness about what Dave had just done. Like opening a rat-infested tunnel and letting the light in, now the world would get a look at what was truly going on inside the Aztec government.

She opened the small cabinet by the window and pulled out a dusty bottle of Mescal, uncorked it, and took a long pull. It surprised her how easy it went down and how quickly it warmed her inside. She was usually a wine girl. She snuggled back into the soft cushions, closed her eyes, and smiled.

Within minutes her peace was interrupted by a harsh knock at the door. This was not the knock of a friend.

At the door were two Quetzalcoatl security guards, not police as she expected.

She was relieved. The regular police force was eighty percent Jaguar devotees and about fifteen percent followers of the Snake order, which was not much better if you valued the right not to be smacked around on the way to a holding cell. Only about three percent of the official police force was Quetzalcoatls, who tended more toward the scientific, judicial, medical, or teaching fields. Jaguars were more often to be found in the military, police, financial industry, and heavier industries such as resource extraction and manufacturing. Since 1520, the Jaguars and Quetzalcoatls dominated society. Other orders—Snake, Corn, Moon, Fire, and Fish—shrank over the centuries as it became more advantageous for families to align with the leading houses of worship. Becoming a Jag or a Quetzal meant better jobs, more slots at superior schools for children, and better housing choices.

Each main religion was allowed to have its own small security force, guards that were loyal to the religion first, the state second. Since the aims of the state and religion were never in conflict, there was never a time when a Jaguar or Quetzal would have to choose his order over the state.

"Miss Ixtapoyan," the smaller guard said. They were wearing electric blue European suits with crimson capes. At their ears were the telltale red, gold, and green feather earrings.

"Can I help you?" T'shla asked. She knew exactly why they were here; she just thought the Jaguars would get to her first after Decoyan's accusation on television. Nobody took down a door like the Jaguar regular police or temple security forces. She was happy it was the Quetzals.

"My name is Tich, and my large friend here is Xhatl. We have come to take you to the Quetzalcoatl temple complex for questioning. Your uncle is keen to have words with you about this data situation and the beheadings." Xhatl stepped through the door and looked around the room to ensure she was alone and there was no immediate security threat.

T'shla did not want to go, but she knew she had no choice. "Do I need to pack something?" she asked. "How long will this be?"

"Toiletries," Tich said. "There are plenty of robes for women at the Temple. Also, all the work material you have related to the health ministry data breach."

T'shla grabbed her bag and went into her bathroom to quickly gather her teeth detergent and brush. Xhatl silently lurked behind her to make sure she wasn't bringing anything sharp that could be used as a weapon.

"That it?" he asked as she turned to leave the bathroom.

"Yes," she said. "Let's go."

Downstairs and out the front door two more Quetzal escorts stood guard watching traffic and making sure no Jaguar police rolled up. A small crowd of neighbors had gathered near her apartment building to see what was going on.

"Quickly," Tich said, opening the car door and gently pushing T'shla in. She was not happy to be going to see her uncle, but he was probably better than what the Jaguars might have in store.

Once they were all inside the vehicle, Xhatl engaged the engine and eased out into traffic. T'shla was sitting between the two outside guards in the back seat. She leaned forward to be able to look out the window. She saw the looks of concerned neighbors and sensed a general tension and fear in the air.

§ § §

Back in the courtroom Dave walked over to Santiago.

"I don't understand what's happening," Santiago said as a Jaguar guard came up and took him by the elbow. "What does it mean to be taken into the custody of a temple?"

Dave didn't have a good answer. "Just hang in there," he said, eyeing the Jaguar guard uneasily. "Don't trust anyone. I will be back at the Temple first thing in the morning to check on you and plan the next steps of your defense after I talk to the consulate."

"I would rather go back to my cell," Santiago said as the guard began to pull him toward the door.

"Hey," Dave said to the guard, "everyone is watching you—don't forget that. If my countryman does not make it safely out of here…"

"Pardon me, sir," the Jaguar cut him off. "I am a professional."

Dave relented, feeling better that Santiago would soon be in the hands of a Quetzalcoatl security officer, even if there were questions about this Jidge Axtulla character.

When Santiago was gone, Dave turned back to the courtroom and saw that it was emptying out. Media were still standing by the side, waiting for an interview. He had given them enough material during the hearing and quickly scanned the room for an alternative exit. Decoyan was just finishing dressing down the prosecution, and Dave averted his course to intercept him before he left.

"Judge Decoyan," Dave said.

Decoyan turned and acknowledged Dave. Dave reached into his pocket and handed Decoyan his visa. "Per your official order," Dave said.

Decoyan smiled. The seizing of a visa under these circumstances was usually just a formality—a gentleman's agreement. The crown did not necessarily need to physically confiscate the visas from men of honor.

Decoyan took the small leather-bound packet. "You don't really need to give up custody of your visa documents," Decoyan said.

"I insist," Dave said.

Decoyan waved for a clerk to come over and take the visa. "I was impressed by your performance," Decoyan said. "Your work today is going to resonate throughout the empire."

"I'm just trying to represent the interests of my country's citizens," Dave countered. "If that means shining an unwanted light on something that's happening here, then so be it."

Decoyan chuckled. "Yes, my boy, of course, you, the bold David Aragon, were going to shine that light. There were no agitators behind you, egging you on."

Dave flushed a bit.

"Oh, don't worry," Decoyan said. "It's not hard at all to figure out where you got your information about the stolen personal and medical data. I'm only surprised our government was so stupid not to connect it to these beheadings before today."

"Exactly what I was thinking," Dave said. "How does something like that happen? Your country is so locked down. I am still amazed that no connection was made until our investigator discovered it."

Decoyan put his hand on Dave's shoulder. Dave knew the cameras across the room would take notice of this. "Sometimes it takes an outsider to point out holes in our system," he whispered. "We have judicial police, city police, an army, and each religious sect has a security force, etcetera, etcetera. They all have jurisdictions, they all arrest and detain people, and not one of them talks to any of the others. It's a mess."

"I'm sure to the detriment of a lot of innocent people," Dave said.

Decoyan nodded gravely and shrugged, indicating that if there was something that could be done to fix things, it would not be Decoyan to do it. Decoyan turned toward his separate exit.

Dave saw an opening. "So, why did you assert in open court that the killers were Jaguars?" Dave asked.

Decoyan stopped and slowly turned around. "Much like how certain agitators used you to get out their information, I used the opportunity to make life difficult for the Jaguar Order. Your countryman implicated Jaguars under questioning. If you weren't going to say it in court, somebody needed to. Hopefully soon we will be able to put down the whole violent, backwards order."

Dave was shocked by Decoyan's words—'put down'—he almost sounded like a Jaguar himself. Decoyan waved to another court clerk who ran over. He whispered an order into the clerk's ear and the clerk ran off.

"Hold here a minute, I'm going to get something for you," Decoyan said.

Dave took the opportunity to collect his briefcase. While there, he checked his phone—fifteen voicemails and twenty-two new text messages. One call from Marta, finally. But still nothing from Johnny. He put the phone back in his pocket and returned to Decoyan, who had been joined by the clerk.

"Mr. Aragon, here is a little something that might be of interest to you," he said, handing Dave a thin and very old leather-bound book. "This book has been in my family for generations. It tells the story of my family and the time Quetzalcoatl originally came to save us from Spanish invaders," he said. "This is a story we do not ever tell your people, and it explains why the devotion to the one true lord, Quetzalcoatl, rings so strong even today. Quetzalcoatl lives."

Dave took the book and carefully put it in his briefcase. He was disappointed Decoyan was proving to be just another religious fanatic. "Thank you. I will be sure to read this," Dave said, with all appropriate reverence.

Decoyan nodded. "I will, of course, want it back before you leave," he said, smiling. "After all, it's priceless, and I do have your visa."

Dave held out his hand and shook Decoyan's in the European style. "I will be sure to trade you this book for my visa when the time comes."

With that, Dave bowed a final time to Decoyan, and exited the courtroom.

As he walked out, he kept his head down to avoid the media. He didn't notice the media had already gone outside to cover the crowd that was growing in the street. Their live coverage had brought out a few hundred Aztecs, curious about the spectacle they had seen on their televisions. Aztecs had never engaged in a public protest or civil action, so the idea of gathering in a large group was foreign to them. So they stood, row on row, quietly eyeing the courtroom building, many not even sure quite why they were there, just that they were there because it was important to bear witness.

Dave emerged and saw hundreds of eyes immediately go to him. He unconsciously clasped his suit jacket closed, suddenly feeling like he must be naked. He eyed the line of cars in front of the courthouse and spotted Tlacatan standing outside their black sedan.

He hurriedly trotted down the steps in Tlacatan's direction. Nefarayit got out of the car to open Dave's door. It was just the two of them. Dave assumed the third muscle was out looking for Johnny.

Just as he got to the bottom step, Dave heard screams through the crowd and car tires squeal. A red luxury sedan raced up, knocking several people off their feet and skidding to a stop, blocking in Nefarayit's car. Nefarayit turned and tried to reach for his shoulder holster, but it was too late. Two large men in Jaguar suits were already outside their car, handguns drawn, blazing away.

"Jesus!" Dave exclaimed as he saw Nefarayit take two bullets to his center mass, the loud pops of the handguns sending the crowd scrambling in every direction. Nefarayit crumpled to the ground. Tlacatan jumped for Nefarayit's body to try to get to his gun, but he too was hit in the shoulder and back before he could reach it.

The gunmen quickly came around the back of the cars and were up on the sidewalk nearing Dave. Dave instinctively held his briefcase up over his head as a shield, but one large Jaguar man was on him, ripping it from his hands while the other drew a collapsible club, held it high, and swung it down on the top of Dave's head. It was a sharp blast of pain, a bright light, and then darkness as Dave fell to the ground unconscious.

The assailants quickly gathered up Dave and carried him to their car. They sped off, and within ten seconds were racing toward the Western Causeway.

CHAPTER 15

February 1519, an amazing sight over The Grand Tenochtitlan

AS SOON AS the blue light cut out, the *Cyrus-Alexander* began to free fall through the bright sunny day, dropping toward the lake at an increasing rate of speed.

"Silvestre, engage the thrusters!" Boddington called out, as the lake got closer and closer. The altimeter showed they had started at 14,000 feet, but were now falling so fast it was impossible to mark their current altitude.

Silvestre held up his hands. "Need power!" Theodora Kopplewicz was feverishly working at her station, trying to punch the engines back online.

"Theodora!" Boddington called out.

"I'm on it—hold on," she said.

Brian began to feel the effects of the free fall. His legs came out from under his seat, held aloft by the weightlessness. Theodora punched in the final relay bypass, rerouting power from the time engine to the thrusters. Above her the reactor lever glowed blue, indicating it was operational.

"All right, Silvestre, engaging power. You should have thrust in five seconds," she said, pulling the lever out and slamming it back home. The crew heard a loud boom as the thrusters became engaged, taking the crew from near weightlessness to being dragged down into their seats by the thrust of the slowing *Cyrus-Alexander*.

Brian leaned over as the entire contents of his stomach came up and spewed out over the metal floor. He wearily looked around to notice that all of them—except Silvestre, Sir Ian, and Vargas—had thrown up. The smell of puke mixed together to create a sickening stench in their cramped quarters.

The ship was now stable, hovering at 2,400 feet above the lake. Silvestre depressurized the cabin, letting in fresh air from outside vents and reducing the vomit smell considerably, though it still sloshed on the floor.

"We are above the island in the lake," Silvestre reported.

Sir Ian undid his buckle and rose to his feet to get a better look out the window. Below them was the untouched city of Tenochtitlan—colorfully painted buildings, floating gardens, and the bustle of river traffic. It was magnificent.

He put his hands to his mouth as tears welled up in his eyes. "We are here, Tenochtitlan, 1519." He looked over to Hans, who was reviewing data on his computer. Hans swiveled in his chair and nodded confirmation.

"Magnificent," Sir Ian said.

Below they could see people starting to gather and gaze in awe up at their craft. More and more were coming outside of their homes and vendor stalls.

Sir Ian motioned to Brian. "Please check on the rest of the crew," he said. "Make sure they weathered the journey."

Brian undid his belt and went to the back compartment where he found everyone to be in good health and spirits, despite some more vomit on the floor. They were all glued to the small windows, looking out over this lake city that stretched as far as the eye could see.

Back on the flight deck, Vargas unlatched his harness and came up behind Sir Ian. "So, what now?" he asked.

"How long can we hover here?" Sir Ian asked Theodora.

"I don't know—five, maybe six years," Theodora said, not bothering to check her instruments. "We're talking cold fusion here."

"Okay," Sir Ian said, "let's hover here for at least an hour to make sure they have all seen us. Then we'll move across the lake and find a flat spot near one of the causeways. There will be no mistaking us. We're not here to hide; we're here to liberate these people from future oppression."

Sir Ian then walked to the back of the flight deck and headed to the rear. "I will be in my cabin getting ready. Hans, Theodora, please prep a rundown on how the ship performed and report to me in fifteen minutes. Silvestre, hold steady. Vargas, you and Brian are with me."

Vargas followed Sir Ian back through the crew cabin and into the main hold of the *Cyrus-Alexander* where the supply pallets, jeep, and aircraft were tied down. On the left side of the main hold was a false wall and a suite of cabins that made up the entire left third of the main cargo hold.

Inside there were five rooms. From front to rear they were bunks, galley and eating space, bathroom and shower space, office space, and finally Sir Ian's private cabin. It was a fairly simple cabin, certainly not befitting the first billionaire to successfully accomplish time travel, but it did have a full-size bed, lightweight metal shelving, and a dresser built right into the bulkhead of the ship.

Sir Ian opened the drawer of the dresser and pulled out his bottle of Macallan 1939 and five crystal glasses. Brian entered to join Vargas and Sir Ian.

"Crew doing well?" Sir Ian asked.

Brian could barely contain himself. "Incredibly excited," he said, "even the mercenaries."

Sir Ian put the glasses on a shelf and began to pour the scotch. "They should be. They are now going to be in the history books forever," Sir Ian said. He recorked the scotch and sat on his bed. "We all are."

Brian went over to a small window in the cabin and saw the people, unmoving, staring up at them. On the island, he saw men standing on the three largest temples. They were just a few hundred feet below. Brian reached for Sir Ian's binoculars, which were on top of his dresser. Through them he could see that the men on the temples were wearing bright white robes fringed with a gold color, their long black hair shining in the midday sun.

"Can I see?" Sir Ian asked. Brian handed him the binoculars.

After a few moments of scanning the city, Sir Ian smiled. "Magnificent." He handed the binoculars to Vargas, who eagerly took them and stepped closer to the window.

"How's your Nahuatl?" Brian asked Vargas.

"My family is originally from Orizaba. They were native speakers of Spanish and Nahuatl. I'd spend summers with my grandparents down there, er, here," Vargas said.

"So?" Brian asked.

Vargas shrugged. "My Spanish is much better than my Nahuatl."

Sir Ian rolled his eyes.

"But my Nahuatl ain't bad," Vargas said.

"I just need a few nouns and verbs," Sir Ian said. "I'm sure you can pick it up as we go along."

"The language has probably changed a great deal," Vargas said.

"You'll figure it out," Sir Ian said. "I have faith."

Hans and Theodora entered Sir Ian's quarters. "My geniuses," Sir Ian said, reaching for the scotch and handing Hans and Theodora each a glass. He then passed out glasses to Brian and Vargas and held the final one up at eye level. Brian, Hans, Vargas, and Theodora all joined him. "To my team," Sir Ian said.

"To the team," they repeated, clinking glasses and taking sips.

"Take it easy," Sir Ian said. "Best to sip one of the finest scotches in the world." Sir Ian swirled the scotch in his glass. "Is it too much of an understatement to say this beats rowing across the Atlantic alone?"

Sir Ian was staring into his glass, a glint in his eye. Brian watched him and wondered how all of Sir Ian's other accomplishments and records stacked up to this one. As his Chief Financial Officer, Brian had read Sir Ian's biography before ever taking the job at 12:36 Adventures. He knew most of Sir Ian's accomplishments were solitary. This was the first time Sir Ian was truly part of a team, relying on the expertise of others to make this adventure possible.

Brian procured the rhodium, Theodora and Hans handled the science, Vargas bought the gear and hired the muscle. This wasn't just Sir Ian's show, it was a group effort—and that's what must have given Sir Ian true satisfaction. *Not too shabby for a sickly boy who always dreamed of playing with all the other kids in the neighborhood*, Brian thought.

111

"Okay, what's the word?" Sir Ian asked after finishing his scotch.

"I will need to inspect the rhodium skin upon landing," Hans said, "but internal diagnostics point to a successful test. The skin effectively shielded the radioactivity from the fusion reaction, pushing it outward and creating a time pocket—like my paper said it would. Radiation levels inside the ship were minimal throughout."

"Excellent," Sir Ian said. "Power plant?"

"We used slightly more reactor power than anticipated," Theodora said, "but it was still just nine percent as opposed to my assumption of seven percent. The loss of power upon exiting the time pocket is a mystery. If we materialized 10,000 feet lower we'd all be sleeping at the bottom of that lake tonight."

"Any idea on the cause?" Brian asked.

"I can't say, exactly, but now that we know what to expect, we can get the engines back online in about half the time," Theodora said.

"Better than nothing," Sir Ian said. "When we land, let's have the mercenaries and Silvestre work on cleaning up and airing out the ship. Wait, hold it. On second thought, I'll take three of the mercenaries with me, Brian, and Vargas when we go out to meet the natives. We will use the Jeep. Theodora and Hans, you both stay behind and work all the possibilities for projecting when we can jump home."

"Will that be hard?" Brian asked.

"Timing the jump back home will be trickier than timing the initial jump," Hans said. "But don't worry. Once we have our touch-down location established, I can calculate the return."

"How does that work?"

Hans patted Brian on the shoulder. "I call it Gaummer's Triangulation Theory. Since our touch-down location won't be known until we actually set down, there is no way to calculate how to get back. Yet."

Brian began to feel queasy again, only this time it wasn't caused by the time travel. Hans chuckled. "Easy, boy, I said 'yet.' You see, I need a starting coordinate on the ground here so I can find suitable jump points from here that, in turn, have a correlation with the Whitestone facility. You know where you are coming from. You know where you are going. Getting back requires travel to a third space-time coordinate that corresponds with both."

"I don't want to sound like I am doubting you..." Brian started, but Hans held up is hand in a professorial wave of confidence and dismissal.

"I have cataloged about 423,000 such potential corresponding coordinates on earth at different times that connect us to the Whitestone facility at a time just after our original launch. Sure, not having GPS satellites here in 1519 is a slight complication, but we have some pretty whiz-bang computer mapping software that will help me get it done."

"And, we have to return to Whitestone after our launch, of course," Theodora chimed in. "Otherwise, the incoming ship would occupy the same space as the ship from the earlier time. Hans has postulated that such an event might permanently cause a disastrous tear in the space-time continuum with the results either being an irreparable hole in the universe at worst, or the deaths of everyone at the facility in a calamitous explosion at best."

"Science," Brian said.

"Science, indeed," echoed Sir Ian.

Theodora and Hans finished their drinks and headed back to the flight deck while Sir Ian went to the bottom drawer of his dresser and pulled out a white silk robe with gold edging. "Depending on the return triangulation, we'll probably be here for a few weeks at the very least."

This shocked Brian. "A few weeks?"

Sir Ian chuckled as he stripped down and started changing into white robes. "Yes, but when we get back it might just be a few minutes or hours after we left. So, you won't really miss anything."

"But isn't there a paradox that says if we even step on a bug here, we will change the course of history?" Brian asked.

Sir Ian draped the robe over his body. It was a little big. He sighed. "I told them to take this in," he said under his breath, picking his pants up off the bed and pulling his khaki woven belt out of the loops. "Talk to Hans about that," he said. "We believe that we're now creating a completely new timeline and a new universe just by being here. What happens from now on, right here, will create a new world. Once we return to our place in time and space, it should all be the same because we will cross back to our original universe." Sir Ian wrapped his belt around his waist and fastened it.

"You seem pretty sure about all this," Brian said.

Sir Ian looked up from his belt and held out his hands. "What do you think?" he asked.

"Looks fine," Brian said.

Sir Ian put his hands on his hips. "Oh come now, boy," he said. "Hans and Theodora are the best in the business. Like you are the best in your business. If you tell me not to execute that stock swap, what do I do?"

"You do your own thing," Brian said.

Sir Ian put a reassuring hand on Brian's shoulder. "I listen," he said. "That's what I do, I listen to my experts. Hans is confident it will work and I have faith in him."

Sir Ian went back to the bottom drawer and pulled out what looked like a showgirl's boa. It was festooned with red, gold, and green feathers from exotic birds. Finally, he pulled out a three-quarter motorcycle helmet. On it was painted the image of a shiny green serpent. He strung the boa around his neck and donned the helmet.

He looked ridiculous.

"What do you think?" Sir Ian asked.

"You look like a mental patient," Brian said, as Vargas re-entered the room.

Vargas cast a sideways glance at Brian, obviously having a hard time keeping a straight face. "Do we have to, ah, dress up, too?" Vargas asked.

Sir Ian adjusted the flowing sleeves on his robe. "No, I'm the one that matters here. I am Quetzalcoatl." There was a long silence in the room as Brian and Vargas cast uneasy glances at one another.

Sir Ian cut the silence. "We have to convince the Aztecs that I am the returning serpent god of knowledge and wisdom. Is the Jeep ready?"

"Yes sir," Vargas said. "We have Collins, Drake, and Chagal on the detail. Collins is the driver. They all have rifles."

Vargas reached into a satchel that was hanging over his left shoulder and pulled out a black semi-automatic handgun. He handed it to Brian. "It's a Colt 1911, loaded but on safety," he said. "I have no idea what we are going to run into. It's just for an emergency. Worst case, I'm sure a shot into the air will pretty much scare the shit out of them."

Brian took the gun and placed it in the ample cargo pocket of his pants.

"Vaccines?" Sir Ian asked. "Make sure the entire crew gets another booster before we land, especially Brian."

"Will do," Vargas said, turning to the door. He stopped and turned back. "And Sir Ian?"

Sir Ian looked up. "You know it's going to be better for the artifice of it all if you start referring to me as Quetzalcoatl at all times. That way we won't screw up," Boddington said.

"Okay," Vargas said. "Quetzalcoatl, I wanted to also say that Silvestre has found what looks like a complex of empty ball courts near the Western Causeway. He thinks we can finagle a landing there."

"Excellent," Quetzalcoatl said. "Tell Silvestre to move us into position and prepare for landing."

§ § §

The *Cyrus-Alexander* lumbered slowly from the complex of tall temple pyramids, markets, and narrow streets of the main island and traveled along the Western Causeway toward the shore of Lake Texcoco. People on the causeway ran underneath, following in the direction of the ship.

In the flight deck, Theodora was helping Silvestre keep an eye out for alternative landing spots. Vargas entered the flight deck and sat in the row of seats behind Silvestre and Theodora, who were seated in the pilot and co-pilot seats, respectively.

"I think we just need to goose the thrusters right before landing—that might do it," Theodora said.

"Do what?" Vargas asked.

Theodora turned to acknowledge Vargas. "We're not interested in crushing any of these Aztecs. It would make a bad first impression. Is Ian ready?"

"You mean Quetzalcoatl?" Vargas asked.

"Oh God, really?" Theodora asked.

"Yeah, he wants all of us to start referring to him as Quetzalcoatl," Vargas said. "He thinks it will help us keep up the appearance that we are visiting gods."

Silvestre chuckled as he reached up to deploy the landing pads. He flipped the switches lowering the pads into place—two aft, two central and one forward. They were round, rhodium-coated disks six feet in diameter. When the pods began coming out of the ship, the Aztecs who were close by began to scatter.

"I guess we might not need to goose the thrusters after all," Theodora said.

Silvestre eased off the throttle and the *Cyrus-Alexander* began to descend.

"Seventy-five feet," Theodora called out, craning her neck out the side windows to ensure the Aztecs were still keeping their distance.

The *Cyrus-Alexander* slowly came down straight and true, landing pads making contact at exactly 2:43 p.m. on February 13, 1519.

Silvestre powered down the engines as Theodora disengaged the power plant. Silvestre stood and stretched as Sir Ian entered the flight deck wearing his Quetzalcoatl outfit. Brian trailed behind.

Theodora put her hand to her mouth, concealing a giggle.

"Meeting in the cargo hold," Sir Ian said, waving his finger in the air in a circular motion that meant 'round up the entire crew.' He exited, and Theodora and Brian cast short glances at each other. Brian shrugged.

§ § §

Out in the cramped cargo hold, the small crew assembled tightly around the Jeep. Sir Ian/Quetzalcoatl stood on the driver seat, his helmet mere inches away from the Black Hawk's rear fin.

"We have all—together—just made the most remarkable journey in the history of humankind," Quetzalcoatl began. "Some of you might be asking yourselves, why here or why now? Well, before we set out to meet our new friends, I want to answer those questions.

"In 1519, the Spanish Conquistadors began their conquest of Mexico. Using Native tribes allied with their cause, they landed on the Gulf Coast and marched inland. The Aztecs, here in the city of Tenochtitlan, had such a strong network of communication they were able to get daily reports of the Spanish advance.

Rather than take up arms and push the Spanish out, Emperor Moctezuma invited them in. You see, the Spanish and their leader, Hernán Cortés, arrived right at the same time as Aztec prophecies foretold of the return of the light-skinned serpent god of wisdom, Quetzalcoatl. Cortés used that to his advantage. With a much smaller force, he was able to get into the main palaces, kill Moctezuma, and within two years, this beautiful city would lie in ruins. Tens of thousands of people would be dead by war or disease, and the Aztec Empire would be finished.

"The city in which we have just landed—at this time—is larger than the largest cities of Europe. Now imagine more than seventy-five percent of the innocent women and children all around us today murdered in the next two years if we don't do something about it."

Brian hazarded a look around the room to see if this was resonating with anyone. He felt deeply conflicted. What happened here was a crime, but was it right to 'do something about it' as Sir Ian was saying? It seemed to him the answer would be much easier if they went back to Germany in the 1930s and killed Hitler. Those atrocities were closer to all their experiences. Those atrocities had been caught on camera.

Theodora and Vargas were not looking at Sir Ian, but the rest of the crew was dutifully nodding at their boss, who was paying each of them a minimum of 500,000 pounds for this one journey, alone.

"I read these stories with horror as a young boy," Sir Ian continued. "I dreamed of being able to come here and make a difference. Well, today we have the tools to stand up and make that difference. Today, we are here to introduce ourselves to the Aztecs and convince them to take up arms against the Spanish, who will arrive on the shores of the gulf coast in mere weeks. Do you have any questions?"

Their mission's sole mechanic, William Ritter, raised his hand.

"Yes, Ritter?"

"Sir, can you explain your get-up there?" Ritter asked.

Sir Ian beamed and did a little fashion-model twist on the Jeep's seat to show off the outfit. "I crafted this based on my research of what Aztec Priests of the time wore as well as a headpiece to create the impression of a serpent." He took off his helmet and held it aloft for all to see. "The feathers are also the color of Quetzalcoatl, and that is why I also had our flying equipment painted in red, gold, and green."

"But why?" someone else asked.

"Good question," Sir Ian said, putting the helmet back on his head. "We are going to use the same coincidence Cortés used, only this time, our mission is one to help the Aztecs, not destroy them. I will pose as the returning Quetzalcoatl, win an audience with the Emperor, and convince him to mobilize against the Spanish using our weapons, training, and expertise."

116

Brian noticed the hint of a sickly expression cross Theodora's face. Ian had likely told her of his plans to visit this place of his childhood imagination, but this whole changing history thing was way beyond the pale. She looked around and her eyes met Brian's. Brian looked away quickly and raised his hand.

"Yes, Brian," Sir Ian said.

"Yes, I asked this of you earlier, and I felt it might also be important to ask it in front of the whole crew," Brian began. "What assurances do you have that us messing with the timeline in the past will not create calamity for all of our individual futures and the people we love?"

Hans Gaummer, who was standing near Sir Ian, raised his hand and got Sir Ian's attention. "I've got this one," Hans said. "Brian, great question. I know it's something many of you were probably thinking. I have done quite a bit of academic research about time travel and the implications of the time-travel paradox. What I can say is that all the best scholarship—including my own—points to the fact that we are now creating an alternate branch of the space-time continuum. Meaning, what we do here to change the future will change the future of this universe, not our own original universe that we can return to using the power source created by our esteemed colleague, Dr. Theodora Kopplewicz."

Hans stopped and began clapping, leading the others in a hearty round of applause for Theodora, who smiled awkwardly, cheeks flushing.

"What we can do here is create an alternative timeline, right a wrong, and then go back to our original home," Hans finished.

Most of the assembled crew in the cargo hold were nodding, likely still too stunned or giddy by their journey to fully grasp the gravity of what Hans just explained to them.

"All right then," Sir Ian said, taking back the center of attention. "Brian, Dr. Vargas, and I, as well as Collins, Drake, and Chagal from security, will drive over the Western Causeway and, well, knock on the palace door. As for the rest of you, let's make sure the Black Hawk is ready to fly in case we need another demonstration of our 'magic.' Theodora—you're in charge while we're gone." Sir Ian came down off the Jeep and went up to Theodora, grabbed her, and kissed her in front of the crew. This made her seem even more uncomfortable.

"Here is a Walkie Talkie—we will be on channel eleven," Sir Ian said.

"All right," Theodora said, pocketing the radio and wiping her lips.

Brian walked up and sat on the back seat of the Jeep. Vargas sat in the passenger seat. Sir Ian took a standing position in the back. He was flanked by Chagal and Drake, who each had their AK-47s at the ready.

Sir Ian gave the signal, and Ritter pressed the release, opening the back of the *Cyrus-Alexander.* Collins fired up the engine as the back hatch lowered to the ground letting in the cool damp air of the Valley of Mexico in late winter.

§ § §

The Jeep slowly came down the ramp and rolled onto the soft, wet turf. The air was thick. All around them were people, many of them children. The men and boys were largely shirtless, the women and girls in tunics and robes. They all stood silently watching the Jeep come out and begin rolling on the wet grass toward a cobblestone path.

Sir Ian held up his hands. "My children," he said in stilted Nahuatl. "I have returned." He reached down and picked up a satchel filled with jelly beans and M&Ms. He grabbed two handfuls and flung them in the direction of the crowd. "A gift for my children."

An Aztec girl reached down and picked an M&M off the cobblestone. She looked at it quizzically and then looked back at Sir Ian with a furrowed brow.

Sir Ian smiled, pulled another M&M from his satchel, and ate it.

The girl looked back to whom Brian assumed was her mother. Her mother nodded. The girl put the candy in her mouth. She smiled broadly upon breaking the candy shell with her teeth and looked back at her mother in glee. Soon other Aztecs had begun reaching down to pick up pieces of candy, tasting them, breaking the already small pieces into smaller ones to share.

Sir Ian held his hands aloft again in triumph.

Vargas tapped Collins on the shoulder and pointed the way forward to the Western Causeway, which was about 50 yards directly up ahead. The Jeep inched forward, and the people who were gathered in front of them moved out of the way, staring in amazement at the magical mode of transport.

"These people have no wheels," Sir Ian said, still smiling broadly for the crowd, "much less pack animals that could propel such a vehicle. As far as they are concerned, we are being powered by divine magic."

The Jeep reached the causeway and came to a stop. It was about 100 feet wide and about a half-mile long. Collins stood up in his seat and looked out over the front.

"Do you think it can support the weight of the Jeep?" Brian asked.

"Cortés' horses and men made the trip, and their combined weight was much more than us," Sir Ian said. "Proceed."

"Hold it," Brian said. "Let's be safe—distribute the weight. Drake, Chagal, Vargas, and I can walk—that's 750 pounds off the Jeep. Just to be safe."

"Very well," Sir Ian said. "Just make your dismount look purposeful. You are in the service of a god—be infallible."

Brian, Vargas, Chagal, and Drake all dismounted from the Jeep and started walking over the causeway in front of Collins and Quetzalcoatl, who remained in the vehicle. Aztecs lined the bridge, which was surprisingly sturdy. Brian looked beyond the people and saw that canoes crowded either side of the causeway, people in them standing up and stretching to get a better view of the returning god.

§ § §

Across the causeway, ensconced in his opulent palace, Moctezuma II was getting moment-by-moment reports from his palace guard.

"They have begun crossing the causeway," Macuiltan said. Macuiltan was a high priest of the Jaguar Order, a Jaguar pelt draped over his shoulders and the head of a Jaguar resting on his head, as if swallowing him.

Moctezuma had heard the rumblings in the court. Quetzalcoatl's return was supposed to happen any time, so the high priests of the Quetzalcoatl devotion had foretold. But all the various devotions foretold of things all the time with only a spotty record of accuracy at best. The fact that this magic beast had appeared over their skies and now had disgorged gods who were on approach was undeniable. Macuiltan's fidgeting and pacing was a sign to the emperor that his old friend was clearly nervous. On the other hand, Sep Tarantan, head of the Quetzalcoatl Order, was elated, sitting in his rightful place to the left and down several steps from Moctezuma's throne.

"My lord, I beseech that we commit a sacred sacrifice on this occasion, before our visitors arrive, so that we can divine some guidance from the blood about how we proceed," Macuiltan requested.

Moctezuma nodded. Just about anything they could do to provide more insight would be helpful at this point. He looked around the court; the gathered piplitzin, or nobles, were silent, shocked by the unprecedented events of the morning. All fidgeted and whispered worriedly among themselves except his proud young warrior nephew, Cuauhtemoc, who stood in full war dress, polished shell necklace, deep green cape, and fiery feather headdress, a long gold-tipped spear at his side.

Macuiltan motioned for an aide to bring a sacrifice to the top of the Pyramid of the Sun. He drew his bone blade, touched it to the bridge of his nose in salute, and exited for the Pyramid to conduct the ritual.

Once Macuiltan was out of the throne room, Sep left his seat and came before the Emperor. He bowed. "You may speak," Moctezuma said.

"My lord, in all your wisdom, you know that Macuiltan's blood reading will not provide any more insight than what is right in front of us. A flying beast. A serpent-headed white god wearing the colors of my order. It is unmistakable. Macuiltan is merely looking for an opportunity to create doubt in your mind. For me and my order, there is no doubt."

Moctezuma waved a slave servant over and whispered in her ear. She left through the red curtains behind the throne and emerged seconds later with a cup of pulque, a fermented, thick, pasty drink created from the Agave plant.

"Maybe there is no doubt," Moctezuma said. "But we have time. Let's see what Macuiltan's sacrifice yields." He then called out to Cuauhtemoc at the back of the room. "Temoc, my boy, come to me."

Cuauhtemoc approached. He was a strapping twenty-four-year-old and such a natural leader that Moctezuma at times quietly envied his grace, strength, and personal touch with people, both in the court and out among the lower masses. Cuauhtemoc bowed, but instead of returning upright, he took one knee and looked upon his master.

"Macuiltan is conducting a sacrifice to provide more information about these visitors—who they are and what they want from us. But regardless of his findings, they are coming. I want you to be prepared to stop them. Make sure we have our finest archers on the walls of the Sacred Precinct. I also want you to personally greet them at the gates. Take a measure of their character, and if their intentions are pure, escort them here for an audience. But, be prepared to kill every single one of these visitors if you perceive a threat. Have a steady hand. I do not want to risk the divine retribution of loosing our arrows on a god and his attendants."

Cuauhtemoc stood. He notoriously avoided the stuffiness of court life and was likely thankful to have an opportunity to get out and see this threat for himself. Palace life was stifling: listening to priests argue back and forth, trying to win favor with the emperor—inch by inch, day by day—it was exhausting.

"I will obey, my lord," he said.

§ § §

Cuauhtemoc rose and strode out of the main throne chamber. Waiting just outside the chamber was his chief lieutenant and friend, Tuxla. "Suit up, Tux," Cuauhtemoc said, barely breaking stride. "We are the designated welcomers."

Tuxla nodded as he stood and slung his shield over his shoulder. He trotted to catch up to Cuauhtemoc, who was already nearing the main doors of the palace. They exited just in time to see Macuiltan up on top of the Sun Pyramid, blade in hand, strike swiftly onto the chest of a writhing sacrifice. Cuauhtemoc sighed. More posturing by priests. He turned to Tuxla. "What's the latest report?"

"They are halfway down the Causeway, moving very slowly. There are four, what appear to be men, walking on foot. There are two others—one appears to be the god, Quetzalcoatl, and one seems to be controlling the beast they are on top of," Tuxla said.

"Are they armed?" Cuauhtemoc asked.

"A few appear to be carrying some kind of short staffs, brown and black. I think they may be weapons of some kind, but…" They were now at the walls of the Sacred Precinct, near the gate that opened to the Western Causeway.

"I want twenty of our best archers on the walls," Cuauhtemoc said. "Also, gather two files of our tallest and most intimidating spearmen. I want to personally greet this god."

§ § §

Back in the throne chamber, Macuiltan reentered, his hands still bright red with blood. Moctezuma rose in his chair. "Well?"

Macuiltan held up his hands, showing them to the entire court. Sep rolled his eyes. Moctezuma descended from the throne and took Macuiltan's hands in his own, studying them.

"The blood tells me this visit is momentous," Macuiltan said. "But it's inconclusive as to whether these visitors are Quetzalcoatl himself or merely emissaries of the plumed serpent."

Disappointed, Moctezuma stepped back toward his throne and waved for a slave to come over and clean his hands. "So, we didn't learn anything, for sure," Moctezuma said.

"Well, this is a very important matter," Macuiltan said sheepishly. "We may need ten to twenty more sacrifices to truly learn what this happening signifies."

Moctezuma washed his hands in a golden bowl provided by his slave valet. "It's too late for that, my friend," he said. "These visitors are upon us. I have dispatched Cuauhtemoc to greet them and escort them here for an audience."

§ § §

Brian and Vargas were the first to set foot on the island. In front of them was a stone wall and wooden gate about twenty feet tall. On top of the wall, on both sides of the gate, were Aztec archers standing at the ready. Vargas hazarded a look back at Sir Ian, who indicated it was okay for him to speak.

Vargas cleared his throat and reached into his pocket for a cheat sheet of Nahuatl that covered some of the common words and phrases. "Great defenders of Tenochtitlan," he began. "We approach as friends. We follow Quetzalcoatl, plumed serpent and god of wisdom."

Vargas looked back to Sir Ian, who nodded approvingly.

Just then, the group heard wood creak as the door began to slowly open. Behind it were two immaculate lines of soldiers, full green-feathered headdresses and white tunics with red woven leather belts. All had gold-tipped spears that were at least 8 feet tall. They heard an Aztec voice from the rear order a command and, moving as one, the lines trotted out and encircled the six visitors and their vehicle.

"Easy," Sir Ian said, reminding his men not to move too quickly.

From the back of the two columns two men approached. One was dressed like the other soldiers, while the other was dressed much more flamboyantly, with a shock of red and yellow feathers in his headdress and gold jewelry, polished-shell chest armor, and broad golden wrist cuffs with Jaguar-spot patterns hammered into them.

This was Cuauhtemoc, a legendary prince of Tenochtitlan. Cuauhtemoc, who in the standard timeline was the final leader of the Aztec people after Moctezuma's death and the death of Moctezuma's brother Cuitláhuac. Cuauhtemoc was the transcendent hero of Mexican history, organizing the resistance against the Spanish until he was forced to capitulate 1521. Sir Ian knew immediately who he was and was awed to be in the presence of such a towering figure.

"Cuauhtemoc!" Sir Ian called out.

Cuauhtemoc's head quickly spun to take in this strange white creature in robes and shiny helmet. He squinted at Sir Ian as if trying to make him out.

"Cuauhtemoc," Sir Ian said again, getting down from the Jeep and walking toward the Aztec prince. Sir Ian strode right up to Cuauhtemoc and touched his face. Cuauhtemoc recoiled.

"Who are you?" Cuauhtemoc asked in perfect, noble Nahuatl.

"I am Quetzalcoatl, and I have returned to help you and your people fend off a great enemy," Sir Ian said. His Nahuatl was terrible, but apparently understood by Cuauhtemoc, who nodded. Sir Ian cast a glance in Vargas' direction. Vargas shrugged, indicating that Sir Ian had done a passable job.

Cuauhtemoc appeared to be very confused by the whole situation, but not flustered. Sir Ian surmised it would take a lot more than the arrival of a celestial being to rattle this fine specimen of Aztec greatness. The Aztec prince looked beyond Sir Ian and sized up Brian, Vargas, and the mercenaries, before whispering something to one of his men.

"Bring them inside," Sir Ian, even with his limited Nahuatl proficiency, heard Cuauhtemoc say to one of his men. With scarcely another look back at the visitors, Cuauhtemoc turned and headed back in the direction of the palace. Sir Ian looked quizzically at Vargas.

"They're letting us in," Vargas said.

"I got that part," Sir Ian said, a smile crossing his face. "Alert the others. Let them know we have an audience." Brian got on the walkie-talkie to tell Theodora of their progress.

Sir Ian pulled Vargas to the side. "We have to be spot on now with our language. Remember, Cortés had translators and loyal Indians—it was fundamentally easier for him to communicate."

"Maybe we tell them their language is an old tongue to us. Being the God of Wisdom, you know many tongues. Then it will stand to reason that we'd be rusty at theirs," Vargas said.

"That's a good angle," Sir Ian said. "Tell them all that by way of introduction when you announce me to the Emperor. Can you handle that?"

Vargas' eyes got wide. "Sure, I guess," he said.

"Good enough," Sir Ian said, getting back on the Jeep.

Brian came up to Vargas as the Aztecs made an opening for Quetzalcoatl's party. "You all right?" Brian asked Vargas.

"For a momentous occasion such as time travel, I have to admit, the boss sure likes making things up as he goes along," Vargas said.

Brian chuckled. "Maybe that's what makes him a genius."

Directly ahead in the Sacred Precinct were the steps to the main palace. To each side, towering above, were the pyramids of the sun and moon.

Cuauhtemoc stood on the top step of the entrance to the main palace, awaiting the visitors. "I will show you to your quarters," he said. "You will be housed in the apartments of the Eagle Order. We know there are others in your group. You can send a runner to tell them they are welcome to stay here as well."

Sir Ian stiffened upon being told what Cuauhtemoc said. "I thought we would be able to see the Emperor," he said to Cuauhtemoc, clearly not happy. "Any delay may be extremely costly."

"Apologies," Cuauhtemoc said, "the emperor wanted to ensure his guests are well rested and well fed before he meets with them. This is the way it has always been. Enjoy our hospitality."

"Then it is we who must apologize," Vargas said. "No need to send a runner." Vargas got on his walkie talkie to radio back to the ship and tell the rest of the crew they were going to be guests of the emperor. Cuauhtemoc and his men appeared intrigued but not frightened by the strange black device Vargas was using to communicate.

"Yes," came Theodora's voice back through the walkie talkie. This must have appeared magical to Cuauhtemoc and his men.

"We are going to be put up and treated to dinner here at the palace tonight before meeting with the Emperor," Vargas said in English. He looked at Sir Ian, and Sir Ian held up two fingers. "Leave two people behind with the ship—Silvestre and a mercenary—otherwise lock it up and make your way across the bridge. Bring weapons just in case."

"10-4," Theodora acknowledged.

Cuauhtemoc had inched closer to Vargas to get a better look at the walkie talkie. Vargas offered it to him to inspect, but Cuauhtemoc refused, instead calling one of his lieutenants over.

"Tuxla will show you to your apartments," Cuauhtemoc said. "Welcome to the Grand Tenochtitlan. You are honored guests of His Holiness, Moctezuma II."

Cuauhtemoc bowed and left them in Tuxla's care.

§ § §

The Apartments of the Eagle Order were a complex of rooms surrounded by a tiled courtyard. It had seven bedrooms and a large seating area at the far end for meals. It was constantly staffed by a complement of fifteen slaves, who were on site to meet every need of the guests. Two Aztec guards were stationed at the entrance portico. In the center of the courtyard was an ornate obsidian sculpture of an eagle.

Sir Ian took the largest bedroom for himself and Theodora. The others had to make do with smaller rooms. The beds were stone slab benches set into the walls. Soft cotton cloths were woven together to create mattresses that were stuffed with feathers. It was about as luxurious as one would expect from a 1519 bed. Down and microfiber it was not. Vargas and Brian decided to room together.

A flight of slaves entered the Eagle Apartments from the portico, arms full of pots and clay cups. Within minutes, the slaves had laid out a spread of tortillas, maize mash, stone-roasted fish fresh from the lake, and two huge jars of pulque.

Following right after the slaves was the rest of the *Cyrus-Alexander* crew minus the two who were back at the ship. They were escorted in by two soldiers wearing royal green capes and Jaguar-themed jewelry. Theodora walked up to Sir Ian, who was pouring himself and Collins a pulque. Brian and Vargas came out of their room and rejoined their comrades at the eating area.

"Was your trip over acceptable?" Sir Ian asked, pulling out extra cups for the rest of the crew.

"Escorted the entire way," Theodora said, eyeing the soldiers and waiting for them to leave. "Are we prisoners here?"

"I don't think so," Sir Ian said. "Plus, they don't know what these are." He pointed to Theodora's rifle, which was slung over her shoulder. "If we get in a tight spot—which I don't think will happen—they have no idea what kind of awesome power they have just let into their temple."

Brian took a sip of the pulque, but immediately spit it out. Sir Ian smiled. "You'll get used to it. Rough going down, but the effect is quite pleasant when it kicks in."

"So, what's our play?" Brian asked after he recovered. "I know how you handle the 12:36 Board of Directors, but I don't think flying by the seat of your pants is going to serve us well here."

Sir Ian scoffed. "Playing it fast and loose got me here, so I won't stop now. I think the emperor and his inner circle are trying to figure out what to do. They have seen an incredible happening in the skies above their city. Is our arrival a good thing for them, or is it a bad thing? They don't know. They are buying themselves some time to think it over, I suspect. Tomorrow, when we have our audience, we will get to show them our magic and win them over."

Hans emerged from his room and came to the seating area, taking a space on the bench next to Sir Ian, who passed a bowl of the maize mash to him. Hans put a ladleful of mash on his plate and reached for the fish tray. No one else was eating.

"I think I have made a very interesting discovery with the ship," Hans said, grabbing the mash with two fingers and sprinkling it into his mouth. "I was testing the Rhodium decay on the ship's systems and found that the catalyst decay rate is a lot slower than we anticipated, meaning the ship may be able to handle much more time travel without needing a reskinning," Hans said.

"Well, that sounds like music to my ears," Brian said. "The less Rhodium we have to buy, the better, especially in the current commodities market."

"Certainly. But that's not all I discovered," Hans said. "You see, the Rhodium is somehow holding onto, and conducting, some of the residual energy from the time travel. We don't have all the equipment here, but I would like to do more tests when we get back to Whitestone Manor. It appears that, by charging the rhodium as we have, we are somehow conducting energy to rhodium elsewhere in the world."

"What does that mean?" Theodora asked.

Hans tried the pulque and grimaced as he gulped it down. "Take a look at your ring," Hans said after wiping his mouth and moving his pulque cup far away from him.

Theodora took off her rhodium ring and held it up. It still had a faint blue glow, similar to the glow they had all experienced when the time travel engine had been engaged.

"Fascinating," she said. "It seems to have retained some properties from the fusion energy source."

"More than that," Hans said. "I believe it has the properties to record and conduct experiences as well as energy. I believe, seeing how the glow persists in the rhodium—and the fact that the charge impacts rhodium that is not physically part of the ship, such as your ring—indicates that rhodium can be used as some kind of an antenna to broadcast or communicate."

Brian took his rhodium ring out of his pocket to inspect it. It also glowed blue, but only inside the circle of the ring.

Sir Ian waved his hand dismissively. "Lovely find, Dr. Gaummer, but I maintain that digital downloads are much more inexpensive and efficient for delivering content than conducting data through one of the rarest minerals known to man. Imagine the costs."

Hans laughed, "Good point sir. Yes, having a rhodium iPod would not make sense economically. But how much would the top universities or entertainment companies pay for a Rhodium looking glass that can see live into the past and watch events unfold? Maybe even record them for television broadcast and sell the rights to major networks? Now, how much would wealthy people pay for their own personal rhodium time mirrors to be in their parlors to educate their children and entertain their guests? Imagine this: tonight at 8 p.m., tune in to the Boddington History Network to watch Napoleon make his last stand at Waterloo."

Sir Ian put down his drink and looked upon Hans with wonder and surprise. "Now you have my ear, good doctor," he said, patting him heartily on the back. "That's an idea that pencils out. You see, Brian? If we didn't take this little jaunt today, we would never have learned all the unintended benefits. Much like how the U.S. space program brought us Tang and freeze-dried ice cream."

Brian chuckled. "Bad examples, but yes, a history-viewing time mirror is certainly something that would revolutionize just about everything. Not to mention the time travel and the fusion—those are pretty big, too."

CHAPTER 16

1999 Aztecan time—480 years later in the same general vicinity.

JIDGE AXTULLA TURNED for the Northern Causeway, which was not necessarily the most convenient way to get to the Quetzalcoatl Temple complex. Q Temple, as the locals called it, was located on a piece of reclaimed lakefront between the Southern and Western Causeways—jutting out into the lake and with a magnificent view of the Emperor's palace on top of Chapultepec Hill. The shootings at the courthouse and ensuing pandemonium in front of the Judicial Complex had closed down all but the Northern Causeway, so the path back to the Q Temple would be more circuitous.

Santiago Esparza sat in the passenger side, happy to be out of the detention center, but having no idea what lay before him. Most of all, he was uneasy about Jidge—his old friend, who was now a zealously religious devotee of Quetzalcoatl. Sure, it appeared as if a Jaguar killed that poor man at the bar, but Santiago had a feeling he couldn't trust anyone.

Jidge easily merged onto the causeway, taking the immediate right hand lane. "The radio said the disturbance in front of the courts has island traffic completely shut down," Jidge said, his voice oddly strained and higher pitched. "I'm surprised the Northern isn't backed up like crazy." Santiago continued to sit in silence, looking through his window out onto the lake.

Jidge continued. "Police closed down all the ways off the island except the Northern. If it's important enough, they'll probably close this bridge, too, huh."

They made it off the bridge and were now on the mainland. Santiago saw highway signs written in the Aztec language. He couldn't read them so he didn't even try. If he could have read Nahuatl, he would have seen they indicated that the North-South highway was coming up and they needed to exit left to head south back into Central Tenochtitlan and the Temple District, including the Temples of Quetzalcoatl, the Snake, the Eagle, and the Maize Queen.

Jidge veered right, to the north—in a direction that would eventually take them out of the city.

Santiago did not notice this—he was never good with directions. He was too preoccupied by the emptiness of his life. How did he get to this point? During his time in lock-up there was no attempt by any family members to reach him. He felt completely alone. Maybe this was what he needed to turn it all around.

Santiago turned to look out the front window and noticed they were traveling in a direction that was away from Downtown. "Are we going to your house?" Santiago asked.

Jidge was silent. He left the highway and turned down a side street, slowing the car to a stop in front of an overgrown vacant lot filled with discarded appliances and other trash.

"Listen," Jidge said. "I am sorry I invited you here and got you involved in this."

Santiago, not noticing a dark sedan pulling up behind them, shrugged. "It's not you. You invited me, but I came here, and I made stupid decisions that got me into this mess."

Two men walked up on either side of the car.

Jidge was now crying. "Forgive me, my friend," he said. He looked to the roof of the car. "Forgive me, Quetzalcoatl."

Santiago leaned forward and noticed the man standing at the driver's side door. He saw the man swiftly pull a pistol out of his jacket. *POP, POP, POP.* The glass shattered, and blood from Jidge sprayed onto Santiago. Reflexively, Santiago turned to exit the car and came face to face with the barrel of another pistol. *POP, POP.* It was over.

§ § §

Across town, in another car that was able to make the Western Causeway before police shut it down, Dave's lifeless body bobbed in the back seat. But in his mind, he was back in that old familiar place.

He looked out on a gray sky, rain forcing him to squint as he lay there, motionless. The heads of other commuters circled around him. They were not speaking Spanish. English, maybe. Unlike most dreams where settings shift in a matter of seconds, this dream seemed to happen in real time. It took forever for the ambulance to arrive. He didn't feel pain, just a general numbness. His head and shoulders were still on the ramp, his legs and feet on the pier. In the periphery, he saw people treading past on their way to work, probably annoyed by this clumsy idiot who slipped and fell. The paramedics eventually arrived. He could clearly make out their faces—a kind-faced African woman and a bearded white man.

"Are you aware of what is happening?" the female paramedic asked, looking him squarely in the face from what was no more than three inches away. She spoke English, but somehow he understood her as if he were a native speaker.

He blinked and made a sound that was halfway between "yes" and a grunt. The paramedic nodded and made eye contact with her partner, who had gotten out a spinal-stabilization board. Together they strapped him to the board, carefully lifted him to a gurney, and rolled him into the ambulance. Before they rolled him in, he noticed a sweet-looking grandmotherly figure approach him. She took out a kerchief and wiped his face clear of the rain.

The paramedics loaded him up, and he heard the sirens begin to shriek as the door closed and they made their way to the nearest hospital.

Dave felt someone grab his shoulder and pull him upright. Groggily, he awoke to muffled darkness and realized he had a loose-fitting hood over his head. It was dark, and he could tell he was in the back seat of the car. He heard and felt the car come to a stop, the driver turning off the engine and opening the door. The thug in the back seat grabbed Dave by the crook of his elbow, forcibly pulling him from the car and dragging him out and onto his knees. Dave fell to the ground, his hands breaking the fall.

"Get up," came the voice, speaking Spanish, but with an accent similar to Johnny's—an English accent.

"We need a positive ID," one of the men said in what Dave could tell was English.

The hood was harshly yanked off Dave's head. He didn't need to adjust his eyes, as they were in a deserted and dark parking garage. Dave's eyes focused on a man in a forest green suit. He heard the man behind him go to the trunk and open it.

Dave rose uneasily and took a step back. "Whatever you're going to do, you don't have to do this," he said in broken English, holding up his hands.

The man who had been behind him came around to his front. Dave could make out he was of European descent, but was wearing foundation makeup to make his skin look darker, browner. The same went for the other man, who Dave could now clearly tell was of African descent but was disguising himself as well, using a lighter makeup than his natural skin tone.

"I am an official representative of the Spanish Colonial Crown," Dave said.

"On your knees," the European said in Spanish, putting his right hand on Dave's shoulder and pushing him down again. In the man's left hand Dave saw the glint of a long sword in the dim light.

Oh shit, Dave thought, feeling warm piss wet his pants and run down his leg. He couldn't believe this was happening.

"Put that away," the African man said. They were speaking English now, exclusively. Dave could make out generally what they were saying but not the entire conversation.

Apparently, they were supposed to bring him back alive to someplace, but the extraction at the courthouse was unnecessarily messy, forcing them to find a place to lie low. They were clearly not Jaguars. The European said Dave's head was important and that Quetzalcoatl demanded it—why not make the best of a bad situation and deliver the head? The African was adamant that they stay and follow orders, trying to move their prisoner alive once the commotion died down.

The argument grew heated with what Dave could tell were curses and insults.

These guys were rattled, pacing back and forth. Dave heard the sword scrape the floor several times behind him.

"Let me call," the African said, walking to the car. The African went to the driver seat and sat down. He pulled out a cell phone and began dialing.

The European raised the sword and put it to the back of Dave's neck. Dave shivered at the feel. The European moved Dave's collar down and pushed the back of his hair up to increase the target area for a clean hit.

Dave tried to make out what the African was saying on the phone, and in the distance he thought he heard the faint sound of a car somewhere above them in the garage. Maybe he could run—he'd have a better chance running from bullets than waiting for the sword.

He could tell the European heard the car too, because he felt the sword draw away from his neck. "Hey, someone's here," the European yelled to his partner. "Too late, too late." He raised the sword in striking position.

"Hold it!" The African yelled, quickly turning away from the phone and bounding out of the car to stop the European, who was about to strike.

Dave began crumpling to the ground as the sound of an engine roared up and a green Incan Spider squealed to a stop less than 10 feet away. The African had his hand on the European's right arm and forced the strike off course, missing Dave's head and sending the sword skidding across the concrete.

The African and European were off balance and delayed in reaching for their weapons. Two men and a woman were already out of the other car, guns drawn. Loud cracks of gunfire reverberated through the garage, bright muzzle flashes illuminating the space for a brief moment. Eight shots in all, and Dave's two abductors lay bleeding on the ground.

One of the rescuers knelt at Dave's side and put his hand reassuringly on his shoulder. "You all right, partner?" he asked.

"Johnny?" Dave asked, voice trembling.

"Yeah—sorry, I missed the hearing. But you did an amazing job," Johnny said.

Dave sat up, noticing for the first time the offensive smell of his urine. "I think I need new pants," he said. Johnny laughed and helped Dave to his feet.

"Wha, what is all this?" Dave said, suddenly feeling the pain of his earlier head cracking at the hands of the now dead Jaguar imposters.

"This is some crazy-ass shit is what it is," Johnny said. "Let's get you some-place safe to give you a full run down. At least the full rundown as I know it."

Dave noticed the woman was riffling through the dead mens' suits while the other man was going through the car—they appeared to be looking for some-thing. Johnny helped Dave to the rescue vehicle, and Dave noticed a familiar face standing by the driver side.

"Tototl?" Dave asked.

The little cab driver smiled broadly. "Aye, Spanish," he said, "how much you gonna pay me now for saving your life?"

Dave smiled and collapsed in utter relief against the side of the car.

"Tototl saved your life, buddy boy. He was watching you for me and called me immediately when the shooting went down at the courthouse. He trailed you and joined up with us outside the garage," Johnny said.

Dave looked at Tototl, who was clearly uncomfortable being called a hero. "Ah, just get in the car Spanish—you're not going in my taxi smelling like that with your piss pants."

"Let's get my guy some food and new clothes," Johnny said to his comrades.

The man and the woman left the Jaguar imposters' car, but only after they moved the bodies and put them in—one in the back seat, one in the front seat.

"We have to move," the woman said. "Geoffrey was on his cell phone when we got here. The call was engaged, so they might have been able to hear what happened and trace the location of the call."

The male rescuer carried a black duffel containing what they had been able to take from the abductors' car. He opened the trunk of the Incan Spider and put it in. "Tototl," the man said. "Can you get us to Xochimilco without too much trouble?"

"Sure thing," Tototl said.

The man was slight with dark rimmed glasses and brown hair that was going gray. The woman was attractive and fit, dirty blonde hair pulled back in a ponytail. She had small features and seemed to be in her late thirties.

"Are you going to introduce me to your friends?" Dave asked as they settled into seats in the car. Tototl flipped on the car's headlights and started navigating out of the garage.

"Sure," Johnny said. "This is Dr. Theodora Kopplewicz and her associate, Mr. Brian Deneven."

"Pretty handy with a pistol for doctor," Dave said.

Kopplewicz smiled. "I'm not that kind of doctor."

For some reason, Dave started to laugh. It was a laugh that he could not control. Soon his shoulders were heaving and he felt tears building. He broke down completely, crying uncontrollably.

Johnny reached over and put his hand on Dave's head, pulling him in close, reassuringly. "It's okay pal, you're safe now," he said.

CHAPTER 17

THE SHOOTINGS AT the courthouse had thrown the capital into complete chaos. The situation was exacerbated by the media—both local and Spanish Colonial—who were right there, covering the entire ordeal. Aztec official media, never accustomed to having any freedom, ran with the chaos and took advantage of the disorder by broadcasting everything from the courthouse steps before the Ministry of Information could pull the plug. The Ministry of Information was paralyzed because half its leadership were Jaguars who went into immediate bunker mode at the sight of these Jaguar Warriors committing this ugly crime out in the open for all to see. The switchboards at the Jaguar Order Temple Complex at the northern end of the sacred precinct were melting down with calls from angry non-Jaguars, concerned Jaguars, and worst of all, Jaguars ready to take up arms and begin wiping out all the Quetzalcoatl devotees.

To make matters worse, there were reports throughout the capital of random acts of sectarian violence occurring sporadically across the city.

T'shla missed all of this—the news, the graphic video of the shooting and attack on Dave, and the official Spanish response, which was forthcoming any minute from the consulate. Instead, she was being driven in a luxury stretch vehicle, guarded on either side by large Quetzal security officers and cocooned in a sound-proof cabin. She noticed they weren't going to the Quetzalcoatl Temple complex as Xhatl had earlier said, but instead were heading toward Chapultepec Palace.

The guards on either side of her were stone silent and clearly not interested or authorized to speak, so T'shla knocked on the window partition. Xhatl lowered it.

"Yes?"

"What gives?" she asked. "I thought we were heading to Quetzalcoatl Temple."

"Change of plans. There was an incident in the Sacred Precinct. The bridges are closed. We have been instructed to head to the Palace," Xhatl said.

The car entered Chapultepec Park and wound its way to the main gate of the palace, which was situated at the base of the hill. The Cuauhtemoc Gate slowly parted. Just inside were four armored vehicles and crews standing guard. T'shla had been to the palace before and had never seen this level of militarized security.

The car climbed the steep grade from the gate, around the north and west sides of the hill soon cresting it, coming upon the second gate which ringed the top and the actual palace complex.

This was the Louis XVI Gate, named after the French king who famously put down a popular uprising in his country, in part by cutting a deal with the Aztec Emperor in 1792. The Aztecs paid the French government twenty galleons filled with gold and treasure to solve the French financial crisis in exchange for the French taking a more aggressive posture toward Spain. The alliance made it harder for the Spanish crown to directly rule their Western colonies and ultimately set the stage for the creation of the semi-autonomous Colonial Spanish Government based in Cuba and Hispaniola.

As a symbol of their enduring friendship, King Louis XVI commissioned his architects to design the New Aztec Royal Palace at Chapultepec, hence it being popularly known as Chateau Chapultepec around the world. It was completed in 1805 and had been the official residence of the emperor ever since.

As a reciprocal gesture, Aztec botanists created the Floating Gardens of Tuileries, where water from the Seine was diverted to create a magical floating landscape of flowers and trees just off the Louvre Palace in Paris.

The car drove up to the main entrance and came to a stop over the black-and-white checkered marble tiles. Xhatl got out and opened the car door for T'shla. Standing at the main entrance was Coaxoach Ixtapoyan, her lifelong tormentor. T'shla was not surprised at all. He wore the white robes of a Quetzalcoatl priest, and his head was adorned with green, red, and gold feathers. Around his neck was a huge gold chest piece highlighted by a gold medallion bearing the image of the plumed serpent. And, as always, he wore his stern, disapproving pinched face.

T'shla made a brave face as she approached him. Coaxoach, for his part, tried to smile, his weathered face cracking with strain. They embraced, coolly.

"My girl," he said, deep voice reverberating through her. "The gods have been good to you."

He put his arm around her and quickly led her inside, past the public meeting rooms and up a flight of stairs to the private areas. She saw no one in the opulent halls—no servants, no guards, no members of the royal family or court. Just Coaxoach and her. Upstairs, they entered a well-appointed bedchamber that was decorated in the French style of the 19th century. T'shla put her bag down on the bed and sat down.

"Is that where your, ah, work is?" Coaxoach asked, eyeing the bag.

T'shla put her hand on the bag and drew it closer to her. She knew he could get his hands on the results of her investigation at any time, but still didn't want to make it easy for him.

Coaxoach laughed. "Don't worry little one, I am not here to steal from you. I am here to watch over you and keep you safe. There are many people in the capital that want you dead for what you found. There are also many people who have taken a keen interest in your ties to that filthy Spaniard. Just look at today—one liaison with him, and our country is on the brink of civil war because of it."

T'shla had had enough. An entire life of his condescension and holding a sword over her head finally pushed her over the edge. Emboldened by how she had earlier handled the morality police and by Dave's performance in Decoyan's courtroom, T'shla rose slowly and steadily from the bed, rage beginning to bubble through her.

"Enough," she said, pointing a finger in Coaxoach's face. "You may have my body and my life in your hands. You may have goons throughout the city violating my privacy. But you will never own my spirit. I know the truth. I know you are a sad and pathetic man, always groveling to whoever is in power. When I was a girl, you lived the Jaguar way, overseeing the sacrifices of countless innocent people—captives of the regime, with a few sweet sacrifices of unsullied blood like myself peppered in. When the Emperor changed his views on sacrifice, you saw the change in the winds and were first in line to leave the Jaguars and join the Quetzalcoatls. And now you've weaseled your way to the top of that order. You're not a leader, you're a survivor—like a rat or a roach."

Coaxoach, unaccustomed to being spoken to this way, recoiled. "Of all the insolence," he bellowed. "My ears do not hear these words of sin coming from the mouth of a Spanish-loving whore."

T'shla began laughing. "So, you—high priest of the realm—must sink to name calling. That tells me all I ever needed to know about you. You are not some magical being with all-seeing powers. You are just an aging, angry little man," T'shla said, reaching into her bag and pulling out the spreadsheet of names. "I want to know the truth. Why are you ordering the sacrifices of these people—these innocents—who did nothing to anyone?"

Coaxoach quickly snatched the list from T'shla and stepped away, walking over to the desk under the lamp. He hastily flipped through the list, stopping by each name that T'shla had circled in red. The look on his face showed T'shla that Coaxoach was puzzled.

Coaxoach put the list down with what T'shla took to be a defeated sigh.

"I have ordered no sacrifices," Coaxoach said. "And I do not know who these people are or why they were sacrificed. Maybe it's as Judge Decoyan announced—Jaguars are committing these crimes. Don't blame me."

T'shla gathered up the papers and put them back in her bag. She could tell Coaxoach was upset he did not see some kind of pattern or familiarity in the list. It was almost as if he was looking for something that would give him some kind of information that would improve his standing in the royal court. Maybe by knowing who was doing all of this killing, he could either hold leverage over someone or ingratiate himself to someone else. Either way, the depths of Coaxoach's crookedness were on full display.

"Well, then, what are you good for?" T'shla asked, sighing and sitting back on the bed.

They both sat in silence for a long moment.

Coaxoach finally spoke. "I was, I was...I...was instructed by those...above me...to bring you. They wanted you under protection—not necessarily because of what you discovered, but more so as a bargaining chip, a bit of insurance of some kind. Exactly why, I cannot say."

At Coaxoach's level, there were very few "above" him in society. The head of the Quetzalcoatl order and the Emperor as the living embodiment of the divine on earth were about it. "Why am I so important to all this?" T'shla asked.

Coaxoach shrugged. "I have no idea." He got up and crossed the room to a small bar by the fireplace. He pulled out a bottle of mescal and two glasses and began pouring.

"I know there are some who know I still have contacts in the Jaguar Order. Maybe they think I can talk to them and get them to reconsider their recent aggressive and embarrassing actions, like those beheadings and what they pulled off at the courthouse today."

T'shla perked up. "What do you mean? What happened at the courthouse?"

Coaxoach handed her a glass. "The shooting," he said, a creepy smile crossing his lips. "You likely didn't see, but it's all over the television. After the hearing, two Jaguars shot up the courthouse steps, killing at least two official Foreign Service bodyguards and injuring Mr. Aragon before abducting him on camera for all to see."

T'shla nearly dropped her drink. The news came like a gut punch. She felt her breath leave her. "No. It can't be..." Her voice trailed.

Coaxoach nodded gravely. "Official police and members of the Quetzalcoatl Security Force are scouring the city looking for him. This could be an international incident." The crooked old priest reached into his robes and pulled out his cell phone. He opened it and began scrolling through his text messages.

"Still no official statement from the Spanish, but the Colonial networks are saying one is forthcoming any minute," he said.

T'shla took a sip from her mescal and stared vacantly at the wall.

"I will turn on the television for you," Coaxoach said.

"I need to try and find him," T'shla said.

Coaxoach clicked on the television and stood to leave. "You can't do any better than the Judicial Police and our own forces," Coaxoach said. "I have been instructed to have you spend the night here, under the protection of the Emperor's guard. The Emperor is spending the night at the old palace in the Sacred Precinct tonight. There was a fear that Jaguars may attempt some kind of coup—so best to keep his whereabouts quiet."

"Do the Jaguars have that much power?" T'shla asked.

"They control the military and most of the police," Coaxoach said. "The only thing really stopping them is 750 years of loyalty and the Quetzalcoatl Security

Force. Both can easily be over-matched by someone mad for power and looking for an opening to grab it. You know, someone like the Emperor's son."

Moctezuma 27 was the Emperor's eldest son, who generally shunned the Capital and the royal court. He preferred his country estate. He had a dour wife with Jaguar leanings, and there was great worry in the Quetzalcoatl Order—and frankly in T'shla herself—that once he was emperor, Moctezuma 27 would rescind the reforms of the Green Revolution and go back to the old and bloody ways. Such was the case with the royal family. The people rarely saw, and almost never heard from, their leaders. The whole system functioned on rumor and gossip. No one would ever know what type of a leader 27 would be until he actually assumed the throne.

"But that makes no sense," T'shla said. "You once told me that the leaders of the Jaguar order are fiercely loyal, even though this emperor has put them in a submissive position below the Quetzals."

"I have not been in the Jaguar inner circle for many years, so I cannot say what's driving this unprecedented uprising. All I know is I have orders to keep you safe until I get other instructions," Coaxoach said, starting to walk for the door.

"You never really answered my question," T'shla said.

Coaxoach turned at the door. "What question?" he asked, a tinge of impatience in his voice.

"Why me? Why am I so important in all this?"

Coaxoach put his hand on the door handle. "Like I told you, I have no idea," he said, and T'shla could tell in this moment how frustrated he must have been. A man of such power and influence now relegated to baby-sitting duty and service as an errand boy.

He opened the door and left the room. T'shla heard the door lock from the outside. Defeated, she turned back to the TV and crumpled on the bed, hoping Dave was okay.

§ § §

Outside in the hall, Coaxoach placed a call to his royal-court contact. "The girl is secure," he said.

"Wonderful," the contact replied. "Thank you for making Jidge Axtulla available to us—he did as ordered, and the Spanish criminal is out of the picture."

For a split second, Coaxoach felt sad about Jidge, hoping the poor fool had taken his advice and put the money somewhere safe before his ultimate sacrifice.

"And what purpose did involving a two-bit Spanish criminal in all this serve?" Coaxoach asked. He knew he was well beyond his authorized role, but felt no harm in asking. Maybe T'shla's rebellious spirit was wearing off on him.

The other side of the line was silent. "Quetzalcoatl is on the rise," the voice said. "The Jaguars are being driven into a fiery pit, and now the international community will have to take notice and condemn their unlawful and heinous actions."

Coaxoach nodded. "I stand in service to the one true god, Quetzalcoatl, and the light of wisdom," he said, removing the phone from his ear and ending the call.

CHAPTER **18**

Efraim Ramirez's account of 1519

The royal court

MY COMPATRIOTS AND I were given modest quarters in the main palace complex of the Aztecs. For three days we waited. We were well fed, clothed, and even given Aztec spirited drinks. But the waiting was interminable.

By the end of our third day, we were thankfully reunited with our injured countrymen—Sanchez, Ventura, and Morales—who were all bandaged but were miraculously in good health.

Sanchez said they were taken to an even larger vessel of some kind across the lake. There, they were tended to by Vargas with mystical tools of healing—strange elixirs that took away their pain, salves and sutures that bound their wounds. It was astounding to hear their stories.

On the fourth day, I alone was summoned to the royal court. It was early in the morning, and the sun was rising over the lake. On the twin-spired tallest pyramid I saw ten men being led to the top, bound by ropes at the hands. The Pyramid's white plaster gleamed golden in the morning light. My guard wore a Jaguar pelt around his shoulder. He led me past the front of the pyramid. I could see a high priest at the top sharpening his blade for the morning sacrifices. I remember thinking how such ugly brutality could be accompanied by such progress in medicine and technology.

I could hear chants coming from the top of the pyramid, but they quickly blended into the sounds of a city waking up—merchants stocking their stalls, farmers hauling in their goods from floating fields, and children running and playing on the cobblestoned streets.

We stopped at what I would later learn was the steps of the main palace's throne chamber. I cannot explain why, but I was nervous. It struck me because I had faced death at least three times in the past four days. Why now should I have more fear than before? I could not say.

Vargas emerged from the front gate of the throne chamber. Seeing him eased my unsettled state. "Señor Vargas, thank you for caring for my men," I said.

Vargas smiled. "They were good patients, but I was lucky that none of their injuries were life threatening."

"So, what am I to expect here on this morning?" I asked.

Vargas considered my question, and it was apparent he did not know quite how to answer it. "In all honesty, I do not fully understand the Aztec ways," he said. "They are as much a mystery to you as they are to me."

"I do not understand," I said.

"In case you haven't noticed, my comrades and I are not Aztecs. We are visitors who have come here…" Vargas took a moment to clear his throat, "in the service of Quetzalcoatl, the Aztec god of Wisdom."

I did not know what to think. A lifetime of Catholic obedience had withered in the face of this awesome magic and technology shown by these people. But still, I could not fully believe that this man was a servant of a god, especially since it seemed like Vargas himself didn't believe he was serving a god.

A guard inside the palace chamber exited to let us know it was our time. "I will help translate for you," Vargas said.

The guard who had escorted me here and the guard who opened the gates lined up shoulder to shoulder in front of us. In lock step, they entered the chamber. Once inside a few feet, they rapped the heels of their pikes on the stone floor three times in unison. The guard in the jaguar skin turned and faced us, yelling out something in their strange tongue.

Vargas leaned in. "My lord and protector, light of the realm, I present to you and to our guest deity, Efraim Ramirez, a captain of Spain and the commander of our prisoners." It was quite a promotion for me, but then again, I was representing my entire country and my king at this moment.

The guards stepped aside to reveal a large room lit by torches and four openings in the thatched roof. Around the room were nobles—I assumed—by the finery, amount of gold and feathers, and fine pelts that adorned them.

At the far end of the room, across from the entrance, sat the Emperor on a raised platform. To his left was Quetzalcoatl, who I had met earlier and who had touched my face. Behind him were the familiar members of his retinue—the slight man with spectacles and the woman with light hair. This morning, Quetzalcoatl was still costumed in his robes and shiny green helmet. His assistants were dressed much more like Vargas and the European and African warriors who helped the Aztecs defeat us days before at the shore. They wore beige, loose pants with many pockets and shirts with muted colors of blue and green.

Joining them was an Aztec in robes similar to Quetzalcoatl.

To the emperor's right were priests representing their orders of society—the Jaguar, the Eagle, the Fish, and the Corn Maiden priests all sat in a line. All were in the middle of their morning meal of fishes, plums, tortillas, beans, and mashed maize.

I approached the center of the room with Vargas at my side. The Emperor spoke softly. It was almost a whisper, and I could not tell if it was directed at me.

Vargas whispered in my ear. "He's asking what gives you the right to invade his country."

I bowed to the emperor. "Please tell him that I and my surviving comrades are lowly servants, foot soldiers in this. We have no desire to conquer anything. We just want to go home."

Vargas gave me a look of concern. "I don't think that's a good idea. I don't know much, but my guess is if they perceive you as lowly, it will be easier for them to stick you on top of that pyramid. You don't want to go on top of that pyramid."

I cleared my throat and reconsidered. I wasn't sure whether Vargas was right, but his approach made sense to me. "Tell him I represent the Spanish Crown, the greatest nation on earth with dominion over the seas. We march on his country to bring his people the glory of our Lord, Jesus Christ, so that their immortal souls may be saved."

Vargas nodded and began speaking in their tongue for quite a long time. When he was done, the Emperor nodded and waved for some servants who entered the room from side chambers and laid cushions and food by our feet. The Emperor motioned, letting us know it was acceptable for us to sit and eat.

The meal lasted nearly half an hour, with nobles eating, staring at me, and talking quietly among themselves. I could see the emperor, who I learned was named Moctezuma, whisper several times to the Green helmeted Quetzalcoatl, as if confiding in him. They looked to have an easy, friendly relationship. The people behind Quetzalcoatl barely ate and looked uncomfortable the entire time.

"The Emperor and the court are trying to determine what to do with you. No one knows how to handle this development. There were supposed to be no survivors," Vargas whispered.

"Can I ask to be set free?" I asked. "We can walk out of here toward the sea."

"That's a long walk," Vargas said. "With delays, mountains, and jungles it could take you a month, maybe longer, depending on whether you run into unfriendly natives."

"And these natives are friendly?" I asked.

Vargas chuckled and took a bite out of a plum. "These natives are on the verge of creating a very powerful nation-state, something to rival the crowns of Europe."

"So, how shall I proceed?" I asked.

"Admit your transgression. Tell them, as a noble person, you and your men beg for mercy and will abide by their wise ruling," Vargas said. "And this next part is the most important: Tell him you are a man of faith, and that you respect men of faith. You understand Moctezuma is a living god, but there is another god in the room. Tell him you would like to follow Moctezuma's most excellent example and put your fate in Quetzalcoatl's hands. Then, cross the room and kneel at Quetzalcoatl's feet. Moctezuma will have to defer, and Quetzalcoatl will not order your execution."

141

"How do you know?" I asked.

"I know Quetzalcoatl. He may be a strange serpent, but he is no monster."

When the time came, I dutifully followed Vargas' instructions, and to my surprise it played out exactly as he said it would. Moctezuma happily deferred, and Quetzalcoatl said we should be spared—but that we could never return to Spain or even the islands.

"What do you do?" Quetzalcoatl asked me in broken Spanish. Moctezuma looked genuinely impressed that this deity had mastery of so many languages. "Aside from being a captain of Spain, I mean," Quetzalcoatl finished.

"I work with wood," I said. "Carpentry."

Quetzalcoatl nodded. "Do your compatriots have similar skills?"

"Yes," I said eagerly. "Juan Pierre is a blacksmith, and the others all have some kind of useful skills."

Quetzalcoatl leaned in and whispered to Moctezuma, who nodded along. Moctezuma faced forward and spoke to the crowd. I looked around and saw a number of people raise their hands, a few shrug, and some shake their heads.

Moctezuma pointed to one man sitting along the side wall—a man who would, in time, become my friend, mentor, and one day, my father-in-law. He approached the emperor and kneeled at his feet.

"What's happening," I asked.

"I'm not sure," Vargas said. "From what I could make out, it seems like you are either being auctioned off, or given as a gift to loyal nobles."

I would later learn that slavery was common in this society. Poor parents who sometimes couldn't afford food for their families would sell their children into slavery to at least ensure they were well fed. It was very different than our view of slavery and what we were doing to the natives on the islands.

The Emperor motioned to Quetzalcoatl, and the kneeling man rose, stepped over to Quetzalcoatl, and kneeled again, this time in front of the god. The god gently stroked his head and let him rise.

"I think all of you will be given as gifts to piplitzin who swear allegiance to the new god in town," Vargas said. "At least I think that's what's happening."

Vargas was right. One by one, my friends were led in and given off as gifts to nobles who knelt at the feet of both Moctezuma and Quetzalcoatl. I could see the Jaguar men and the representatives of other sects standing, arms folded, almost in disgust and contempt that their god had not returned to give them such favor with the Emperor. It was as if a bright light was going to shine on anyone who followed Quetzalcoatl in this court.

The man who claimed me, the first to kneel at Quetzalcoatl's feet, approached. He had short, black straight hair that hung down from his head like a bowl turned upside down. It was time for me to join him. He spoke softly and kindly, but I did not understand a word. I looked at Vargas quizzically.

"He said he has something for you," Vargas said.

I smiled and bowed.

The man produced a blade of obsidian, shiny and sharp. He handed it to me, apparently with no fear that I would harm him. With his other hand he reached into his robes and pulled out a small block of soft wood he had been whittling designs into. The man was a noble, but he enjoyed the common practice of wood-work and carpentry. I would later learn it would soothe him as he struggled to manage the affairs of his people in the Xalapan region where he was a wealthy, well-born man, and where I would soon call home.

I graciously accepted the blade and block. I had no more need to see blood and violence. I had seen enough for one lifetime.

"He wants you to come back to his estate and work with wood," Vargas said. "Apparently it's a good business in his region with great profit to be had."

I looked at the Aztec and knew my life's course was set—at least for now. Though my freedom was taken from me, my life was spared. For that, I expressed deep gratitude to this Vargas. As a token of appreciation, I gave him my last and only possession of any value—a pewter ring bearing the crest of my family—the Holy cross, the pine tree, and the cannon.

I turned my attention to my new master, who had kind eyes. "Efraim Ramirez," I said, introducing myself.

The man, who was about half a head shorter than me, put his hand on my shoulder. "Tzixtuc Decoyan Xalapan," he said, though I would only know him as Decoyan from that day forward.

CHAPTER 19

Same exact place about 8 weeks earlier

QUETZALCOATL STOOD AT the gate to the main palace throne chamber. It was about 8 p.m. on the same day as their arrival. Maybe it was the pulque clouding his judgment, but he was growing impatient. He was a god, and he waited for no man. Antonio Vargas fidgeted nervously at his side.

"Are you sure about this?" Brian, ever the voice of reason, asked.

Quetzalcoatl smiled. In the business world he was a legendary breaker-down-of-doors, and he saw no reason why he should act differently here. His first rule of negotiation was to own the high ground, and he did not want Moctezuma to perceive him as weak. Quetzalcoatl felt the need to take back the upper hand.

"We are not going to sit politely and wait for them to debate the meaning of our appearance. I am a god," Sir Ian said.

"I hope this works," Theodora said under her breath. They were seriously under-manned, with two of their mercenaries holding four Aztec guards hostage back at their quarters.

Sir Ian looked her way and gave her a boozy wink. She hazarded a look at Hans, who was looking every bit like he had never held a rifle before.

Quetzalcoatl put his hand on the gate and pushed his way inside the dimly lit chamber. The rumblings and conversations of the assembled nobles quickly hushed as all eyes turned first to Quetzalcoatl and next back to Moctezuma. Moctezuma, who was speaking to some nearby priests, straightened up in his seat as he looked on Quetzalcoatl for the first time.

Quetzalcoatl stayed in the doorway, Vargas right behind him.

Moctezuma motioned for Cuauhtemoc to approach the god and escort him back to his quarters. Dutifully, Cuauhtemoc picked up his spear and started walking across the great room toward Quetzalcoatl. Quetzalcoatl reached into his robes and pulled out a flash grenade. Quickly, he pulled the pin and rolled it on the ground toward the center of the room.

Bang!

A loud flash of smoke and brilliant light filled the room. The assembled nobles screamed and edged back against the walls, but they did not leave. In the smoke and confusion, Sir Ian's team took up positions around the room, guns out. Sir Ian and Vargas walked to the center, calmly and slowly. Cuauhtemoc was on his back, stunned by the display. Sir Ian nodded to Brian and Hans, who helped Cuauhtemoc to his feet and moved him to the side.

Moctezuma was now standing. He spoke to them.

Vargas whispered in Sir Ian's ear. "He's asking what the meaning of this is."

"Tell him time is short, and we did not come here to rest. We came here to do important work for his people," Sir Ian said. Vargas struggled, but was able to relay the message.

Sir Ian gave the signal to his team, who all pointed their rifles to the ceiling and each fired one shot, jolting the crowd with the power of their fire sticks and likely alerting everyone in the Sacred Precinct that something extraordinary was happening.

Sir Ian then addressed the crowd himself. It was a speech he had practiced, so he did not need Vargas to translate.

"There is a great force coming from the sea. It will destroy all of you and kill nearly everyone you know—including your esteemed emperor who stands before you. We have come from the heavens to help you defeat this force. We have brought magical weapons that we will teach you to use. With our help, you will preserve your society and *our* religion."

A Jaguar priest standing to Moctezuma's right stepped forward and spoke— gesturing wildly and pointing at Quetzalcoatl. Sir Ian could not make out most of it, so he leaned in to Vargas.

"He's saying that, if there was a true threat to their empire, the gods would have sent Huitzilopotchli, the god of war, to come and defend the people. Sending the god of wisdom makes no sense. This is either trickery or a misunderstanding among the gods," Vargas translated.

"God of war versus god of wisdom," Sir Ian said under his breath.

The Jaguar priest, Macuiltan, was quickly cut off by a man in Quetzal robes. Sep Tarantan strode across the room and embraced Quetzalcoatl, then fell to his knees prostate. Sir Ian put his hand on Sep's head. About four or five others in the room followed Sep's lead, standing behind Sep and waiting their turn to demonstrate their supplication.

Moctezuma watched all this with curiosity. Quetzalcoatl was winning the room. The emperor looked over to his nephew, Cuauhtemoc, who had recovered from the shock of the blast and now, bereft of his golden spear, observed the proceedings impotently. Cuauhtemoc's faithful lieutenant, Tuxla, got in line to pay his respects to this new god in the flesh.

Quetzalcoatl whispered in Vargas' ear. Vargas thought for a moment about how to structure the sentences, and then cleared his throat.

"The plumed serpent, god of wisdom, Quetzalcoatl, appreciates the fidelity and friendship he has been shown. The light of wisdom will always shine on those who heed him. It is through wisdom and the magic of our weapons that we will defeat the invaders. Brute force alone will not work."

Quetzalcoatl motioned to Macuiltan and bowed his head. He whispered more into Vargas' ear. Vargas spoke again. "Quetzalcoatl does not mean to denigrate the other gods and spirits who guide us. Were it not for the Eagle spirit leading our people here, we would still be wandering the wilderness."

It was a reference to the founding of Grand Tenochtitlan some 200 years before, when the original city founders, wandering the high countries, came across an eagle eating a serpent while perched on a cactus. It was a sign for them to found their city here in this abundant lake region surrounded by snow-capped peaks.

"The eagle, the jaguar, the gods of day and night and harvest and earth—they all have a fitting place. But the day of the plumed serpent has arrived. We are entering an age of wisdom, and it begins by repelling the invaders who will soon arrive."

Moctezuma stood and looked out on his nobility. A few more approached the line to pay their respects to Quetzalcoatl.

Quetzalcoatl gave a signal to Hans, who spoke some words into his walkie talkie. Within seconds the low pounding of helicopter blades began to thump through the sky, getting closer and closer. In the dark of night, people through-out the temple complex of the Sacred Precinct stirred as a bright spotlight from above zeroed in on the plaza just outside the throne chamber.

Quetzalcoatl turned his back on the emperor and walked out of the throne room and to the plaza. He walked to the center of the spotlight and stood arms held out. Moctezuma followed, walking past kneeling and cowering subjects, stopping at the portico of the throne chamber. Quetzalcoatl looked back at the emperor with a kind, welcoming smile.

All eyes were on Moctezuma and Quetzalcoatl.

Moctezuma walked slowly at first, and then picked up the pace until he was at a trot, stopping right in front of Quetzalcoatl. Both were now bathed in the impossibly bright light of the helicopter. The emperor embraced the god tightly, stepped back, and then fell to his knees in worship. All around, Aztecs followed the Emperor's lead, even Macuiltan, who grudgingly bent down.

All assembled Aztecs bent their knees in worship except Cuauhtemoc, who faded back into the darkness of the throne room.

Quetzalcoatl tapped Moctezuma on the shoulder, letting him know he should rise. He saw tears streaming down the Emperor's face. Quetzalcoatl then looked back up into the light, held up one finger and pointed it to the ground.

Immediately, hundreds of chocolates and liquor minis rained down on the crowd. Quetzalcoatl picked up a small bottle of peppermint schnapps, unscrewed it, took a small sip, and gave it to the emperor, who took a swig without hesitation. The warmth and sweetness immediately brought a smile to his face.

"Better than pulque?" he asked, putting his arm around the emperor and leading him back to the throne room.

"Nectar of the gods," Moctezuma said.

And Sir Ian understood exactly what he said.

Chapter 20

1999—Aztecan Time

THEY MADE THEIR way to Xochimilco in separate cars, Dave and Tototl in Tototl's cab, Johnny and the rest in the Incan Spider sedan. Xochimilco was far south of the island in the part of Lake Texcoco that was the most taken over by floating gardens. It was the Venice of the Aztec Empire. Before the 17th century, it was considered its own lake even though it was connected to Lake Texcoco. It was rezoned by Emperor Moctezuma 11 in 1679 to be officially considered part of Lake Texcoco.

Once they entered the tangled lanes and dense overhanging flowering plants of the Xochimilco neighborhood, Dave was completely lost. He sat back and closed his eyes, still trying to process what he had just gone through. Tototl sensed this was not a time to talk, so he turned the radio to a classical station and let Dave be.

Dave suddenly remembered Marta and that he was due to meet up with her after the hearing. He checked his phone—thirty missed calls, three were from Marta. His mailbox was full—mostly friends and family who he assumed were checking on him after seeing the drama of the hearing and the scene on the court-house steps. One of Marta's voicemails made it through before his mailbox was full. She left it about the time the hearing was going on. That's the one voicemail he listened to.

It was surprisingly sterile.

"David, good luck in the hearing. No word on Fiver. Let's meet tomorrow morning at the office—something came up with the trade talks that I have to put to bed. See you at nine."

Dave disengaged his voicemail and looked at his phone. "Am okay—call you later—Love," he quickly texted his mother, before returning the phone to his pocket.

In about five minutes they crossed a rickety wooden bridge over a canal and turned down a quiet lane on a small island. For centuries, the floating gardens actually did float—they were barges on which the Aztecs grew their produce. But over decades and centuries, the soil and roots in the barges stretched down and grabbed hold of the lake bed—locking the barges in place and creating a dizzying complex of man-made islands and canals.

They came to a stop in front of a compound of four simple buildings that looked like they had been abandoned for quite some time. Flowers and vines grew up and over the white-plaster structures. It would only be a matter of years before the island and the lake had completely reclaimed them. They got out of their cars and were immediately assaulted by dank, heavy air. Johnny pointed to the main building, indicating to Tototl and Dave that this was where they needed to go.

Dave and Tototl entered the building and found the interior to be a small but surprisingly luxurious and well lighted modern home. In the kitchen, at the far end of the main room, a man was making food in a large pot. As he cooked, he watched the news. Johnny, Brian, and Theodora settled into the house, dropping their bags and putting their pistols on the table.

"Shh," the cooking man said, pointing to the television. "Spanish statement is coming up."

They all turned to the big screen which dominated a wall of the living room. The camera was focused on a podium with a Spanish Colonial seal. To Dave's surprise, it was Marta who approached the podium. She was wearing the same outfit he had seen her in that morning. She looked uncomfortable. The chyron under her image read, "Marta C'de Baca, Spanish Colonial Consular Spokeswoman" and "Spanish gov't reacts to courthouse shooting."

She took a sip of water before beginning.

"Good evening," she said, casting her eyes down briefly to her prepared notes. "The Spanish Colonial government is deeply concerned about the safety of our citizen and foreign-service attorney, David Aragon. We are fully cooperating with the Aztec ministries and authorities working this case and are confident of Mr. Aragon's swift and safe return. As visitors in your country, we respect the sovereignty of the Aztec government, its supreme ministries, and the office of the Emperor, Moctezuma 26. The colonial government of Spain has no comment on recent sectarian strife within the government of the Unified Aztec Empire, only to say that we regret our citizens have somehow been caught up in it. This spate of recent unrest among various sects does not impact our government's intention to enter into a cooperative trade agreement during the Regional Trade Summit next week. Thank you."

Marta took a step back from the podium, straightened her jacket, and exited the way she entered. A few reporters tried to ask questions, but Marta was gone. A consular staffer came up to the podium and told the assembled press she would not be taking any questions this evening.

"Well, that was anticlimactic," the cook said, reaching into a cabinet for some bowls.

Dave reached back into his pocket again to call Marta and tell her he was safe.

"What are you doing?" the doctor, Theodora Kopplewicz, asked.

Dave motioned to the television. "You saw. I need to let Marta know I'm safe."

Theodora had a contorted, concerned look on her face. She quickly reached over and snapped the phone out of Dave's hand. "No, don't call her," Theodora said. "She's with them."

Johnny had found a pair of dry, clean pants about Dave's size in one of the back bedrooms of the house. He handed them to Dave. "Freshen up," Johnny said.

Dave, holding the pants, was still trying to process Theodora taking his phone. "She just took my phone," Dave said.

Johnny said nothing.

"Marta C'de Baca is with the enemy—the ones who were trying to kill you," Theodora said.

Dave was stunned. Everyone in the house was looking at him, waiting for him to react. The cook picked up the stack of bowls and walked over to the table.

"Clear off your shit," the cook told Theodora and Brian, who went over and moved their bags and weapons off the table and onto a nearby sofa. The cook put the bowls down on the table and wiped his hands with a towel that was slung over his shoulder.

"We have a lot to talk about," the cook said, holding out his hand. "I'm Antonio Vargas, and welcome to our clubhouse."

Once Dave had washed up and changed his pants he rejoined the group, which was now eating dinner at a large round table. It was tortilla soup, with roasted chicken and local vegetables. Dave did not know what to make of these strangers, but they did save his life, and Johnny and Tototl seemed to trust them.

Dave finally regained his mental footing, though he was unsure he would ever truly be the same. He rubbed the top of his head and felt a large bump two inches away from his skull plate. He was sure he was concussed, but the effects were seemingly mild, at least as far as he could tell.

"Okay, so what's really going on here?" Dave asked. It was a question mostly directed at Johnny. "What happened to you?" Johnny was mid-bite, and Dave waited impatiently for him to finish.

"Listen, I know it's going to take a little bit of faith, but hear these people out," Johnny said between chews. There was a long moment while Johnny swallowed and took a swig of beer.

"Ok…well, I'm waiting," Dave said.

Brian cleared his throat to get attention. "There is a movement afoot by some in the Quetzalcoatl order to completely destroy and discredit the Jaguars and capture total control of the government—including gaining more power in the industries and institutions that have traditionally been dominated by Jaguars."

"So you're saying this is a coup?" Tototl asked. Tototl had served as a lowly conscript in the Angola war and was an unobservant Jaguar, but he was a Jaguar nonetheless.

Vargas shook his head and ladled some more soup into Tototl's bowl. "Not really," Vargas said. "The Emperor is pretty checked-out—he's already inclined to back the Quetzals; this is just being executed to push him further into their camp. If the Jaguars are degraded in power and prestige, then the Quetzals will be able to steer more resources and money into the scientific goals of their order."

Brian cut in. "You saw those men who were killed? You were up close to them. You noticed they were not Aztec."

"I noticed," Dave said. "One was European and one was African. But then, all of you are clearly not Aztec—why do you care? Why are you involved?"

Brian put his spoon down and sat back in his chair, a sickly look coming over his face. "Those men we killed. Those men were our former associates. We killed them because they are following the orders of the leaders of this plot." He stood up, clearly shaken. "There has been too much killing—too many beheadings."

"What do you know about the beheadings—other than what was revealed in the court?" Dave asked, turning his attention from Brian to Vargas.

"I know that the people who were behind the plot to snatch you are responsible. Much like the attack on you, the assailants in the beheadings were outfitted as Jaguars," Vargas said. "That means the men who committed these awful crimes are likely people who the three of us know." He motioned to Theodora and Brian.

"How do you know," Dave asked more insistently, "and why kill those people."

"Because dressing as Jaguars is something we saw our former associates do many times before—to blend in and act with impunity. It just makes sense that it was them," Theodora said. She then went silent, lost in deep contemplation. "They killed those people—the ones who had their personal health data stolen— as a part of a scientific experiment. Those beheaded people were unwitting subjects of a nasty science project."

Dave put down his napkin and turned to Johnny. "So, how the hell did you get caught up in all this?" Dave asked.

Johnny pointed to Theodora. "These guys, they saved my life just like they saved you," he said. "The two men from the garage tonight accosted me on the sidewalk as I was leaving the jail this morning. I can only guess they thought they were grabbing you. Brian here, used some kind of electronic stun device to zap one of them—and Theodora hustled me into a getaway car. They said they were tracking the Jaguar pretenders and saw them make a move on me."

Vargas opened a bottle of beer for Dave and slid it across the table. "For some reason, David Aragon, you're the key to this whole enterprise," Vargas said.

Dave took the beer and looked at the bottle for a long moment. "Yeah, but why? Why me? It makes no sense."

"That's the 25,000-peseta question. Why you, indeed," Theodora mused. "Our only intel is that it's somehow connected to Marta C'de Baca. She knows you and she arranged to get you out here for this case."

Dave didn't buy it. "That makes no sense. I am a lawyer for the Spanish Foreign Service—this is a part of my job."

Johnny chuckled. "Is it? How many field assignments have you had in your career?"

"None," Dave admitted, sheepishly.

"And this one?" Johnny said. "Marta specifically asks for you. Why? She's had cases here before? She could have had Dina Lopez or Ignacio Martinez fly out. Those two have had dozens of courtroom hearings in the Empire. Why you? Why an underachieving desk jockey for an important case before a trade negotiation?"

Dave understood all this. He knew he was on the B-Team. In fact, he, too, was quite surprised when he got the call for this case. But that still proved nothing.

"Marta is a loyal public servant—and a friend. I won't sit here and stand for this character assassination without proof," Dave said.

"She's the lover of the head of the Quetzalcoatl Order," Theodora said, flatly.

Dave was struck, exasperated. "What? Is that even allowed?"

"Anything is allowed," Theodora said. "They met at a private Chateau Chapultepec event more than a year ago."

"How would you even know?" Dave asked. "This is crazy."

Theodora was growing irritated. "I know," she said plainly and adamantly. "I was there when she was introduced to him."

Dave folded his arms and exhaled loudly out of his nose. "Who's the head of the order anyway? I thought the emperor was the official head of all orders and sects."

Theodora shook her head. "Nope—the head of the Quetzalcoatl order is Quetzalcoatl himself."

"*The god?*" Dave said, half laughing. He looked to Johnny. "Are you listening to any of this? It's insane."

Theodora closed her eyes tightly and slammed her palm down on the table. "Okay, Spanish colonial lawyer, I have no reason to justify anything to you—ever. You are a creation that may not even have ever existed were it not for me, Brian, or Antonio here. We come from a place that created you. *We created you.* Your existence is a cosmic joke that we unwittingly played. This Empire? This world and the petty men who rule it? They are all our playthings. That's why it doesn't matter when a few people get beheaded along the way. It's all happening in the amusement park that I helped create."

Vargas slapped his palm forcefully on the table, making their stew bowls and silverware clank. "Theo, stop it," he snapped. "You do not believe those words, and you certainly don't co-sign the atrocities of Quetzalcoatl or Gaummer."

This fierce and crazy woman seemed chastened by the cook's words. She sat back in her chair and looked off into space.

"You're absolutely right," she said after a few moments had passed. Her voice was just above a whisper. "But even though they were the ones who believed they created this universe to do with as they pleased, and even though they treated the people living here as their playthings, it was you, Brian, and I who enabled them and played along with them for so many years."

Dave was almost amused. "What the fuck are you all talking about?" he asked.

Theodora turned back to Dave. "You want the story? I will tell you the story. The whole story. Brian. Get the proof. You're in for a doozy."

"Try us," Dave responded.

Theodora took a drink of water as Brian left the table. "About 480 years ago a Conquistador named Hernán Cortés began his invasion of Mexico by landing on the Cempoalan coast—about five hours east of here by auto."

Dave punched the table. "Stop it right there. Everyone knows Cortés' fleet disappeared in a storm, never to be heard from again."

Theodora held up a finger and glared icily at Dave, signaling to him it was not the time to talk. "From there," she continued, an edge in her voice, "he and his company of about 400 men marched relentlessly toward Tenochtitlan, gathering allies among some of the tribes that had grown weary of Aztec rule. Also accompanying them were strains of virulent diseases such as smallpox. These were diseases the Aztec people had never been exposed to."

"They were particularly deadly to the local population," Vargas chimed in. "In fact, diseases killed many more than Spanish steel ever could. They literally ripped Aztec, and all native societies, apart."

Theodora nodded and looked at Tototl, Johnny, and Dave, who all sat speechless, watching her. "Cortés' arrival coincided with a prophecy about the arrival of Quetzalcoatl, the white-skinned plumed serpent and Aztec god of wisdom. Cortés used this coincidence to convince the emperor at the time that he was the god. The emperor invited him into the court, and after many reversals, court drama, and hostage taking, the emperor was dead and the Spaniards were chased from the city. What ensued was a two-year war for control of the empire with Cortés claiming final victory when the last Aztec emperor, Cuauhtemoc, was captured. That's it. Aztec culture was destroyed, and the Spanish filled in the lake and founded Mexico City on top of the muck."

Dave considered what Theodora had said and looked questioningly to Johnny and Tototl for some kind of support. Both seemed as confused as him. "Are you our captors?" Dave asked.

"No," Brian said, holding a strange looking device he had produced from a back room and was starting to set up on the table. "You're free to go if you want."

Dave sat back and put his napkin on the table. "Ok then," he said. "We have work we have to get back to." He pushed back from the table.

"Then," Theodora said, in a louder and more serious tone. Dave paused.

"Then the world went on. Countries were built, countries fell. Technology advanced—both for good and evil. Finally, hundreds of years later—in the year 2013—a mad, impossibly wealthy genius decided he wanted to travel back in time. So, he amassed a fortune and gathered a team to solve two major scientific problems. One, how do you travel through the time continuum, and two, how can you generate enough power to effectively and reliably do it. This mad genius was able to solve these problems, in part by using my services and those of Brian and Vargas here. Together, we joined him in this exciting journey to go back in time.

"Now, this mad rich genius is a bit of a crusader, so he decided his first trip was to come back and right what he saw was a historic wrong—the raping and pillaging of the Aztec Empire. So, he showed up with his team a few months before Cortés, calls *himself* Quetzalcoatl, and arms and trains the Aztecs with modern weaponry to destroy the Spanish fleet before they ever make landfall."

"Are you done?" Dave asked, convinced these people were complete kooks.

"Hey," Vargas cut in. "How do you think I feel in all this? I am a proud Mexican. That's what the people who lived here in my time were called. I know Cortés was no hero, but I also know his invasion created the Mexican race—my race. By destroying Cortés, I played a role in the genocide of my people before they ever came to be. So don't take this lightly."

"You believe this nonsense?" Dave asked Johnny.

"Listen partner, what I know is these guys knew an awful lot about the danger you were facing. I can't really say much about this time travel stuff, but they've been right so far about a lot of things," Johnny said.

Theodora got up from the table and took the device that Brian was setting up, looking it over quickly to ensure it would operate. She put it back on the middle of the table. It had a round, brown plastic base about 20 centimeters in diameter and two shiny telescoping metal spokes protruding out about 20 centimeters. In the middle of the brown tablet was a shiny metal medallion that looked thin as foil. On the base was an inscription: *Gaummer Time Window, Version III.*

"The men we killed were two mercenaries who were with us since our initial expedition," Brian said.

"Collins and Ben Agabe," Vargas said. "Good men, but ever loyal to the boss, even when it seemed like that boss had no plan at all."

Tototl leaned in while Theodora and Brian worked on getting power to the device. "So, you're saying Quetzalcoatl is this same rich man? And he's here, living in Tenoch?"

"He has dinner with the Emperor three nights a week," Theodora said. "When he isn't working on a way to get back home or romancing his new girlfriend, he's busy building a business empire and controlling more and more wealth of the country—all in the name of the Quetzalcoatl Order, which he owns. Why do you think his liaison with a high Spanish official is so important? You can bet their pillow talk will be used to the Aztecs' advantage in the upcoming trade talks."

Theodora motioned to Vargas to get on the light switch that was behind him. "Okay," she said, "we have only a few seconds. When I turn this on, Gaummer will know it's been activated, and he might be able to triangulate our location if we're online for more than two or three minutes."

"What is this," Dave asked.

Theodora stood up straight to stretch her back. "It's a device that allows users to peer into another time or another dimension. We can't quite program it to pinpoint momentous historic events—but we can peer in on random slices of time. It's made of a rare metal, rhodium, which acts like an antenna, allowing us to tune to other rhodium throughout the space-time continuum."

"I'm a lawyer, he's a cop, and that one's a cabbie," Dave said, pointing to Johnny and Tototl.

Theodora sighed. "It allows you to see into another time—generally. We're trying to figure out how to use it to better allow us to travel through time and navigate our ship back home—Fall 2013, southeast of London. But right now, all we're able to do is look through it."

"But that's in the future," Johnny said. "It's 1999."

"We know," Vargas said. "In our time, it was 2013 when we left and originally came to 1519."

"So, you're saying you created the time machine in 14 years?" Tototl asked.

Dave was following, somewhat, so he held up his hand. "No," he said. "They're saying they created a time machine in 2013 in their timeline and then went back to their 1519—which was also our 1519. But, their changes created an alternate timeline which changed everything, including making possible our existence. In our time it's the year 1999."

Theodora patted Dave on the shoulder. "That's about right," she said. "What allowed us to crack the space-time barrier was the rhodium skin on our ship. What we have discovered since then is that rhodium is the constant." Theodora nodded to Johnny. "Where are you from?"

"New Amsterdam, originally, the island of Manhattan," Johnny said.

"Good enough, Brian's hometown," Theodora said. "Bri, can you program it?"

Brian had opened a laptop computer and plugged it into the base of the Gaummer Version III. He input the map coordinates and the geolocation. The computer came up with several dates and times that could be accessed. "October 13, 1979 seems to offer clear visuals," Brian said, giving Theodora a thumbs up.

"Okay, Antonio, hit the lights and flip the switch," Theodora said.

The lights turned off. Theodora affixed the thin rhodium medallion to the two spokes so that it hung between them, like a floating screen. Brian hit return on his computer, and the metal glowed blue, illuminating the table. Dave immediately felt a strong vibration at the base of his skull and a ringing in his ears that blocked out any other sounds in the room.

On the screen was a faint glittering image of a city with impossibly tall buildings. It looked like a live feed. They could see boats moving on the river. The screen gave them a vantage of the city from the shore across the Hudson River. Dave, Tototl, and Johnny were mesmerized.

Inside Dave's skull, car horns were honking as if they were in the room. The image jumped out from the screen to him, and he was able to somehow fly through it, across the river and among the buildings. He could not explain why, but he knew this place and knew it intimately.

The screen went black. Johnny and Tototl blinked. Dave kept staring, the images persisting in his mind. *Snap, snap, snap.* Theodora was snapping her fingers in his face. "Hey, Aragon, you all right?"

Dave shook himself out of it and mentally pulled himself back into the room. "Wha, what?" he asked.

Theodora came around and sat next to him. "You were out of it, man," Johnny said.

"For how long?" Dave asked.

"At least three minutes after we shut down the machine," Theodora said, quizzically. "What did you see?"

Dave put a napkin up to his face. "A city. The city. New York City."

Brian and Theodora looked at each other. "You mean New Amsterdam."

Dave snapped to. "I need a drink." He took a sip of his beer. "What did you see?" he asked Johnny and Tototl.

"I don't know, a city of tall buildings across a river. It could have been the Hudson, I guess. But the New Amsterdam I know has no tall buildings like that. Especially in that part of the city—down by the water."

"And nothing else?" Dave asked. "You didn't fly to it?"

Tototl and Johnny both shrugged. "It was interesting, but it was fleeting and short," Tototl said.

"Wow," Dave said.

"Wow what?" Vargas asked.

"I just…I just had a much different experience. It was like I was somehow floating through the city. I knew the city—the smells and the sounds. It was incredibly familiar to me. I can't explain."

"What is New York?" Johnny asked. "Sounds like someplace in England."

"It's like it took over my body," Dave said, looking up at Theodora who studied his face, brow furrowed. Dave took a minute to breathe and re-acclimate himself to the room. It was truly like he had been taken away, out of his body.

"Maybe that's part of the reason why they're so interested in you," Brian said. "The transmission lasted exactly one minute and 41 seconds," Brian added, looking at the computer.

"And you were transfixed—sucked in—for a good three-and-a-half minutes after we cut the power," Theodora said. She was now kneeling down, at eye level with Dave. "So, what is it about you? What makes you special?"

"Nothing," Dave said. "But, I have to admit—that city, the city I saw. I have seen it before. I knew it. It was so real, like this recurring dream I have been having for years now. I'm certain it's the same place."

"Can you describe the dream?" Vargas asked.

Dave relayed his recollection of the dream—the boat, the city, the rain, and then the slip and fall with the interminable wait for an ambulance. He told them he started getting them about twelve years before and that the latest, most intense version was just that morning. Tototl corroborated Dave's story, telling of how Dave's eyes had rolled back into his head and his mouth started to foam.

But most important, Dave tried to relay how it was always so much more than a dream—it was somehow real, like he had been transported each time and sentenced to re-live that awful clumsy accident.

"Have you had an injury or major surgery to your brain?" Theodora asked.

Dave reflexively felt his skull. "I did," he said, "a major skull fracture when I was a boy. I fell off a horse on a remote part of my grandfather's ranch in Cuba. It required major reconstructive surgery and the insertion of a metal plate."

Theodora stood up and went around behind Dave. "Do you mind?" she asked.

Dave shook his head. "Not at all," he said.

She gently ran her fingers through his scalp and began feeling for the demarcation of the plate. "About 6 centimeters by 9—it's a big one and located near the occipital lobe—perfect location."

Dave straightened up and moved his head away from Theodora's hands. "Wait, wait, wait," he said. "Perfect location for what?"

Theodora came back around and sat at the table. "There is likely rhodium in your skull plate, and that means your brain acts as a tuning fork for temporal vibrations. So, any time we powered up the time engine and jumped somewhere, you either had a dream or a seizure—taking you back to a touch point in our original time," Theodora explained.

"Rhodium?" Dave asked. Theodora sucked in her lips and sat back. She cocked her head uneasily. "What?" Dave pressed.

"Well," she started, casting a glance at Brian. "When it became apparent we were going to have trouble getting back home, one of our associates, Dr. Hans Gaummer, started developing a helmet made with a Rhodium skin to allow him to better control how the ship moved through space-time. It improved the ship's performance, but not enough to allow us to pinpoint a path home. That's when Hans convinced our boss…"

"Quetzalcoatl," Johnny interjected.

"Yeah, Quetzalcoatl, or Sir Ian Boddington, as we knew him," Vargas said.

"Well, Gaummer convinced him to go back to a point in your timeline and provide critical medical research on skull and brain injuries using technology not seen before. Somewhere around your 1940s, your doctors across the world made huge leaps in caring for people with severe brain injuries. They were able to do this because we were there for three years—1939 to 1942—and Gaummer spent his time presenting scientific papers across the world on the subject. He even won a Czar Nicolas Genius Prize in 1944. In absentia, of course, because by that time, we had jumped back here."

"Unknown scientist comes out of nowhere to revolutionize brain research," Brian added. "It was his way to plant the seeds for rhodium being used in brain protective devices and skull plates around the world. A medical-device company we started back then, GBKD-Corp out of Geneva, provides more than sixty percent of the brain injury devices used in medicine today. I was the first Chief Financial Officer for the company."

Theodora put Dave's head in her hands. She looked into his eyes. "So, here you are—the result of that effort to put rhodium in the heads of people in an effort to…well…cultivate people who can better control the time engine. You're the result of an ambitious and insane scientific experiment six decades in the making."

Dave pulled away. "This is too much."

Theodora stood up. "I know, maybe you should rest and we can come at this tomorrow. You know, put together a plan."

Johnny came over and put his hand on Dave's shoulder. "All this legitimate?"

Dave considered for a moment. "I can't explain what I felt or experienced when she turned that thing on, but it was as real as you and me right here, right now. I can't give you a logical or legal explanation but, I know in my bones they are telling us the truth." Dave stood and stretched. "I need to rest," he said. "Did you get my bag from the back of that car?"

Brian pointed to the couch, "It's over there."

Dave walked over and picked up his bag. He looked inside for the spare toothbrush he always kept in his briefcase for those late nights at the office. He noticed the ancient leather-bound book from Decoyan. He pulled it out. It was a fragile volume handwritten on very thin, aged parchment. It made him think of Decoyan and what his role could possibly be in all this. He asked the group about Decoyan.

"From what I know about him, he seems to be a devoted Quetzal supporter—comes from a good family. I've seen him at a few Palace events," Brian said. A phone on his belt chirped. He pulled it off and looked at it. "It's the boss." He took the call but walked into the other room.

Dave looked puzzled.

"Quetzalcoatl still thinks Brian works for him—he's our guy on the inside—we needed a man on the inside," Vargas offered. "Theodora and I—we're wanted criminals in Quetzalcoatl's view. We've turned against him and stole vital technology. We couldn't deal with the awful methods anymore. Quetzalcoatl believes he created this universe, so there is no harm in killing people who otherwise wouldn't exist were it not for him. People here are his toys. He literally believes that."

"That's twisted," Tototl said.

Theodora had grown silent. Dave could tell from her watering, distant eyes that she had seen some of this up close. "I was a part of it," she said. "I am no better than those monsters who sacrificed people on tops of pyramids for hundreds of years."

"You can't take that on yourself," Vargas said. "I let him destroy my whole race the minute we got here. My proud blood is the result of the coming together of Spanish and Native cultures. By joining Sir Ian on this madness, I played a role in preventing the creation of my people."

Brian re-emerged from the bedroom. "What's up?" Theodora asked.

"He needs me back at the Temple. They found the bodies of Collins and Agabe—they had a tracker on the car. They also sensed a temporal disturbance just a few minutes ago—emanating from southern Tenochtitlan – meaning here."

"Our use of the device," Theodora said.

"Yeah," Brian said. "They haven't pinpointed it, so we're still safe for now. I will get a read on things back at the Temple and send word when I can. Sit tight."

"But wait," Dave said. "Marta must now know I am not in the custody of those men. She's probably already tried to call me."

Theodora went to her bag and pulled out Dave's phone. Sure enough, four missed calls over just the past few minutes. "Looks like she has been trying you." Theodora handed the phone to Dave.

"How should I play this?" Dave asked.

Johnny went over to look at the phone. "As far as she knows you don't know she's a part of this. I think you call her—tell her you are all right, you escaped the shootout, ran out of the garage, and are in hiding. Tell her you're freaked out and you'll lay low and set up a meeting with her in the morning. That'll buy us time to figure this out."

"What's that?" Brian asked, looking at the book in Dave's hands.

"I don't really know. Judge Decoyan gave it to me," Dave said, sitting down on the couch, phone in hand, preparing to dial Marta. He handed the book to Brian.

"The Account of Efraim Ramirez. It's dated from May of 1536," Brian said.

Vargas, who had taken his dish to the sink, dropped it upon hearing the name. They all looked up at him.

"I know that man." Vargas said. "He was one of the survivors of the Cortés battle. You remember him—he was their leader—the one who spoke for them. He was the one who was claimed by the nobleman Decoyan and taken away."

Vargas walked over to look at the book and began leafing through it. "It must be a written account of the attack, but from the Spanish side."

"Why would Judge Decoyan give it to me?" Dave said. "It's priceless."

"Maybe he wanted to connect with you, get you on his side," Johnny said.

"Don't trust him," Brian offered. "I know these guys. I see them in the temple. If he's truly a Quetzalcoatl devotee, I wouldn't trust him."

"I wonder if I'm mentioned here," Vargas said. "You mind if I read it first?"

"Not at all," Dave said with a shrug, already too overwhelmed to take in any more information, much less read an ancient handwritten book.

Theodora tapped Dave on the knee. "Make the call," she said.

"Right, right," Dave said, activating his phone.

Chapter 21

T'SHLA'S EYES OPENED to the lavish French decor of a palace bedroom. The walls were covered by ornate gilded wallpaper that she did not notice in the darkness of the night before. She was lying on top of the covers, still in her clothes. She must have just fallen asleep right there and not moved all night long. She slowly sat up and looked out the glass double doors of the bed chamber.

She walked over and opened them, letting in chilly morning air. The sun was coming up over the mountains, and a breeze blew in the sweet scents of the palace flower gardens. She shivered and rubbed her arms, regretting not throwing a sweater in her bag as she was being hustled out of her apartment by the Quetzal guards the night before.

Clang. Clang. Clang. A loud reverberating sound of metal on stone came from the hall. Quickly she turned to see the door to the hallway fling open. Four women in white and green robes entered and bowed their heads, holding them down. Behind them, he entered in a flash of shiny red satin and golden jewelry.

"Good morning, my dear," he bellowed, bounding into the room. Behind him were three more flower bearers, bringing in new arrangements of white lilies to brighten the room.

T'shla immediately fell to her knees, eyes on the floor. "You grace me with your presence, your highness," she said, uttering the standard greeting of any common Aztec when in the presence of their emperor.

Moctezuma 26 put his hand on her head. "Arise, my girl. It has been too long."

T'shla had not been in the presence of the Emperor for at least five years—an official Palace function to commemorate the Green Revolution and the enduring productive lives of the Saved Ones.

She stood up slowly and looked him in the face. The palace pamperers had taken good care of him. He was mid-sixties but looked at least ten years younger. He wore red satin pajamas, but he was the emperor in his house; he could wear whatever he wanted.

"How have you been?" he asked, walking over and sitting on the bed.

"I…I have been well, your grace," she said, nervous to be in the presence of the one man who truly held her life in his hands. In some ways, she was glad he looked so young and healthy. His son, Moctezuma 27, was much more unpredictable and had taken a high-born Jaguar wife from one of the fiercer warrior clans of the south. She did not look forward to the day he ascended to the throne.

"Sit here, girl, and let me look on you," he said, patting the bed next to him. T'shla approached and sat on the bed next to the emperor.

"I see you slept in your clothes—that won't do at all," he said. "B'he, please bring this daughter of Eagles some togs befitting her status as a Saved One." A short, middle-aged woman, one of first to enter the room, bowed and exited, walking backward.

"Thank you, my lord," T'shla said, voice cracking with nerves.

"I do so want to catch up—will you please join me for breakfast?" he asked.

T'shla knew she had no choice in the matter. "It would be an honor," she said.

"Fantastic," he said, hand patting her knee. "You are my guest." He leaned in conspiratorially. "No need to worry anymore about your fuss-budget uncle. He's been sent back to the Temple." T'shla smiled, glad to hear it but not completely comfortable being so close to the emperor, either.

The emperor stood. "Good. Freshen up, my sweet. Breakfast is in a half hour." He turned toward the door.

"Wait," T'shla said. "Why was I taken here?"

The emperor turned back to her. "I always look out for my children," he said, "my dear sweet children."

"Can I leave if I want?" she asked.

"Why ever would you want to leave the Palace? Thousands would kill to take up residence in the palace."

"Residence?" she asked.

He smiled. "Dear, sweet girl, there is so much to discuss," he said. "I want to hear all about your exciting work in computers. You know I can barely turn the things on—to know you have become somewhat of an expert is thrilling to me."

T'shla gulped.

"And how..." the Emperor started, seemed to consider his words for a moment, but then plowed ahead, "and how the reports I'm getting are that you have been a naughty, naughty girl."

T'shla looked down, not ashamed, just not wanting to have this conversation.

"And with a non-Aztec boy, no less," he said. "Our gods can do these things because they're gods—they've created all people and as such, can consort with all people."

T'shla looked up at him questioningly. The emperor seemed to T'shla as if he entered a bit of a momentary fog. "What?" she asked.

The emperor shook off the fog and the smile returned. "I do so look forward to having you join me for breakfast," he said, turning quickly and leaving the room.

Coming in immediately behind him was an attendant with fresh court robes, colors and fabrics she had not worn in ages.

§ § §

"Oye, man, move it!" Tototl said, punching the dash of his car. There was a tie-up on the Cuitilac Expressway heading into the center city. They were running about five minutes late.

"So much for getting there beforehand to scope out the scene," Theodora said from the back seat.

"Eish lady, give me a break here," Tototl said.

According to the news, the authorities had only opened the causeways about three hours before—at 5 a.m. Now the streets were full of delivery trucks that had been stuck on the lake shore the night before. Most deliveries to island businesses and government buildings happen between 11 p.m. and 4 a.m.

Dave had agreed to meet with Marta at Pietro's Cafe, a Greek breakfast place located near the shore between the Palace district and the Sacred Precinct on the city's main island. Johnny and Antonio Vargas had left about thirty minutes earlier to scope out the location and report back any evidence of agents or mercenaries. So far, no word from them, as they were probably late to take up their positions, as well.

Theodora's phone buzzed. It was Vargas. "Yeah," she said. "Okay. You guys set up? Where? Did anyone spot you? Got it." She disengaged the phone.

"What's the deal?" Dave asked.

"They got a table at another cafe across the street. Marta is at Pietro's. She appears to be alone," Theodora said.

"No Spaniards?" Dave asked. In his heart he hoped she would be joined by staff members of the consulate. That would mean she was clean.

"Alone," she said. "You see, I told you. She has no interest in announcing that you're safe. She's there to get you back to Gaummer and Boddington."

"She's not stupid," Dave said. "She has to know I reached out to someone, anyone else to let them know I was okay. If I disappear, they will certainly counter her story."

Theodora settled back into the seat. "Sure," she said, "unless, of course, she drank the Kool-Aid and believes, as Quetzalcoatl does, that this universe is merely his creation and there are no consequences to reckless actions here. Remember, she's fucking the god who created this world." Her words sounded angry and bitter.

The thought chilled Dave. If someone truly thought that way, they'd be incredibly dangerous and unpredictable. "You getting all this, Tototl?" Dave asked. It was a lame effort to alleviate his own anxiety. "By the way, what's Kool-Aid?"

"Okay, stop and let Dave out about two or three blocks before the cafe," Theodora instructed Tototl. "You good?" she asked Dave, reaching forward and giving his shoulder a gentle squeeze. She then went through her duffel, pulled out her pistol, and handed it up to Dave.

"Got any weapons for you?" Dave asked. "I mean, if it gets hairy."

"Nope, just memos about Gaummer's research and activity reports from the mercenary team. All the evidence we'd ever need to blow the cover off Quetzalcoatl if he ever made a direct move against me, Antonio, or Brian. These documents are our aces in the hole. I never let them out of my sight."

Dave's heart was pounding and he felt heat building under his collar. He was still not completely comfortable with the idea of carrying a gun.

"All right then. Let him out here," Theodora told Tototl. "We'll circle the block and stay at a distance. If things aren't safe for you in there, run back through the kitchen and out the back..."

"...and into the alley, turn right and meet up with you, Johnny, and Vargas in the Shoreline Pub. I got it," Dave finished.

"Good deal," Theodora said, "and it's an awful, sugary drink that a crazy cult leader used to poison about a thousand of his followers. In my timeline, of course."

Dave looked confused.

"Kool-Aid," Theodora said. "When someone drinks it, it means they've..."

"I got it," Dave said. "Sounds all too familiar. Maybe this cult leader was just a god from yet another timeline."

Theodora laughed. "Now that's a mind fuck." And then, "Seriously, take care of yourself—that melon of yours is incredibly important to this whole thing. How, I have no idea, but we need to try and get as much as we can out of Marta, but without jeopardizing you."

"Okay," Dave said.

"Most important," Theodora said, "we need to know more about what Gaummer and Boddington have planned for the heads they have collected. Obviously, learning what we learned last night from your live experience with the device, it's clear that the head is much more valuable if it's still attached."

The car stopped and Dave exited. He crossed the street and walked the last two blocks to Pietro's. This was a part of town that he was not too familiar with. Its proximity to the Palace and the Sacred Precinct always put T'shla off, so it was never a place they frequented back in the day.

Dave was hyper aware, looking at each person he passed on the street, hoping to recognize at least one face from the consulate. Nothing. Just busy people heading to work and stopping for coffee and sweet pastries.

Pietro's was about two-thirds full. Marta was unmistakable, sitting in the front window, glued to her phone. She was striking and beautiful. A lifetime of memories welled up inside him. He could not believe she was responsible for any of this.

He opened the door to the cafe. She looked up and smiled brightly, standing and nearly bounding over to him to offer a bear hug. "Thank Jesus you're okay," she said. "I was beside myself with worry."

Dave accepted the hug, eyes closed. Her hair smelled of flower nectar.

"Sit," she said, "tell me all about your ordeal."

"It's hard to explain," he said. "You must've seen the TV coverage. They cracked me on the head," he bent over to show Marta where, "and the next thing I remember is we're in a garage. These men, they started arguing about whether to chop my head off, if you can believe that. Insanity."

Dave went silent, staring down into the white tablecloth. Marta reached over and grabbed his hand, reassuringly. "Then, boom, a car screams up, bullets. I run— faster than you can ever possibly imagine me running. I went upstairs and out into the street—it all must've been no more than a half mile from right here. I get into the first cab I see and have the cab take me to a seedy hotel. That's when I contacted you."

"I just cannot imagine," Marta said, signaling for the waiter to bring more coffee. "This is unacceptable treatment of our citizens. We are exerting strong back-channel pressure on the government to distance itself from the Jaguar Order. They're animals."

"Are you sure it was Jaguars?" Dave asked.

Marta put her napkin down, disgusted. "They're terrible. This country has such a divide—the Quetzalcoatls have moved the entire society forward so much, but the whole place is dragged down by brutal Jaguar filth. And to think, they tried to pin those murders on one of our citizens."

Santiago. Dave hadn't given one thought to him since the afternoon before. "Santiago," he said, "did he check in to Quetzalcoatl custody?"

Marta looked down. "Jaguars," she said.

"What?" Dave asked.

"They found his body and that of his Aztec sponsor north of the city yesterday evening. Both had been executed."

Dave couldn't believe it. "No," he said, crestfallen.

"It's all the more reason for our government to make an official statement recommending the Aztec government decertify the Jaguar Order and label it a terrorist organization," Marta said. "There was nothing you could have done for Mr. Esparza. His fate was sealed, somewhat, when he started down his path of crime and violence."

"Santiago wasn't violent," Dave said. It was almost a whisper. "He was just a petty, shit criminal looking for some kind of a path."

Marta took a deep breath. "Be that as it may, his death and what happened to you will be enough for the General Assembly to indicate it will not enter

167

into any trade relationship with the Aztec Empire unless the Emperor cuts off the Jaguars—funding, official recognition of the order, the whole deal."

"That's about thirty-seven percent of the population—disenfranchised," Dave said. "I can't imagine the official Jaguar Order approves of any of this. Plus, I'm a lawyer. There is no definitive proof that these were Jaguars."

"What?" Marta asked. "You heard Decoyan in court yesterday. You interviewed Esparza. You saw the Jaguars attack you and shoot government security workers on the steps of the courthouse. They're out of control."

The coffee arrived. Dave treated his with cream and a sugar stick.

"What if it's a set up?" Dave asked. "It's all too perfect. What if someone is purposefully trying to set up the Jaguar Order? I imagine some people would benefit a great deal if the Jaguar Business Consortium lost its preferential position in the mining and fuel industries. Who benefits if the Jaguars take a fall?"

Marta straightened, looking incredibly uncomfortable in her seat.

"What?" Dave asked, the lawyer in him sensing he had struck a nerve.

"I'm just, I'm surprised is all," Marta said, her voice clipped.

Dave said nothing. He took a sip of coffee.

"After all that happened to you," she said, "I figured you would be clearer of mind about it and what needs to be done."

Dave smirked. "What needs to be done?" he asked. "We're Spaniards. What do we care what needs to be done here. Our job is to keep our citizens safe and out of the news. You know, look out for the best interests of the Spanish Colonial Government and its people."

"And what if our best interests are served by having an Aztec government dominated by the Quetzalcoatl Order?" she asked. "They're good for business."

"Is that the official position of our superiors?" Dave asked.

Marta fidgeted.

"Are you freelancing this?" Dave asked.

Marta folded her hands in front of her on the table, lacing her fingers together tightly. "I do not entertain this line of questioning," she said.

Dave sat back. "Okay," he said, changing course. "So, when do we announce that I have been recovered?"

Marta shook her head. "I think we're going to have to get you someplace safe—quarantine you to make sure you are properly debriefed before we announce your recovery."

Dave's heart sank. This was it. He knew right then that if he went with her he might never live to leave the country.

"Have you communicated with anyone but me?" she asked.

"No," Dave said, "not at all—just you."

"Good," she said. Her cell phone buzzed on the table. It was face down.

She turned it over to see what it was, pulling it close to her. It was a text. She read it with no expression. She put the phone down and looked into Dave's eyes. She smiled. "A lot of history between us," she said.

"Sure is," Dave said.

"Like family, way back when," she mused, stirring her coffee.

"I'm not going into quarantine, am I?" Dave said.

"Oh, David, you are a very important piece to a puzzle that, well, I suspect you know all about already," she said.

§ § §

Across the street Vargas saw it all going down. He stood abruptly, waving his napkin in an effort to get Dave's attention. Johnny quickly caught on and joined in, but they were helpless.

§ § §

"You mean the beheadings and the connection to the health records?" Dave said.

"No, I mean the time travel," she said.

Dave flushed, heart beginning to race. Marta cocked her head toward the window. Dave glanced and saw Theodora standing in front of the window, fear in her eyes. A large white man was standing behind her. He turned slightly to reveal a gun pointed at her ribs, concealed by his overcoat.

Shit, Dave thought, fight or flight mechanisms beginning to kick in. He looked back to Marta.

"I'm sorry it had to be this way," she said. "But you really can't believe these rogue elements—they don't have the full story."

"Then why the need to threaten them?" Dave asked, knowing all the cards were on the table. "Why let goons wild pretending to be Jaguars, killing innocent people? I can't believe the Marta I knew would stand for any of that."

Marta signaled for the man to take Theodora away. Before he did, Dave saw Theodora mouth the word '*corre*' or 'run' before being dragged back into a waiting car. Another large man got out of the car and walked slowly to the restaurant. Dave knew the man was coming for him—setting up to nab him the minute he stepped out to leave.

Dave stood.

"Don't run," Marta said. "There's no point. You have something Quetzalcoatl wants, and when he wants something, he eventually gets it." Marta wiped her mouth with a napkin and put cash on the table.

"And there's something else," she said. "We have your Aztec girlfriend, T'shla.

She is now safely under our roof." Marta shook her head. "None of this would have happened if you had just come to me that first night."

The news about T'shla was crushing, made more devastating by knowing he was responsible for her being in danger. Without a word, Dave bolted—farther in to the restaurant. This took Marta and her muscle on the street by surprise. Dave snaked quickly among waiters and patrons. He was fairly nimble for a thirty-two year-old desk jockey. He entered the kitchen by the time the goon was in the restaurant and was out into the alley before his pursuer was just a few steps inside.

Dave sprinted according to Theodora's instructions, quickly darting from the alley to the street, to another alley, and finally to the Shoreline Pub, which was just opening its doors for their famous English breakfast. Dave slipped inside, his lungs burning. He walked briskly to the back of the pub, found a dark booth, and sat, back to the door. After a moment, he heard the door to the pub open again and then heard footsteps on the wooden floor of the pub. It was either Johnny, or they had somehow followed him. It was Johnny.

Johnny and Vargas sat down as Dave sighed in relief.

"They got her, man," Vargas said, his panicked voice cracking. "We've been running rogue for nearly a year, and they got her."

"I know," Dave said. "Did they ID you? Did they follow you?"

Johnny craned his neck and looked out toward the front door. "I don't think so. I think we're clear."

"What happened to Tototl?" Dave asked, while really only thinking of T'shla and her safety.

"I don't know, we only saw Theodora out in the street," Vargas said. "Shit!"

"What do we do now?" Johnny asked. "Marta's in with them. We're fucked."

"They also have T'shla," Dave said. "Marta said she's safe 'under their roof.'"

"At the Q Temple?" Johnny asked.

"I don't know," Dave answered, "that's all she said." Dave looked up at the ceiling, trying to catalog everything. "Okay, let's try to piece all this together," he said. "Marta is in on this—and she is definitely connected to your former boss, Quetzalcoatl. I think I can do one of two things. I can show up at the consulate and announce my return to the press office. Marta has power, but she can't keep a lid on my safe return. Not when there's been so much media attention."

"But the downside is there's no telling what they might do to Theodora and T'shla. That gives them quite a bit of leverage," Johnny offered.

"Or?" Vargas asked.

"Or, we push for a one-on-one with Quetzalcoatl. We negotiate, Theodora and T'shla's safe return in exchange for me. Along the way, we tell them that it's best to use live subjects to try and better calibrate their time engine. That should spare my life. Heck, I might even be able to get a new career out of the deal."

Vargas looked away as the waiter arrived with three waters. Nearly a year of being on the run had likely taught him to not show anyone his face. "We have to move," Vargas said, "back to a safe house we have on the main island near the Temple district."

Johnny waved off Vargas. "Okay," Johnny said. "I think your first option might be good because it makes C'de Baca's life uncomfortable—she'd essentially have to either welcome you back with open arms or immediately defect to the Aztec government. This would be a grave embarrassment. But, if she has been convinced to think like this Boddington character—that this is just a sandbox of a universe where life doesn't matter because it's been created by him—well then, it doesn't really matter if we mess up her professional standing with the Spanish government. She's literally fucking the creator of the universe. So I guess I'm full of shit—maybe it's not a good option after all."

Dave exhaled heavily, confounded by an array of bad choices before him.

"Plus, she's a smart cookie. She probably has muscle watching the approaches to the consulate, prepared to tackle you and take you away before you get within ten meters of the building," Johnny said.

Dave pulled out his cell. "But I do have this," he said. "I already texted my mother. I can call the press."

"That's good," Vargas said, appearing to grow antsier as the moments passed. "We really need to go underground, get back to a safe house and plan this thing out. Also, I think your option two is a last resort. I would never trust a one-on-one with Boddington. Gaummer has his ear, and he is a sneaky son-of-a-bitch."

Johnny went to the front of the pub and looked out on the street. He came back. "Looks clear," he said. "You guys have good luck."

"What do you mean?" Dave asked.

Johnny held up his hands. "You forget, but I'm still officially missing, too," he said as he ambled back to their table. "They don't know we've been together. I can easily report to the consulate and say I went on a bender, got all fucked up, heard this crazy news, and wanted to report in. That way I can be on the inside and relay information to you and Antonio."

Vargas and Dave shared glances. It made some sense to have a man on the inside watching Marta.

"Is that story believable? You would almost certainly lose your job for such a screw-up," Dave said.

"My friend, I never mentioned this, but it's in my personnel file. I've been to employer-sponsored rehab three times. Booze and pills. I'd for sure get booted for a fourth screw-up, but with all the activity going on in Tenoch since last night, they'd probably keep me around on desk duty seeing as how they need all hands on deck."

Dave searched Johnny's face. "That all about ends your career. Are you prepared for that?"

"Well, if this 'god' you speak of actually did create this world as an alternative universe and none of this matters, then who gives a shit if I get fired," Johnny said, flashing an easy grin. "I'll try to keep an eye out for what happened to Tototl, too. What do you think?"

"It's risky," Vargas said, "but it would be good to have eyes on Marta." Vargas looked to Dave as if deferring to him to make the decision. Dave squeezed his eyes tightly. Johnny could be walking into at best, a firing, and at worst, a deathtrap.

"You sure?" Dave asked.

Johnny shrugged. "Not really, but it seems like the best idea I've had all week, so…"

"Okay," Dave said. "Do it. But be careful, amigo."

Johnny embraced both Dave and Vargas and headed for the door. Dave and Vargas stayed in the pub a few minutes more, with Dave passing the bartender fifty pesetas for his trouble.

"Okay, the car's back over by the…*shit*," Vargas said.

"What?" Dave asked.

"Theodora's phone—if they got her, they got her phone. It probably has a ton of calls between her and Brian. Once they go through her phone, they're going to know he's working with us."

"Jesus," Dave said.

Vargas whipped out his phone and shot Brian a quick text. *Theo caught—probably being taken to Q Temple. They likely have her phone. You are compromised. Get safe.*

CHAPTER 22

BRIAN FELT A buzz in his pocket indicating he just received a text. He was sitting alongside Hans Gaummer, who was enjoying his breakfast—eggs, bacon, chiles, and fresh tortillas. As had become tradition, he and Gaummer sat immediately behind Quetzalcoatl at a smaller back table, but still facing the rest of the court. Quetzalcoatl sat at the large round table to the immediate left of the Emperor, the most esteemed position. To the Emperor's right, in the space designated for the Jaguar order, sat his son, Moctezuma 27, and his son's wife, Katherine.

On this day they *Jaguared it up*, proudly wearing the colors of the order—black, red, and gold. Moctezuma 27 wore a tunic that left his bulging tanned bicep uncovered. It bore the tattooed image of Cuauhtemoc, the patron and transcendent hero of the Jaguar Order and of any Aztec who saw fit to question the status quo. Cuauhtemoc was a martyr, questioning the rise of the Quetzalcoatl order and the imbalance it had cast on the whole of Aztec society. Legend had it that Cuauhtemoc was not a pure Jaguar and detested human sacrifice, but the Jaguars took up his cause and placed him at the center of their religious iconography as the Quetzals began their rise nearly five hundred years before.

The rest of the large round table was filled out with the usual suspects—the tiresome hangers-on and relatives that made up the inner-circle of the court. Quetzalcoatl had been effective at freezing out dissenting voices and shrinking the circle around the Emperor over the past few years since he had returned this third time. It was now a core group of loyalists and people with family ties.

It was uncommon to have new faces at court breakfast. But joining the group this morning was a stunning Aztec woman who Brian immediately recognized as one of the Saved Ones, T'shla Ixtapoyan.

Brian grew depressed when he saw her there. He knew her presence meant that Boddington had more leverage over Dave. *Boddington always wins in the end*, he thought, looking at the back of his master's head, his hair now completely dyed a deep, rich forest green to allow him to forgo the silly helmet.

"I am so pleased to have a few guests here this morning," the emperor said in his upbeat and vapid way. He had once seemed like a god, young and strident, committed to improving the lives of his subjects. Now he was fat and jolly, letting Boddington and the fiercely loyal Quetzalcoatl high priests guide much of palace life and policy. That's what unquestioning trust gets you. The whole court was on auto-pilot, which allowed Boddington and Gaummer to manipulate everything.

Brian pulled his phone out of his pocket and looked at the text from Vargas. It was more terrible news. His heart sank, and he felt the air of what hope was left seep out of him. He also needed a Plan B.

"What's that?" Gaummer whispered, trying to get a peek. Brian knew Gaummer never fully trusted him.

Brian slipped his phone back into his pocket, now realizing it was only a matter of time before he was found out. "The Texian oil and gas company we're buying. Just got word there are new financials coming over this afternoon."

Gaummer nodded and got back to his breakfast.

"...my boy, Moctezuma 27, has graced us with his presence," Moctezuma 26 was saying. "What brings you out this fine morning?"

His son was slouching at the table in disdain for the whole charade.

"Come now, boy," 26 said, "you're now what, thirty-eight? You're not a moody teen anymore. Sit up straight."

His son shot his father an icy look and sat upright. "Thank you, father," he said. "I came because there is much worry out in the country about what is happening in the capital." He was referring to the fact that the Quetzalcoatl religion was most deeply held in the urban areas, with there being a much more even split of devotions out in the more rural parts of the empire and in the Southern Continent.

The emperor chuckled. "The Capital is fine, my boy. It has stood proudly for 730 years and will stand proudly for three times that more." The assembled court members grunted their approval and offered a smattering of applause.

"Still," 27 said, "We do not serve our people well when one devotion stands above all others."

At this, Quetzalcoatl stopped eating and looked at 26, who cast a worried glance his way. Brian knew Quetzalcoatl had an inkling that 27 was going to be a problem if anything ever happened to the current emperor. Quetzalcoatl had tried to win him over, but the boy and his wife were stubborn and, Brian suspected, just plain didn't like Boddington or believe he was a god.

"As Emperor of the realm and associated territories and islands, I represent all faiths equally. All faiths come from the beginning, birthed unto earth at the same time by gods of power and wisdom," 26 said. "That noted, I can count one god who has favored us, time and again, with his presence. One god who helps us in our affairs and shows us the path to light." He then motioned to Quetzalcoatl, who nodded humbly.

"You embarrass me with your praise," Quetzalcoatl said. "I am a being of immense power and light, this is true, but I am also a being of humility."

Brian had trouble keeping a straight face and put his napkin up to cover his mouth and nose.

"That's just it," 27 said. "Why this god? Why has he come to visit us time and again? Where are the others? He comes here nearly 500 years ago, he returns nearly twelve years ago and, again, he comes back nearly three years ago. Why the frequent visits by him and no visits by any others?"

The Emperor twisted in his chair, becoming frustrated. "What exactly are you getting at, boy?" he asked, impatiently.

"I guess I'm saying the gods—all of them—are a way for us to order our lives and contain the way we explain the world. They are not beings. They are philosophies. I believe we are being taken by charlatans and their tricksters in the court, and it's tearing our society apart so that very few can profit," 27 said, his voice rising with each word.

The emperor sat back, exasperated. "Do you believe what I have to put up with?" The crowd, generally all sycophants of the Emperor and the Quetzal Order, snickered and sneered.

§ § §

T'shla observed this exchange, and though a little worried about 27's Jaguar leanings, began to feel the emperor's son was an honest, thoughtful person.

Quetzalcoatl rose and took a position in the middle of the circular arrangement of tables. "As a god, you can still learn some things," Quetzalcoatl said, as if starting a sermon. The crowd seemed to settle in for a stem winder.

"I have learned that there are great men on earth, men with forgiveness in their hearts, men like our very own Moctezuma 26," he said to solid applause. "It's true, I came here 480 years ago and saw a people in need of defense." He pointed to a brightly-colored mural on the wall to his left which showed a white-robed green-cowled god stepping down from the pyramids of the old religions.

"And then, again, I returned twelve years ago, and I found a society about to explode with potential but being held back by ancient and outdated brutal ways that had turned our beloved country into a global pariah. That was the Green Revolution. The end of sacrifice. The opening of trade. Your Emperor, Moctezuma the 26th, had just assumed the throne, and he had the courage to make a change no one before him had the temerity to do. His decree ended barbaric human sacrifice and opened society to the rest of the world."

Quetzalcoatl walked over to T'shla and stroked her hair. "We are joined today by one of the Emperor's Saved Ones, T'shla Ixtapoyan, Third on the List." He let the words sink in. "Third on the List."

T'shla shifted in her chair, visibly attempting to avoid Quetzalcoatl's touch.

"I left again for a time, returning three years ago, to be where I belonged, at the side of my friend, Moctezuma 26, and in the greatest nation the gods ever saw fit to create—the Aztec Empire."

175

The assembled courtiers loved the patriotic pandering, jumping to their feet in wild applause.

"So, as a god, what I learned is that not only do you serve me, but more important, I serve you. I serve my friend, Moctezuma 26, and I will be at the ready to serve Moctezuma 27—if he calls on me. If not, I will fade and come back to my favored people in their times of need."

Funny, T'shla thought, *there must have likely been no fewer than a thousand times of need between godly visits. Where was this god during all those times? Famines, outbreaks, wars. A lot can happen between divine visits.*

"No turning back, no turning back, no turning back," the assembled nobles began to chant.

The Emperor held up his hand to silence the crowd. He looked to his son. "Would you take us back?" he asked, pointedly.

Moctezuma 27, now sulking further in his chair, threw his napkin on his plate. He chose his words carefully. "The Green Revolution has been good for our people, but I do not hold that gods must pave the way for us to be decent to one another. We have it in ourselves to be decent. I would never reverse the reforms of the Green Revolution." He looked T'shla in the eyes and nodded. "I would not have a flower so lovely be cut down under my rule."

§ § §

From his vantage, Brian contemplated the power of this moment for the striking young woman in the center of the table. For the first time in her life, she must have felt the burden of impending execution truly leave her soul. Depending, of course, on long and healthy lives for both Emperors 26 and 27. He also wondered how the prince's wife, Katherine, took the remark, but he didn't have a clear view of her face.

"Then why do you wear the colors of an order that has recently been implicated in a rash of beheading executions?" Quetzalcoatl asked the prince.

Moctezuma 27 and Katherine stood. "You may be a god, but you do not make accusations at me in my future palace," 27 said.

"I am not accusing you of anything. I am questioning why your order has acted so violently of late," Quetzalcoatl pressed.

Moctezuma 27 smiled. "You're a god," he said. "Shouldn't you know the answer to that question?"

Quetzalcoatl for once, seemed at a loss for words.

Moctezuma 27 and Katherine bowed to his father, but not to Quetzalcoatl, and abruptly left the chamber. Before leaving completely, he stopped and called back into the chamber from the doorway. "My place is with the people who question all this palace intrigue—the people who want truth and answers." And with that, he was gone.

All eyes turned to Quetzalcoatl, who made his way back to his seat. "There are times I do not choose to look in on the dark hearts of men," he said, regaining his composure. "It is a mystery."

"Well, that was eventful," the Emperor said, turning to Quetzalcoatl. "The boy will learn, I promise you."

Quetzalcoatl and the Emperor shared a few whispers as T'shla and the court finished their meal. After the servants cleared the chamber of dishes, the Emperor clapped, and everyone looked upon him. "Please clear the chamber. Quetzalcoatl and I would like to have a few private words with the Ixtapoyan girl."

The chamber emptied quickly with just the Emperor, Quetzalcoatl, T'shla, Brian, and Gaummer remaining.

"My dear," Quetzalcoatl said, "I bet you are happy to learn of the next emperor's intention to keep the Green Revolution reforms going."

T'shla sat obediently. "Of course, my lord."

"Good, good," he said, getting up and crossing in front of her. "When I came back twelve years ago and again three years ago, I was careful to not reveal myself to the public. The only people who know about me are the high-born to the Quetzal Order, my spiritual family, my servants, and members of the Royal bloodline. You are one of the few outsiders in modern times to ever be in my presence."

"Why is that, my lord?" T'shla asked, studying his face.

"Why is what?" Quetzalcoatl said.

"Why do you hide yourself from the public when you didn't do so in the past?" She motioned to the mural, which clearly showed him out among the people.

Quetzalcoatl nodded. "Good question. I suppose it's because I understand the modern mindset of tearing things down and approaching the world with cynicism and disbelief. I cannot reveal myself because the modern heart is not equipped to believe. So I must do my good works in secret."

"Best to not let the masses see behind the veil," T'shla said.

Quetzalcoatl smirked. "So, you are now protected. The next emperor will not kill you. This must be good news to hear."

"It is, my lord," T'shla said.

"But there's something the young and cocky number 27 does not know," Quetzalcoatl said.

"What is that, my lord?" T'shla asked.

Quetzalcoatl wheeled on her, eyes fiery with rage and his voice a bellow. "I AM THE GREEN REVOLUTION."

T'shla started and was glued to her chair.

"With a word, I can bring back death and the bloody temples," Quetzalcoatl said, his voice now much softer. T'shla hazarded a glance at the Emperor, who kept his eyes down. She then looked at Brian, who tried to offer her a sympathetic face.

"So, I am going to need your help, Saved One," he said. "I need you to deliver your Spanish man to me."

"David?" T'shla asked.

"Yes," Quetzalcoatl said, "this rapist, this defiler of a sacred virgin. David Aragon."

Brian noticed T'shla become flush and saw her demeanor change from fear to anger. "I was never raped—I joined with David by independent choice." Her hands were balled into fists.

Quetzalcoatl dismissed her and turned back to the Emperor. "He's brainwashed her. She is his courtesan slave—that's how he was able to steal the medical data from her."

"I beg your pardon," she said, rising from her seat.

The Emperor also rose from his chair and walked toward T'shla. "Poor girl," he said, "a pure Aztec flower defiled by a Spanish monster."

"Not hardly," T'shla said, a growing tinge of contempt in her voice.

"We will redouble our efforts to catch this menace," the Emperor said, ignoring T'shla completely. "See to it that she is given an even nicer room in the palace." The Emperor turned and left for his ten a.m. tennis match.

Now she was alone with Quetzalcoatl, Brian, and Gaummer.

"Brian," Quetzalcoatl said, "see to it our Aztec flower is well taken care of." Brian stepped forward. He was immediately joined by two palace guards.

Quetzalcoatl came up close and looked down at her. "I saved your life," he said. "Today you will repay that favor either by telling us all you know about Señor Aragon's whereabouts or serving as bait to lure him here."

"He was abducted. Everyone saw that on the news," T'shla said defiantly.

"Somehow he got away. He had help from some criminals. They killed two good men to break him loose."

"You ordered the attack at the courthouse?" T'shla asked. "You captured David?"

Quetzalcoatl did not answer. He turned and left, joined by Gaummer.

"I got it from here," Brian said in perfect Nahuatl to the guards. It was only a matter of time before Theodora would be brought before Sir Ian and Brian would be found out as a traitor. If he was going to help this woman—and their cause—it was now or never.

Brian escorted T'shla back to the guest wing of the palace, past the room she stayed in the night before, and down a grand corridor. Its walls were covered with murals of the greatest moments in Aztec history. He stopped at a door that did not look like the door to a bed chamber. It looked more like the door to a mop room.

He looked up and down the hall to ensure they were alone, opened the door, and hustled her inside. It was an empty servant hallway, poorly lit and painted a drab off-white. Trays and service carts lined the narrow hall. T'shla tensed up, and Brian sensed he needed to reassure her after the uncomfortable breakfast.

"Don't worry," he said, softly. "I am here to help you." He knew there was no reason for her to believe him. But he had no time for small talk, so he cut to the chase. "I helped rescue Dave last night," he said.

T'shla exhaled but still kept one hand on the door back into the hallway. "What, what is all this about?" she asked.

"We have to get you out of here and get you to safety. Some of my friends have been captured, and I'm about to get found out by Quetzalcoatl very soon. We don't have a lot of time," Brian said. Then, considering T'shla needed something, anything more to go on, he added, "We are not from here—Quetzalcoatl, me, the man sitting next to me this morning." He didn't want to get into the whole time travel thing, plus he knew it would immediately make her suspicious and think he was a lunatic.

"Quetzalcoatl is not here to do good. He's here to rule things—your country, all of its businesses and industries, the whole of society. When he said he is the Green Revolution, that part was true. It was all his idea, impressing those changes upon the new emperor when he ascended the throne twelve years ago."

"The Green Revolution has been great for our society, for women, for me," T'shla said.

Brian sighed in concession. "I agree, it was good. But the man you just saw is not the same anymore. He has lost his mind and feels as if your whole world and the people in it are his toys. He's the one behind all those beheadings that have been happening. The ones Dave mentioned in court yesterday. The ones you connected to the medical-records theft."

"Why?" She asked.

"Because he needed to find Aztecs who have had brain injuries or operations. The man I was sitting next to? His name is Dr. Hans Gaummer, and he's a scientist doing research on the impact of a particular type of metal skull plate and how it might stimulate brain matter under certain circumstances. It's very complicated, and like I said, I don't have time to get into all of it."

"And they want Dave because he's on to them?" T'shla asked.

"That, and because he, too, has a metal plate in his head—and it is in an area near a part of the brain that allows him to do some pretty remarkable things."

"Like what?"

"Hopefully you'll get to ask him yourself," Brian said, putting his hands on her shoulders and physically turning her into the corridor. "But that won't happen unless you get moving. Take this corridor to the end. Behind the next door is a staircase. Take it down until you can't go any lower. At the bottom—there's only one way—is a red door. Take it. That's the cellar level and Gaummer's Palace lab.

There, you'll see some of the things I'm talking about. Gaummer won't be there yet; he has a standing after-breakfast meeting with Quetzalcoatl.

"Go through the lab. At the far end, you'll see a fire door. Go through it—there is no alarm. On the other side is an entrance to the lake-bed access tunnel. It's about one mile under the city and the lake. At the other end you'll find stone stairs leading straight to a door. Go through—it'll place you right smack in the Quetzalcoatl Temple main lobby off the cloak room. From there, exit to the street. We have a safe house apartment on the corner of Moctezuma 6 and Avenue of the Eagle. Apartment 905. Here's the key."

Brian slipped a small key into her hand. "Try to find Dave. When I last saw him, he still had his phone," Brian said.

"How can I ever thank you for this?" she asked.

"Don't get caught or killed," he said. "This is all about leverage. We have to stop Quetzalcoatl's further descent into madness, or it will be the ruination of your whole country and maybe your world."

"My world?"

"Just go," Brian said. With that, he slipped back into the main corridor, leaving her there.

CHAPTER 23

Apartment 905

DAVE AND VARGAS easily made it to Apartment 905. It was a cozy two-bedroom in a building that had been built in the 1920s. They settled into the living room. There wasn't much to eat, as Theodora and Vargas had only used the apartment as a safe-house stop on their way to the Xochimilco compound. Just a few cans of beans, some seasoning, and frozen vegetables.

Vargas always loved to cook because it made him feel closer to his grandmother and his childhood in south Texas. He put a pot on the stove, determined to make something out of what they had.

One thing that was available was plenty of stale German beer in the refrigerator. Dave popped one open and moved to a stool off the breakfast bar. "How long do we wait?" he asked.

"Till dark," Vargas said, "or until we hear back from Johnny or Brian."

They were in the dark with no good options. Dave sat on the stool. "So, why did you rebel?" Dave asked.

Vargas was twisting the opener on a can of beans when he stopped and looked forward to consider the question. "Sometimes, you see the handwriting on the wall and realize you need to act, or you become no better than those you work for."

He resumed twisting the opener. "I was in the military in my time, the greatest military in the world. Our country was a great power north of here. I was a medic and later a field doctor. Our country invaded some other nations across the world—near the Ottoman Empire. I went. I served. I didn't agree with why we were there, but there were young kids—my countrymen—being blown apart, and I felt I had to go over there and help. I didn't question my superiors, I just did my duty."

He emptied the contents of the first can of beans into a stew pot and grabbed the second one.

"My whole life has been keeping clean, doing right, following directions. When Boddington hired me, he got the best candidate in the world—military and medical background, and I could speak Nahuatl because of my father's side of the family. They're from a little village about 40 kilometers south of here. I spent nearly every summer down here. I was like three people in one for Boddington—by hiring me he could keep his team small. So I made him pay me the salary of two people."

Vargas smiled at the thought. "He paid me without batting an eye," he said.

"You didn't ask for enough," Dave said. Vargas chuckled.

"So with unquestioning loyalty I came on board, put together the logistics, staffed the sick bay, and brushed up on my Nahuatl never even imagining for an instant that the whole thing was a time-travel gig. I mean, who could ever conceive it. Boddington confided in me only a few days before launch. I was very uncomfortable, but I had a job to do, so I did it."

"When did you start questioning?" Dave asked.

Vargas emptied the next can of beans into the pot and went rooting through the cupboards. "I started questioning immediately," he said, pointing to his head and then to his heart. "But I never said a word."

Dave nodded. "Sometimes I feel I do the same thing—never questioning—never making waves. Only I've never had to make life or death decisions before."

Vargas nodded and a long moment passed between them. "Then we got here, in 1519," Vargas said, continuing his tale. "And I stood back as Boddington's plan, a plan I helped carry out, destroyed the world that would create me and my people. All along he convinced me and our team that he had the riches and the scientists to get us home—back to a world we recognized.

"But something happened. Turns out our science wasn't so sound, after all." Vargas said, reflecting on the day, in an Old Palace anteroom with Boddington, Gaummer, Theodora, and Brian when they all finally realized there was no easy way back to the universe they knew.

"Gaummer had just told us that the change in dimension and our movements within the new timeline had essentially created ripples obscuring the pathway back to our original 2013," he said. "That was the sick joke of it all. Gaummer had been able to give us time travel, but once we stepped across the void, everything we did in the new time created reverberations throughout the continuum. Meaning the more we traveled, the harder it would be to get back because we wouldn't be able to pinpoint locations at exact times."

"What did you all do then?" Dave asked.

"Boddington decided he needed a scapegoat to keep the mercenary crew on his side. With help from a loyal Aztec warrior, Tuxla, he was able to set up Prince Cuauhtemoc and make it seem as if Cuauhtemoc sabotaged our ship. Cuauhtemoc had been a problem for us from the moment we arrived. Something about him— he just didn't buy Boddington's bullshit and refused to lead the Aztec troops in the attack on Cortés. Boddington, as Quetzalcoatl, presented his 'proof' of sabotage to Moctezuma II, and the emperor grudgingly agreed to imprisoning Cuauhtemoc on the charge of high blasphemy and interfering with the work of a god. Cuauhtemoc died in a dungeon a few years later. As you now know, Cuauhtemoc would go on to become a patron icon of the Jaguars and their 'Serve, but Question' motto.

It was Boddington and Gaummer's scheme, but we all were just as guilty because we said nothing and went along with it."

"How did he set him up?" Dave asked.

"Boddington invited Cuauhtemoc to the ship, got some video of him touching a few buttons here and there and that was it—video proof of sabotage, at least enough to convince the crew and the Aztec leadership. Moctezuma II was more dazzled by the video playback—it essentially wowed him into the reluctant conviction."

Vargas looked down into the pot of beans in shame. "That was also the roots of our ugly belief that somehow the lives of people in this world didn't matter as much as our lives. Almost like you don't even count at all."

"But we do count," Dave said. "We are people. We feel, we bleed, we have babies. I can't imagine this Boddington, or Quetzalcoatl, would turn so far away from his humanity."

Vargas heard a faint commotion emanating from the living room window. He went over to raise the sunshade. Below he saw a throng of humanity organize itself and head northward toward the great temples.

"Come look," Vargas said, "it looks like the Jaguars are starting to organize."

Dave came over and looked down and beheld a crowd of at least one thousand people, some carrying signs such as "JAGUARS UNITE" and "THEY COME FOR US NOW, THEY'LL COME FOR YOU NEXT." They both knew enough about Aztec culture to know that such public demonstrations were unheard of. What they were witnessing was historic.

"I'm not sure the Quetzals or the secular authorities will know how to handle this," Dave said. "If more and more Jaguars come out they'll have to respond."

"I never pinned the Jaguars for a weaker class," Vargas said. "They have the guns, and they still have large portions of the military."

Both Dave and Vargas took up seats near the window, with Vargas leaning over to open it to let in more of the ambient sounds from the street. They were nine floors up, but the faint chants reached them in a rhythmic chorus of protest.

"You do vacate your humanity when you are treated like a god and come to believe it," Vargas said. "I would be lying if I said I wasn't somewhat drunk with power, too. As a doctor, treating people with ailments easily rectified by modern medicine made me feel like a miracle worker. God-like myself." Vargas reached for the television remote and clicked it to a news channel. It was covering a story about a large theater festival happening on the western coast of the country.

"Quetzals control the media," Dave said. "Few people out in the country will see this demonstration."

"There will come a point it cannot be ignored anymore—something called a 'tipping point' in my time," Vargas said. They both sat there, absently watching the demonstration grow in the streets while their pot of beans warmed on the stove.

"You're right," Vargas said after a long while. "You do count. I mean, you proved it to me last night with the way you interacted with the time mirror. You had a connection to that place—hell, you knew it was called New York. That means there is some kind of a cosmic link."

Dave shook his head. "I could have read a sign telling me that was New York."

"Search your thoughts and feelings—is that true?" Vargas asked. "You also dreamed of that very same place for years and years. How could we, by activating the machine, implant dreams into your head from a thousand miles away? We activated the machine; we didn't know we'd be giving people dreams or tell them what to dream about. Right? Somehow you had those visions of that city—a city that was incredibly similar to what you identified as New York last night. You do matter, because you have just proven a real and biological connection between our timelines. You're some kind of a touchstone. Maybe you bear a genetic or familial link to someone in my timeline that made the vision stronger with you."

"I'm just a simple, underachieving lawyer," Dave said, taking a sip from his beer.

Vargas laughed. "True, very true." He got up and went to his backpack and pulled out the Gaummer Time Mirror. "But I want to investigate how much of an underachiever you were in my time."

Dave looked at the machine warily. "You said they can track us when we use it."

"I don't think they'll be able to easily get through the demonstrations—plus, this is too important. If you can navigate and control the visions in my home timeline, then you can possibly navigate our ship home," Vargas said.

Dave put up his hands, as if fending off the idea. "Whoa, friend, I did not sign up for any of this—navigating a time machine?"

Vargas put the time mirror down on the table. "Oh yeah, that's right, I forgot. We can't ask you to leave your wife and kids and all your possessions here in this timeline," Vargas said.

"I don't have a wife, or kids," Dave said.

"I know," Vargas said. "You also have a dead-end job, and it seems to me you also missed the boat on truly living."

"So, I'm supposed to give up everything I know to drive your crazy machine?" Dave asked, defensively.

"Hell, I don't even know if it would work. That's why I want to put you under the influence of the mirror again—to see if there's any chance whatsoever," Vargas said. "If there is, I just appeal to you to make a decision that works for you. Remember, you are a free man."

§ § §

T'shla followed Brian's directions to the letter. She knew she entered Gaummer's lab because she immediately felt unsettled. It was dark and filled with low-hanging cabinets. She moved her hand along the wall until she felt a light switch. She flicked it on, and the fluorescent lights slowly buzzed to life. As the lights came up, she cautiously began walking through. It looked very much how she would imagine any scientific research lab would look. It was long and narrow, like a galley kitchen, with black stone countertops on either side. The countertops were a mess of metal scraps, computer equipment, glassware, and papers. At the far end, near the exit, she saw a large industrial freezer.

She had a sickening suspicion that this was not a freezer for food. She was at the door and knew she could leave, but something kept her in front of that freezer. She did not want to open it, but felt duty bound to do so. Her right hand clasped the handle, and she gave a soft tug. It opened and became illuminated. Inside, with no attempt at secrecy, was the head of an Aztec woman, dead eyes and the top of her skull peeled back to reveal a small metal plate near her right temple.

T'shla shuddered. Under her head was a hanging clipboard affixed to the freezer rack. T'shla took a look at the top paper of the clipboard. It was clearly in English, which she did not read. She took the top paper from the clipboard and folded it quickly, never taking her eyes off the poor woman's face. She put the paper in her robes. Behind the woman's head, she found what she assumed to be the heads of three others, wrapped in butcher paper. She also found other biological samples and vials of liquids that she assumed needed to be frozen. She always thought she would throw up in a situation like this, but she did not feel ill, only immense sadness and anger. She knew she couldn't take the heads with her to repatriate them to their families, but she did want to do something to sabotage this wicked 'research.'

She looked around the lab and found a pair of wire cutters. She unplugged the freezer and clipped the cord, ensuring that the contents would thaw and hopefully be unusable by this Gaummer monster.

It was all she could think to do.

She opened the freezer one last time and bowed respectfully, saying a silent prayer for the dead. She left the freezer door open and left the lab, continuing on her way out of the bowels of the palace and toward freedom.

§ § §

Across town, on the Southern Causeway, Marta was finally getting into the office. She buzzed through the security desk and made her way up the three flights of steps to her office.

Jorge Torres was waiting for her with her daily coffee and briefing folder. "Good morning ma'am," he said, joining her fast pace as she made her way to her office. "Here is the briefing on the Esparza death, and below it is the latest on the Aragon disappearance."

Marta took the files. She knew more about the Aragon disappearance than she wanted to. "Anything else?" she asked. "Fiver? Has he turned up anywhere?"

Torres cleared his throat and motioned to her office. Her eyes widened.

"Checked in this morning," Torres said, becoming uncomfortable. "I think he's been, well, he's not quite right."

Marta rolled her eyes. "I'll handle this," she said, dismissing Torres and entering her office. Inside she found Fiver slouching on her couch; his clothes reeked of liquor. She entered and loudly slammed her morning briefing folders on her desk. Fiver groggily roused.

"Are you serious?" she asked.

He sat up, head in hands, rubbing his face. "Sorry boss," he said.

"Where the fuck have you been, Fiver?" Marta demanded.

Johnny exhaled mightily. "We got in. Dave had a dinner date pop up out of nowhere, so I was, well, left to my own devices. I had a drink at the hotel bar, and then the next thing I know I am out on the town."

"You called Dave from the jail in the morning—checking on the prisoner. I heard the voicemail. You said you were going to compare notes," Marta said.

Johnny shook his head. "Yeah, I guess. I was fucked up. I woke up in a run-down hotel downtown—I figured I would meet Dave at the jail, but I was a mess—I reeked, I was still inebriated. Then some jail guards grab me to throw me off the property, saying I was being a lout—right while I was leaving the message—so I told Dave to meet me at the consulate."

"But then you didn't come here," Marta said.

"In my state?" Johnny asked. "I was afraid I'd get fired, so I found a whore and some cocaine to get my head straight and the cycle started again."

"Another bender," Marta said, shaking her head. "Did you even know your partner was missing?"

"I saw the news and read the brief," Johnny said, gruff voiced. "I came in as soon as I learned. Any intel on where he might be."

"I should drum you out on your ass—next flight out—fired," Marta said.

Johnny looked up and their eyes met. "You said 'should'?"

She sighed and handed him her cup of coffee. "I've already had mine."

Johnny sat up and took a sip. "Thanks."

"The country's blowing up, the trade summit is hanging on by a thread, and our media superstar from yesterday is missing. I need all the seasoned field agents I can get," Marta said, going to her desk and sinking into her chair. "You were once one of the finest agents in the Foreign Service. What the hell happened to you?"

"Addiction," Johnny said, "she's a cruel mistress."

Marta seethed. "No crueler than I'm going to be if you fuck up one more time."

"Yes ma'am," Johnny said, rising to his feet. "I assume I am on desk duty considering my, ah, transgressions."

There was no reason for Marta to suspect Johnny was in cahoots with Dave. The two hardly knew each other before this assignment and had probably spent no more than a few hours together before Dave took off to see his ex-girlfriend. Plus Fiver had a reputation for disappearing.

Marta shook her head. "You're not leaving my side. I have a pre-summit planning luncheon at the Palace today. You're my driver." She tossed her keys to Johnny who caught them. "You will be sober enough to drive in two hours, right?"

"Yes ma'am," Johnny said, slipping the keys into his pocket and straightening his rumpled suit.

"We're done here, Fiver," she said. "Get with Torres. He can get you some clean clothes. After things cool down here, you're probably still going to be fired, but I need everybody I can get right now. So consider this your last chance."

CHAPTER 24

THEODORA WAITED PATIENTLY in the receiving room of Quetzalcoatl's complex at Chateau Chapultepec. The guards had patted her down for weapons and emptied her pockets of ID and most important, her phone. Thankfully Tototl had grabbed her bag and ran the moment Marta's goon punched through the cab window and yanked her out by the hair. She hoped beyond hope that he, and more important the papers he now carried with him, were safe.

Quetzalcoatl's complex at the palace consisted of a twelve-room out building just south of the main palace residence and official public meeting areas. She had lived here before, so she was well acquainted with every detail of the place. She had picked out most of the furniture herself.

She was apprehended by Drake and Chagal, men she once knew as friends and compatriots, now stone-faced with hatred, rightly blaming her for the deaths of Collins and Agabe the night before. They stood watchful at the entrance to the building, knowing Theodora couldn't run, but also not wanting to take their eyes off her. So Theodora sat for the better part of an hour, waiting and wondering what would happen to her next.

The door on the opposite side of the room opened, and Quetzalcoatl stepped through. He was joined by a small boy who was no more than four years old. The boy held tightly to Quetzalcoatl's robes.

He had to do this, Theodora thought, a wave of emotion drowning her.

"Tlaloc," Quetzalcoatl said, "you remember your mum." The boy stepped out from behind his father's robes and looked questioningly at the woman wearing a dusty brown jacket and military-style cargo pants. "She's one of the smartest ladies in the whole wide world," Quetzalcoatl continued. "Go and give her a hug."

Theodora now had tears streaming down her face as she looked on this beautiful young boy. In his eyes she could see herself at that age. She scooted off the chair and fell to her knees as the boy approached.

"Mummy?" Tlaloc said, still hesitant.

"Yes baby," she said, touching his face, "it's me, deary. I have been away, but I am here now." She grabbed him and held him tightly, never wanting this moment to end.

"Can I show you my trains?" The boy asked after they parted.

Theodora wiped the tears from her face. "Of course you can, sweetie," she said. The boy's face lit up with excitement.

"Very well," Quetzalcoatl said, "let's let mommy and I have a few grown-up words." The boy looked to his father questioningly. "Mommy will be along in a bit," Quetzalcoatl said. "Go on up to your room and play."

With that the boy was gone in a flash, bounding out of the room, down the hall, and up the stairs to his bedroom. Theodora stood, brushed off her pants, and tried to regain her composure for the fight that was about to happen.

Quetzalcoatl poured himself water from a pitcher at his desk. He emptied a pocket from his robe and placed her cell phone on the desk in front of him. "You broke a rule, Theo," he said. "I am very disappointed in you."

"You are not a god, Ian, so let's stop with this imperious approach to everything. You're a businessman, a nerd like me who struck it rich. You don those robes and trick these people into believing you, and you start believing it yourself."

It probably had been a while since anyone had spoken to him in this manner—about one year, to be exact—right before Theodora and Vargas ran off with one of Gaummer's time mirrors and Theodora's code to the fusion drive.

"I may not be a god in the way you define it, but were it not for me, this place would not exist as it does," Quetzalcoatl said. "The last time I checked, creating worlds is part and parcel of being a god. But I didn't keep the party to myself—I have always recognized the roles of those on my team—you, too, are godlike—like me. Brian, the god of finance, you, the god of power, Gaummer, the god of time—it all makes sense when you look at it that way. That's why what you did to Collins and Agabe will not stand. Do what you may to our creations, but the deicide you committed against your former friends is appalling and true murder."

Theodora had been through this battle many times. Ian was too far gone, justifying his bad behavior and chalking it up to his god-like status.

"What are you going to do? Execute the mother of your child?" Theodora asked. "You may not value the lives of people here, but I do. For too long I believed you and Gaummer were honestly trying to help us find a way home. Now I know the truth: You never had a clear plan to get us home. You suckered that poor noble Cuauhtemoc. You had us race around this timeline seeding the world with rhodium skull implants, and now you're what, going around experimenting on people, cutting heads off, doing dissections? What's it all for?"

"Well, when you put it that way, it does sound a little off," Sir Ian said, sitting down in his chair. He waved to dismiss Drake and Chagal, who obediently left the room.

"Do you think I don't want to go home?" he asked. "Imagine the adulation—that we successfully crossed the space-time continuum and came back to tell about it. You know, I have at least six billionaire friends who would give their businesses to me to do as we have done. Imagine what they would pay me to take them to create their own worlds where they were gods? Think of the possibilities?"

Quetzalcoatl softened; he probably knew this line of argument would not work with her. "I cannot bear to have Tlaloc separated from his mother anymore. But don't forget you were the one who left."

Theodora sat back down in her chair, folding her arms. "I left because I could not, in good conscience, keep up this charade. I have followed you across time in harebrained schemes, literally, and where did it lead us?"

"In this universe it led us to the top of the mountain," he said. "I own twenty-six percent of the world's oil resources and am this close to signing a deal to control the world's largest uranium reserves."

"Uranium?" Theodora asked. Way back in the 1520s, when the Spaniards couldn't make headway along the Mexican coast they were able to grab a sliver of land between the French holdings in the north and the expanding Aztec Empire to the south. Their settlements stretched north of the Aztec Dry River Territories along the Dividing River up into the high deserts and forests of the northern continent. There they discovered a yellow rock of little use to anyone for hundreds of years until Quetzalcoatl came back to open up Aztec society, warm relations with the Spanish, and look into a long-term trade and mutual-development pact that would hopefully allow the Aztecs to mine what many viewed as a useless element with radioactive properties.

"Yes, about that," Quetzalcoatl said. "I can do it without you, but I'd love to have your help. Gaummer and I have a five-year plan to bring nuclear power to this universe. Your expertise will help us get it done faster. Imagine, a lab of your own 30 miles north of here. Tlaloc could stay with you."

Theodora hated Boddington with all her heart, but she could not deny the thought of being with her boy all the time might make her happy enough to give up on the quest to go home.

"Just power?" she asked.

Sir Ian shrugged his shoulders. "Well, you know there are other uses for atomic energy," he said. "It's the year 2000 here, and they haven't had the world wars to push technology forward like in our time. There are no satellites or space exploration…"

"And no nuclear weapons," Theodora said.

"Not yet," Boddington mused. He saw he was losing her. "Someone is going to develop this technology at some time. It might as well be us. We could use it for good—restore more order to the world."

Theodora exhaled vigorously, her lips motor-boating. "I can't believe I ever entertained this. You might as well lock me away in some room here, because I am done. I'm fine staying here, house arrest forever, but I'm not going to help you with your insane plans."

"Then what use are you to me at all?" Quetzalcoatl asked. "Tlaloc has an army of governesses, and Marta C'de Baca gives me sex and uranium. Why would I keep you here taking up space? Someone who abandoned me, tried to destroy me? Just because you are Tlaloc's mother? I thought you were so much smarter than that."

"Then do it because you're still human," Theodora pleaded, knowing there was little point in trying to change his mind.

Sir Ian's eyes were gray and cold. The case was closed.

"I never loved you," she said. "I always thought you were some kind of a pathetic and lonely man. But the checks cleared and it was fun for a while."

Sir Ian snorted dismissively. He put his finger hovering near the button on the desk to call for the guards.

"I know you're beyond trying to get home and that you've created the ideal life for yourself here, oh Emperor of the world. But why all the effort to capture this Spaniard? If his brain plate doesn't matter anymore, why try to bring him in?"

Sir Ian took his hand away from the button as he considered this. "This Aragon intrigued me when Marta spoke of him. She had access to his medical file, and when I shared it with Gaummer, he felt strongly that Aragon's brain plate placement and type of injury might mean he would be a good test subject for dissection," he said, musing on the thought. "You remember we seeded the whole world with our product, but finding people with brain plates large enough and placed just so is like finding a needle in a haystack. One just happened to drop in our laps. But, the experiences with the others proved to us that there was no way the brain plates made a difference or would improve navigation of the *Cyrus-A*. So, sure there was an initial curiosity to see if this man's brain plate over the occipital lobe made a difference, but I was frankly more concerned with him finding out about our project. Obviously, my fears were well founded with that court charade yesterday."

"So, you're just trying to disappear him, now?" Theodora asked.

"Well, two for one," he said. "Disappear a problem and get a dissection to further Gaummer's science while we're at it. I really should never have listened to Marta about pulling strings to get Aragon here. My lovely Spanish-African girl always trying to be helpful. All he's caused so far are complications." Quetzalcoatl reached for Theodora's phone. He activated it and looked at the screen, straining without glasses. He smiled and pushed the button to call the guards.

The guards entered from the back of the room. Theodora heard the muffled shuffle of a struggle and turned to see the guards dragging Brian in, his face bruised from a pummeling.

"Deneven, you disappoint me, too," Sir Ian said. "Too many Judases, too many Cuauhtemocs." The guards pushed him forward.

This emboldened Theodora. She had nothing to lose. "Chagal, Drake, I know you hate me for what happened to Collins and Agabe, but know this—this man," she said, pointing at Sir Ian. "This man cheated and tricked you. He has given you riches, but he knew all along that there was no way home. He set up an innocent man with the sabotage of the *Cyrus*. What he didn't tell you was that the ship was always flawed. Its navigation back to our universe was rendered useless by the very act of our time travel and its impact on the continuum." She stopped, noticing her words were falling on deaf ears.

"We can't go home…until now," Brian piped up. Theodora looked at Brian with surprise, trying to figure out where he was going.

This got Quetzalcoatl's attention.

"You hurt us, you kill us, and it will never happen," Brian said, turning his attention to his now former boss. "Gaummer's long-term experiment worked. Aragon can manipulate the time engine. He can control the mirror better than anyone ever."

"Is this true?" Quetzalcoatl asked Theodora. Theodora shrugged.

"Well?" he pressed.

"He showed an uncanny connection to the time mirror, I'll give him that," she said. "Properly plugged into the machine and given enough information about the location and time, and he may very well be able to guide us."

Quetzalcoatl looked beyond Brian and Theodora to Chagal, who was standing menacingly behind them. "Go get Gaummer," he said, "immediately."

Chagal left the room. Quetzalcoatl rose and walked over to the wall-length window overlooking the garden, waiting in silence while Theodora and Brian sat, passing each other troubled looks.

"We never intended for the test subjects to interact with the live time mirror," Quetzalcoatl said, as Gaummer entered the room quietly from the back. "The plan was to study how the plate interacts with and grows into the brain. After more research we were going to implant a plate into Gaummer in just the right location to ensure he could navigate the time engine—mainly because he knew the workings of it. I frankly don't believe that someone from this timeline can effectively interact with the engine. Isn't that right?"

Brian and Theodora turned to see that Gaummer had entered the room.

"We really don't know," he said. "It's all theoretical. That's why we need a large enough sample size of subjects out there with our brand Rhodium-coated nanotechnology plates in their heads. All of our post-mortem investigations have led me to believe we can still flow energy through the plate. If the subjects were alive, I can surmise there would be a modicum of ability from the live subject to interact with the time engine."

"So you didn't have to behead those people?" Theodora asked incredulously. "You could have taken out an ad in a newspaper and brought people in voluntarily to test this?"

Gaummer scoffed as if the thought was insane. "You're a scientist, Kopplewicz.

All good science follows a sound process, and my briefs for this research were clear: develop a model for creating enough subjects with the plates, conduct research on how the plates are incorporated into the body, which required dissection, and finally start investigating with live subjects before I undergo the procedure."

"Unbelievable," Brian said.

"Traitor," Gaummer retorted.

"Enough," Quetzalcoatl cut in. "How the study has been conducted up until now is all water under the bridge. The fact is, there is promise, and that means bringing the Aragon fellow in is all the more important. I will use Theo's phone to get word to Vargas that we have Aragon's girlfriend. Let's see what kind of a man he is."

Brian chuckled.

"Something funny?" Chagal said, putting his hand roughly on Brian's shoulder.

Brian squirmed away. "Good luck finding her," he said. "She's got a forty-minute head start on you—she could be anywhere."

Quetzalcoatl took a glass off the table and heaved it across the room, shattering it against a 300-year-old painting. "Lock these two away," he bellowed.

§ § §

Chagal and Drake dragged Theodora and Brian out the back of the room and closed the door, leaving Gaummer and Sir Ian alone.

"Do you believe that," Sir Ian said, exasperated. He didn't expect an answer.

"I thought we had deprioritized the brain-plate research in the wake of the revelation in court yesterday and the Aztec girl uncovering the connection," Gaummer asked. He noticed that Sir Ian was truly upset.

"I can understand Theodora being upset," Sir Ian said. "I obviously broke her heart. She's been separated from her little boy—her choice, of course—she was replaced as my chief science adviser by you, replaced in the bedroom by Marta. I can understand."

Gaummer began to fidget.

"But Brian," Sir Ian said. "If you are my right hand, he was certainly my left. I am devastated by this betrayal."

"His knowledge of business with the uranium deal on the horizon would certainly be helpful," Gaummer said.

Sir Ian sat down again, crestfallen. He waved Gaummer's notion off. "No, I have Marta; she will give us and the Aztecs great terms on the uranium. It's just more of a personal blow—a real bummer."

Gaummer walked over to his master and put his hand on his shoulder. "About the time research—can I re-prioritize it and move forward, maybe actually try to find a way back?" Gaummer asked. "I'd like to get my hands on this Aragon chap. If Brian was correct, we may be able to make progress."

"Always a dreamer, eh, Hans," Sir Ian said. "But I need to kill this Aragon—more so because we must make sure what he knows about us is never found out. I frankly don't care too much about your time research. We have the power to be larger titans here than we ever could have been in our time. And for me, that's saying something. I have no intention of going back. I plan to take care of this world and see how far I can take humanity as a god and benevolent ruler."

A device on Gaummer's belt buzzed.

"What's that," Sir Ian asked.

Gaummer looked at it and became very excited. "Someone has activated a time mirror again," he said. "I need to get to my computer to see if I can trace its origin."

"Vargas," Sir Ian said.

§ § §

Dave was disconnected from the machine after being plugged in for only about 45 seconds. However, this time he spent an additional four minutes and thirty-seven seconds transfixed. Vargas studied him closely. He held up a small penlight to his eyes and noticed that a blue glow completely permeated both his eyeballs.

"Remarkable," he whispered, clicking the light off. He gently tussled Dave's hair, slowly snapping him out of the trance. "David," Vargas said, voice rising a bit.

Dave blinked and shook his head to snap back.

"Long, strange trip?" Vargas asked.

Dave stared ahead blankly. Before activating the time mirror, Vargas and Dave agreed to see if he could explore the visions of his dream. They calibrated the settings to the New York area and used a wide time window of 1970 to 2013—any moment in a forty-three-year window. That's a possible 19,447,200 minutes. Vargas was curious if Dave could connect to that singular moment in that rainy city of his dreams.

"I made it," Dave said, still wispy and lost. "I was there, a man, going to work. I was riding the Staten Island Ferry. All this time I thought the ship was named the TATEN."

"Good, good," Vargas said, grabbing his pad. "Tell me every detail." Vargas was not a Ph.D. researcher, but he was a doctor, and though he could not engineer a time machine, he had spent enough time with Gaummer and Kopplewicz to become handy in the lab.

"Bernard Christie," Dave said. "That's my name."

"Your name?" Vargas asked.

"I can't explain," Dave said. "I was there, it was me. I felt my hands slip on the metal railing. It was as real as I am sitting here."

Vargas leaned back, putting his hands on his head and looked to the ceiling. "What does it mean?" Dave asked.

"I don't know," Vargas said. "Something in you, here, is connected to that man, over there."

"Connected," Dave said.

"Or maybe the same person, somehow," Vargas said. "I don't know. Some kind of consciousness-connection may be stored in your DNA. Something—but whatever it is, you are inexorably tied to this Bernard Christie fellow."

Dave stood to stretch. "Does that mean I can only go to places this Christie person can go? Places he knows? Like this New York, this traumatic event?"

Vargas shook his head. He didn't know. He turned suddenly at the sound of a key sliding into the apartment door. He got up quickly and went to his bag, pulling out a pistol and cocking it.

"Dave, gun," Vargas whispered, pointing to a vantage that had him covered in the hallway. Dave hurried over and pulled out the gun Theodora had given him earlier. He hadn't handled a gun since he was a boy on his grandfather's ranch—and that was a small .20 caliber rifle.

The door creaked open and T'shla walked in. She turned the corner to the barrel of a gun leveled at her forehead.

"Wha!" she exclaimed, dropping the key and jumping back.

"Who are you?" Vargas demanded, his voice becoming a harsh growl.

Dave came from the other hall. "Lower the gun!"

Vargas complied. T'shla saw Dave and ran to him. He grabbed her tightly.

"They said they had you," Dave said, pulling apart and searching her face. "How did you get away?"

"I was locked in the Palace. I met him, I met Quetzalcoatl—he is an evil man. I also met a man named Brian. He let me go—he said they were going to find out about him," T'shla said, still shaking. "I'm, I'm just so glad you're all right. I was so worried when I heard the news."

"Please," Vargas said, "sit, have some water."

T'shla walked to the dinette and took a seat on a simple wooden chair. "You won't believe what I have seen," she said, staring forward. She reached into her robes and pulled out the paper she had taken from Gaummer's freezer. "There is this other monster, a man named Gaummer. He works for Quetzalcoatl—he is somehow behind these beheadings. I saw some of the heads in his laboratory." She handed the paper to Dave. Dave couldn't read English well, so he passed it to Vargas.

"Nazca Ledi," Vargas read.

"She was one of the names on the list—a teacher," T'shla said.

"Plate location over temple makes subject unsuitable for operation," Vargas read from the sheet. "It says here she had the plate for six years."

"Following a car accident," T'shla said, "I remember her health record."

"Where are these heads?" Dave asked.

"Deep under the palace—there would have been no way to easily get them out to return them to their families," T'shla said. "I feel so terrible about that."

Dave and Vargas passed looks back and forth as T'shla pressed her palms to her knees and looked toward the ceiling. After a moment she stood and walked toward the window to look out on the street.

"It's getting very tense out there," she said. "When I was coming over here, I heard someone saying that Moctezuma 27 was going to speak at a Jaguar rally today at noon. Do you believe that? The son of the emperor speaking at a political rally?"

The significance was somewhat lost on Vargas, who came from a place where it was common for leaders to be seen. In the Aztec world, the Emperor or his family were only seen maybe once a year at the annual national harvest festival, and the only time anyone had ever heard the Emperor speak was for that short shining moment during the Green Revolution. Even then, Palace insiders had deep reservations about the Emperor speaking in public. However Quetzalcoatl, ever the media showman, pushed the idea of Moctezuma 26 appearing and speaking in public as a way to cement real change. Being a god, the lower nobles had no choice but to relent and let the emperor go to the markets that fateful day twelve years before.

"Did you see anyone else when you were in the palace? A woman, a white woman?" Vargas asked.

T'shla shook her head. "No. It was my uncle, the Emperor, servants, family, and then this 'god' and his two minions—one was Brian, the other Gaummer." She trailed off, and a quizzical look crossed her face. "And, I'm sorry David, but who is this man who just pointed a gun at me?"

"T'shla, this is Antonio Vargas," Dave said. "He's an associate of Brian and is a friend. He's a good man."

She took a breath and looked down at her hands. Dave approached her and put his arms around her again. "I said incredibly harsh things to you yesterday. When I thought I may never have the chance to take them back, I, well, I deeply regret it all—everything I said. You were very heroic in that courtroom," she said.

"I can't believe I, for an instant, thought about my stupid career or my standing when I knew you were putting your life on the line. I should be apologizing to you." He leaned in and gave her a soft kiss on the lips.

Vargas handed T'shla a glass of water, breaking in on the moment and trying to get everyone back to business. "You should know that Quetzalcoatl is no god."

"Yeah, I kinda figured that one out," she said. "But if he's no god, then what is he, some kind of a huckster, a pretender cozying up to the Emperor?"

"That's about the extent of it," Vargas said, his eyes telling Dave he didn't want to get into the whole time-travel thing right then.

"T'shla is safe," Dave said, "that's all that matters to me right now. And it also makes our next move a lot easier."

"What are you talking about?" Vargas asked.

"I'm going to turn myself in. I think I can negotiate the freedom of Brian and Theodora in exchange for helping Quetzalcoatl with his experiments," Dave said.

"No," T'shla said. "I can't bear to see you in danger again—this is an Aztec matter. You should not be caught up in it."

Vargas went back to the Time Mirror and turned on his laptop. "It's not that simple," he said. "David has already gotten the attention of the god and his pet emperor. He knows too much about us and about the level of corruption rotting the royal court. This thing won't end until we stop Quetzalcoatl and end this nightmare of human experiments."

Vargas waved Dave back into the living room. "First things first," he said. "Let's see how well you can manipulate this machine when we are not focusing on some place where you are completely comfortable and familiar."

Vargas turned the computer so that Dave could see the screen. He had it opened to a file that said, "Whitestone Manor." Dave put the computer in his lap and began to scroll through a file of saved images from the lab and grounds, pictures taken by Vargas originally meant to be e-mailed to his mom back in Texas to show her the amazing place where he worked.

"What is this?" Dave asked.

"They're photos I took at the place where we built the machine, Sir Ian Boddington's estate south of London," Vargas said, reaching over and pulling up a detailed map of England and Whitestone's location.

T'shla had gotten up to watch the commotion out the window.

"What am I supposed to do with this?" Dave asked.

Vargas shrugged. "I don't know—I'm flying on a string here. I guess I want you to see where this place is, try to project to it, and see if you can find it through the mirror."

"Sure, I'll give it a try," Dave said. "Nothing to lose."

"The crowd is really growing out there," T'shla said, her forehead now against the glass looking down. "I see no signs of security, either."

Dave and Vargas turned their attention from the time mirror and joined T'shla at the window. Vargas reached for the remote control and turned the TV back on. No more arts and crafts. This time, it was showing a live feed from the Jaguar Temple steps, the center of the protest.

Jaguars, not typically the savviest when it came to media optics, were still setting up a makeshift podium on a rickety table. Quetzals would have had a banner up and pyrotechnics at the ready in minutes. Vargas looked at the time mirror and back to the television.

"What?" Dave asked.

"We already activated the time mirror once today—one more time at this location and we're going to have to be ready to move fast," Vargas said. "I guarantee Gaummer has a pretty good idea where we are already. At least our general vicinity."

"Shh," T'shla said. "Someone's going to start speaking." On the television, an impossibly tall man proudly wearing a Jaguar cowl about his head and shoulders approached the podium.

"It's Guichava Zempolutla," T'shla said, "head of the Jaguar Order." This was completely unheard of. The heads of the orders never spoke in public.

Guichava had a soft voice and began with a series of low incantations in Nahuatl, calling upon the powers of the earth and the heavens to give him and his people strength. He punched his fist on the podium, shaking the microphone.

"I am a loyal servant of our beloved emperor and stand with him always," he said, voice shaking. "But I also invoke our patron, Cuauhtemoc, and his commitment to the truth above all—truth above gods."

The line got a surprisingly strong positive reaction from the crowd.

"I support the Emperor and the Green Revolution," he said. "I do not support unseen elements in the government working to discredit Jaguars and paint us as bloodthirsty heathens. We are decent people who abide by the laws. We love our families, and we will no longer stand for this character assassination. But most important, we cannot stand by and let our country be taken away from us."

"He must have something up his sleeve," T'shla said, "otherwise he would never say these things."

Guichava cleared his throat. "Just a short time ago, I heard from a simple man, a simple hardworking Jaguar man. He gave us information and documented proof that there are outside forces in the government. These forces have the ear of the Emperor, and they are leading us down a path to ruin."

"It has to be Tototl," Dave said.

"This simple and brave cab driver—is just like any of you. This morning he showed up on the doorsteps of our temple, out of breath but with a story of outsiders posing as fine Jaguar soldiers. In his hands were proof that there is an outsider in the palace, pretending to be a god and poisoning the mind of our beloved leader. This brave hero stands in the crowd today—not afraid anymore. His name will last in our Empire as long as Cuauhtemoc's. His name is Tototl."

The camera panned into the crowd and Tototl stood uncomfortably as the crowd roared.

The scroll at the bottom of the screen began running some of the details from what Tototl had. "Man posing as 'God' may have infiltrated Emperor's inner circle…Documents suggest use of treasury to enrich companies linked to shadowy figure…Three tech companies and two energy companies linked to holding company run out of Palace…"

"Whoa," Dave said, "Theodora's bag. She had it with her in Tototl's cab. When they got her, he must've been able to hold onto it. He probably felt he couldn't trust regular security and went straight to the Jaguar Temple instead of the United Imperial Authorities."

All three began hearing the din in the streets below grow louder and louder. They looked out the window again and watched as the unrest swelled before their eyes. Down the Avenue of the Eagle, they could see armored carriers approaching. They were coming from the Quetzalcoatl temple complex, while at the other end of the avenue they saw a column of regular army troops, which was largely made up of Jaguars, and protesters gather and begin to move cars and vehicles to block the road.

"We bear no ill will toward anyone," the voice at the podium said. It wasn't Guichava anymore. "Eagles, join us; followers of the Corn Maiden, join us; Quetzals of good conscience, please come down and join us too. Stand together with your fellow Aztecs. We can extend the revolution and bring freedom and equity to all."

"Who is that?" Dave asked.

"It's Moctezuma 27," T'shla said, her voice cracking. "I had breakfast with him this morning. He said I had nothing to fear when he becomes emperor. He has lifted the shroud of death from my shoulders."

The crowd erupted at the words and the sight of the young future emperor.

"My friends in the tanks. The ones coming down the avenue toward us. If you can hear my voice—listen to the people, listen to me. Put down your arms. We have no quarrel with our countrymen."

For an order that was never good at public relations, this was a very solid production. Getting a future emperor to speak at your rally trumped all the theatrics money could buy.

"Fuck it," Vargas said. "Dave, get in position in front of the time mirror. We have to test if you can visualize Whitestone." He hustled Dave to the table.

"Wait, won't they be able to pinpoint us?" Dave asked.

"There's a revolution happening out there," he said. "I'll take our chances that they're a little preoccupied."

Dave squeezed T'shla's hand, gave her a quick kiss, and took up his position in front of the mirror. Vargas quickly connected the laptop back to the time mirror.

"Ready?" Vargas asked.

Dave nodded.

"OK, I am inputting a three-month range from between August and October, 2013. Try to find the place from those pictures and tell me everything you can about it," Vargas said, inputting coordinates and temporal data into the computer.

"All right, let's go," Dave said.

Vargas flipped the switch. Almost instantaneously Dave was sucked in. So much so that he didn't notice T'shla heading for the door. Vargas noticed and got up from the computer. If Dave truly had any gifts, he'd be able to locate the place without an operator helping him.

"Where are you going?" Vargas asked. "There's no way any Quetzalcoatl agents will be able to get here with all the commotion downstairs."

"I have to go," she said. "I can't fathom what the two of you are doing here. I have to imagine it will help us somehow. But just now I realized that a life of hiding behind a computer and waiting for death has led me to this moment. My place is down there in the streets. I don't know where this thing will lead or if it will be good for me or for the country—but I know there is a roiling energy in my people down there and I must join them. I am a human symbol of the Green Revolution—one marked for death and saved by civility. I have lived the last twelve years free to live but not completely free from fear."

Vargas stepped back. "I don't know you, but I have seen the stories about you and your unique situation. I cannot imagine what it must've been like to have the sword hanging over your head your whole life." He held out his hand. "I am proud to have met you, if only for such a brief moment," he said as she took his hand, firmly and confidently.

She smiled. "Please tell Dave I love him. If it is meant to be in the future then it is meant to be. But now, I must join the struggle in the streets."

She opened the door and left, walking hastily down the hall. Vargas closed the door and looked back on Dave, his consciousness still sucked into the time mirror.

CHAPTER 25

QUETZALCOATL AND THE emperor watched the protest rally and television coverage together in an anteroom to the throne chamber. Both sat in stunned silence.

"Are you with me?" Quetzalcoatl asked. "My friend."

Moctezuma 26 stiffened. "I am no puppet. My son will get a stern talking to."

Quetzalcoatl breathed a sigh of relief. "He is a problem, your grace," Quetzalcoatl said.

"He is still my son" the emperor responded, plainly, putting an end to any exploration on Quetzalcoatl's part that some cosmic accident befall the prince. Quetzalcoatl did a quick calculation in his head. They could try to purge the media. He, of course, could still kill the prince by some 'accident.' But would this uprising blow over? That was the question.

"You are a god," the emperor said. "You have shown me things that I know— if you were to show the people—they would surely believe your divine grace."

Quetzalcoatl considered his predicament. He might still have the emperor with him, but this revelation of the corruption and profiteering was a complication. It meant that the days of unquestioned emperors and this form of government might be numbered. Quetzalcoatl looked Moctezuma up and down. His old friend didn't see it. The final rulers are always the last to know when their time is up.

"They will not believe, my friend," Quetzalcoatl said softly. "It is a modern world of technology and questions. When we opened the box with the Green Revolution, we created great things and enormous power for you and for your people. But we can never again close the box once it is opened. What's happening today is an outgrowth of what we started twelve years ago when I returned to my Aztec people and guided us on this path to freedom."

"All I'm asking is one simple show of divinity to wow my people and push them back into their regular lives," the emperor said.

Quetzalcoatl knew this protest was now being broadcast nationwide. The coverage of the court hearing the day before had set the media running wild. Too many moles popping up out of holes in the ground and too few hammers to pound them back down.

"A show of divinity would now be lost on the people," Quetzalcoatl said, noticing that the emperor was becoming desperate. Quetzalcoatl seized on it. "That is why—more than ever—you must display *your* faith."

The emperor fidgeted in his chair and exhaled forcefully. "That will not do as long as there are riots in the streets."

Quetzalcoatl rose. He knew all about uprisings and civil disobedience from his time. "People want their regular lives," Quetzalcoatl said. "Riots, civil unrest—these are not altogether unhealthy. They are also quite exhausting. Many of the rank and file people out there will probably go home and only a core group will push forward. What's important is to react appropriately."

"You mean put them down?" Moctezuma 26 said.

Quetzalcoatl's eyes widened and he wheeled on the Emperor. "No," he said, adamantly. "A violent response will only further inflame the people. And remember—the world is now watching."

"So what do we do?" Moctezuma 26 asked.

"Speak to the people—yourself—on television. Allay their concerns. Show them your love and your glory. Wrap yourself in the Green Revolution and embrace further reforms. The people will love you if you get ahead of them and show them you are with them," Quetzalcoatl said, moving ever closer, almost nose to nose.

"What do I say?" the emperor said, still utterly lost.

Quetzalcoatl sighed and backed away. His meal ticket needed some work. "I will write something for you. Have your press office announce that you will be speaking to the people this afternoon. That will steer a good deal of the media coverage away from the unrest. And, most important, send word to all the forces under your command to not engage in any violence. The last thing we need is blood in the streets."

"Very well," Moctezuma 26 said, "write me a fine speech, my friend. I hope this works."

Quetzalcoatl left the anteroom and exited to his compound.

§ § §

Marta and Johnny had arrived at Chateau Chapultepec to find that the guard had tripled and the troops looked antsy. "Are you sure your meeting hasn't been canceled, you know, considering the riot downtown?" Johnny asked.

"No," Marta said, "It's still on."

They crested the last hill in their olive-drab consular van and passed the final internal gate to the main palace complex. Johnny was impressed the guards let them pass without a word upon seeing Marta.

"Obviously, you're a frequent flier here," Johnny said, trying to make a joke but at the same time needle Marta a bit. From what Theodora said, Marta spent about three nights a week at the palace.

Marta didn't take the bait. "The negotiations have me here quite often."

They pulled right up to the smaller, but no less impressive complex just off the main palace. It was a small estate made of rose-colored stone and vines growing up the walls. It was surprisingly lightly guarded. There was a visitor spot right next to the building. Such lax security would never be acceptable anywhere else in the world. Imagine an unchecked car being allowed to park right next to a vital and iconic government building. Unheard of.

Marta exited the van. "Wait here," she said. "This meeting should last about two hours. There's a cafeteria on the first floor in the main estate."

"Yes ma'am," Johnny said.

She pointed to his phone on the dashboard. "Make yourself useful—do a round of calls to our field agents to see if there is any progress on finding Aragon. We have to get him back safe." She turned, straightened her jacket, and walked across the gravel to the main entrance, fancy shoes crunching the rocks under her feet. Strange that she carried no briefcase.

Once she was out of sight, Johnny grabbed his phone and called Vargas. Vargas picked up immediately.

"Yes?" Vargas said.

"Hey, it's Johnny. Crazy shit. I'm driving C'de Baca around today—my punishment—and lo and behold, I'm at the palace."

"You're kidding me," Vargas said.

"What can I do from here?" Johnny asked. "Any chance they took Theodora or T'shla here?"

"There's every chance," Vargas said. "But Brian was able to help T'shla sneak out this morning—she's safe. Theodora is likely being held in the guest palace complex—pink building. Probably upstairs somewhere. Be careful—Boddington and Gaummer have the run of the place. They have mercenaries and regular palace guards at their disposal."

Johnny checked the pistol in his shoulder holster to make sure he had a full clip. "I'm sure Dave's happy about T'shla," Johnny said. "Okay, how do I get out?"

Vargas was silent on the other end for a moment. While he was waiting, Johnny quickly looked around the grounds. Four guards by the gate, six milling by the entrance to the main palace. Probably at least four on the roof.

"Everything Okay?" Johnny asked.

"Yeah, yeah," Vargas said. "There's a tunnel in the cellar of the main palace, but that would be particularly hard to get to, considering that's how T'shla got out this morning." Johnny heard Vargas sigh audibly on the other end. "I don't know. Be creative."

Johnny rolled his eyes. "Thanks, that's helpful."

"Sorry, it's been a year since I've been there. I'm sure many of the security protocols have changed," Vargas said. "Look, I have to take Dave off the machine. Hopefully C'de Baca and Boddington will be engaged long enough to give you a chance."

"Got it," Johnny said.

"Good luck and stay in touch," Vargas said, ending the call.

§ § §

Marta entered Quetzalcoatl's private quarters, promptly undoing her jacket and putting it on a gilded hook. Quetzalcoatl was in the small office just off the bedchamber, sitting at the desk and banging out something on his laptop.

"Darling?" Marta inquired, stepping hesitantly into the suite.

"Over here," Sir Ian said. "Your little friend has certainly made our lives complicated."

Marta entered the office. "I'm sorry. He just didn't reach out to me when he got here—if he did that, we could have taken him right then."

Sir Ian looked up from his computer, eyes peering over his glasses. "I warned you to have your own men meet him. Those official judicial minders are way too pliant and accommodating."

Marta was genuinely hurt, but she knew she had some leverage in this relationship, and she knew how to play her cards. She turned away quickly without a word as Sir Ian returned his attention to his computer screen. He stared at it for a second before turning his attention back to Marta.

"My dear, wait a minute," he said, getting up from the computer and going into the bedroom. Marta was already pulling her jacket off the hook. "Don't go. I'm just under a lot of pressure. We have to make the emperor's response an event of epic poetry or else our little project is in real danger."

Marta paused. "Are you sure that's it?" she asked.

"What do you mean?" Sir Ian asked.

"I don't know. Your goons and I were able to grab your ex-girlfriend this morning. I figured, with her back in your custody, things would change between us," Marta said.

"Oh my dear, you have no idea," he said. "Theo may be the mother of Tlaloc, but she is not the kind of woman I see myself with. She's certainly no Caribbean goddess." He walked up behind her, putting his hands on her hips and drawing her close. "That ship sailed a long time ago."

Marta smiled, feeling his breath on the back of her neck. "Very well," she said, drawing away, "Let's talk about this uranium you're interested in."

"Really?" Sir Ian said. "We can talk about uranium later."

Marta cleared her throat. "The last time I checked, you had a lot on your plate today. My government needs the full financials on this arrangement before they sign off on giving you the rights to mine 100,000 tonnes. We need to get that done—today. With, of course, a negotiating fee deposited to me in my Dutch island account."

Sir Ian smiled. "The toil of a time-traveling god is never done." He spun her around and kissed her full on the lips. "Just give me a few minutes dear so that I may finish the emperor's script."

§ § §

"Dave, DAVE!" Vargas said, shaking him clear of his time-mirror trance.

Dave blinked and came out. "Eish, I need some eye drops," he said, shaking his head and squeezing his eyes shut.

"You're going to have to splash some water from the bathroom. I have no eye drops," Vargas said.

Dave took his hand away from his face and looked at Vargas with complete confidence. "I got it," he said.

"You do?" Vargas asked, brightening considerably.

"It's clear as a bell—you come over white coastal cliffs and zero in on a beautiful mansion with a completely ugly metal outbuilding."

"Yeah?" Vargas goaded.

"I was drawn to it like a magnet. There's a helipad and exactly 106 meters away is the door to the hanger. I saw you, October 6. You were loading a trailer of supplies into the mouth of an impossibly huge vehicle—like a Cargo airship, only fatter and uglier," Dave said. "I also saw Theodora and another man working in a laboratory—that's where the feeling was the strongest. You were all noticeably younger."

Vargas chuckled and stroked his graying chin. "You got that right," he said. "You got it all right. It must've been the concentration of rhodium on-site that made the vision so clear."

"But then why is the Bernard Christie vision so clear, too?" Dave asked. "I can't imagine he had rhodium on him."

Vargas slowly shook his head. "That's a mystery. But what I do know is I think you can get us home, my friend."

Dave sat back, suddenly becoming aware that the apartment was emptier than it had been before. "Where's T'shla?" Dave asked.

Vargas scratched his head, his face contorting into a pained look. "About that," Vargas said. "She wanted me to tell you that she loves you, deeply. I could tell that myself, for sure. She just, I guess, well, with all the activity and the uprising happening, she was swept up in it."

Dave's brow furrowed. "What do you mean?" he asked.

Vargas walked over to the window and looked at the protest below. "She went down there," he said. "She joined the revolution, I guess."

Dave slouched in his chair. A sudden feeling of depression came over him, but he ultimately felt a sliver of satisfaction knowing that T'shla had taken a bold step in controlling her own fate. He thought back to her speech of hopelessness and despair in the restaurant almost exactly twenty-four hours before. Dave brightened a little, feeling like he had helped her in her journey toward personal freedom. And now, by walking away, she had given him the same help. His destiny may or may not be with her. It may or may not be with these strange travelers, either. But he now knew for sure it certainly was not in a musty bureaucratic office somewhere in the bowels of a government building.

"What now?" Dave asked. It was not necessarily a question for Vargas, but a larger one about his life and its direction.

"Johnny called me," Vargas said. "He's at the palace—he's been assigned to be C'de Baca's driver of all things. He's going to try to free Theodora and Brian."

"Then what?" Dave asked.

"Then we get to our ship to see if we can start it," Vargas said.

Dave nodded slowly. "All right, then, where's this ship?"

Vargas went to the window and looked north, far down the avenue. He pointed to the spires of the Quetzalcoatl temple, which had been completed ten years before as an Imperial gift to the Most Holy Order of Quetzalcoatl.

"The Quetzal temple?" Dave asked. "But how, did…"

Vargas shrugged. "It's not hard when you have unlimited labor resources—slavery was just being abolished, but Sir Ian slowed that reform by a few months so that the temple could be completed. He had our ship, the *Cyrus-Alexander*, disassembled from our hidden landing point and reassembled in a cavern under the temple. The only people who can enter the area are the highs—high Quetzal priests, high-born Quetzal piplitzin, and the high god and his servants."

"So clever," Dave said, his voice trailing off. "The last time I checked, though, you're no longer the servant of a high god, and none of us fit the other descriptions."

Vargas patted Dave on the chest. "There may be a chance, my friend" he said, crossing the room to his duffel. He pulled out Decoyan's leather-bound papers. "I couldn't sleep, so I read this last night," Vargas said. "It's the story of a Spanish survivor of the massacre of Cortés' fleet. I knew the man, Efraim Ramirez. I remember he seemed to be a decent, simple man, not a man of hate or prejudice."

"What about him?" Dave asked.

"He and the surviving Spaniards were given away as tribute to nobles who knelt at the feet of Quetzalcoatl," Vargas said. "The piplitzin who claimed him? A man named Decoyan, a land owner and furniture maker from the Xalapan region."

Dave coughed.

"I remember clearly—I translated the whole transaction because I know both Spanish and Nahuatl. How about that?" Vargas said.

"So what does this Decoyan connection mean and why would he give me the book?" Dave asked.

"Well, I know my eyes were crossing last night and Ramirez's handwriting was awful, but there is a passage that says, I think, the original Decoyan became Ramirez's father-in-law. Which means, our Decoyan might be a direct descendant. A true Mexican," Vargas said, eyes alight. "A person of mixed Aztec and Spanish ancestry."

"So, he was giving me a signal that he is on our side?" Dave asked.

"It's the best chance we have," Vargas said. "Let's ring his bell and see how much he'd be willing to help us."

CHAPTER 26

DOWN IN THE streets, T'shla reveled in the electric excitement. There was a slight lull in the protest when the Emperor's press office announced he was going to speak to the nation in just a few hours. But an expectant energy soon overcame the lull, and the crowd continued to build around the Jaguar Temple. T'shla was pleasantly surprised to see people from all walks of life there. Workers, office salarymen, people there just to watch, and people committed to change. It was as if all the quieted voices of the city had gathered to express the hopes of an entire country all at once.

T'shla easily made her way through the crowd toward the gold-painted towering Temple of the Jaguar order. She approached the main steps. At either end were two pure gold jaguar statues standing twelve-feet tall, gleaming in the midday sun. She had never spent much time here after her release from custody so many years before. It was weird to be back—returning to the scene of her original torment.

She made it to the steps where she beheld him, Moctezuma 27. He seemed so much larger than before, standing upon the temple's first main terrace, speaking with aides and directing the protest.

He turned and saw her, his eyes growing wide in surprise. He strode over to her. "I see you went and got yourself released from the palace," he said, greeting her warmly.

"Are the words you speak true?" she asked him. "Are you committed to changing society for the better?"

He leaned in, becoming serious and looking at her intensely. For a second, she felt as if she was the only person in the world. "They are as true as I am standing here," he said, holding her gaze. He then backed off a bit. "But you never know how long that may be, what with Quetzalcoatl's masked assassins lurking around every corner." He smiled, letting her know it was a half-hearted attempt at humor.

"I love my father," he said. "This is no coup. It is an attempt to jar him free of the forces that surround him. You saw those forces in action this morning, and you probably didn't like what you saw."

"I'm here to do what I can," she said. "I know I add value to your movement, but I need an assurance that you support more opportunity for women and girls. And that you mean it when you say you don't support a return to the old ways."

"I have three daughters," Moctezuma 27 said. "Katherine told me she is done having children. That means it is my sincere hope that someday one of them becomes the first Aztec Empress. And I will change law and religion to make it happen."

The answer satisfied T'shla. "To get there, you're going to need strong women high up in government," she said.

Moctezuma 27 grinned broadly. "Then walk with me," he said.

He stepped away and walked back to the podium and took the microphone. "Listen, listen, my people, hear me," he said into the mic. The crowd quieted and turned his way. "We have just been joined by one of the sacred Saved Ones, T'shla Ixtapoyan!" he proclaimed, reaching for her hand. She gave it to him, and he held it aloft as the crowd roared in approval. T'shla felt as if the cheer lifted her off her feet and into the air. "Join me," he said. "Join us as we walk over to the temple to meet with our friends, the Quetzalcoatls. Should they not join us in Aztec unity, too?"

He linked arms with T'shla and gave her a reassuring look as he handed the microphone to an aide and began walking down the stairs.

§ § §

Johnny entered Quetzalcoatl's retreat on the Palace grounds. An Aztec guard sat at a small table in the foyer.

"Can I help you?" the guard asked.

Johnny held up his phone. "I need to make a report to my boss," he said. "She got an important message from the home office and is not picking up her phone."

The Aztec guard looked back down at his paperwork. "Next level—third door on the right. Be sure to knock first. You know…"

"Got it, thanks," Johnny said, moving past the guard and toward the stairs. As he climbed the first level, he texted Vargas. *Where would they be held?*

He slowed his pace, hoping for a quick reply. At the top of the first flight of stairs he saw another guard sitting down the far end of the hall, reading a newspaper. He turned for the flight to the third level, acting as if he belonged there. The guard said nothing or did not notice; either way Johnny kept on moving.

Third-level bedrooms. Look for doors with outside locks, Vargas' replied.

Good, he was on the right track. He made the top of the stairs at the third level and saw another guard. This time it was a European, a mercenary Johnny surmised.

Shit, he thought, exhaling heavily, his heart beginning to race in anticipation of an impending physical confrontation. He slowed his pace as he approached the man, who was big but not a mountain. The man noticed him and stood with a questioning look on his face.

"I'm sorry, sir," Johnny said, walking closer and making a quick assessment he only had one chance. "I might have made a wrong turn…I'm looking for…"

Without notice Johnny quickly punched the man square in the throat. The man gagged and reached for his neck. Johnny lunged forward and gave the guard three quick, hard punches to the face, bringing him to the ground. The combination of throat punch and head blows knocked him groggy. Johnny crawled on top of him, searching his pants and coat, removing a gun, keys, and a knife. He was now past the point of no return. He looked up to the door knobs nearby and saw one with a lock. He fumbled through the key chain and began trying them on the lock. The third key opened the door. Inside the room, he saw Theodora sitting on the bed. Brian was by the door, holding a lamp menacingly.

"Johnny," Theodora said, rushing to help him. Brian looked out into the hall to see Chagal bloodied on the ground.

"Help me get him in here," Johnny said, breathing heavily from the adrenaline of the attack.

Together Brian and Johnny dragged Chagal through the door. Once inside, Johnny handed Theodora Chagal's pistol and slumped on the inside of the door.

"I really don't want to kill this guy," Johnny said. "We gotta get out of here, now, but we have to do something with him."

Brian got up and searched the room. "We have some cords from the lamps."

Johnny surveyed the room. "Quite the luxurious setting for two dirty criminals," he said.

"We have to tie him up and gag him. Get me a washcloth from the bathroom," Theodora said. Brian headed to the bathroom.

"All right, now how do we get out of here?" Johnny asked. "My plan went as far as right here, right now. I'm sure what I did was caught on camera somewhere."

Theodora shook her head. "Quetzalcoatl's retreat—no cameras. He never wanted any video footage of him acting like a human leaked anywhere, ever."

"That's a relief," Johnny said.

Theodora straightened and surveyed the room. She went over to the window. "Hey, Ian's on the move," she said. Johnny came over to see Marta and Quetzalcoatl leave the compound and head in the direction of the palace, Marta never even giving one glance at their car to see if Johnny was there.

"Hey, help me get him in the tub," Brian said, starting to drag Chagal across the suite. Johnny and Theodora came over to help.

"So what's going on?" Theodora asked.

"It's all over the television and radio," Johnny said. "Jaguars are protesting downtown en masse—they've closed everything down. The effort is being led by the emperor's son. And get this, Tototl took your bag from this morning and gave the Jaguars all the information you had on Quetzalcoatl and his dealings. He's becoming some kind of a folk hero."

Theodora chuckled incredulously. "The Jaguars are the good guys?"

Johnny shook his head. "Who knows—I'm not sure there are any good guys."

Theodora blew a strand of hair out of her face. "I've been in and out of this culture for centuries, and I still don't quite get all the back channels and cross-currents of who's screwing who over. It's 750 years of secrecy exposed all at once. The Aztec power class wasn't—and still isn't—ready for the attention that comes with an open society."

"You should hear the coverage of what's happening downtown," Johnny said. "It sure seems like the people are ready for the cameras now. And that Moctezuma 27, he's a real charismatic guy. I heard a little bit of his address on the radio on the way over here."

"27 addressed the crowd?" Theodora said, sounding truly surprised. "It makes me happy to hear that. I always liked him. He was one of the few in the court who I could talk to and goof around with at all those stuffy palace events."

"Done," Brian said, quite satisfied with the bind-and-gag job he pulled on Chagal. "I knew Boy Scouts would payoff someday."

"What's Boy Scouts?" Johnny asked.

"Never mind," Brian said. He now had Chagal's gun and placed it in his front pocket. "Now, how do we get out of here, and where do we go once we do?"

Johnny took out his cell and texted Vargas. "Got them—trying to find way out. Where can we meet?" Johnny held up his phone. "I just texted Antonio. We'll see what he says."

"Keys?" Theodora asked. Johnny reached into his pocket and tossed Chagal's keys to her.

"Where are you going," Johnny asked.

"I'm not leaving here without Tlaloc," she said, getting up and heading to the door.

"What's Tlaloc?" Johnny asked.

"Her son with Sir Ian," Brian said. "Come on, let's stick with her. When she's on the move, she can be hard to keep up with."

Johnny drew his gun. "All right, lead the way."

They entered the hall and saw that Theodora was already down at the far end, entering a room slowly. Brian and Johnny hustled to catch up. They entered and saw Theodora kneeling down next to a small blond boy who had been playing with trucks on the floor. Johnny quickly hid his gun and nudged Brian, motioning for him to also put away his weapon. Brian nodded and complied.

Theodora cradled the boy's face in her hands and smiled. "Pack up your favorite toys," she said softly and soothingly.

"Mommy, are we going somewhere?" the little boy asked with a poise and diction beyond his years.

"You and I are going to take a little trip," she said. "These guys, back here, they're my friends."

Quickly, she packed a bag of clothes while the boy stuffed some of his toys into a backpack. He tried to stuff a toy panther from his bed into the backpack, but it wouldn't fit. Johnny held out his hand.

"I'll carry this for you, little guy," he said. Reluctantly, the boy handed the panther to Johnny. "Don't worry, I'll take good care of him," Johnny said, gingerly holding the stuffed animal in the crook of his arm.

"It's not alive, you know," the boy said.

Self-consciously, Johnny readjusted the panther so that it was more secure under his arm. His pocket buzzed and he grabbed for his phone. It was a text from Vargas. "Heading to Q-Temple to the ship. Tell Theo that Dave has it down."

Johnny relayed the message, and upon hearing it, Theodora turned and sat on Tlaloc's toddler bed. "He's got it," she echoed, sitting down with palms on her knees. Johnny could see tears welling in her eyes.

"What is it, Mommy?" the boy asked.

She looked into the boy's eyes. "We're going home," she said, gathering him up in her arms.

Brian checked back into the hall. "That's great, but we still have to get out of here first."

Theodora's face brightened. "Can we get Gaummer up here?"

CHAPTER 27

DAVE AND VARGAS were lucky they caught Decoyan before he left for the day. The protests and the impending Imperial speech had caused all court hearings to be postponed and the courts to close by 1 p.m.

Dave and Vargas milled about by the exit of the court complex's staff parking garage awaiting a sign of Decoyan as he drove home. Sure enough, about twenty minutes before 1 p.m., Decoyan, in a rather smallish, green three-wheel sedan came rumbling up the ramp.

Dave, from near the garage entrance, nodded to Vargas, letting him know it was the right car. Vargas was a little ways down the street where Decoyan would have to stop before merging into traffic. Decoyan exited and turned left in the direction of home. Vargas was waiting near the first stop indicator. When Decoyan stopped, Vargas leaned close to the driver-side window and brandished his weapon. Decoyan froze. Before he could react, Dave had come up on the passenger side and let himself in the car.

Decoyan turned quickly to see Dave sit as Vargas slipped into the back seat, gun drawn and pointing in the direction of Decoyan's back. "Mr. Aragon," Decoyan said, "this is most irregular. If you are looking to get your visa back, there are proper channels."

Dave chuckled nervously at the remark. "We came to you because we need your help," he said.

"Brandishing a firearm in the face of a judge is no way to secure that judge's favor," Decoyan said. "Besides, weren't you taken hostage? What are you doing now, taking hostages yourself?"

Dave looked back at Vargas and gave him an indication it was all right to put the gun down. Vargas complied, sticking the gun back in his jacket. "We need you to get us into the Quetzalcoatl main temple," Dave said. "And to drive, *now*."

Decoyan put the car in gear and engaged the gas, heading out into the streets that were now nearly empty of car traffic.

"I have no access to the Temple," Decoyan said as he maneuvered the car through the empty city streets. "I am but a lowly magistrate judge priest. I am not high enough on the pyramid to get you more than past the front door."

Vargas took out the book and passed it to the front seat. "These writings here say otherwise," Vargas said. "You're piplitzin, noble stock, all the way back from the good old days of the early empire."

Decoyan shrugged and looked at Vargas through the rear view mirror. "Well, if you read that, you probably also could surmise that my blood is not pure Aztec. That we may share some things, you and I. In the Decoyan family, we recognize that we only have a drop of Spanish blood, but we are all told from the earliest of ages to celebrate both our cultures, even if we have to do it in secret."

He turned to Dave. "That's why I shared this important family story with you. I wanted you to know that I understood and appreciated the Spanish as well as the Aztec natures. That those natures can co-exist, and our peoples can find a measure of peace and collaboration."

"There are no natures," Dave said. "We're all just people. We may believe different things or have wildly different upbringings, but at the end of it all, we all love, we all like to laugh, and we are all stirred by things like art and music. All this concentration on blood and different natures does nothing but build walls between us—and for no good reason at all."

"What exactly are you getting at?" Decoyan asked.

"What I'm getting at is you didn't need to prove to me you would be a fair judge because you share a speck of ancestry with me or with Vargas here. You prove it by being a decent human who considers things based on facts, not biological traits." Decoyan pulled into a parking space on an abandoned commerce street that any other day would be bustling with vendors and lunch-goers.

Dave pressed. "Why did you do their bidding, telling everyone on live television that it was likely the Jaguars who were chopping peoples' heads off? We now know it was people very high up and connected to the Quetzalcoatl Order who were doing it as some kind of a sick science experiment."

Decoyan kept his hands tightly wrapped around the steering wheel, his eyes glued forward. "I could not, in good conscience, convict that Santiago Esparza fellow knowing full well that he was merely a petty criminal just off the plane and likely not the murderer. But, there were some in the order, people high up like Coaxoach Ixtapoyan, who approached me, urging a fast conviction. They never planned on the Spaniard leaving that alley, and the fact that he was in custody was trouble for them. They wanted him gone—quick conviction and next-day death. They were prepared to deal with the diplomatic challenges. But I couldn't do it. That's where I took the moral high ground. But this is Tenochtitlan, and when you take the moral high ground in one place, you have to be willing to cut a deal in another. So, I cut a deal with them. I would do a lesser favor for them in exchange for keeping my judicial scruples."

"Announcing in open court that it seemed Jaguars were to blame," Dave said.

"That was my deal with the devil," Decoyan said, "and now look at what it's done for that poor Santiago fellow. Dead anyway. Horrific."

"Dave, this is Tenochtitlan," Vargas whispered. "You can't trust anyone."

"And who is this?" Decoyan asked, almost as if remembering Vargas was in the back seat.

"This is Antonio Vargas," Dave said. "He's the man who helped save the life of Efraim Ramirez, and he was there when Efraim met the original Decoyan for the first time."

Decoyan turned in his seat and looked upon Vargas in disbelief.

"It's true," Vargas said. "How else can you explain the Aztec possession of such advanced weaponry and flying machines as described by your ancestor in his book?"

"I never did try to explain it," Decoyan said. "I attributed it all to flights of fancy on the part of an incredibly interesting ancestor. If an ancestor says he flew in the belly of a metal beast, you take that with a kernel of maize."

"Well it was true," Vargas said, reaching into his pocket and pulling out the ring Ramirez had given him hundreds of years before. "Here." He handed Ramirez's ring to Decoyan, whose eyes got wide as he inspected it.

"What?" Dave asked.

"It's the family seal of Ramirez. We have ancient carvings of this in our country home in Xalapa, carvings made by Ramirez for his grandchildren so they never forgot his story." Decoyan held the ring out for Dave to see more clearly. "See here—the pine tree, in particular. Elements of this seal have been incorporated into my family's crest."

Decoyan was still studying the ring, his eyes glistening. "But how," Decoyan said. "Are we related?"

Vargas shook his head. "I'm afraid not. Before embarking for Xalapa with his new master, Ramirez sought me out and gave it to me as a token of thanks for showing him a sliver of humanity when others clearly weren't."

"Remarkable," Decoyan said. "That means you are either very old or somehow have traveled through time."

Vargas nodded. "For good or ill, we were the original ones to arm your people with those incredible weapons Ramirez wrote about."

"I cannot pretend to understand all this fantastical information," the old judge said. "But this ring, this ring is very real, and it is telling me I need to help you."

"You can keep the ring," Vargas said. "It belongs to your family, and I always felt like I was only holding it for someone else all the time I had it."

"Thank you," Decoyan said. "You have no idea what this means to my family." Decoyan slipped the ring on his right ring finger. It went on a little snug, but ultimately fit. "All right," he said, "if we're going to get you into the temple, you'll need the right robes."

CHAPTER 28

T HE EMPEROR SAT on his golden throne as a sound tech worked to affix a microphone to his breastplate. A makeup artist was touching up his forehead. Moctezuma 26 was quietly reading the statement aloud as Quetzalcoatl leaned in closely to make sure he was getting it right.

Moctezuma 26 put down the papers in a huff. "I'm sorry," he said. "No offense, but why does the Spaniard have to be in here?"

Marta stiffened.

"All right, your grace, if it makes you more comfortable." Quetzalcoatl turned and gave Marta a pleading look. "My darling, can you please wait in the Great Hall. It shouldn't be too long."

Marta shrugged. "All right, I will check on some other work," she said, leaving the room.

"Thank you," Moctezuma 26 mouthed to Quetzalcoatl. "You know, I just don't like the artifice of it all—the television—it does not treat me well."

"Perhaps if you wore clothes that were more common and regular—like your subjects—perhaps then you'd be more comfortable," Quetzalcoatl suggested.

Moctezuma 26 considered. "Very well." He clapped his hands. "Have more selections for my wardrobe brought in immediately."

Quetzalcoatl straightened and squinted his eyes in frustration. "Let's keep it to two or three choices—we're already running behind."

Moctezuma 26 scoffed. "I'm the emperor."

"Yes, but, I'm a god, and even I know you don't keep the media waiting," Quetzalcoatl said. "Plus, the tensions seem to be growing."

§ § §

Marta exited the palace altogether. She wanted no part of that puffery; she had done her TV time the day before. Across the parking lot, she noticed that most of the regular security at the palace proper were not around. They had probably gone inside to gather around the televisions to watch the protest and wait for the Emperor's speech. Marta went over to the consular van and noticed Johnny was gone, too.

She checked her watch and looked in the direction of the palace cafeteria. Too late for lunch. She wheeled back and headed in the direction of Quetzalcoatl's apartments only to see the guard missing and Johnny, Brian, Gaummer, Theodora, and Theodora's son slowly coming toward her. Not knowing what to make of the scene or Johnny's involvement, she walked toward them with furrowed brow.

"What is going on here," she demanded.

Johnny was the first to notice her. He pointed his pistol at her. "Sorry boss," he said, "we're busting these people out."

"Dr. Gaummer, you too!" Marta exclaimed, but Gaummer gave a worried look, and she noticed Brian had his pistol jammed into his back.

Theodora walked up to Marta. "We're leaving, honey," she said. "I'm walking out of here with my boy, and you're going to help us."

They quickly exited the building and got into the Spanish government van. Marta was behind the wheel with Johnny furtively pointing a gun at her ribs. Theodora climbed over the far back seat to the small space between the back of the seat and the rear door of the van. Tlaloc climbed over and nestled on Theodora's lap. Brian and Gaummer sat on the bench seat behind Marta and Johnny. Brian, too, kept his pistol out of sight but pointed at Gaummer's side.

"Fiver, you are going to spend the rest of your days breaking rocks in the desert," Marta said under her breath.

"Easy," Johnny said. "Just say negotiations are done for the day and we're going to watch the broadcast from the consulate."

"Really?" Theodora asked from the far back. "How does that explain Hans joining her?"

"What, you have something better?" Johnny said.

Silence from the back.

Slowly, the van made its way to the first set of gates. The guard there recognized Marta's face. He smiled and waved them through without even stopping them.

Johnny sighed. "I apologize for that frequent-flier crack I made when we first got here."

They easily cleared the other two checkpoints with nary a second look from the guards, who were either preoccupied by the news or familiar with Marta. In moments, they were free and out of the palace.

§ § §

Arm-and-arm, 30 people across, the human chain marched through the streets up Quetzalcoatl Boulevard toward the gleaming Q-Temple. The Q stood 50 stories tall, a modern glass pyramid with purple metallic spires jutting out at each corner. It was the last public construction project to incorporate slave labor, even though ground-breaking occurred three weeks after the official abolition of slavery and sacrifice.

T'shla felt a strength inside she had never felt. Next to her was the future Emperor, Moctezuma 27. On his other side was 27's wife, Katherine. T'shla was joined on her other side by an Eagle general, General B'shcutt, who was master of the city defense. Behind them and alongside, a peaceful mass of about 40,000 people filed by, holding signs and signing songs. They were Jaguars, Eagles, Corn Maidens, and even a few Quetzals sprinkled in here and there.

§ § §

A few blocks away Decoyan, Vargas, and Dave were now hopelessly caught up in the jam of humanity created by the protest and the spill-over of bystanders.

"I never thought I'd ever smile to see Jaguars peacefully marching on the Sacred Q-Temple," Decoyan said. "Growing up, I was always told they were violent brutes. If I ever dreamed this day back then, I would have assumed they'd be in tanks instead of this human chain."

Dave was standing on the trunk of Decoyan's car trying to get a glimpse of the path forward. "Well," he said, hopping down, "it looks like we're not getting in via the front door."

They were wearing Quetzal robes hastily bought from a religious supply store near the courthouse. Such stores were common in the Sacred Precinct because of the number of temples and courthouses requiring religious dress to conduct official business.

"Yes, and in these robes—if we join that march, we will never be able to get in. The Quetzalcoatl's in the temple will see us as traitors," Decoyan said. "Let's try to go around back—it'll be about ten blocks out of our way, but we should be able to gain access via a service entrance. Let your friends know."

Vargas took out his phone to text Johnny.

§ § §

In the van a few miles away, Johnny got the text with Vargas' update. "What's the word?" Theodora asked.

Johnny looked at Marta, not wanting to give anything away to her. They were safely away from the palace and through the park, approaching the Western Causeway, which was the shortest.

"Pull over at the causeway," Johnny said.

"What is this all about?" Marta asked, pulling over and slowing to a stop on the causeway. The traffic was incredibly light, as most Aztecs were gathered around televisions waiting for the Emperor's speech.

"Out of the car," Johnny demanded as he, too, exited the vehicle. Marta got

223

out of the car. Johnny put the pistol back in his belt. With his hand, he motioned to the wall of the causeway and the sparkling lake on the other side.

"What are you doing? I'm going to have your fucking head for this—this is treason," she said.

"Stop threatening, stop talking," Johnny said. "Give me your phone and get on the railing." He touched his pistol for effect.

Exasperated, she took out her phone and handed it to Johnny. Johnny took it and heaved it as far as he could into the lake. "Now, go get it."

"What?"

"You heard me," Johnny said. "There are two ways off this bridge, and neither of them are on foot or in the van."

"What do you want?" she asked. "I can give you enough money to buy your own private island."

"I want you to have not sold out Dave," Johnny said, shaking his head. "Now jump or I shoot you."

Marta climbed the railing and looked around. Johnny saw the desperation in her eyes, but felt nothing for her. And there was no one to help her. She looked down at the water of the lake 20 feet below, and her eyes met Johnny's one more time. Johnny offered her no appeal and no remorse. She nodded and jumped off the edge with little fanfare or drama.

Splash.

Johnny looked over the side to make sure she wasn't dead, and once satisfied, got back in the car. Theodora had already climbed from the rear and had taken over the driver's seat.

"Nice. Awfully humane," Theodora said. "Probably more kind than I would have been."

"Eh," Johnny said, "she didn't steal my boyfriend, so I have much less invested in punishing her."

Theodora smirked and lightly punched him in the shoulder. "Let's go."

Brian heard a familiar buzz and reached for his pocket. No phone. It had been confiscated. He looked at Gaummer, who betrayed nothing and was largely silent through the ordeal.

"Phone?" Brian asked.

Gaummer sighed. "I do not know what you all are hoping to accomplish by any of this," he said. "Let my science take its course—I can find a way back home. I just need more time."

"Quit your bullshit," Theodora snapped. "We both know Sir Ian gave up on going home years ago. The time mirrors and your sicko skull dissections were all a sideline. He wants to rule this universe, and he's sucked up all your time developing atomic power and training Aztec scientists to be nuclear engineers."

Brian pushed the gun deeper into Gaummer's ribs. "Phone," he repeated, more forcefully.

Gaummer slowly reached into his pocket and produced the phone. Brian took it and, not wanting to take his attention off Hans, handed it to Tlaloc, who had also wiggled himself to the front of the van.

"Give it to your mom, buddy," Brian said.

Tlaloc, who was now between Theodora and Johnny in the front seat, looked at the phone for a moment before handing it to his mother. Theodora took the phone and smiled warmly at the boy. She flipped it open.

"Hey, watch the road," Johnny said.

"I can multi-task," Theodora said, taking a second to look down at the phone. She read quickly and then looked at Gaummer through the rear view mirror with a glint in her eye. "Coaxoach Ixtapoyan is helping you? Really?" she asked, shaking her head.

Gaummer stiffened. "He's loyal."

"For a price," Brian said.

Gaummer cleared his throat and fidgeted. "He gets things done, he knows everybody, and, well, he fit in with the operational team we had—especially after you and Vargas abandoned us. He has been an extremely valuable asset—getting our mercenaries into places and connecting us with other useful added muscle when we needed it."

"He's a slimy crook," Theodora said. "I can't imagine Sir Ian would..."

"Sir Ian has nothing to do with it," Gaummer said. "Quetzalcoatl wants results, and I get him results, by any means necessary."

CHAPTER 29

BACK AT THE palace it was go time for the broadcast. Because there were never any broadcasts from the palace, the audio-visual team had last-minute trouble linking their camera to the media feed. But with the bugs finally worked out, the palace was ready to go live. Quetzalcoatl stood off camera and gave the emperor an encouraging smile.

The emperor grimaced uncomfortably.

The camera went live.

"Hello, good day to you, my children," he said in a stilted tone.

Quetzalcoatl's heart began to sink.

"I…am…here today to talk about all of the grand things we are doing to improve the lives of our people." The emperor swallowed hard, as if his mouth was impossibly dry.

Quetzalcoatl looked around. *Where is Gaummer?* he thought. Gaummer was always a good security blanket for the bad times.

"The…the Green Revolution. The Green Revolution was, ah, started…" He was lost in the text. The emperor looked down at his papers.

Quetzalcoatl backed off a bit, craning his eyes to see if Gaummer was somewhere in the room. Instead he saw Chagal enter from the back, helped by an Aztec guard. Chagal's face was bruised and bloodied. Quetzalcoatl eased over to him, not wanting to call attention to himself or further distract the fumbling, mumbling emperor.

"…there is no need to have fear or mistrust in the regime…"

Did he say regime? Quetzal asked himself. Bad choice of words. There is no regime. Regimes change. There is the emperor and the emperor is eternal. 750 years of Imperial power could be undone in one telecast. *This was not my best idea.*

"What happened," he harshly whispered to Chagal.

Chagal struggled to speak. "It was a man," he said gravelly. "Sucker punched me—took Theodora, Brian, and the boy."

An icy fear shot through Quetzalcoatl's bones. "Come. Now!" he said, striding out of the room, leaving the Emperor to clean up the ruins of the speech. *Maybe this will be his test of faith*, Quetzalcoatl thought.

"Where to?" Chagal asked.

"The lab and through the tunnels," Quetzalcoatl said. "I'm pretty sure I know where they are going."

§ § §

Dave, Vargas, and Decoyan met up with Johnny and company just outside the back service entrance and loading docks of the Q-Temple. After a few moments of hugs and recounting their journeys, Decoyan held up his hands to silence everyone. The Emperor's speech had begun and was echoing through the streets on radios, loud speakers, and various television monitors.

"Please, please," he said. "The emperor is speaking. We only have a few minutes where everyone's attention will be completely on him."

The group snapped to and followed Decoyan to a back entrance along the lake front, down a service ramp, and to a metal door beside a loading dock. He pressed the ringer. A loud buzz briefly sounded. They waited. The emperor's words were unintelligible as they bounced around the nearby buildings. After a long while, an older man with long stringy white hair appeared in the window of the door, looking annoyed to be disturbed during the Emperor's speech.

Decoyan held up his Quetzal ID and the man opened the door.

"His grace is speaking," the old priest said, curtly. "What is the meaning of this intrusion?"

"I am an officer of the court, a judge priest. I have been given instructions by the head of my judicial order to give these people a tour of the public parts of the holy temple," Decoyan said, making it up as he went along.

"I don't recall this on any manifest," the old priest said, "and besides, his grace is speaking."

Decoyan shrugged. "I am a just a simple officer of the court. I was given an instruction, and these people showed up in my office expecting a public tour. We had to use the back entrance because of all the commotion out front. Maybe you weren't alerted because there was a mix-up with the courts closing early today. I think they are from the Spanish crown, in town for the trade negotiations."

The old priest, definitely growing more agitated by the moment, closed his eyes in frustration. "Fine," he said. "You know the rules—stick to levels three through five. The museum on Quetzalcoatl history is closed until the emperor's speech ends."

"Thank you," Decoyan said. "Quetzalcoatl's spirit is embodied by you."

"Yes, yes, very well, on with you, then," the old priest said, shooing them inside and returning to a nearby monitor where several other temple workers were gathered around trying to discern what, if any, meaning could be derived by the emperor's nonsensical rambling.

Decoyan led his group to an elevator. They entered. Floors three through five were the only floors that had buttons. Decoyan reached into his robe and pulled out his key ring. He singled out a golden skeleton key and inserted it into a small unmarked slot above the buttons. With a clean swish, a panel on the elevator opened, revealing about 50 additional buttons.

"Level B4," Theodora said. They had always entered the Temple via the palace tunnel. This was new for her.

Decoyan looked back at her. "I've never been down that far," he said. He pressed the button, and the elevator began to move downward.

CHAPTER 30

OUT ON THE Q-Temple steps, the protest march had stopped, and the crowd grew quiet so that they could listen to their emperor. There were now two lines facing off against each other. Quetzalcoatl priests, bureaucrats, and agents were standing in front of their temple, and against them were the masses, led by Moctezuma 27 and the heads of several orders. The crowd behind them now enveloped the entire front and two sides of the enormous glass pyramid.

For seventeen minutes, the emperor droned on and on, and at no point in his speech did he come close to making a point. T'shla looked upon 27, who showed an obvious look of disappointment and sadness at the empty words of his father. As the speech limped along, many in the crowd began to grumble and murmur and turn their eyes to him.

T'shla squeezed his arm and he looked at her. "You can clean this up," she said. She saw deep doubt in his eyes. "Trust me. When he is done, take a microphone, honor your father, but tell the people a new day has come."

Montezuma 27 nodded very slowly, and T'shla saw the confidence return to his eyes. On his other side, Katherine glared at T'shla.

§ § §

The elevator beeped when it stopped at Level B4. The doors slid open to reveal a cavernous room, dimly lit and with mossy wet walls moisturized by the lake. It was a chamber nearly 400 meters by 200 meters. In the middle, looking somewhat small in the enormous room, was the *Cyrus-Alexander*, sitting unkept and tarnished by the water and mold in the air. Above and around them were catwalks and balconies of levels B1-B3.

Decoyan looked back at Theodora. "It's incredible," he said. "All this time, I had no idea it was this big down here."

Brian pushed Gaummer forward, gun still in his ribs. "All right, you have me, you can let me go. Where am I going to run?" Gaummer said, a hostile tone in his voice. Brian put his gun in his pocket.

Gaummer answered Decoyan. "We needed a hidden place in the city where we could land it," he said. "We had such a strong temporal connection to this place, we could easily come and go from this chamber without fear of materializing in the bedrock. For some reason, time travel in this timeline that we created has always been easier—pinpointing our returns to the meter. It's so damn hard, I might say deadly, to try and get back to our original time."

Theodora put Tlaloc on the ground and took his hand. "Let's go check out the time ship," she said, running forward with the boy, who excitedly charged ahead with her. The rest began to walk toward it, the *Cyrus-Alexander* looming larger as they approached.

Vargas put his arm on Dave's shoulder. "You ready for this?"

Dave looked at the ship, now almost towering above him. He was awed that he lived in a world of such wonders, and how lucky he was to be in the presence of an actual time machine. He thought about his life and his job. His apartment and his stuff. None of it mattered to him anymore. Only T'shla mattered. He so wished she could be here to see this amazing room and this otherworldly vehicle.

Dave looked off for a second, and Vargas could tell he was becoming wistful. "That girl's a firecracker," Vargas said. Dave didn't understand the reference. "She's a good woman. I have a feeling T'shla is going to be just fine. And, hell, maybe you will come back to see her."

"Well, I certainly can't go back to Colonial Spain," he said. "I'd probably like to text my mother and tell her I'm going to be okay and not to worry."

"Sure," Vargas said, "I hope you can get service..." *bang*—a bullet tore through the meat of Vargas' calf, taking him to the ground with an unholy grunt.

"Antonio," Dave called out, catching him and beginning to drag him. Johnny and Brian drew their guns and hit the ground, eyeing the catwalks and levels above them for where the shot came from. Theodora used her body to shelter Tlaloc and push him closer to the vehicle.

Gaummer ran full sprint toward the sound of the weapon and his salvation. The fast, unexpected movement caused another shot from the darkness. The bullet hit Gaummer center mass, and he fell to the ground, blood gurgling from his chest.

"Hold," they heard a deep British voice yell. They turned to see Chagal and Sir Ian emerge from the shadows.

Sir Ian ran to Gaummer, his most loyal and trusted friend. He slid to his knees and cradled his head. "Hans," he said.

Gaummer looked up at him, eyes losing focus, blood starting to trickle from his mouth. "I, I tried," Gaummer said. "I tried to get us home."

Sir Ian began to cry as he held Gaummer even tighter. Theodora took the chance and hit the release button opening a ramp into the ship. The loud cranking of gears and hydraulics began to wheeze as the ship's cargo bay opened.

"This is your fault!" Sir Ian screamed in anguish, pointing a bloody hand at Theodora. "You left. You set into motion this ruination!"

Theodora held up her hands. "I just want to take my boy home, if we can find it. I'm tired. So many years. It's been enough."

Sir Ian stood. His white robes were now black and red from the chamber's slime and Gaummer's blood. "Kill her!" Sir Ian yelled like a madman at Chagal, who stood, confused. "She killed your friends. Collins. Agabe. Kill her!"

Chagal raised his rifle. Theodora pushed Tlaloc into the ship.

Bang...bang bang. Three shots, two from Johnny and one from Dave, who was covering Vargas, echoed through the chamber. Chagal fell to the ground, and Dave and Johnny wheeled on Sir Ian, leveling their pistols at him.

"We don't know this guy," Dave said. "He's no god to me."

"Is deicide even really a crime?" Johnny asked.

Sir Ian fell to his knees.

"Give the word," Dave said, cocking his pistol.

Decoyan stepped forward and gently put his hand on Dave's pistol, lowering it. He walked over and did the same to Johnny.

"Please," he said, "care for your injured friend." He motioned back to Vargas, who was now being tended to by Brian. Decoyan then moved forward and went to Sir Ian, who was crumpled on the ground.

"It's all over," Sir Ian said.

Decoyan knelt down by Sir Ian. "My boy," he said, "it's never over. There is always time for forgiveness."

Dave and Johnny helped Brian get Vargas up and into the ship. Dave then came down to see Decoyan and Sir Ian, who were kneeling beside Chagal and Gaummer giving them last rites and using the Aztec traditions. Dave stood silently and watched for a moment before impeding.

"Theodora says you can't come," Dave said, approaching Sir Ian and Decoyan. "But I think you probably had an inkling."

Sir Ian nodded gravely. Two confidants taken from him. His son being taken away. Dave knew everything was crumbling for this 'god,' and a part of him felt sorry for him.

"You can still find Marta," Dave said. "My partner, Johnny, said she should be by the Western Causeway. He said she's probably wet."

"I have nothing," Sir Ian said.

Dave shrugged. "Not really," he said. "I'm sure there are plenty of hidden accounts floating all over the place for you. Probably warehouses of gold, too."

Sir Ian looked up at him, ruefully. "I will kill you someday, sometime, Mister Aragon" Sir Ian said, rising.

Decoyan put his hand on Sir Ian's shoulder. "Quetzalcoatl does not teach us hate," he said. "You of all people should know this. Where did it go so wrong?"

§ § §

233

Outside, the emperor's confusing speech finally ended to a smattering of applause, but mostly grumbles and confusion. Even the loyal Quetzalcoatl priest-hood and their well-armed security force seemed less than inspired.

T'shla stepped between the two divided groups and went over to the nearest, highest-ranking Quetzalcoatl priest, whose brow furrowed as she approached him. "Do you have a public-address system?" she asked.

Still appearing confused, the high priest summoned over a lesser priest, Coaxoach Ixtapoyan, who came forward, red faced.

"Please, Coaxoach, get this lady access to our microphone and public-address system," the high priest said, dismissing Coaxoach to do his bidding. Coaxoach would not look T'shla in the eye. He turned to fetch the microphone.

T'shla closed her eyes, feeling ultimate satisfaction. She returned to Moctezuma 27, who was standing among various staff and close friends. "They are getting a microphone for you," T'shla said.

Coaxoach returned with a long corded mic and handed it to T'shla without ever acknowledging her. She took the mic and handed it to 27, paying Coaxoach no mind. She instead focused on 27.

"Heal us," she said. "Bring us together."

Moctezuma 27 took the mic and looked at it. He then handed the microphone back to her. "I will speak," he said, "but you get us started. It's about time the people heard from a smart and brave woman."

T'shla felt a flush of exhilaration at the compliment as she took the microphone. Moctezuma 27 smiled. "Make it hard for me to follow you." He pushed her forward to face the crowd.

She grabbed the mic tightly, cleared her throat, and began to speak.

§ § §

Brian, Theodora, and Vargas were back in the old familiar cockpit of the *Cyrus-Alexander*. Like second nature, Theodora entered the reactor security codes and spooled up the long dormant fusion reactor. In no time, the ship began to hum.

Brian was tending to Vargas' wound as Vargas sat in the pilot's chair and re-familiarized himself with the manual, handwritten by Silvestre Arenas when it became clear the path home wasn't going to be easy and the entire crew needed to cross-train on other jobs. Poor Arenas and their sole mechanic Bill Ritter had been killed a few years back when the Black Hawk crashed during a terrible storm. Vargas was no Arenas, but he could fly the boat, even with a gunshot wound to the calf. The morphine helped, and Brian assured him there was an exit wound and luckily no bone appeared to be hit.

Johnny came up from the back cabin where he had been playing with Tlaloc, trying to get the boy's mind off what he had just seen. Dave was seated at Gaummer's old station. In front of him was a time mirror interface wired into the ship's main reactor. It was a gerry-rigged console that Gaummer had added to over the years.

Dave finished sending a text to his mother and turned to Johnny. "Are you staying or going?" he asked.

Johnny moved forward and strapped in next to Vargas. "Somebody needs to help this bum-legged burden fly this thing."

Vargas smiled.

"Besides, I am fired, so fired. There is no returning to Colonial Spain for me—especially if Marta gets to them first," he said.

Theodora retrieved Tlaloc from the rear of the ship and made sure he was snugly latched into his seat. She stroked the hair from his eyes and kissed him gently on the forehead. "This is going to be a fun ride," she said. "And I'll be right over there, running the show."

Brian administered another hit of morphine to Vargas and stood up next to him. "As soon as we get somewhere, we need to get Antonio back to sick bay so I can get some sutures on that wound."

"Is there an exit wound?" Theodora asked.

"Yeah," Brian said, "that's the good news."

"What's the bad news?"

Brian shrugged. "That I'm the one who's going to have to sew him up."

Johnny laughed. He was now buckled in. "Instructions?"

"Just do what I say," Vargas said.

"Mark 90 seconds to full power," Theodora said. She walked over and gave Dave a reassuring hug, kissing him on the top of his head, right where the plate was located. "For luck." Dave flushed.

"You got this?" she asked.

Dave cracked his knuckles. "Let's see," he said.

Theodora went back to her seat and buckled in, reaching over to squeeze Tlaloc's hand. "All right," she said, "thirty seconds."

Dave felt a wave of confidence wash over him as the ship began to glow bright blue. He turned his attention to the time mirror on the console and felt as if his eyes were seeing beyond it and through time and space itself. He felt a strong, now comforting vibration course through him. He was locked in and right where he belonged.

Theodora reached up to flip the reactor switch that would divert power to the time engine. The ship began to rock gently, shaking off years of neglect.

Critical mass.

"Engage," Theodora said.

All went white and the *Cyrus-Alexander* slipped through time and away from Tenochtitlan 1999.

CHAPTER 31

Four months after the Aztec popular uprising that brought Moctezuma 27 to power...

THE COMPUTER SCREEN glowed with crystal-clear images of the empire in all its glory—its beaches, its mountains, and its jungles. In the center was an image of Moctezuma 27, standing tall with his gold-tipped spear in one hand and his wife and daughters proudly by his side.

"This is fantastic," T'shla said, sitting back from her chair as the programmer tweaked the display for maximum contrast.

"Really?" Senior Programmer Brektosh Catalpa asked, sounding unsure.

"Yeah, I think this looks amazing, but what exactly is the purpose?" T'shla asked to no one in particular. There were about five staffers in the room.

A junior programmer at the far end of the conference room cleared her throat. "Ma'am, we call it an Inter-Con page. It is a page that will live on our home servers but can be accessed by any computer that is networked via phone or data lines. It has information about our country and its people and is in keeping with the new emperor's directive to be more open."

T'shla nodded slowly as another junior programmer navigated the page. "So, anyone can access it?"

"No, well, not yet, at least" Brektosh said. "We reverse engineered some of the programs on one of Dr. Hans Gaummer's computers and dug through his notes. Apparently he lived in a time where they had something they called the Internet, which was a web of interconnected computers and programs where people could share ideas, engage in commerce, and generally learn about the world around them."

T'shla felt her heart skip a beat at the possibilities. Three months into her new job as head of the Ministry of Information, and her team was on the verge of creating a revolution in the sharing of information.

Moctezuma 26 had been the first Aztec Emperor in 347 years to abdicate and retire to the north after the peaceful uprising of the early spring. A mere few months into power and his son, Moctezuma 27, was changing everything. All religions were now given equal standing, and women were no longer shunned from the higher levels of government service. Not so much for the priesthoods—those would be harder to crack. But still, the divine wind of Moctezuma 27 had blown off a lot of the caked-on corruption that festered around his father's regime.

"So right now we're the only ones who can do this?" T'shla asked.

"Yes," someone answered. It was another junior programmer.

"But we have ideas about building better networks using existing communications hard lines and mobile infrastructure," Brektosh cut in. "This idea could be huge—we'd like to pitch it to the emperor so we can build it out, teach others, and see where it goes."

T'shla rose from her chair and folded her arms in satisfaction. "When I took this job, I told the emperor I would do it on the condition that we would always be allowed to push technology forward. That means pushing way past my level of comprehension—and sometimes, past my level of comfort," T'shla told her team.

The assembled programmers in the room fidgeted and adjusted in their seats.

"I have a pretty good handle on this," T'shla continued, "which tells me we might not be pushing hard enough."

"But ma'am," Brektosh started to break in.

T'shla held up her hand with a reassuring smile. "Don't take that the wrong way. What you're showing me here is world-changing—I can see the applications already. Build it. Grow it. Let me handle the emperor. But you all are on the right track—don't stop. Just let me know the budget you need and I'll work to make it happen. Now, if you don't mind, I have something I need to get to."

T'shla rose from her chair, left the room, and was immediately greeted by her old coworker Shetla, whom T'shla had brought along as her senior assistant when she was promoted.

"Girl, you have thirty minutes until your next appointment, so slow it down a bit," Shetla said, catching up to T'shla, who was bounding down the hallway.

"I know, I know," she said. "I just don't ever have too much time to myself these days. Every spare moment is precious."

"You should maybe go on a date," Shetla said. "It's been four months."

"I will, don't you worry," T'shla said as they approached her office door. "I know you're staffing me this afternoon in the oil and gas industry meeting, so why don't you take some time, have a nice lunch—I can take care of all my meetings and calls till then."

"You don't need to tell me twice," Shetla said. "I'll see you at 1400, Eagle Hour."

Once Shetla was off, T'shla opened the door to her office and entered. She closed the blinds and sat at her desk.

To her side was a simple cardboard box containing contents from Gaummer's lab. T'shla had the box brought up from storage that morning. She leaned over and opened the box, not sure what she'd find. She knew the human remains had been properly repatriated to the families, but the rest of Gaummer's and Quetzalcoatl's belongings had been cataloged, boxed, and put into storage for future research.

T'shla sat back and considered for a moment. *Why am I doing this?*

Maybe going through this stuff made her feel closer to Dave. Maybe she could unravel the mystery of Dave's disappearance and find clues about what happened to Quetzalcoatl and his Spanish lover, Marta C'de Baca.

Moctezuma 27 had de-prioritized bringing Quetzalcoatl and Marta to justice in favor of turning the page. Still, there were too many questions about what happened and about where these strange visitors had come from.

T'shla took out a laptop computer from the box and opened it. It was a model familiar to her. It was the same model as the one she saw so many months before in Apartment 905, a slim, silver device with the glowing image of a chewed-on apple on its cover.

Under the computer was a pile of notebooks and another device she remembered from that same day—one of those table-top projection machines, but a slightly different and seemingly more advanced version than the one Dave had been staring into when she left him.

She put it on the table and assembled it much in the same way she had seen it set up in Apartment 905. She looked into the box and pulled out a handful of cords, leaning back in her chair to untangle them and figure out where they went.

Once she had affixed all the cords and linked the computer to a power source, she turned on both the machine and the computer. The thin metallic medallion began to glow blue. For a split second, she considered disconnecting it, but then saw a twinkle of an image that immediately drew her closer.

It was a man in a park sitting with another man playing a game of chess. She blinked and moved in closer. She was sure it was Dave. He was there smiling and talking to a man who appeared to be in a wheelchair. *Where was he? What was this? A recording of some kind?*

"Dave," she said, softly, feeling a bit silly and self-conscious. "Dave, I am here."

§ § §

In another universe, at a simple park on Staten Island, Dave felt a tingling at the back of his neck that he now recognized as someone, somewhere, activating a time mirror. It was probably Vargas or Theodora back in London, messing around or doing some kind of experiment. Then he heard a faint, familiar sweet voice. He cocked his head and felt a warm wave wash over him.

"You okay?" Bernard Christie asked, wheeling back a bit from the chess game.

Dave snapped to. "Yeah, sorry, I was pulled away by a weird thought or feeling; it's hard to explain," he said in his ever-improving but still broken English.

"It's your move," Bernard said.

Dave turned his attention back to the board, but still felt the tingle. He moved his bishop into a stupid position, and Bernard immediately took advantage, claiming it with his knight.

"Hey, if you're not into it, we don't have to play," Bernard said. "It's just nice to get out of the house—away from Beth and the kids for a bit."

"Are you sure?" Dave asked. "My head's not in it today."

"Listen," Bernard said, looking down. "I've only known you a short time, but I have to thank you—and I'm sure Beth and the kids thank you for getting me out of the house—I really do look forward to hanging out when you're in town. It's the most non-family human interaction I have had since going on disability."

Dave smiled. "It's no problem at all—I love hanging out when I'm in town."

"When do you have to head back to London?" Bernard asked.

"A few days," Dave said. "The boss is a real task master."

They both sat in silence for a moment as Dave continued to feel the tingle, his ears searching for more lovely sounds. After a moment he closed his eyes.

"Take heart that we live under the same moon, my love, it's just in a different phase," Dave incanted in perfect Nahuatl so it could not be misunderstood by his watcher.

"What was that?" Bernard asked.

"Hey," Dave said, opening his eyes and changing the subject. "Did I ever tell you about my girlfriend?"

The Entropy of Knowledge
Mark Dellandre and Britton Learnard

We've all had moments when we felt like we were surrounded by idiots...Babylon Briggs feels that pain every day because his town, his planet, even his galaxy, is jam-packed with the most thick-headed simpletons imaginable. So when his home world is invaded by a group of equally clueless conquerors, it's up to Babylon to save the day. The only question is:

Is he smart enough?

Time Starts Now
Michael Walsh

Professor Cal Sutherland's research on the philosophy of time and time travel elicits only snide remarks from fellow philosophers and rejection notices from journals. Even Cal would admit that time travelers probably aren't real—until he encounters one inside his neighbor's burning house. Cal is destine to take a trip back in time with a man who is both a bank robber and murderer, where only one of them returns...